ALSO BY HAROLD BRODKEY

First Love and Other Sorrows (1958)

Women and Angels (1985)

Stories in an Almost Classical Mode (1988)

The Runaway Soul (1991)

Profane Friendship

PROFANE

FRIENDSHIP

HAROLD BRODKEY

MERCURY HOUSE
SAN FRANCISCO

Published in the United States by Mercury House, San Francisco, California, a nonprofit publishing company devoted to the free exchange of ideas and guided by a dedication to literary values. Originally published in 1994 by Farrar, Straus & Giroux. PROFANE FRIENDSHIP was written at the invitation of the Consorzio Venzia Nuova and printed privately in December 1992 in an edition not for sale to the public. Grateful acknowledgement is made to the Consorzio Venzia Nuova for permission to publish this revised and enlarged edition.

This is a work of fiction. Names, characters, places, and incidents either are the product of the author's imagination or are used ficticiously. Any resemblance to actual events, locales, or persons, living or dead, is entirely coincidental.

UNITED STATES CONSTITUTION, FIRST AMENDMENT: Congress shall make no law respecting an establishment of religion, or prohibiting the free exercise thereof; or abridging the freedom of speech, or of the press; or the right of the people peaceably to assemble, and to petition the Government for a redress of grievances.

Mercury House and colophon are registered trademarks of
Mercury House, Incorporated

Printed on acid-free paper
Manufactured in the United States of America

Library of Congress Cataloging-in-Publication Data

Brodkey, Harold.
Profane friendship / by Harold Brodkey.
p.   cm.
ISBN 1-56279-071-4 (paper)
I. title.
PS3552.R6224P76   1995
813'.54 — DC20   94-40443
CIP

FIRST PAPERBACK EDITION
5   4   3   2

For Ellen,

with all my heart

Contents

◈

Profane Friendship

A PROLOGUE

OF A SORT

I APOLOGIZE for the narrative I am offering. It attempts a portrayal of the true nature of love in one example which might not be a true example of love and one that anyway I am not competent to portray, being a criminally interested party.

Moved by some songs and some paintings—and by memory and the architecture of some houses and churches which seem to indicate the power of emotion—and moved further by a hatred of absolutes and of thoughts of perfection, I have gathered together surface signs and remnants and clues and symptoms of feelings into a narrative I haven't had the heart or skill or time to finish . . . I am as imperfect and unabsolute—as unomniscient, as democratic even with written characters—as that.

The world is, as usual, crapulous with politics and with famines and violence as I write this. That must be folded into the sentiment. To write without sentiment or lying seems impossible.

I will attempt it but with provisoes such as that in the middle of the attempt I may change my mind about what I am attempting. And I may change my mind about the characters who are hardly typical or archetypal and who are certainly not archetypes of love, and I may try to make them archetypes after all, mere puppets of mine and yours, and not people we compare our own lives to, and so on.

PROFANE FRIENDSHIP

And then they were not lovers, after all. And yet they were.

Now that I am establishing the contract, for discretion and for the sake of order I will put it that I will limit everything in this account to Venice and the Lagoon as far as Iesolo, and to a simpler kind of love than the kind usually described. I will play fast and loose with fact and dates and some elements of geography and with places and names and streets in Venice but I will not engage in fantasy. And I reserve the right to be pornographic. Without shame.

And I reserve the right to be mistaken, to be merely a crazy old man yelling at you that "love . . . love . . . love . . . Love exists . . . I say so . . . But it exists only in reality and only without fantasy and only in the ways that reality permits it to exist . . ."

ONE

1 / 1991

THE AIRPLANE'S COURSE from Rome to Venice—a long cross-wise swirl and then a spike going north with a small half-circle at the end—went from side to side of the peninsula from the Tyrrhenian to the Adriatic and up half the length of the boot of Italy past Ravenna and Ferrara to the foot of the Alps.

At one point, the plane banking over the Adriatic in clear air was suspended above the dimpling and restless glare of the sea, one sun-washed section of which was a dancing, unpictorial, pallidly gold mosaic, unimaginably far below.

All in all, the ancient ages and the Gothic moment and the *Rinascimento*, all the historical past, whispered briefly, foreshortened and terrifying below—the stone monuments and deaths—a moment of flight time here, a few seconds there—in the plane's raven-like shadow. The flight lasted an hour, actually sixty-three minutes. It represented a new Italian meaning of eagles and gods, *dei ex machinis* and angels-turned-demons spilled from the realized City of God and become air travellers in the wan hubris of vacationing or on business jaunts. Or returning to their childhoods.

My Italy now is a tangle of flight times, suburbs, superimposed cultures, a country caught up in affluent hysteria, modern but hoping that the modern was something that could be played at.

But the modern moment is unforgiving, no matter whether it is also unforgiveable.

When the plane landed, the old-fashioned clock tick before quartz, or even medieval time animated by brute noise and church bells, seemed for a moment to have been restored and to rule still over footsteps and travellers and my life. We had returned to the other story, the other story still existed—or might resume—at any moment. But I realized soon that here too, even on earth, on dry land, time was modern.

On the motorboat I hired to bring me into Venice, where I had lived for a large part of my childhood and then again in adolescence, the heavyset boatman, the water chauffeur—dressed like Humphrey Bogart in *The African Queen*—opened up the engine, opened the throttle when we came near the mouth of the airport inlet, and the bow lifted; and we went skidding and sliding thumpingly across the gray water of the Lagoon in the lane set out by new channel markers. And apartment complexes, factories, smokestacks, bridges, and the chemical pall of terra firma were dimly visible in the distance all around the shore of this part of the Lagoon in the gray light. A rainy, clouded afternoon with motionless, shroud-like light, weighted as if by rain.

So, the story here too was of a new order, much as I would have liked to be comfortably held by the old description.

The motionless almost-stillness of the gray light is an illusion. One knows the light is unstill, more unstill than the boat or plane, more unseeably unstill than the mind which broodingly *ticks* or sput-sputs and glides and slimly speeds and flatters itself that the light of thought is swifter and steadier than light itself. To be honest, one's eyes, not as young as they had been, do see the raindrop-clouded light as a haze of grayly luminous motions, see this while my body is shaken by the mechanically solid jazz of the motorboat engine and while I hear the not entirely muffled noises of other engines in other boats not far off from us in these channels.

And the whisking movements of the eyelids, and the shift of images on the retina and in the mind, are part of the web of restlessness in which one approaches Venice, part of the variable and moist and tickling instantaneities of dimmed and jostling rhythms and emotions . . . Here is the self and the hovering moment; here is the trembling, nervous, seemingly near motionlessness of the surface of the water; here is the rustling bow-wave and wake; here they are in subduedly echoing canals in Murano; then here is the Lagoon again, Venice ahead obscured; here is *San Michele* on the left pretending that the dead are silent and are not numberless; here is the gouging and choppy passage of the white motorboat over gray fluidities, the lighted grayish rain-teased air holding a glow as of a decomposing moon, and I am enveloped in flitters of memory which I resist of the canals in Venice itself, the wrinkled water in the *rio* behind our house, the secret hushes and whispers there, time's indescribable motion on a Venetian afternoon. I was a child here. And here is my history of love. I see eternity-in-reverse now, welling up as reality, a reality which is particularly Venetian and which is mine, no part of which is eternal, my Venetian reality in a modern moment.

It is a sense of time and of my own life on which my mind is sailing so wildly, time emerging from *the direction* of my father and moving in the direction of my death and bearing and containing my life.

The day brightens infinitesimally, and here is the *Sacca della Misericordia*, in which at once the motorboat slows and the bow comes down. To the left, quite high, are statues in the air, on the roof on top of the delicately subsiding fabric of the *Gesuiti*, stone versions of angels riding in wonderful absurdity and suggestive of belief in the gray-blue air—blue because it is brightening somewhat, only a little, but somewhat. In the damp air, in the pause in the rain, buildings here rise on either side in pink and worn rosy walls and terraces forming abrupt, closed-in, yet somehow grand perspectives. Proud Venice. When I was adolescent I woke sensually each morning nearly always as an experience of falling into this world. In the narrow *Rio Noale*, the wind kept out and light obscured, the boat putt-putts in the shadow. At the end of the long open-roofed shadowed tunnel of this *rio* is a half-strongly lit, horizontal-but-as-if-tilted slab of wavery water in the Grand Canal, into which after a moment or two of heartbeat we ride. Which is to say, into the wider view we come.

And the motorboat slues and heaves in the bright, sharp chop of the *Canalazzo*, in a sudden unfurling of a broad reality of gray-lit water and tilted palaces. Really, it is like a gathered thought, the scene, half-worded, incompletely visible, greedy toward reality, to hold it, and full of a will to display itself, and beautiful.

The boatman let me off at *Sant' Ortellia*. The porter sent from the palazzo where I will stay waits with a two-wheeled hauler where he stows my suitcase and my briefcase and my notebook-computer. I hurried ahead of him.

Now I move into the narrow shadow of the *calle* and I come at once into the shade of a number of fragments of memory, and then after a hundred yards or so to a narrow canal, the *Rio Piotin*, with water too low for the motorboat and with thin sheaves of somewhat brightish, somewhat yellowish light visible here and there among the walls. On the heavy, tossing silk of the unclean water, seabirds, white, and black-headed, beaked, float: small, living gondolas. Jiggling necklaces of light move on the damp lower walls of the palazzi. An ocean has been funnelled into greenish mirrors among walls softly and narrowly lit like this. In this city much of the direction of my life was established.

In the cold shadow where I stand, I grin inwardly and move over the high-backed curve or stone curl of a *ponte storto*—distorted bridge—and I come to the *Campo Marinention*. (I am giving it a fictional name.) The old, many-windowed, double-loggia'd palazzo, handsomely bent and cleverly restored and so gently conceited and airy, bears the Venetian imprint, is an expression of the Venetian theme of secular grace. It has two trees in front of it, leaves fluttering in the wind, and a Renaissance wellhead; and part of the façade and the center of the *campo* is touched by a spread of clear light.

I gaze at the palazzo façade in the light. I move toward the light, and my heart shifts its weight when I pass into it, into the clear light—I feel myself in Venice to be at home in the amoral grandiloquence of the light.

I have come to Venice to write a little book . . . And it will be about these things.

2 / CHILDHOOD PASSION

SOME CONSTITUENTS of an early awareness of love are a salt arm of the sea and the glowing light above the water outside the windows of a room. The walls of the room and the sounds from outside and the footsteps and games and presences and voices inside. And nursery indecencies, the invadeability of one's body and one's being able with one's voice and hands and lips and smiles to invade the privacies of others and to stir the air, and to disturb the others. And the astounding concentration on physical matters in infancy and early childhood, such concentration clothed in concern, and all of it mingled with the creation of the world: *See, that light is sunset . . . No, you little angel, you cannot hold it; it touches you; you cannot touch it . . .* The barge outside in the shadow of the *rio*, the watery air—how *indecently* and totally we love people and moments then and attention and light, how we try to bring under control and rule the causes and guardians of desirable sensations.

In the age of exhibitionism when one is small the color of the soul is reflected luminously outward—the skin is, after all, merely a film of water over one's innocence which comes and plays on others like a light from barely underwater. The faint radiance of an undine, or child-naiad, the waiting permissiveness, or even quiet invitation in the child is like a glimmer in dark or brightly dancing water. The world itself, all of it, to the child is as inviting as water.

Then, you see, a child has to learn to be ugly.

The water-light comes through the high windows of my parents' pretentious house, a palazzo.

A long time ago, in 1935, when I was just preparing to start school, we lived in Paris not far from the Parc Monceau, among other expatriates. We came to Venice; and we stayed for a month with friends who had rented a modernized little palazzo with a loggia and a large garden—this was on the *Zattere*.

It had a garden in front, and one saw through a screen of

trees the water at play in the *Giudecca*. My father was a writer whose works sold. He was an acquaintance of John O'Hara and of Hemingway, but his books sold much better than theirs; his work was, I am afraid, despised; his project was a very long historical romance about Venice and the barbarian Turks—they were, Lord knows, sadistic, flaying one Venetian admiral alive —and my father, I was saying, decided to use the Marciana Library and to inhabit the true atmosphere of Venice, and we were having a long visit.

One brightly lit twilight then, the air was full of the watery floating illumination of a Lagoon sunset for a long sequence of somehow both-shadowy-and-bright moments. This was before the shadows of pollution were as bad as they have become. The sunset was in the old colors, sweet pale yellows and clear pale blues and a very un-orange red and harsh and eery mauves and unlikely acid gold, with shades of more metallically golden gold—a child's delight of a famous sky. It was, you know, a famous light and actual and its colors, in part, lay like ghostly worn flags on the outside walls of the house, the palazzo.

A bird is singing a very ornate song. And white gulls with sickle wings and some with slightly curved dagger-like wings are swooping and gliding in the yellow and salmon light which stains them. They sweep through the shadows over the glimmering and dimpled and partly shadowed and partly lit, wetly murmurous *Giudecca*, which to the west has still its own haze of rebounding light and seems still day in the half-shadowed twilight.

The cat leaps up on the garden wall, which is stucco over brick with some of the stucco worn off. A bird goes chittering in the alteringly sharply yellow, partly mauve air. It is purple twilight lower down where the children are, where I am, the almost carnivally masked lower air. The pretty paths of the garden under trees that seemed very large then—but which were small and Venetian—are mostly dark. In the arcade, in the shadow mostly—only part of them was in the light—my oldest brother, Carlo (Charles, really), perhaps seventeen years old, with a great fall of brownish-reddish hair over part of his very thin face, and a girl who was pinkish-dark in the arcade in the as-if-shadowy glare of that hour, were facing each other with their arms around each other. They were embracing.

It is, among the bushes, almost night. Those two are kissing. Kissing? Well, they were looking at each other and grinning, maybe even half-laughing and then experimentally (I think) trying out this or that sort of kiss with some excited embarrassment. The degree of their silence was notable. I think they were actively resisting any further silence, any deep slide into more sexual silence. Or into sensual tantrum. Or into a nervous or unnervous fit or too sharp spasm of sensation. I think I echoed with their imploding heat and their backing off from it.

In the aura of pallor of my fifth year on earth, after the considerable frenzies of my earlier years, I saw them kissing in the shadows, the sound of the city's bells ringing, clanging, and then in the succeeding silence the pantomime continued. I watched. I had seen people kiss before, I myself had been dandled and tousled and strenuously played with, had felt bodies near and had kissed faces with feelings in them. Every face in my familiar world had a romantic saga behind it and contained hints of its erotic destiny.

I half-recognized jealously the degree to which this trespass was not so laughable as my trespasses were. Perhaps I recognized this other form of my desires. I saw the sexual coloration, the tincture of real affection in actuality, felt the sexuality of the world in all its moments.

The direct kisses and fondlings I had experienced, the hugs, the being carried, the moments on one of my brother's shoulders, or on my mother's chic breast, her moving or removing her pearls for me, so that I could put my head against her neck. The inner colors of feeling and flashes of odor and the sweeping washes of sensation, my mother's powdered cheek, my father's beard-stippled chin, my nurse's starched blouse, my brother's hair. Sensuality was not strange to me.

A ringing and drumming bowered in heat is what I felt at the expressive caresses of hands or lips and the whispers of affectionate words. The feel of the inexplicable grown-up bodies, shifting solidities, muscular and river-like, and the dimensional mass of such large torsos and thighs, and the tough seaweed of hair. And the hard currents of muscle in motion even on softer bodies and the emotion coursing in them, all of it was motion, was emotion and unstillness and familiar.

But the emotion of seeing the lovers in the garden was different. It had more stillness. My distance from the lovers became a territory to be traversed in my life. Much of my life was to be an exploration of these matters. I would say I saw the world newly, not a new world; I believe that no other world exists, that there is no other world at all but one of time and of caresses.

In *the rosey pearliness* of early latency in me, the coded silence of the unexplained spectacle in its low splendor of passionate meanings seemed to be the center of the actuality of grown-up distances from me. Grownups were very separate from me in my comparative innocence.

The sounds of water beyond the garden, the clack of footsteps in a stone *calle*, a vaporetto chugging to a landing accompanied the sight and feelings in those moments. Childhood is enclosure in a familied fate. Being this child in this house, I have had the fate of someone who always consciously loved and who desired love often sulkily but also often with amusement.

My family, members of it, say I was spoiled.

People around me applied the word, the term, *love* (in French, in Italian, in English) to what they felt about various things such as wind and silence and certain colors—*I love ecru, puce, and blue, do you?*—and Christ and springtime and Venice—*do you, sweetheart?*

A stuffed animal, spaghetti, this person and that one, women's voices under leaves in the garden, the marvellousness of windows, my father's feeling for his handsome friend Hemingway—and for a white motorboat that we had—my mother's for black singers and certain movie stars and for some palazzi and for pretty fabrics, sweetly or hotly: this love. Sometimes the feeling was mentioned coolingly, sometimes angrily.

The young people kissing seemed fever-limbed and seethingly jocular and a bit sour. It was recognizably a passionate event—the very thing that the movies have never gotten right.

I thought, but not in words, *So that is love. So that is what love is.*

3 / LOVE

MY FATHER, Dennis O'Hara, wrote a short story with the title "Love" in 1923 for *The Saturday Evening Post.*

He used the title but not much of the story for a silent movie he wrote in 1927 for Vilma Banky at Carl Laemmle's studio, Wilson Ewarts directing.

In 1933, he had a chapter called "Love" in a novel, an historical epic of early Christians in Rome. A book that was named *The Cross and the Dove*, and it had a virtuous but fiery Roman maiden who loved an unvirtuous and very fiery centurion.

Then, a chapter was entitled "Love" in a book about Sir Francis Drake, *Dear Ocean*. A sprite of a girl, rosy-cheeked, utterly windblown, entirely irresistible and very highborn and a bit fast and very temperamental, loved Drake and was tormented by the Virgin Queen who was jealous.

He was, my dear Dad, an ex-Catholic who in life spoke of *the form and substance of love* and, after a drink or two (or five), as a paganized ex-Christian spoke of *fucking.*

As an arrogant and sentimental Platonist he spoke of *the desire to become whole* as being love.

And among intellectuals he spoke of *sexual maturity* and as a liberal he spoke of *the escape from death* in love as if one had a choice not to love. He was my father, and I paid far too much attention to what he said. And then in reaction far too little. What he knew that was true and the bullshit as well, I ignored or took too personally.

Still, he was the primary determining force in how we lived and love was the determining force of his presence in our lives. We went to Venice that first time after my Dad quarrelled with Hemingway. Everyone quarrelled with Hemingway. Hemingway was lunatic, drunk, vain, power-mad, treacherous and filthy-minded, androgynous, seducible, pathetic, and unbearably clever, a towering figure, a genius, and an awful man, who, perhaps because he was rotten, because he had so many aspects of rottenness that he was like a relative, became a truly great media figure, the journalists' Everyman.

I am not exaggerating much. Well, my father was similar but smaller, less driven, although he was driven, and less able. And then he imitated him. Actually, that was too hard, and, so, he imitated John O'Hara whom he also "loved." O'Hara is a terrible writer with good moments and impossibly false. I say I saw this as a child, but all of us children saw it, and we lied about it to each other. Hemingway could not bear the portrait of him in anyone's imitation, in any lesser man's imitation. The reality of what my father's love for him was did sicken Great Hemingway. My father could not really bear just how talented and just how vile the great man was; the love was partly false.

Part of the grace that Hemingway had lay in the way he suggested that his own marvellousness was stolen, was *The* Stolen Greatness and not something intrinsic to him.

But in the androgyny, the nerved-up and nervously masculine Hemingway style, he turned his life into a party, and that was taken up by my father in his life . . . This was at the beginning of the Media Age.

Tiziano at the end of his life painted Marsyas flayed by Apollo, having lived it, the artist flayed for his pride.

Hemingway was flayed and naked and bested—by art, by fame . . . by his farcical presumption.

But he was quite amazing, perhaps the greatest writer of male complaint of his time. He was not the sort of writer he wanted to be. And he was the measure: my father was a much, much, much, much lesser Hemingway. My father was a minor figure of solipsistic masculine narcissism. Of course, he was widely read. In my father, Hemingway saw as in a reflecting pool himself in a fool's version; and his eminence and his sweetness skewed and the amateurish limitations both reproduced and distorted. He insulted my father, picked a fight; it was an actual fistfight, and he beat my father fairly badly although not before being hit hard enough in the head that my father, perhaps self-servingly, blamed himself for having damaged Hemingway's brain and helped bring on the lunacy of the last years and the suicide.

History is hard to come by, and it is not wise to believe the source and the interpretations. My father in Hollywood, twenty years later, spoke to me about these matters—this was long after he divorced my mother. And Hemingway had begun to stay in only Catholic countries most of the time. And my father, ill with diabetes, a chain-smoker and an alcoholic, and tensely on the wagon supposedly and full of mental derring-do and with an avid appetite to recount to me important scenes from his past, said that he and Hemingway had *loved* each other, but that Hemingway changed his wives and his friends for each book. He made it sound glamorous.

"And," said my father, "it was our fault . . ." The fault of his friends. "We none of us understood the man's pride or how much he wanted to be Hemingway." Then he said, "And we wanted each other dead . . . I began it, I suppose. I may be giving myself too much credit, but I think we at least helped kill each other . . . And we led each other to Venice. I went there first. Now he has discovered Venice and he goes there to write just as I did."

Hemingway in Venice after the war, I saw him again then and truly was scared of him. He was a travesty human, a great figure, a huge soul, mad.

So we were in Venice. My father in Venice wrote a book on Venice and the Turks, human violence and the infinite sadism of actuality. It was a book of sea battles and of men and women alike in pearls and it had that odd dialogue of the 1930s, dialogue at once chic and conventional and either muttered or expostulatory.

We consisted of my mother Clemmie and Dee-dad and Madame, our French housekeeper (from Arles), and my brothers, my sister, and myself, and a secretary, an Italian, Paolo Zixi, who, my father said, reported on us to the *Questura*, and my nursemaid, Zilda Gildinigro, and a cook, Carmenina Paxo, and we had a boatman also named Paolo. This was in 1937 and we stayed until 1939.

It was important to be rich, to have style. Actually, Hemingway had another sort of style. So did Pound whom we met and to whom I said, *Do you like cake?*, not in imitation of Marie Antoinette but because I liked sweets, *pound* cake, of which he had never heard or had forgotten, or he chose to play the great man with me when I was a child. I think he was beyond love in his lunacy and in his excellence as a poet.

Poor Dee-dad, so ungreat and, often, so in his cups, so malicious about these other men and their mannerisms and vanity and beliefs.

In college in America, years after the above, I read a Russian novel, a short Russian novel, in which the narrator as a young adolescent sees his father speak to a young woman who is standing or sitting by an open window or sitting on the windowsill perhaps. The boy observes his father wielding a riding crop, sees the way he strikes his thigh. Something in this suggests *a truth* involving dominance, personal beauty, willfulness, cruelty and hurt of a complex nature, and an apparent rapture—supremely intense interest—a supreme force, love.

As I read, I was jealous.

Of what? The riding crop?

I don't know of what. I was jealous of the knowledge of such things in the writer, of that writer, so much better a writer than my father. And of the characters, the force of the father, the power of the girl, the luck of the boy having the privilege of observing such a passionate moment. I don't know. It was not as sternly written as Hemingway but in most ways it was better than Hemingway, truer about love certainly. Hemingway was a bestselling liar about love. I was never as fond of any of Turgenev's other books or of any other passage in that book.

What is it you most desire?

As someone who was exposed to Catholicism, I say one desires salvation because salvation is everything. Of course.

And one desires a final answer, a meaning that contains with finality the naturalness and unnaturalness of the world in a never-to-be-corrected statement.

One desires peace, tenderness, intelligence, fame perhaps, and to have been brave and to have done good work—and perhaps to have astounded the world.

One desires love in various forms.

One desires a naked world of love to replace the one of lonely dailiness, a world which has a heat of emotion and genital heat, and such warm, shocked brightness spreading through it that it might as well be Hell.

MY MOTHER
AND THE REST
OF US

☙

SO, WE WERE in Venice in no simple fashion and in no simple sense.

My friend Amedeo who may one day be pope, who is *papabile*, and who is theologically distinguished, said, *Terrestrial love comes to us from God through the mother*. Amedeo is very complex in his purposes and always means something obscure and hidden.

My mother, Martha Brower O'Hara, was sometimes called *Clemmie* because she had been My Darling Clementine in an unfinished dance of Martha Graham's performed as a fragment, but later dropped from the repertory although it was much praised at the time . . . She always denied her emotional nature. She said of me as if I was *entirely* different from her in this, *He's a younger child; all he's interested in is love.* Così fan tutte—*as the wind listeth, fickle, fickle, fickle.*

Like Amedeo she always meant more than she said but unlike him she liked to speak nonsense, and she did not necessarily ever quite mean what she said or all that she said. Her style was that of a tough-wicked fluffy blond who had married a writer who made money. She was vain but in a workmanlike and hardworking way. Her father had been a workman in Wales. She had left home at fourteen to study dancing. She had been a sweet-faced dancer but with somewhat heavy hips. She had an air of being a very polite person with a tremendous will for getting her own way. She was a tease.

She had a tremendous ego but she was cleverly deferential toward men—my father liked that in women, perhaps in everyone. He liked it in Hemingway, too. Of course, I cared about love. I was the baby of the family, and my mother doted on her baby for a while between appointments, flirtations, the thing of being someone people talked about.

She was palely blond, so often flushed as to appear scratched, bleedingly reddened, she was so fair-skinned. She said, *Of course, I lost my coloring early, when I had children—blonds do.* But she had splendid coloring or pallor; she drew attention to it by denying it. She was a performer and a personality. She pretended to be giddy.

I remember her best in relation to the sea and this city. In the winter in Venice, I remember the spidery nervousness of response to the cold and the way her body flinched at the force of the wind in the channels formed by the walls and the canals.

In the winter, the susurrus and throbbing of engines is muffled and echoing in snowfalls and fog. Bell sounds shiver in the cold air. The cold is watery and changeable but occasionally fixed and icy. I was a child in the cold, bundled up, and chaperoned by my mother.

So much of the city is circumference that one often arrives at the edge of the city, at the edge of the water, into the cold wind in gray light, the freed, large wind. In some blinking moments in the wind on our motorboat with my mother or on our dock, me warmly dressed and holding her hand, glimpses of feeling choke me like swallowing salt water. My mother's politics of emotion with her children, her husband, her friends always amazed me. Her moods were terrible, but she was clever about them. My blond, sweet-faced mother was very largely clever, I am afraid.

On the dock at one of the innumerable edges of the city, the straitened, *interested* breath of the child in the throes of naked feeling, naked sensation, is part of her life. "Are you cold?" She hugs me to her leg, her coat.

My uncontrollable breath is a gasping as in sobbing or laughing, such a potency is in her. She is displeased with all the others. She says, *You at least are nice to me, Nino. And* you *are interesting.* Each softly blond laugh of hers in the cold carried a puzzling echo of her other laughs, as in the echo of reflection in the water of the buildings in their varicolored geometry in the gray air along the *Giudecca.*

The clouds of innuendo of further sensation gust in the sensation of love at the sound of her laugh and drive me along as if I were a small, scudding boat.

"Oh you like me," she says as I tighten my arms on the fur she wears.

Love is in search of a voice, an embrace, a caress. The strange, exhibitionistic arching of the self in her presence, the extortionate soul in its natural cruelty trying to imprison her in lover's pitiability, says, "Don't go." She was going to the mainland for the day. For a while in my life she was the shape and soul of the emotion of consolation. But so was the child for her. And for others.

But we were not the right types for such emotions. This sort of tie did not last. My father said of my mother, *She was never an angel, you know?*

As a small boy, I was permissive toward others—I remember that *nervous* concentration of shaky permission: "It's all right: you can go: have a good time."

Really, how dreadful love is, from the very beginning.

THE LOVE OF
A FATHER AND
A SON: LOVE IN
A FAMILY FURTHER
CONSIDERED

CHARLEY, the oldest of us children, was first called Carlo while we lived in Venice and the name adhered to him ever after. My father doted on Carlo. But he forgot him from time to time. It was as if he practiced at home the omissive omniscience he practiced as a novelist, moving his attention from character to character and from scene to scene. That he couldn't practice such omissiveness and omniscience with his taxes or with critics and reviewers (or with politics) darkened his life and sometimes soured his moods—he was addicted to it, you see.

In his writing, he dealt in physical actions and strong emotions and he decided on the consequences and meanings, on the endings. He decided deaths and madness and fate in general, including happiness. He parcelled out coincidences and disasters and strokes of fortune. He rewarded good characters and condemned bad characters. He did this in his books for whole populations and civilizations like an Old Testament Prophet or one of the grimmer Church Fathers. In seventeen apocalyptic novels and a dozen forceful movies in thirty-five years of authorship, he decreed destinies and rather openly defined social and spiritual reality. He always said that he revered the craft of writing, but I believe it was the practice of omniscience and the intellectual omnipotence that stirred him, and this showed in the texture and bloodiness and clarity of his books and attracted readers, this perhaps inexpensive majesty.

And for us, the children, perhaps in Oedipal resistance to his hubris, a certain horror of *kitsch* apocalypse shaped our style and our responses.

Dad, plain-faced, vain, well-dressed, painfully proud and temperamental and deeply angry, and tall and thin and nervous, was a show-off who was kindest when the newspapers had paid amiable attention to him. As I said, he had doted on Carlo, who was very good-looking. But things change. Dad backed off from a handsome son he was tiring of or was jealous of, and he doted on the youngest child, me. In some ways, my poor gorgeous brother bored my father, and part of that, I am afraid, was that he longed, my brother did, for an ideal attention of the sort presented as love in my father's books. And Carlo found counterfeits of it here and there, enough so that he was demanding and disappointed—and angry. Of us children, he was, in temperament, most like our father.

Then, when this "ideal attention" paid to him revealed itself as theatrical flummery and courtship and swindle, he went to pieces silently as the departing trickery receded in its light. And then the demons arrived, and my brother was monstrous. This happened over and over. My father came to hate my brother's sorrows, my brother's cruelties, his rages, his weaknesses. Later he hated his successes as a financier and as a charmer of sorts, competent and energetic and vicious—and sentimental, an adept at omissively flightly "ideal attention."

My brother's cocaine addiction is of the sort that only the successful and powerful can manage. It is an addiction as a parable, a measure of how great a sense of omnipotence he had, and how he longs to preserve that sense, and it is a continuation of rebellious unhappiness he knew in childhood with the happy-unhappy ending of an effectual vice indulged in over and over.

My brother is generous, and his generosity suits his size, his craftiness. Much of his generosity is reserved for underage girls—well, sixteen, eighteen, in need of rescue, whom he cheers up and suffers with. They tend to look like me or like our mother.

We are, he and I, as restless in our adult lives as the old Venetians were in their marsh. Did he compete for me with our father? In revenge? Or in strong feeling, out of emotion that can't be named? It is very difficult for a smaller boy to resist an older boy—so much knowledge is embodied in the sort of self one hopes one will have someday oneself. I was abducted. I preferred Carlo. Poor Dad.

I know Carlo's shoulders from being carried on them. He taught me to row. I often slept curled against his back or on his lap. Still, in a sense, I had only his company, never his real attention. I never managed to get his "ideal" attention. When I tried, he would panic and turn me over to our mother.

At a certain age, when I was still not yet in school, in Venice the first time, my parents gave a party on the occasion of their buying a Matisse, a bit of ownable modernism. The *piano nobile* was filled with laughing and chattering people. My brother and I sat on the modest stairs that went to our floor; this was behind a padded door. These were not grand or ceremonial stairs, but they were stone. I knelt beside my brother on the stone and quivered with excitement. At a certain point, I grew bored and restless, and he put his arm around me; but it wasn't personal. He was then seventeen, and well grown. I remember I could feel in him a cold density of muscular innocence, the sort there is in a dog or a colt. He sat there in the *cold* reality of being our father's son and the more ordinary reality of being my brother, and I swear I could feel my unreality for him; all my reality for him was in the reality of his arm, of his gesture. He listened to the sounds of the party and occasionally opened the door with his foot and peeked from where he sat, at leg's length. Then he'd let the door close and he would refocus his eyes on a worn tapestry on the wooden wall of these enclosed stone stairs; and I swear I wasn't real to him for a single minute, and he said, *We have a house full of crazy people* and *I wish they were all dead. I wish we were alone.*

And, oddly, then, crazily, for a moment we actually were alone together—it was just the two of us. And then, in the noise of the party I was real to him. The difference was immediately and grossly apparent, the difference when I had his attention; and I was always aware of it.

He nagged me when I was a child and he nags me still. I am to him the very definition of what is unsatisfactory, refractory and wicked, which is to say unreliable—like the girls he cares for. We all fail him. I am what interests him, but I do not ever get his attention. It is as if I had the affectionate and erotic reality for him of having been of importance to our father, of having replaced him with our father, in having the secret of how to hold our father. But that is not me. It is merely a perceived emotional-historical quality.

I suppose he pursues himself in his relation to me, his brother. Jealousy, the web of jealousy. Love never occurs between two people cut off from all other people, so that with love one enters a story of conspiracies and of whispers and of complex responses and tangents and echoes. We daydream of finding each other in solitary circumstances. We create solitary circumstances. Carlo and I did this. We were so attached to one another for a while that for a number of years we slept in the same room, us as a pair, in this daydream state of there-are-only-two-of-us, but that was only very rarely the true emotional reality.

I mean he ignored me most of the time except as a reflection of him. Or as a prisoner or as a hostage he held. He "molested" me a bit. I didn't mind. Well, I did and would stop him. But what I remember is years later, visiting again in Venice, I went to the *Palazzo Camba* and glanced up at the Tiepolo ceiling in the Grand Salon, at the faded blue sky painted there, the painted flags and the suggestion of wind, and the light on the Lagoon brought into paint, and the disembarkation in eighteenth-century Venice, a ship and soldiers, and above them, an enormous male nude, Apollo perhaps, bending over a small cherub, and there it was, Carlo in the dark asking me, in Italian, if I was asleep.

The soft, almost granular night air. He wasn't talking really to *me*, nor did I see him clearly. It was clouded by the dark, *sfumato*, and by ignorance and by dim wishes and feelings. He began to talk about girls, and he sat on my bed, his butt sweaty in his pajamas, and the bed jiggled in a lovely, not quite boat-like way; it jiggled near me a little like a boat in the wake of a large motorboat.

The room was filled with ghosts and with the truths of erotic substitutions, the airy Venetian dark. There is rarely a moment in one's life, no matter how much one feels the opposite, when one is entirely unloved and free or when one is loved enough. One is never morally or ethically alone in one's love. The past will not shut up or shut down or be simple.

My Venetian nursemaid, or governess-nurse, was named Zilda. I preferred her to everyone else, even to Carlo, even to my mother; Zilda saw to this. She was very seductive and fierce about loyalty and possession. I remember her bathing me, her eyes and forehead and her breasts over the edge of the tub, and her hands on me. And I remember being on the *altana* with Zilda under the vines, in the shredded light, with such broad-gauged, spreading, ruthlessly naked sunlight around us on the roof outside the *altana* that I blinked. I felt the pulsations of her fanaticism in matters of love, the desert-island, the prison thing. She gave me a very physical attention that was filled with sounds, her breathing, the noises of her clothes.

My fondness for Zilda was an enormous passion, really. And this bothered my father who was jealous of it and of Carlo and of my mother with me, at least when he wasn't forgetful toward me. And I was jealous of his being a grownup. I was jealous of all of them, if you want to know.

My fondness for Carlo, a handsome boy—that was the category Carlo was put in—my quiet passion, often physical and easily delighted, affected Carlo whose neck would redden with an observably swollen intake of breath. Carlo tended to be blank, wooden, cool. That was an attempt, a manner. I was drawn by the resident and waiting power in this stuff, the power for me, the power to affect him.

And I tried it on the others, to affect them, at least when I wasn't being cool or abstracted or forgetful myself. Carlo and the others said I was a devil, no angel. I was delighted by the stone and paint resemblances that suggested, at least when such references didn't hurt or affront me.

I suppose I was fascinated and perverse to the point of surprised and startled *love* toward what happened and toward these other souls. Every day brought new defenses, new tactics, new events. Temper and sad cynicism about revealed nature and one's susceptibility, one's secretly passionate nature—and hope, rage, justice, will—were enticing and yet embarrassing to a fastidious child.

Carlo drank and drugged a bit, he used the drugs of that day, and he would be chemically emotional, and feel that I had hurt him—*Do you want to make me cry, you little devil?* he would say. Dad and Mother and Zilda and my sister and other brother were not so obvious. Mother said I broke hearts.

The thought of it would fill me with a sensation inside, a silvery fullness. I would choke on the emotional breath in my throat, the private recollection of potency.

I was jealous of Carlo much of the time, but I hid it. I laughed at him in a childishly squinting way. And spied on him. Made trouble for him. I never clearly felt this as love except when found out and accused. Then I would see love as a public thing, see it as seeable and known to others, and I would fill with heat at my badness, with embarrassment, not guilt so much.

Sometimes the forgiveness and reconciliation were so sweet that it was worth going through the spying and the exposure for the moments at the end. I think I loved Zilda in part to be simpler and in order to practice her meannesses and prejudices in a simpler story rather than my story with Carlo.

I loved her to escape Carlo, and that escaped love on top of my feelings for Carlo, on top of the basic or essential *original* love, perhaps belonged to him as well. In a way, he was part of any love I felt. One day or another he might reclaim me and my feelings. One day in a mood he wound up the rubber bands of the plane models he'd made, and he launched them from the loggia, first setting them aflame. They flew over the walk and partway over the water and then fell into the canal, the *Giudecca*. And this was mixed with his saying, *Be nice to me . . . Be polite for once, mostrino . . . Little monster*—summons to the sport, to flames and a noble death, love and death and simplicity of will, or simplification finally.

Coolness.

Heat-teased, Carlo was unpredictable—unpredictable by me. In such a world one was the favorite only *in-a-way* and for a time only. But one forgets that and in each new episode one turns bitter and cynical, until at some point one is habitually bitter and cynical. One has learned this, been taught it. One has come to it. One is a little grown-up about love. One is being a man about it. One has learnt self-control—of a sort and to a limited degree. One has a style, a history.

One is older and one dislikes the role of the favorite. One avoids the royal prince who strikes at you in some large, regal way in the course of his moods.

He erupts anyway—one is hurt . . . Oh, it is awful. Awful. One moves into the sunlit white-plaster-walled rooms of the next phase, a latency. One is a turtle inside a shell of refusal.

Carlo, like a mad prince in history, said of himself, *I'm a lamb*, and was indefatigable in pursuit sometimes when I was evasive and chilled. He was popular in the world and inattentive. He saw me as innocent but irritating-at-times, and I partly believed his judgement. His demands occasionally bordered on the sexual but mostly they were tormented versions, distortions, of tenderness and of a wish to keep his small brother in amative servitude. Carlo's absentmindedness and his absences were so bluntly difficult to bear, his cruelties so abrupt and stinging and resonant, that I preferred to forget him, as our father had.

But then I was vulnerable to being waked by his attentions. He didn't hate me as he hated our parents. I hadn't had a hand in shaping him. He didn't love me as much either, as he did them. I have to admit I thought him beautiful in his power.

As he grew older he was inclined to focus on himself and his wishes with a blindness that seemed royal and stupid but enviable. His notions of love-and-affection were Hemingway-esque as would be inevitable in the oldest son of our father, and absolute, as I mentioned earlier, and extreme—courage and dying for love—nothing reasonable. And his underlying pursuit of our father went on.

He sulks. Carlo often sulks—he sulks in the Italian manner, a young male. He chews on a cigaret, is wholly blasphemous and alive. He sometimes smokes a cigaret in a holder à la Roosevelt and stands hipshot on the loggia and stares out over the canal world-rulingly. Sometimes he wears one of my Dad's white hats in the heat. When Dad took to using a cane, Carlo began to use a cane, too. Carlo grew a mustache in Hemingway idolatry. Carlo was anti-English—he was Irish to that extent. He would not go to church, but he *loved* Catholicism and the *idea* of sin and of real apocalypse. In spite of his rebelliousness, he secretly was an addict of *kitsch* apocalypticism like our father. Carlo was moved by Fascist flags, Fascist buildings, the governmentally decreed fresh paint, all of it—he took it as absolution for the degeneracy of life.

He was not quite pro-Fascist. He said of himself, *I don't kiss asses* . . . an act I asked him about, and he showed me what it was. It didn't seem interesting. Only years later did I understand the humiliation and the humiliated tenderness, the defeat that is indicated in the phrase, the degree of unwise, humiliated love and subservience.

But he was sufficiently a bitter and cynical neutralist that my mother could not bear him when he was in that mode. She hated the emotional patterns he had—Carlo, as I said, was always in difficulties when he cared for someone, a friend or a girl or an older woman, too demanding, too confused, perhaps too self-concerned, too showily moody, a bit boring.

The caroming affection in him and the drama of growing up were mixed with his feelings for Venice which he also loved and hated. He was sad and often drunk, availably limp, available for foolish distraction. Dad, drunk too, wrestled with him one night in the *grande sala*—I couldn't bear the sight of them grunting and fighting for real and then slipping into merely symbolic and yet still more embarrassing and nakedly meaningful combat and then fighting in earnest again. It was unendurable.

It had too much meaning, too many meanings. I was too jealous to breathe.

Whatever Carlo did, I did a version of. I spoke in dialect like him, and filthily. I was disapproving and very Catholic like him. I swaggered and had my own ways of doing things and I sulked like him.

When he hurt me, I went looking for help from our father. I was not a nice child nor a delicate one in my politics yet, although I think I became more delicate later. I carried on so rabidly that my father in mischief—and guilt—punished Carlo by not letting him use our boat. My sister Ruthie snitched in my favor. I was slavering and crying and wouldn't eat, wouldn't move, but kept demanding that Carlo stop hurting me.

You are—uppity, Carlo said, pinching my nose. Carlo was angry too, and contemptuous and sad. He gave me a shove in front of our father who had to choose but chose to avoid us by turning on his heel and leaving the room: *I can't stand either one of you*, he said.

I would not accept my father's affection after that—really not ever again in his lifetime. Oh dear me. Angry with me, Carlo said I was a little whore, which did initiate in me an interest in whores that has never died.

Carlo refused to believe I was as unforgiving as I am, although my mother warned him. With me it is a bodily thing. I find I cannot hug Carlo although we are both old men now. He is quite old, and still difficult. I become rigid, rigidly cold and silent. Obstinate. In his presence.

This would change if Carlo changed. But Carlo and my father until his death were too proud to change emotionally; they simply lied a little bit to get past the scene or my disapproval; they trick you; they expect you to know the world does not permit men to change and to accept their lies about change in a kind of sour brotherhood.

In his cold, almost elegant, stiff-backed, nouveau riche, son-of-a-famous writer way, Carlo refuses to be afraid of me. This is what I feel about him. He refuses to be afraid because of love, I think, paradoxically because he is afraid of me and can be hurt.

And because of regret and doubts about himself. But the regret is not because of what he does, not ever that. It is because of the way it affects others, in some cases, me, the way the child took the act or the man now.

Later that year of the wrestling in the *grande sala*, my worldly Irish Poppa took us, the entire family, to the opera, a *bribe*—a reward—a family festival. He took two boxes. I had no clear idea what an opera was. Carlo, seeing this, and touched by my simplicity and ignorance, by my virginity, enticed and confused me by promising me *green* ice cream before the opera. I could not picture *green* ice cream: *It's like having green hair*, Carlo said; *it comes from Mars.*

At the moment itself, at Florian's, when it was served, the fading sunlight or twilight touching the dimly shabby, erratic façade of the *Procuratie Nuove* while the Christ and Evangelists above the front of *San Marco* and the great horses of Constantinople, green and flecked with gold, motionlessly moved in the long rays of Venetian sunlight still, I felt consciously the power of my feeling less love toward my brother than my brother felt for me. I felt the game of the moment to be the amount of love and independence between my brother and me, of how it would not work to feel no love, and of how it would not work to be full-hearted. Suffering and courtly—and devoted—Carlo is saying, *You see it is green and it tastes green . . .* Carlo is scoffing at me at the same time, and he says, *Only a little green beast of a caterpillar eats green shit. You will eat anything.* He kicked me under the table.

The extraordinary emotion and the extraordinary light that evening, the so-specific light and the sudden emotional illuminations in events as in *Carlo's being mean to me*, as in *Carlo, stop kicking me*, and my specific tone of complaint or of idle, newly boyish *boredom* with his shenanigans—and the grownups' habitual illuminations: *Oh that's just Carlo, aren't you used to it by now, he's a barbarian*—were part of such specific amative momentum that it would require a novel all to itself if I were to present it as perhaps a worthwhile story to tell.

We rode in our white motorboat from the *Piazzetta* in the

twilight to the water steps at *La Fenice*. Liveried ushers helped us out of the boat. The stiff whiteness of my clothes in the darkening gloom of evening Venice and the outdoor light and the moon and the burble of the water and the sweet warmed moistness of the breeze and then the light inside the theater, Carlo holding my hand, having claimed me . . . you see it is love . . . And my resistance when he squeezed my hand and my transferring my grip to my mother's hand and the green taste in my mouth of the ice cream and the great, rising and encircling curves of the green and gold auditorium and the buzz and mumble, bass in tone, the vastly shaking air in the auditorium of people talking and moving around, and Carlo reclaiming my hand . . . it is love still and again . . . And then the music finally beginning—my exclamation of *Oh* . . . the churn of it, of the music, of the dancing sounds, the high sounds wheeled and curled, the low sounds rushed, wind-like, that almost visible music . . . Snowflakes for the ear . . . a landscape rushing *unstably* through the mind, a prompted hallucination of the ear and of the soul, yet real, like Venice itself outside the auditorium.

The opera was the *Entführung*, with its Pasha, a *sweet* half-reality, bright colors, and extraordinary sounds—Turkish, some of the noises, or so I was informed by Momma, and then by Carlo who once again was impossible in his re-established claim to me. But I loved Carlo's explanations. They were nearer to me to start with. I understood nothing; much of the music was a jumble; but I *understood* Carlo, Carlo and me, understood us a bit. I felt moored to his politeness to me, to his voice, in the flooding and impermanent welling up and flights and pressures of the music. My skin felt stroked; my eyes were like ears, I think—*Look, he is all ears*—I opened my mouth and moved my fingers.

My mother was moody that night. She sat in a way that showed her legs. She was in style harassedly brazen, breathless, a blond ex-dancer, a mother and a wife and somehow overworked all-in-all. I think my father's interest in her had changed and was angrier and perhaps lesser. At any rate, she had changed in the last years.

It is the extreme differentness of the moment, the refusal of life to be circular or spiral, it is the absoluteness of the singularity of each moment which I remember. Things happen and situations change dramatically in almost every moment. We live this way even if we don't notice it. Celtically, my mother seemed to react to the music as to a prophecy, to read omens and advice in it for itself, for us, for her . . . Somehow she was always tilted toward what was coming. My father sat absorbing the occasions, but Pasha-like, taking it personally as something he had bought for us. Carlo was a bit like Momma, even more restless, reading atmospheres of refusal, of darkness in the pretty show.

Even as a child I found his vanity of intellect odd. The *Constanze* was pretty or had an air of prettiness, a bit too fluffy I would think now, but she was serious enough singing "Traurigkeit" to suggest an emotional reality that the men singers were incapable of.

She, the woman singing Constance, had recently married the conductor. She was a woman with a rouged and coiffed quality that was one of the styles of the period. She had a rather large bust. And a willful and not entirely intelligent but still brain-driven power of seduction with something a bit grimly *northern* about it—she was from the Piedmont and had greater triumphs later in tragic Verdian roles. Her power of attraction was an issue in the opera, in the story being told on stage.

The tenor had a tragic air of inferiority that night, a sad, pretty-voiced man, young, destined to be famous—famous for his pathos.

They love each other, Carlo whispered to me. *They want to be faithful but the sultan will kill them.*

My mother said, *He wants to kill them because they're too old for those parts* . . . My mother had "conversation" but people tired of her or became angry with her anyway. She suffered from boredom and had many small ailments and was a *prima donna*, Daddy said.

Artful music. All those tonal images, those tonalities, were emotions, were lights and shadows, were shallows and coves of harmony or of unease. The implication of feeling in each separately pronounced melody, voices and instruments conjoined, and the colors of the costumes in the stage light, and the rapid movements and dance and flutter of the plot—how dangerous the moments were! And how strangely like someone thrashing in a canal and swallowing water and then swimming among palazzi. I proceeded in those moments, wading in the light and shadow or tumbling in the noise or mounting as if on water steps or wallowing as in the marshes. A child.

But then a child with the soul of a bird, and unstained by the musical adventures of listening, watching the conductor stir the air and produce the churning sounds in the almost circular hall.

A certain long-held note by the *Constanze* was like a white heron over the mud flats. My mind-obscurity and then the bits of clarity—*Look, he's in a fog*, Carlo said—well, it was like being in a fog on the Lagoon in a *sandalo* with Carlo or Paolo in the shallows with the lights of Murano dimly fuzzy, then suddenly sharp in the mist—but the thing overall placed me in a world, in everyone's world, not just in the family's world. It seems to be human to know something and at the same time not quite know it yet. To live, knowing and not-knowing, in the real air dangerously and in some respects extravagantly—foolishly—is to have an identity.

I was often a good child who sat still and was quiet when told—that was a rewarding thing to be in our family. But now I kept pestering Momma and then Carlo, who held me on his lap, *What is it?*, that is, what was going on, as the opera proceeded. My father inserted himself, his explanations, disregarding Carlo's, telling Carlo he was wrong, as the unstoppable conductor whipped and poked and tugged the music from the gleaming wood and metal *whatevers* in the orchestra pit.

Carlo used often to ask me who I liked best—as he asked our dog. Carlo lived in the deepest concern from time to time on that matter.

Do you like Constanze best? Who do you like best, me or Daddy? Mischievous because of the music and my age, I said, *No one.*

You have to choose, he said, squeezing my shoulder.

Ow, I said. It sounded like a dissonant musical note.

Stop it, you two, Momma said.

I like Momma best but I don't like anyone, I said.

Why do you like Momma best? Daddy asked.

She's more interesting and she doesn't ask dumb things.

Momma said, *Oh my, he's growing up. The show is over; now the trouble begins.*

Momma put on the best show day after day. She governed on the Venetian system, a bit of tyranny, some terror, and lots of briberies and seduction, lots of amusements—and beauty. She had, I say now, in those last years in Venice before the war, a clever focussed importance as a woman with a stylish undertone of moodily corrupt conceit.

And Daddy is not happy with her anymore. Momma is scattered among the difficulties of her story—politic and impolitic love split a half dozen or a dozen ways. Her hidden but never completely hidden favoritisms are a difficulty; her resentment at being forced to be expert in love; her aging; her unreliable temper—what else was her life but love in this sense?

Her manner when you asked her a question tended toward silence around a real answer: *No, I don't love you at this moment; you're behaving hideously—no one can love you when you're like this.*

Dee-dad said to her, oblivious to her legs, her dress, her manner, *You have an opinion on every subject under the sun.*

In the box, he tried to get me to be cleverer and not choose anyone. I refused. I was through with him in some odd way, conditioned to it—I do think others drive us away.

Don't you like the opera best? he asks.

I like it . . . I don't want to choose . . . They asked me . . . Then: *What is an opera?*

My mother says in the noise of the pretty music as it booms and burbles and then swells, sail-like and noble, taut and powerful, in the hall, *It's a big to-do about love—with music.*

I stared out at the lit stage, at where the lights and voices were.

Carlo whispered in his chair, his arms around my chest, *Don't you like me as well as Momma?*

Poor absolutist, poor Carlo. Clemmie pursed her lips and said, *It's no good asking him; he's not a child anymore.* And then she crossed her legs—to the music. Poppa watched, Dee-dad, and he was sour and not impressed—she looked at him: *You bastard*, she said. And leaned over and pushed my hair out of my eyes. It was one of the great, commanding, watershed gestures of my life—her encouraging me to see.

Being seductive, she said, *An opera is heaven for the ears and hell on the tush . . . It's heaven and hell . . . I like it when things are set to music and with very fat singers . . . But then I like music. It is more interesting than the things people say when they talk . . .* She was a gambler and a fighter as a woman when she wasn't being sweet or adorable or baby-talking.

Carlo, who is tougher than I am but softer in some ways, said, *Shush, Momma.* He knew the ship was sinking. He told me so at other times. Now he held his face next to mine and we watched the opera.

I like operas that show a little hell better than I like this one, Momma went on, dangerously I guess.

Dee-dad said, a bit harshly (in his Fascist mode: vain, omniscient, omnipotent) to her, *Well, so much for your tastes.*

The weight of my father's flesh inside his clothes gave off a perceptible heat always. A comparative *shapelessness*, it has odd, wiry fur and a particular sweatiness. I really only understood Carlo's shape and mine. I knew very little about what a lifetime was. Carlo's body was usually cool, Momma's hot and cool in various places . . . She and Daddy felt to me, their touch, their bodies felt old and *shapeless*.

One turns away—from the knottedness, from the difficulty. One is instantly amnesiac, a child aware that he is a child.

The singers were as fat as Zilda. I did not yet realize that emotion was a heat in me as it was in all of them. I was interested in the opera, and then in the noisy bustle of the crowd afterward, and in the boat and the moon on the water when we went chugging home afterward—I was interested in the world.

ONNI

1

TWO THINGS I know about Venice. Nowhere in the city does the eye rest on a human claim to omnipotence and divine right. The jumble of culs-de-sac and sudden unfoldings into small and then large spaces and then curving or twisting, more or less outspread vistas with ultimate perspectives in them of Lagoon and sky don't suggest a single kingly eye. And the haphazard bounding upward of the walkways onto the high-instepped footbridges over the rustling canals, bridges which block your forward view until you mount high enough on their steps, the crowd of unknown people around, all of them on foot—none of that suggests royal divinity. Nothing in Venice represents the ricketty stuff of centralized kingly will, and the pious self-hypnosis of one person who is the living, hereditary embodiment of the entire place and of others who love the place (and their place in it) with a similar and lesser and less pious self-hypnosis of their own.

No. Here is an abrupt commercial canniness mixed with daydreaming and an unbelievable depth of having trafficked in daydreams commercially for centuries. That is the other thing I know about Venice.

Mother's milk and the first crooning sound of breath. Then later, fresh air and wind. And later, in play, squirming on the ground and taking a small clod of dirt in one's fingers and lifting it to one's mouth and tasting it . . . Zilda said something like, "Ah, Nino is at the breast of good Mother Earth."

And then at play in the *Campo San Stefano* with other children, Zilda overseeing it, and then Zilda's successors. The outward world in my childhood had a central core of politics, the Pope and Mussolini and the Blackshirts, new coercive pieties and uniforms, noise and brawl-massacres, a million hideous great indignities of the adults, indignities imposed on further millions debased and slain—and the child, like other children, comically anxious to enter the presence of history, to play at being soldiers or airmen. The extreme foolishness of childhood is terrifying. In the terrifying mute distractibility of youth, one loves—perhaps one loves in a childish way. The category is love-outside-the-family, love-in-Venice-outside-the-family.

First was—ah, I don't remember his name. Then it was Sandra, the second one; she hit me with her doll—it had a large pottery head. She was English, I believe. Then—let me interrupt myself and say that loneliness in Venice moves and shifts and crumbles as the buildings do, and is mutable and like the water. One is lonely and then one's nurse comes, or Carlo, to take you to the *campo* or for a walk along the *Zattere*, or to pull you in a little wagon down to the *Dogana*.

Among the walkers and the workers.

One time recently, a little drunk on a disreputable Merlot, and on a vaporetto that bonged and bounced in the *Canalazzo*, I heard the noise of the banging motor as *Thronging, belonging*. The constantly gathering and flowing crowds of Venice.

Venice was never literary. It could not supply the necessary loneliness. And childhood's kingly hopes are dissipated here among the statues and the frescoes, angels and cherubs, spies and clowns, Pantaloons and panders. And among the myths of dutiful heroes. The rich apparatus of emblems and elaborate façades spotted with carved heads and monsters at peace among the waters is a poetry self-consciously of fools and games.

An ambitious soldier and sailor had to go somewhere else

to gain military glory and bring the news of it here, to the *Rialto*, where the local folk could make money from it.

I asked my father once why some book or other used the phrase *happy Venice*. And he chewed his lip and his at-that-time sloppy mustache, and he said that in his view Venice was a subtrahend, a batch of negatives—that is, it was not grim, not stern, not-a-lot-of-those-things . . . And that added up to happiness or to something like it. And I remember this very clearly—he said that no one who was not Latin could understand.

School. The light is glimmering on the wooden surfaces of desks.

The squeak of chalk and Miss Moon's voice. Children's heads like painted birdhouses into and out of which thoughts and ideas and sensations and perceptions fly and perch like small, brightly feathered vibrant birds. It is a dark day, rain, lightning, and thunder. Here is the moment when Miss Moon switches on the electric lights, and a modern boldness of glare, abrupt, dimensionless, entire, fills the room. We are in a tent of such light.

Inside me, school's *Ideas* scutter and fly and flit, sometimes among vaguely burning clouds of mental perspective. Ghost-shapes, shades, foreign to me, they overrun my eyes, my smallish ears, my open mouth—one listened in part with one's open mouth . . . Mortal, held breath, and the hope of *love* . . . Of childhood friendships.

In the afterflare of a flash of lightning, the door to the schoolroom is flung open—truly—and the galvanically nervous and overenergetic McIlhenny, head of the school, a Scotsman, appeared holding the hand of a small, sharply sculpted child, a boy, who had a lot of light-brown hair and what was both an apple-like and a stoney-arrowhead little face. The mix of effects of flesh and bone and oversized Venetian-pink lips and staring eyes set in shadowed bone scoops gave an impression of great beauty.

"Here is a new student for you, Miss Moon," Signor McIlhenny said. "This is *Giangiacomo Galliani*."

McIlhenny was given to headmasterly theatrics and spoke, often, with strangely conspirational flourishes of his voice.

The children stared at the new boy. The boy was—one guessed, one saw, one knew at once—a too much admired and pawed and mauled and fondled child: children are aware of such elements of fate in another child; children can sense that particular quality of fate in another child, that early knowledge of romance.

He was a year older than the class, two years older than I was. He was put back a grade because his English was not good—I have not mentioned that this was *The English School in Venice*: that was its name.

Even outside in the *calli*, people stared at Onni. Were such stares like pebbles thrown at him? Like small flashes of light and heat? As a child, he lived in a world of stares, of eyes, of the colors of eyes, of such gazes touching him . . . *Everyone* said at that time that *I* was a beautiful child, *tanto bello, un piccolo tremendo ragazzo*—of course, my parents were thought to be rich. But no one ever said it again who had seen *Giangiacomo*. I had been king of the class, *re della classe* until now. At the sight of him I felt my crown, my power among my peers, wobble.

I didn't much mind. He was of another order of physical presence entirely. He had a quite serious early glamor. He was *a little matinée idol*, my mother said after she'd seen him.

At recess in school, taken on the roof of the palazzo the school occupied, he was willful, he was drunk with will in play, largely serious and untalkative, and vivid in movement, and greatly interested in being who he was. On the roof, standing face-to-face with him in such play, I do not idealize or idolize him. Or lie to myself about him. Or suffer the torments of jealousy. Those elements were not present. He simply was a wonderful child, and it was wonderfully exciting to be with him minute-by-minute.

I don't know how he came to be enrolled in *The English School*. His family had moved to Venice from Udine. His father was a government functionary, a Fascist, and a violent one, a rigid-spined and hard-eyed man, handsome but with a sternly lumpy, perhaps muscular face.

Onni's mother, so the gossip ran, was a slut. Venetian gossip is harsh in tone. She was middling-middle-class by birth, scandalous.

Her first husband had been a much older man, a manufacturer of paint in Trieste, a Jew, who died and left her some money. An *enchanting* if strained woman-of-the-world, she'd come to Venice, a monied young widow, and met her future sister-in-law, the unspeakable Contessa Potta, Clarelia, who married her off to her provincial brother, the violent Fascist . . .

When I met his mother, I was startled by what seemed an echo, or remnant, of fragile loveliness, something at once wild and passive, harshly ironic and maudlin, a bit sly and drunken-eyed. She fascinated me, but I don't recall ever liking her.

Standing face-to-face with him, I stared at him. He looked back. Finally I smiled and blinked, blinked amiably. He then smiled a curious, very pretty, openly false, but radiant smile: yes.

As immediate friends, we ran side by side in the narrow *calli*, our satchels pummelling each other's legs or our own. This was among other children after school while the sounds of the bright-hued and dull-hued voices rise in the narrow passages. We didn't always shout. We have discretionary tones among the wild shouts as we run in trafficless Venice.

At certain times of day here still, the dominant sounds are the shouts of children playing.

He was, as a companion in terms of emotions and companionship, intimately stoic, a Fascist's son, a Fascist's beautiful-and-athletic little son, not much more than that. A largely silent object of admiration and physically restless. He was awfully interested in games of cruelty and peril, in how much pain and pressure he could manage, in what could be borne and in what made him or others give up: heroic matters. We all were, the girls too, pre-war, in those last pre-war moments.

One of the districts Mussolini built, or rebuilt, in Venice consisted of modern *calli* in the back part of Venice beyond *San*

Giovanni Evangelista toward the *Stazione Marittima*. Onni lived there in one of the new Fascist Style apartment blocks with a garden and a wall around it. Building, wall, garden and nearby *calli*, all were in a scale new to Venice.

Onni was that Italian rarity, an only child. Before school, I would run through my part of Old Venice to *San Giovanni Evangelista* and wait there, breathing hard, shivering a little, and he would appear, often at a run and silent, or he would begin to run when he saw me, run toward me silently . . . Not a talker, he would not necessarily greet me except with a weird smile or a birdlike toss of the head up and down, sighting and acknowledging me. Often he would slow down or pause and we would then run side by side, Red Indians through Venice, to school. Behind the *Frari* and past *San Rocco* we ran, under a high, fleecy, gray morning sky, in dimmed winter light that was like airy tissue paper. We ran past the garbage collectors and the smocked *calle*-brushers, the morning stir having begun along the canals. We ran past other blue-smocked workingmen carrying hods on their heads. They whistled or sang—or blew on their hands; we ran past them. The cold stung my bare knees. I wore long socks. I had often to stop and pull them up. Onni unkindly told me my legs had no shape. My blue visored cap with a button on top kept blowing off.

February's is an alphabetical light, pale with dark shadows like lines and blotches on a page. We played in the beckoning and slightly motional, slightly *vulgar*, pallid and yellowish light of March. Then in the fresh bright glare of April mornings which makes me squint, we play some more. In different lights and weather we play. And he and I shoulder and shove open the sighing weight of the door at school. Our classroom has two tall windows with flame-shaped tops. In that room we come among the odors of children in school clothes, droplets of rain perhaps on our slickers as we enter. Our wet satchels, we dry them on our legs, against our socks. A pencil box falls to the floor as we do this, and the snap lid flies open and the pencils tumble out. Onni pretends to laugh—but silently. He closes his eyes and picks up the pencils as if he were blind: a test, an elaboration of life.

It was much harder work to be an educated middle-class child then. One had also to go to dancing school, and usually one had music lessons and boxing lessons. Onni sometimes had horseback lessons on the Lido. I had instruction in gymnastics and in fencing.

2

HIS CHILDHOOD ENGLISH was American, not British. I don't know why. I don't know who taught him. His mother's English was odd. That woman was attentive or very inattentive and given to taking sighing breaths. She sometimes had a look as if something *possessed* her, as if she heard voices, demonic conversation; and then, contradictorily, she was *practical* and chatty in a haunted way.

I felt I knew why Onni liked *me* . . . By comparison to his family I was sensible.

When we met each morning at *San Giovanni Evangelista*, he might run up, smile—his emptily radiant smile that contained him peeking at you over his smile—he might say, "I thought of something," and I would say, "What? What is it?" Do you know how you open up blankly when you say, "What?" Watching me narrowly, he would swing his satchel and hit me in the hip or on the side of the knee.

And before I could get angry he would say, "Now you do it to me."

We spent so much time together that people, grownups, older kids would say, *Are you in love?*

The studies in power one engages in, the attempts at mastery, the psychological dexterity are not latent; they are merely limited. They are not adult. One needs help, companionship, against the dissonant and occasionally sweet music of such latency, by which I mean the odd mix of a sense of innocence with the sense of ultimate impotence, the mix of harmlessness with helplessness although one is not entirely helpless, not harmless either . . . it is a comparative matter. One needs help in the intent study of dignity, the intent study of seduction. Onni and I had no vocabulary, merely glances and facial expressions asking to be understood.

Onni knew a great deal about being a child, about being a child in Venice, and around this knowledge spread the otherwise unknown *rest of the world*. Ignorance is an outer darkness around me which, in bad moments, becomes an inner dark blankness. I am often terrified and obstinate. Onni and I signalled our alliance by making confessions to one another about our families. We betrayed family secrets to show that we put friendship first but also to dilute our ignorance and terror in regard to the grownups and their action, the giant's world. We did it in whispers in shadowy rooms or empty *calli*. It was a scary and satisfying and terrifying obscenity to do this . . . we cut ourselves off from willless and obedient childhood and stopped belonging to the grownups and gave ourselves over to our whispers, which we partly owned but which also had a further life, consequential momentum, and history.

Obscenity: we showed each other our bodies in our underwear. We showed each other our bare behinds, our peepees. We went to the bathroom in each other's company. We then, each separately, broke the other's confidence. I remember the scalding heat of remorse or embarrassment when my mother told me she didn't think her feelings about our cook ought to be public knowledge: "Nino, don't you know when to keep your mouth shut?"

I don't know what other potency was available to us. We often played in a dark storeroom on the water level of his Aunt Clarelia's palazzo near *San Stefano*. One of the maids in his aunt's household began calling us *the crows* although I was fair in coloring. We stole, we made messes, we lurked and spied. We sometimes behaved well, but we were as bad as we knew how to be in somberly near-giggling immoderation. I told him about my *mother*'s constipation and did a strangely hysterical (but whispered) imitation of her sitting on the toilet and making noises . . . *"She takes* hundreds *of medicines, ugh—she gives herself enemas . . ."* I said, in a whisper, "My parents fight a lot . . ." I spoke, laughingly, hysterically, or in puzzled sobriety about the punishments my Dad inflicted on Carlo and on Mom. And Onni told me his father stole money from his mother's purse. He said he'd seen his father hit his mother. He imitated, in the dark, without visible emotion except for a dry, quiet childhood air of sad, mean scandal, his mother reeling and saying, "I forgive you, Pietro. You don't know what it is you do to me who loves you."

Onni, when he became excited, would lapse into excited Udinese that I learned to follow. He said he had seen his father kick his mother. We observed our world's secret history. Childhood is a dream in this sense. My father tried to limit the time I spent with Onni. Onni was not always my friend. We fought, physically and in silent demonstrations of dislike.

Some of the fights were heartbreaking and were based on genuine anger. Often then the grownups tried to heal us, not liking to see us so upset. Sometimes the fights sprang from hurt, usually an angry inferiority trying to right itself by asserting that the ultimate strength lay in rage, violence, force, in force backing up disapproval or dislike or objection . . .

Sometimes they arose in spells of emotional languor when I wanted to live freely and not be entangled in someone else's will, or I was past caring about anything and was merely self-willed. The strutting *kitsch*, the utter *utopian-apocalypticism*, the fanatic masculinity of the time influenced us. We were the children of that stuff, children of the age.

Onni and I were not of the same class. "The prince and the pauper," my father said of us. And: "Can't you do better than that pretty little sneak?"

And my mother did not think highly of Onni, but it was a matter of pride to her to fight with my father and see to it that I had as much time as I wanted to spend with Onni despite my father. At other times she goaded me to do what my father wanted.

Onni's father's life was tied up in Fascist Party *brutture*. A hundred and ten different stories were happening in our parents' lives, and the children were a lesser story mostly—and it was better that this was so.

The grownups were concerned with issues of world conquest and their own would-be greatness, and to find and have the great love of their lives, and so on. My father hightailed it to Harry's Bar at four-thirty every day. My father was more and more harried by the *Fascisti*. He did not take a public stand decrying them, at least not a fierce stand. He decried them some. But his crime in their eyes was that he flatly refused to take a publicly pro-Fascist stand—in any form. The propaganda ministry was interested enough that they turned Ezra Pound, among others, loose on my Dad to persuade him. Dad said at home to us that his kidneys were loosening, from the drinking he had to do to be a sport and from the coffee he had to drink to sober up after his sessions with *Fascisti* and pro-Fascist writers, American and otherwise. Pound told my father that he, my father, ought to have better political sense . . . *good sense, horse sense, the old American sense of masculine probity . . . I mean courage . . . Yessir, courage . . . Prose has to be grown-up . . . Children's politics don't make for no grown-up prose . . .*

Hemingway, hearing about these ins and outs, wrote Dad an inflammatorily pro-decadent-democracy letter: *Few things are simple black-and-white but this is . . . The Blackshirts are not white men . . .*

Dad half wanted me to have as a friend the son of a Fascist official, and he was, he said, *Goddamned ashamed* of playing politics *with these two-bit Mussolinis everywhere.*

Onni and I wrestled for national and personal and local honor. Yay, Venice. Yay, Manhattan. My sight is filled with his flopping hair and the writhing pavement. Ah, the pink-tissued, enflamed breath of wrestling. His ears and part of the sides of his face are suffused with blood, purple and pink and enflamed red. "I will kill you," he said in Italian.

In games involving imagination, as when we were soldiers fighting in Albania, the terms of the game would be *logical* or *realistic* for a while, but then, like some narrators in novels, we would tire of the constraints of reality and we would start in on being illogical and fanciful, as illogical and fanciful as a dream or movie is or as the passage of events is in a surreal novel. We might insist on having a number of identities and switching among them; we would start to refuse to be killed in the game but would insist on being in another body; or we would suddenly argue that we had secret body-armor and couldn't be killed, or that the bullet had been stopped by a Bible in our pocket as in some movie or other that we had seen.

We often acted out movies as best we could, actually scenes and groups of scenes that represented what we understood of the plot and the principles of cause and effect in the circumstances of the given plot. I am not sure I ever, even as an adult, got the point of grownup movies except as pornography and distraction or as excitement and a peek into other lives, although I have written for the movies.

He theorized that it was interesting to kiss when you were grown up because your mouth hurt from talking and smoking. Of course, we experimented with kissing. We kissed each other. Outside of pecks on the cheek, it did not make conscious sense to me. I went "Ugh" in English and ran giddily around the room and down the stairs and along the *calli*.

We called each other names, "Oh you pouf," and we called kissing names. "Eat some garbage" meant *Kiss me.*

"Ugh, ugh, buh-ugh/buh-ugh: ugh" meant anything we decided it meant . . . At times it was code for *This is good stuff* and at times *This is disgusting-and-foolish.*

Merda—shit—was code for *murder* which meant very good or very bad back then in slang; and that meant that we were going to chase someone or that we were suffering. We argued whether secret weapons existed; and if the dictators had bullet-proof secret armor or not; and if they were the smartest and happiest men or not.

"Would you do it if your father asked you to hand a bouquet to Mussolini in front of a lot of cameras?"

"Yes," he said.

"Would you kiss him?"

Pause. "Yes," he said.

"That chin—ick—eeeee-ick . . . Would you wipe your mouth in front of the cameras? I wouldn't touch *him* . . ."

He hit me fairly hard, not cripplingly.

But on the whole, not death and not any ideas of any doctrine—or of being bulletproof—were as absolute, were as high-ranking with us as was the absence of loneliness and the freedom to play *good games* and the privilege of having this tangled and imaginative intimacy knottily present once a day a number of times a week, every day really.

Our attachment was a resource and a refuge. And a potency. This potency was the obsession, not each other. Whatever I did apart from him, I described to myself after so that I could describe it to Onni later, and he would understand. And agree with me. He did not think I was cute. He was seriously interested in what I had to say. I spoke four kinds of Italian because of him, Tuscan and Venetian and Roman and Neapolitan. My American took on a British tone (which I have never lost) because he got what I said quickest if I was clipped and formal in enunciation when I spoke to him.

Even back then, in the real moments, it was my impression that potency was the real issue—not the word but the thing-in-real-air. Potency was the great or chief or only real desire, and all else that happened was therapeutic or stopgap until such time as we would be as potent in the world as grown men were.

I have ten men with me—no, twenty, I say. *I have enough men with me that you can't do anything . . .*

He says, *I can beat them to powder using jiujitsu . . . Splock! I can knock out twenty men. I have special training . . .*

Or: *I am a Super Shock Trooper . . .*

All right . . . I have a hundred men here with machine guns . . . And the wizard Merlin—from King Arthur's court—and I put a spell on you and you can't move your arms or legs . . . You can only move your head; you have to confess things when I torture you . . .

Sometimes it was *easier* and more *sensible*, more perceptible to us as feeling to play at being older, merely that, or at being child movie stars making a movie of a battle rather than trying to play out an actual battle with the two of us as field marshals and lieutenants and fighter pilots and infantrymen and super shock troops and infinitely killable and resurrectable.

As a young soldier, of indeterminate, omnipotent age, I capture an enemy soldier, a column of air. I shoot him and shove the invisible corpse toward Onni who makes grabbing and heaving motions saying, *This is a cliff—I throw it over this cliff . . . That is what I am doing now . . .*

Onni and I creep up on another enemy and crouch on the pavement and consult each other's eyes for a signal of when to spring. We run and I feel my breath bursting from my lungs in gasps like foliage being whipped from narrow spaces inside me and through my mouth and into the air. I grab the invisible enemy's hair and say, CUT HIS THROAT . . . In the game Onni does it with a movement of his arm and with a dry-mouthed, childhood grimace . . .

Then the category of dares and suggestions—*Do you dare me to do it?* Were we old enough, able enough, brave enough . . .

So here I am jumping into a moored barge from the railing of a little bridge over a small canal, jumping through the air into the open pit of the barge. I feel the fringed lashes of my eyes as damp with sweat and air-ridden and the weight of my lips on my face and my nose sticking out into the air and sucking in air shakingly . . . I feel my fragility, my transparency, my being made of childish glass and having a glass breast so that people say they know what I am feeling—I feel how breakable I am . . . How heavily I land—and sprawl! And how queasily the barge thunks and moves on its bed of sluggishly resilient water.

Now Onni is flying through the air downward after me. I am gasping and watching. The electrical ruthlessness of one's feelings in childhood, the ruthless emotionalism, the bravura braveries—will one live or die? Will one become a scandal and a pity? In the fantastically wide and dual simultaneity of our present tense, the all-there-is is the world and him-and-me . . . A totality of attention is in these events, in these minutes, these few seconds . . . I am breathingly watching . . . crouching in imitation and anticipation . . . watching Onni's movements in the Venetian air . . . Onni lands and crouches and does not sprawl but is frozen from the jolt, the physical shock for a second. Then he jumps up and grins his wide, dry grin in my direction . . . *Let's do it together—holding hands . . .*

And we do, side by side, hold hands and leap into the yielding air, in fear and bravery, and drop, wide-eyed, into the barge and sprawl in a small-kid-simultaneity . . . *Again*, he says.

Let's go, I say.

The outward day in the flesh of its own light is a body of this companionship of ours.

I was almost willing at times to leave my house and live with him and his looney parents. And yet we were not faithful to one another. We were not even completely best friends. Other kids were often with us. When he and I were not friendly, I often didn't miss him, although often I did. One time after my father and mother and Carlo and I and our brother and sister had a two-week vacation in Klosters at Christmastime, when we came home, when we reached the terminal in Venice, my mother let me go alone from the train in carless Venice to find Onni, I had missed him so that time. I wanted to tell him about Klosters, about the skiing and the snow. I ran over the *Scalzi*, bearing my white message, ran down the mostly new *calli* but cut through *San Giacomo dell' Orio* and *San Giovanni Evangelista* to his apartment house. I ran and walked fast to breathe and ran, so one says *I ran all the way*. My heart pounded, really, my chest ached, so one says *the heart in my chest ached for him*. To tell him about the rush and glitter and speed of skiing.

But a few days later, I was bored by him. Or hurt. He had been jealous of the trip and unforgiving. My father said, *Stop thinking about him so much . . . Even at your age you ought to have a bread-and-butter sense of what people are like . . . But you are so sure you will be loved that you are like a little animal . . .*

I can resurrect the feelings, the desperate or relieved or ex-hilarated caring . . . and, then, the not caring . . . or the caring less. What is clearer, however, is how others thought of us. On a summer day of sun and bugs and a sweaty floodwater of tourists eddying and spilling into the *campi*, I was walking with Onni and his mother back from the *Merceria*. I can feel the heat of his mother's body—it seemed such a big body—and the relative coolness of Onni's smaller being. The size of his mother and my size are such that when I was walking alongside her I had to look up at her as steeply as if she were a statue or as if she were a figure in a ceiling fresco.

She said that we were lucky friends, *gli amici più fortunati*; she said we were *una famosa amicizia*, a famous friendship; and all at once, she is gone, she leaves us, tactfully, and we are alone as if we were lovers or famous friends.

Where is your friend? People would ask that when they saw me. *Only one of you? The cup—and not the saucer?*

Onni and I sat on the low steps on the Florian side of the *Piazza San Marco* and stare heavy-eyed and sophisticatedly at the pigeons and felt the triumphant reality and burden and mystery of having this sort of reputation, of playing this sort of role in the world.

My mother sometimes took me to Mass, and my eyes would bulge out with boredom after a while. I fiddled, I twitched, I told myself stories, drew invisible apples and guns and faces on the tiled pavement of the floor of the church with the toe of my shoe. The errant mind caroms off the absolute in innocent betrayal and then in obstinacy and malicious unbelief . . .

Be still, my mother would say. *This is important to me*. Then: *Be still, pray for Onni: be useful* . . . And she would smile sadly, piously . . . She was in the process of becoming Catholic.

I am nice to him but he's no angel, you know?

I would, sometimes, be useful and pray in my putative innocence for Onni and for others and for peace rather than war. I did it restlessly and childishly . . . I did not in my heart consider God to be more important than Onni—or childhood. Sometimes when my mother said this or that deep thing or errand or duty was more important than Onni, I would, partly in humor but cuttingly, with early male snobbery, say, *It's not*, and give reasons in rapid demotic Venetian, blinding her ears, if I might be allowed to put it like that; and perhaps that was my attitude toward God as well.

You are unappreciative, she said, with her own humor; *God loves you and your father loves you—you are the love of your father's life* . . . She said it with sad rebuke and an edge of dislike for men and me as an example of the male and in disdain toward my notions of love . . . selfish and privileged notions in her view.

And my oldest brother, Carlo, would imprison and punish me whenever he could . . . *You think the two of you are so adorable* . . . And Dad, of course, would not defend me.

My then still-Protestant but wavering mother said to me in church, *Pay attention to the Mass and maybe you'll be a civilized man when* you *grow up . . . and not a little beast like your friend whom you love so much . . . That brat means more to you than the rest of us put together . . . Pay attention to Jesus and learn who your friends really are and what really matters and maybe you won't be a fool your whole life long . . .*

My father said, *You'd throw us all to the wolves for the sake of that Fascist kid if he asked you to.*

Onni's mother, a bit wild-eyed, said, *Venice spoils children, aie, aie . . .*

I preferred Onni to my father usually. But fatherhood has its aura, too. This confusion was part of liking another child in the midst of one's family life.

My mother called it misguided love . . . So it began. More and more I lied about Onni to her and the others, about Onni and then about everything. I lied *tactfully* and blankly, sometimes sourly—I began to lie everywhere, to everyone . . . except him. I did not usually lie to him.

Onni's father, too, began to object at this point. Onni listened to his father. Onni was less rebellious than I was—he was Italian.

I remember saying to Onni, *I wish you were my brother*, and Onni saying only, *Yes*, accepting it as homage but not interested then in a reality other than the one that existed although he often enough had said it before to me and would say it again when things had happened at home and then with me that made him feel like that, but he had no brothers and understood only the temporary wish not to be alone as he felt it and not the true contractual range of accepting the reality of another boy's feelings or the intertwining of lives contained in my more experienced sense of brotherhood, of brotherliness, of brothers.

•

Poor memory. It glimpses the real time of the past but cannot stay in it for more than a flicker of the mind's eye . . . Real time takes too long to recall and is so crammed with reality that it is shocking when it resurfaces—it is so physical, the reality of flesh and of emotions and of light, that it self-destructs before it comes to the end of anything. Or perhaps the mind retreats to symbols and abstractions, to a kind of self-righteous triumph of conclusion and opinion, rather than go on being tortured by the depth and width and brilliance of the real even in the courts of memory.

If I were a *Herr dottore* I might suggest that it was neurally impossible to contemplate actuality, the continuous time in which we live. Perhaps with the help of outlines and thoughts on paper we can glimpse it and run or bounce or carom from glimpse to glimpse. But the true story is lost to us in the errancy of memory which must inevitably shatter and fly about and run off like spray and water splashes from the stubbornness of the reality of continuous time.

I mean that one can only dive in, and not swim there, in the lost canals of an earlier moment, not swim continuously. Perhaps it is spiritually impossible to accept that Time *is* continuous, unbroken and of irresistible majesty. Perhaps one must have symbols whose motion can be altered and gainsaid and denied. One can deny God. But time, ah time, its direction is unyielding and one cannot alter physically the physical dimensions of a moment.

Venice sits among the waves and among the winds and the silent continuousness of time.

The devices and slants and racing improprieties of memory can't retraverse in a real way a single past second and its rich complexities in literal truth. All the tricks of memory and of mind can't picture, in their abstract compressions of real moments, time's truly unabridged continuousness. In that unpicturable succession of events and seasons and moments, the untranslatable realities of our lives occurred.

Perhaps it is impossible for any ego to deal with this obstinate and continuous omnipotence so appallingly present and unhidden, this immediacy of other and motionful power, this selfhood of reality.

One's tears, one's gloom, or one's regret are for the lost elements of the continuousness tucked in silently among the symbols of recall.

So, memory uses dramatic discontinuity as dreams do, and as stories do. Memory is as mad and maimed and bureaucratic and lazy and corrupt as the grotesque masks and figures of carnival and of mocking paintings show dreams to be. Since the distance to the moment before this one cannot be physically traversed, Onni and I fight each other to settle the degree of factuality in each of our skittish memories.

Skittish memory. I wake a little before dawn, a child and an old man mixed, a little like the Virgin as a child among the grownups in the Titian or in the Tintoretto, in the *Presentation of the Virgin*, and I am the grownups too, the rabbi at the top of the stairs, the watching women, the bearded men. In the tidal ebb of eddying moments I find myself in bed in the *Palazzo Marinention* with this other body, it is not the body of my childhood, and I hurry and dress myself, I hurry outside into the loosening dark, the soft, silent air.

Venice is a separate country. It cannot properly be part of Italy, or part of anything. It floats at anchor inside its own will, among its domes and campanili, independent and exotic at its heart, a collection of structures among the waters, monuments of independent will, a city of independent will.

In Venice, here on the vaporetto landing at *Sant' Ortellia* with the façades of palaces visible in an irregular line along the watery, water-carved curve of the *Canalazzo*, time seems to be illuminated in the moist air, an arriving moment is so immediate and obvious in its approach and in its reality as yet another moment of one's life . . . This motion is exemplified in the faint, pale yellow appearing in the east and lying lightly in long rays on the façades and small waves and perceptibly changing moment by moment. Time is different here than on the mainland, in the cities or countryside there. Affection is untied to the departing moment and is perhaps not refastened unless you or events fasten it again, rebutton it. The boundless *medias res* in which we live, and the intermittences of attention when there is no pause of bodily reality—and our unawareness of the basso continuo or ostinato of pulse—and our awareness of the discontinuities of the mind's tenor and soprano and baritone—explain why presence has its quality as beauty for the mind's comfort and beyond it, to the mind's dismay and sense of imprisonment—I mean presence is fidelity and belongs to one's continuing heartbeat and breath, and not to the disjunctures of attention.

The light moves between the buildings and on the buildings and tricklingly on water. Actual light and actual dark is everywhere in sight. The world is real. The glimmer of his small teeth between Onni's lips when we sat on the steps of the arcade behind the *Loggetta* watching the rain, a relentless and loud, smelly, greenish-gray rain. Rain was a larger phenomenon back then—and fell from a higher sky above the Doges' Palace. Onni's hair is damp—damp boyish hair. My mother in a white linen dress is drunk—this is another moment, my mother drunk, near dawn; she had fallen—she was bruised; her white linen dress was torn. The hurt-eyed world of childhood. And school in the Fascist era . . . Lurid and garish public carnival, hatred of England, the sounds of the breath of rapid radio voices . . . All the thrilling *kitsch*. Parades and searchlights . . . Massed formations of warplanes in the air . . . The oratory threatened to shed enough blood to fill the Lagoon . . . The Blackshirts in the narrow *calli* . . . Mussolini's colossal architectures . . . I will tell you a fourth thing about Venice: it is not a city in which black has much meaning. Even the stains here are rarely black. And night, rarely. Black plays little role in Venetian painting. Black as a color for clothes is Dutch and French, Spanish and English, but not Venetian. Black here is luminosity, is color lightly asleep, veiled. Visiting Nazis in black uniform or dressed in regular clothes had the quality even then of a bad sentence or a cheaply excited movie —they were unsuitable in their visored caps in motorboats or gondolas, erectly sightseeing on the Grand Canal, and somehow, in every way, they are out of scale and presumptuous; more like owners than tourists, they are scrawls of discoloration on the surfaces they traverse or wherever they stand.

The Blackshirts too, but more nervously, with a different sense of alertness, a different shade of intrusive black.

Literally, since they often wore shiny black, and the colors of the city and of the air were reflected dimly as in a dirty mirror. I think my brother Carlo felt considerable sympathy toward Fascism and its adventurism. I was immune to spite him. McClure Piersall Caulkins of the consulate advised my Dad to behave with caution, as did Dad's Italian lawyer, the father of Amedeo, the boy I liked who was troubled by a sense of the presence of God even in childhood. My Dad said Amedeo's father spoke of God's mysterious and difficult wishes and the salvation to be found in at first unwanted submission to God's history on earth—i.e., behave and be patient toward the Fascists.

One was a soldier. A little soldier, realistically, among the realisms. In this peculiar era, everyone claimed to be realistic, but the realisms didn't match. It was an era of contest, separating the sheep from the goats, everyone said; everyone had different ideas about sheep and goats. *Pay attention*, my father said. *Be attentive*, my parents advised . . . Carlo taught me how to stand at attention . . .

But now it is the hideous mute distractibility of my schoolroom attention that is real and the impurity of my loyalties is like the impurities of my attention. In the bored-with-class moment of watching Onni's hands as he draws warplanes, I see the shape, the roundness of his childish hands, his fingers holding the pencil—the hands and fingers of a killable, often *mute* boy. How high the ceiling of the room is. How vast the *Bacino* is.

Now I see us from outside, small-faced, visibly white-skinned children . . . Here we are at the movies. I hear the rustlings of our clothes as we sit side by side and shift postures and watch. The pulse of blood and breath in me now is not the same as it was then in the child: my childhood pulse is like sparrows scattering the gravel of a path.

The almost liquidly gold-leafed yellow light of dawn when

we were out fishing with Paolo the boatman on the Lagoon . . . or with one of our fathers . . . or with Carlo . . . The fishing rods were an aspect of fatedness; you wait inside the sense of possibility in each moment . . . The unbroken surface of the water with its streaks of dawn's gold or its paler, flickering, gauzy peach of a later minute and the destiny of fish or a boat, a *sandalo* being rowed toward us, toward this fragment of the Lagoon, are also figures of possibility in the watery silence . . . Leaning against Paolo's side, or next to Carlo on a seat, I slept, my fishing rod propped under me . . . Onni, a better soldier, stayed awake and never napped and never had to eat and drink unreasonably. When he did eat and drink, it was on the grownups' schedule, and he had then clearly a physical hunger and a real thirst so that eating and drinking had a strong, physical quality and did not seem nervous or childish but precociously serious and quite disciplined instead. Carlo and Paolo and my father seemed to admire Onni when they were with him, to like him without sarcasm, with a kind of patient but respectful indulgence that such an erect, alert, soldierly child with such an extraordinary face and manner deserved. Onni's unnervous but somehow neurally taut or kindled, only slightly soft, boyish alertness and readiness, the way he soldiered in the minutes at being a male child at each project, at the ways he was ably focussed in each category of attentiveness asked of him, won their respect, the wide-eyed and as-if-on-tiptoe way he listened in spite of a certain subdued pressure of physical restlessness in him. His readiness and his need to move and to act showed his need to express the life in him, the ability, the superiority of the creature self in him. He was a superior creature, he had an impressive self . . .

But sometimes the grownups were cross about him when he was not there. Behind his back, they dismissed him or were sarcastic. They shook their heads. *He is too handsome*, Carlo said . . .

I was rarely jealous. I felt ennobled by reflection instead and, anyway, people liked me too. I wasn't starved or overshadowed or didn't feel it if I was—or did only sometimes as he did by me, at moments, certainly not so many. But how would I know?

All this had to do with an estimated, a guessed-at value—I mean besides the merits in immediacy of his charming and serious presence, the presence merely of a child. And beyond my value in immediacy was my possibly having this other juvenile, contingent merit in regard to the future, *all in good time*, as the grownups said.

I felt oppressed at times but I admired the superior creature, this idea of rank embodied or exemplified in my friend Onni.

It was a very real matter in that era. Here is Onni in Venice walking toward me near *San Rocco*; Onni, in schoolboy costume, his head cast down, is just such another figure of possibility as the *sandalo* was as it was rowed toward us across the gray and bluing and whitened surface of the Lagoon, he so suggests life and a story, he is so admired by so many people, he is such a promising creature . . .

The quality of early fate in a child is unendurably enticing. A boy in class, Piero Zittoni, could barely speak to Onni, he idolized Onni so, was so impressed by him. Piero's face had so much heat of sensation in it when he looked at Onni that it was embarrassing to see him.

Onni, an idolized boy, surrounded by this sort of event, was often sour and childishly ironic—irony was rare in a Young Fascist, which Onni was. He had a uniform. He kept his feelings at a distance far inside himself as if they were cars stabled on the *Piazzale Roma* while he was in the Piazza. Onni, when he was in his observantly Fascist mode, did not react to me or my emotions. He would just stare at me. Or he would produce a careful smile, almost a professionalism of response in a fine Fascist child. He was rather un-Italian . . . Or a new sort of Italian. In his challenging and guileful, heroic aspect as a very Young Fascist.

Onni and I were social exceptions, exceptional: *An inspiring example of honest international friendship*, his father said, *international friendship*.

You see, the grownups often meddled in the image and in the actuality of our attachment . . . They could not resist the impulses of power in them. They used restlessly their creature superiority and their mental and spiritual understanding, exercised them as if they were stabled animals out for a run on the Lido.

Onni needed me. It is both immodest and grim to outline why. But I was consciously well-meaning and that lightened his sense of things. And one might mention what might be called a basic silence, or helplessness, in him, invisible in his heroically hyperkinetic brilliance, but it was there. I am made of words. I supplied the words. I protected him against his role as a child by putting things into words that formed a childish language that protected him . . . I took him quite seriously.

It was mysterious to us that we affected one another because we did not understand or consciously know much about or even recognize our differences, our individuality, we so took our brotherhood and a generality of being as a given. We were surprised when differences appeared in us, and we tended to treat them as forms of antagonism. We did not admire each other's difference from the other except in the implicit appreciation that was present in our attachment to one another.

We checked each other's faces for affection each time we met. We saw the day's current degree of attachment then. The attachment was not always there.

But when it is there, we run and tackle each other and collapse on the pavement. Collapsed, we don't rise at once. Our breath, our breathing mingles, flowing side by side, childhood and early youth breathing in near unison.

Or we were with my mother at the *Pescheria*, in the smell and the restless crowd, in the heat of the sun, with the stirring of the *Canalazzo* just beyond the stalls and crates and boxes of food and fish. When the bells of the city rang at noon, my mother said, *Where did the morning go?*

It fell into the sun, Onni said.

My mother said, *You are an adorable boy—that's an interesting thing for you to say.* Encouraging him in civilized conversation.

His remark came from games Onni and I played in which our spaceship passed near the sun's corona, and we yelled commands to increase the rocket thrust so that we would not fall into the sun, and we jettisoned things to lighten the ship: those things fell into the sun.

Time was strange in the spaceship, we had been told. Time disappeared or curved, or we travelled in it. Anything that disappeared, but especially time, went into the sun. It had become a catchphrase. We so derived ourselves for a few months that it wasn't clear who spoke when either one of us spoke.

When I sassed my mother in Italian, she said, *Am I talking to you or to Onni Galliani? I don't know which one of you is more disrespectful.*

Onni was often rude. I believe he was derailed at times into nervous madness, not deeply, except for moments or for an hour or a day or two, and then deeply enough to be monstrous in a way. Onni was often monstrous . . . His would become another of the gargoyle heads in Venice, distorted in a silent scream or in will, when he and I—sometimes with other children, girls and boys—would in dark-mooded play strike each other with sticks, with stones, with books to see how much we could bear or stand, each of us, before one of us screamed or squealed and said *Stop* or lowered his or her head or closed his or her eyes in a sign of surrender at the inability to accept any more of this reality.

In this manner, we also beat each other with belts, with sticks from gardens, with our shoes while we stood or danced around in our stocking feet dealing and receiving blows. We used to butt each other, head to body or head to head, do it over and over, and harder and harder until one of us begged off, or until one of us would clutch his head and reel, sometimes exaggeratedly, and fall to the ground sometimes in actual concussed confusion.

Or we would lean against a wall holding our heads.

He often went mad, breathing hard, insistently, and to tell the truth, I did too. It was not quite a game, not quite an entirely serious matter to the death. The lunacy, the battle intoxication shook us, shook our brains loose, shook our brain pans into one another's, or, I think, into hatred, not always a practice hatred, but sometimes it was only that. I think we hated until the sun went black for us. I hated my own mind often, and consciousness.

"The U.S.A. is rotten."
"Your country is rotten."
"No, I mean it."
"No, I mean it."

We stared at the possibility of this as truth for us or as a cause of dislike, but while the subject of Mussolini came up endlessly often, it did not separate us. I'm not sure that had I known of the brutalities it would have been different. My parents did not heavily propagandize. They did not interfere to the extent that they would have if they had *hated* my seeing Onni.

It is difficult to describe this sort of thing, but, you see, the Fascists and Fascism did not proceed in the moments in so disciplined and steady a fashion that one was stuck with a cold, fixed issue in regard to them . . . In the daily and yearly ebbs and flows of politics were lapses of attention and belief and periods of decadence, almost of collapse of that movement as a serious matter or as an earnest one. Then there were crusades of rededication and renewal and reform, but then laxity returned in the Italian manner. Sometimes it seemed to be a laxity from the top, a forgetfulness in *Il Duce* himself. An odd ranting figure, visible only within a glary haze of propaganda, and not seen but only squinted at and never seen humanly and in a dimension of reality, and, so, never humanly discussed. He was an odd emblem or emblematic figure to have as an image in the mind, too odd actually to hate and to fight violently . . . Too odd to fight because of him, for or against. He was there because he was there. I did, in a way, cordially loathe the presence enough that it was ready to be hatred. But it was not clear to me what I felt.

Onni, differently, yet similarly, was *blurred* toward me. As I said, at times Onni and I were a semi-official symbol of Italian–American amity—that was partly why people acted the way they did toward us. Onni's father and my parents, too, at times approved or disapproved or fostered the friendship officially.

For Onni, in his life, his friendship with me had a Party standing and was a source of pride, a term of citizenship. Onni, however, did a few times betray *Il Duce* in talk, and then he was harsh with himself and brooding afterward. It was a time when beauty was self-consciously a national-socialist weapon, but so was death. So was one's mind.

Onni said quotingly: *You should love Il Duce. He is the greatest man in the world. He is the greatest man in Europe since Napoleon. Who likes Napoleon?* I said. *He lost.*

We fought—we started hitting each other, and we fought. Onni looked across-a-gulf and down-into-a-pit at me when we were children since I was apart or alone in his eyes in his Europe.

Another friend of mine, the pious Amedeo whom I mentioned, the son of my father's Italian lawyer—the Amedeo who will grow up to become a priest, or as my mother, a converted Catholic at the end of her life, will say, *An important priest*—looked at me similarly in those months. As did working-class children often. And English children. And some other American children in Venice. One was suddenly regarded differently. In a certain fashion, snobbery is a temporarily still-half-peaceful form of war fever.

Where did my politics come from? I disliked having my life and my mind be at anyone's disposal or at the disposal of an idea. I was sometimes beaten in fights with Fascist kids, but often that was class war more than actual politics, or it was the will of a bad group or of one ambitious boy leading a gang.

But this happens in a life without a Mussolini. The true strangeness was only spectrally visible in Venice. The windows in our palazzo were broken on three occasions. I ran gauntlets of thrown stones a couple of times. A life is full of adventures and traumas; you do not always remember them clearly or name them correctly when you do remember.

In the bad months when the Fascist fever was strong, Onni sometimes shielded me, provided credentials, and twice fought alongside me. We, my family, were half-accepted in Venice, after all. To some extent I took his support for granted.

But Onni is not the only child I love. I love a girl, Albia, who is *very* religious. She, too, goes to our school. A number of Italians in Venice distrusted the State schools and the Church ones and thought the English School was to be trusted, and Albia's parents were among those. Albia did not suffer such prolonged lapses of attention to religion or such absentness or wavering of feeling in herself toward God and the saints as I did, but every day, she slipped, for an hour or two or three, off and on in those hours, away from attention and into errancy, into wildness to some degree.

She was the sort of child believer who creates one real example after another of local virtue in strenuously taut complete-ness—and she showed an enraged affection for the people of faith who guided her. But she slipped up and liked me too, and she had a wildness in her, a fever of intelligence and willfulness and blind courage that would emerge.

But she did love virtue and the idea of virtue—very reli-giously. But there are so many minutes in the day, so many heartbeats that though she most often was animated by love of God and of her mother, she was, also, for a while, off and on, and exasperatedly but loyally and at times meekly but darkly, wildly fond of me.

She was very smart and she was rather an angry child, power-mad and nervy and savvy and meddlesome and dark-souled. When she laughed, she laughed in pain as if she was being cut by knives that also tickled her. She laughed with a kind of self-righteous, affronted horror and completeness of giving herself over to it. She believed in magic, in God and faith, and in character.

And she disapproved of the world. No, she was angry with it. She was a small girl, or person, for whom another, clearer reality—of idea—existed than the ordinary physical one of child-hood. She was vengeful. Even while talking forgiveness, she was alert for vengeance. She was so competitive that if I won out over her at anything, she would stop speaking to me although she would not leave my side. She made me lie prone in the middle of the *Campo San Polo*; and while we were prone she asked me, while voices skittered around us, she asked me if I saw the Virgin's robe in the pale blue Venetian sky. A supernatural Queen, untouched by sexual reality and radiant with power, with the ability to punish. And gifted with mercy, of course. Mercy being a licensed beyondness, you were outside all rules with mercy.

Albia runs over a high-arched *ponte storto* over the *Rio Santa Maria Mater Domini* or moves, windblown, skirt and skinny legs and long braid, in the great Piazza . . . "Say only polite things to me . . . Don't talk to me as if I were a boy—or stupid," she said.

She and Onni were wary of each other.

In real moments, in the abundance of seconds and moments, things change so that contradictions and paradoxes naturally abound. It is not that everything is unclear but that the fixity of names is untrue.

There was triumph in her voice when she said good-by when her family moved to Switzerland. "I love the Virgin and the young Jesus—and God—and the Holy Spirit more than I love you . . . I want to be a saint. Well, I won't see you ever again . . . I love you too . . ." Gloomy, childish, exalted voice . . .

I mean that I was not reliable where Onni was concerned. My mother who was often very nice to Onni and about him said, *Onni is not our sort. His father is a real fascist, you know. Onni can't be trusted. He reports on us to his father.*

My mother's (and father's) choices for my friends were high-flown, positively ducal, the twin nephews of an exiled queen or the son of—as they put it—*an important newspaper publisher* who sometimes came to Venice.

For me, though, the complications of rank with such children and all the negotiations with them made childhood play pallid and formal, *bulky* and slow and ceremonial. Liking-at-sight and friendships that were half-forbidden and improbable proceeded more quickly and were livelier and had more depth and more sudden astonishment in them. Meetings, spending time together, the fact of presence was simpler with such affections.

I went to the movies every week, a Venetian movie theater, a dark cavern in an old damp building . . . Onni and I usually sat apart from the other children. Sometimes a child who wanted to be friends would ask, *Who do you go to the movies with?*

I only go with Onni.

A good deal of one's life is not acceptable and so one refuses to remember it. Sometimes we took a group of children with us but then we sat separately from the group, or at one end, or just behind, a peninsula of special relation.

In the late winter rain of March, Onni and I took the vaporetto to the movies. Sometimes when it rained heavily, we stayed out in the rain to be heroically buffetted and toughened. Or we purposefully ran in the rain in the narrow channels of the *calli.*

This was a dreary rain. The Grand Canal was pocked with little knobs attached in cause and effect to the general slant of the brownish lines of falling drops. I wrestled with Onni, idly, then industriously—I kicked him while being kicked while sitting loose-armed, innocently. Both of us had on caps. The vaporetto seats squealed as we squirmed. The boat groundingly moored at each landing. Outside the dirty rain-streaked window of the boat, the palazzi had their lights on in the daytime on this watery street.

"Are you full of shit?" I asked Onni earnestly and dryly mocking in the manner of childhood.

"No. You are," he said snobbishly but in the Fascist snobbish manner which he sometimes mocked.

Twenty-three desks in the classroom, and rain outside, not a brown-colored rain but seeming black, in blue, black air, and the great desk where Miss Murphy, our new teacher, sat . . . Miss Murphy has replaced Miss Moon who has left the country abruptly. Miss Murphy said *shit* under her breath sometimes, and I liked her. After she said *shit,* she would say, "But you didn't hear me say that . . . Ha-ha . . ." Miss Murphy said in a very sharp, pinching-you voice, "*Giangiacomo*—" Onni she meant. "The beautiful *Giangiacomo* is going to be *Protestant* now. We're going to help him be a true-blue boy." It was something his father wanted, him not to be subject to the influence of the Church. The children said of Miss Murphy to Onni, *That woman is in love with you.*

Onni's father was feuding with the local Cardinal. Onni was to be an Italian Fascist Protestant.

Miss Murphy was to be *understood* in a great gulp or else she vanished into complication and chaos. Erotically pretty and heavily made-up, she was in style and effect a classroom goddess. Miss Murphy had black hair cut short and used white powder and dark rouge and very red lipstick. She had very dark, closely plucked, curved eyebrows and very broad cheekbones—the effect was of painted clay, and of a face of a *femme mezzo-fatale*, my father said in two languages. Hers was an insufferably self-satisfied prettiness, or perhaps one should say big-boned handsomeness.

My father thought her a Fascist assigned to keep an eye on the expatriate English-speaking community in Venice and on the other teachers in the school, most of whom were spies for someone or other, or so he said.

Miss Murphy was fond of the poetry of Walter de la Mare and of Kipling . . . *I must down to the sea again* . . . I am not sure that is quite how the line goes . . . And she said, "I know oodles and caboodles, tons of Kipling by heart." The poem about keeping your head when everyone else was losing theirs was something she recited perhaps too often. "It is time for the multiplication tables . . . *We must down to the sea again* . . . No sighs . . . None of that . . . If we can keep our heads while all about us are losing theirs, we will be sons and daughters of the gods. I am not descended from the monkeys. I don't know about you but I am not an ape. I am descended from the gods. Let's keep our heads even if all about us are losing theirs. Poor Marie Antoinette. Onward to multiplication now."

It was a time when people were losing their heads in more than one sense. She champed her teeth as if on a horse's bit. She was consciously imitating a war-horse. She snorted in a neighing way. "I have my own sense of humor," she said and she folded her arms under jutting breasts; she held a piece of chalk under that jutment. She looked at us ironically-fierily, a personality.

She said, "I don't like smart people. I am not ready to be *wise*. I am ready to be *brave*. Let's do the *eights* . . ." She said, "I like greatness and self-sacrifice. I like people who know the rules, who have spine, backbone, guts. I don't want to teach bankers. I want to teach heroes." It was an ideal she was proposing, a way to live, and did not to us then sound despicable as an ideal. Life and action were attached to this ideal. Her notion seemed a severe and demanding grown-up extension of childhood, of childhood activity. My judgement as a child was, of course, that of someone who had not lived much yet. Miss Murphy was Irish by way of England and bitterness. She was a Protestant and had no brogue. She said, "You have to learn how to be teased . . . I am not going to be led around by the nose by bratty children. I am my own woman. Don't make faces—I can't hear myself think when I am looking at ugly, stupid faces—I want to hear myself think. I enjoy my own thinking, whatever anyone else says . . ."

It wasn't personal madness quite but was a broad madness of universal ambition . . . She had tremendous energy and she was fiercely living life but as a teacher restlessly active and striving to be heroic, looking for dramatic meaning. The momentum of energy and ambition and activity did not allow her much open doubt; I have never known anyone as boldly sure of herself. I believe she did love Onni and me but me less than she did Onni, or more, but more disapprovingly in her fierce momentum. And her love was all momentum, was in a rush and as if in passing even when she looked at me head-on.

Love as grievance and contamination is peculiar, the angry wish to make public a privacy of infection, to enlarge the small community of infectious mutual release of feeling, and to be a local star, day after day—the hypnotic and seductive familiarity of it is strange; it seems dusty and death-ridden. It seems it can end only in death, in disaster, in a great crash.

After a while you can smell how dirty a victory is, and you want to die. A community of death-feelings, intricate feelings, sprang up . . . The class, too, was affected. Was influenced.

At a certain point, Onni withdrew from me. No: I began it. In a way, it doesn't matter who did it first. He had jealous grounds, fastidious grounds. He had his pride. He had his own ideas. I was very unhappy. The accumulation of hurt makes the child staringly, agonizingly, consistently recessive, quiet, a boy of gestures. Onni talked more and more. I was less than of use to him.

Onni was vividly tireless in school games. He was increasingly royal. He had an entourage of boys, and, more and more, in the classroom or in the small dank indoor exercise room, or on the roof, or after school, he was well-mannered, darkly blasphemous, smart and undisciplinable, and shrewdly alert, so alert that his wide-awakeness was perhaps an extra quality of personal beauty. He was darkly open, an entire eye.

He was not a very good leader. The class became brutal, a mass of sullen or active factions. And Miss Murphy was more and more absentminded—a tilted goddess. Onni was not very much like what he had been in private when we played. As I said, he played while Miss Murphy imprisoned me in her moist grip and was talkative, and the games, the recesses became febrile and torn with unhappiness for me.

Everyone involved was *human* and mistaken—but not equally. The mistakes were in no way equivalent. To take refuge in quick judgement is to be stupidly apocalyptic. I do not want to throw life away as violently and as universally as the *Fascists* did who claimed that such blood sacrifice was better for everyone than to have meaningless lives.

To think, to feel, to care is a kind of nervy gambling, isn't it? Each moment is a roulette—and history is guesswork. Ambition, love—one's own survival—these are elements. Onni was noticeably and precisely snobbish toward me. And he was snobbish toward me in a general way, in a Fascist class-leader's way. I couldn't believe he was throwing our friendship aside, but so long as I was "entangled" by Miss Murphy I was helpless toward him in this matter.

But it was a case of him being visionarily snobbish, heroically so. He did not see Fascism as banal. He was heroic and *sinful* —but sad. And he had a dark-eyed faith in redemption through death someday—many of the children did—and that was heroic, if stupid. I don't mean that we knew what it all was about, but

we guessed at it, childishly, boyishly-erotically. And it was a
literal reality, a metaphysical plague, the contaminated wistful-
ness of the styles of *heroism* at that time. It infected all of us.
Our sense of intellectual order, our childhood doctrines, shaped
our faces—people had a certain look then, and children too.

No one knew how the contests of that time would come out.
Everyone was gambling heroically whether they wanted to or
not. We children wanted to. The dictators said courage would
decide. Whether it would be courage or economic strength or
military genius, no one knew. The planners and the soldiers
guess. Everyone had to guess. Everybody had, to some extent
complicitously and bewilderingly, to play for high stakes, for very
high stakes, the stakes being the world and everyone's notions
of right and wrong as they would be taught in schools and lived
by and one's own life and other people's lives in quantity. The
very silence of the Lagoon seemed to pulse with a sense of tidal
blood and death; the dim clang of water against the hull was like
that of martial machines. Flags were everywhere; they flapped
and crackled in the wind; that too seemed to mark the martial
pulse.

And children's eyes and breath were part of that pulse. He,
Onni, was taken up as if by an eagle, abducted by the doctrines
of Mussolini that supposed realism and greatness. About him
hovered the ghosts of dead heroes, he was so heroic in manner.
He had an air of unworldly issues; his forsaken Catholicism was
now his Fascism, such as it was, along with his Protestantism in
its warrior form. Miss Murphy had been lying in wait all the
while to gobble up his little soul. Growing up, getting from childhood to manhood, is a gruesome adventure. He had a quality of
having otherworldly presences present to him in this world. He
had a romantic quality of being important to people although he
was a child.

And he had a quality of concision in his judgements that
argued that if he was not Alexander the Great or the equivalent,
he was an awful fool. Not dumb: a fool . . . In the too-quick
judgements he made . . . merely a boy and dark-faced, an as-if-
sculpted and admirably athletic young boy.

Miss Murphy, drawn on by her maneuvering as a Fascist of

some importance, a ruler of the school, a *goddess-alighted-here*, foisted Onni on us as a political leader, *re della classe*. He accepted the role without responsibility, with mostly only a ceremonial or posing-in-the-role responsibility. He was independent, even wild inside himself still—I know that much. But he *loved* these outward roles . . .

"Wherever I go, I try to improve things," Miss Murphy said. She and Mussolini left a trail of *improvements*, mementoes of the improved world, of their time in power. She was, after all, Fascist-colossal, too, out of scale with the city. Miss Murphy's procedures were of searing, scalding interest to me. I was not, of course, starved to death. But she affected me so strongly it was unendurable. She said, "You will become a strong man or you won't last long, which will it be in this time of decision, my little American *friend?*"

Onni and I still exchanged glances and invitations, "You want to go to the lunchroom with me?"

He was a big shot in class. He had his own standing independently of me. He liked kids I hadn't cared that much about, and it happened that Onni and I weren't such good friends anymore on those grounds as much as on any other. We were not often in each other's company alone anymore. Angrily solitary, I saw that Onni wanted me to *accept* my own unimportance. I disliked him for that.

Children. Children's cruelty. The wars of childhood. But to demean someone—ah, you see, Miss Murphy knew my type. I hadn't the heart to fight, or perhaps the interest, having seen him as this person, fight to go on being friends, or to be angry at the dissolution of the friendship.

He and I had walked to recess side by side exclusively with each other. In games too we had almost always been side by side. No more.

Miss Murphy said, "Don't look at me like that . . . I don't care if you dislike me . . ." She said to Onni, "Go run and play—and be natural . . ." Or: "Go to lunch with your own kind, dear . . . *Caro* . . ."

She cared that I disliked her and disapproved of her and

that I was hurt. Grownups usually care what children think of them. And children offer their affections, don't they? Or withdraw them. Children do act toward grownups. Or operate. It is very difficult—and partly sexless. Mostly children respond helplessly—isn't that what makes children seem so sweetly lifegiving? That they are so sweetly available to your strength and ability.

She said, "Try to understand me . . . I want to be *very proud* that I once knew Nino O'Hara."

I began to be silent with a dull, minimal, gestural politeness. If asked I would have been unable to say what I felt but it was dismissal and a kind of boredom, a bored agony. Momma said, "Everyone has had a nightmare teacher and a faithless friend."

I did not clearly know how to dislike Miss Murphy while I still was drawn to her. The knowledge she had and my ignorance in our interchange, the blackly interesting dialogue, struck me as wicked since it had lost me Onni's regard, and I felt a kind of awed contempt, an *I-bet-you-will-be-punished* sort of contempt for her, but I did not have in me a mechanism of final rejection.

I hardly knew what my feelings were, but they were obvious as so much unhappiness that I was crippled and could not be proud or playful or endure other children. Or consolation at home. In Venice it is not easy to be alone but one drags along at the edge of things or turns down a side route and is alone briefly. Or one sits in the *Piazzetta* staring at nothing . . . And perhaps Onni will come marching by, literally, in some rehearsal march of Young Fascists. Or with his retinue.

We spoke. We greeted each other—minimally-maximally with so many degrees of glance, of distance, of patient blankness, briefly-staringly that it was hateful. It did induce headache and nausea, a vertigo at the depths of things now.

I rather think I thought he was loathsome and a fool and too easily bribed and not sensible and to be avoided, but for a while I loved no one else. And as my father pointed out—"Poor lonely Nino . . . We don't even have a dog."

My attitude toward Miss Murphy did influence the class, some of the kids and then all of them—even Onni—grew tired of the goddess with the painted clay face. I had not expected others to be influenced by my state, but when I saw this boredom with her develop I grew firmer in my disapproval of her—this too was without conscious thought.

In the city, I saw her with different men. One was a soldier in one of the Alpine Regiments . . . I saw her with him in the Piazza. She waved to me and signalled for me to come over to her table where she was with him, but I shook my head and broke into a clumsy run toward the *Loggetta*.

She began to be more and more lackadaisical in class and to have headaches. It is strange for grownups when children refuse to like them. She spent a good deal of time writing notes to other teachers and having us read to ourselves and write themes in class: "I need some time to myself. I need to think . . . Leave me alone . . . Teach yourselves for a while . . ." She never had been good at instructing us.

She was bold, brave, and ruthless still but without energy and chronically ill the last winter with a cough, perhaps bronchitis or from smoking too much. McIlhenny, the headmaster, and she were feuding—she spoke of the feud in class.

I grew a bit plump, from not playing outdoors as much, and gray-faced similarly from too little exercise and loneliness, the only pale child in a class of Venetian children, pale with hopelessness; and I grew somber and untalkative.

Miss Murphy believed that her ideas were worth dying for —*I need a serious life . . . Everyone here is too young to die for anything . . .* Her defeatedness became that sort of speech. I swear I understood how heroic she was—just as I understood, in a way, straight-legged, growing Onni, a bit taller after a sudden spurt of growth in those weeks, Onni with a differently shaped head and altered face running up the *Merceria* followed by his gang, his grim happiness, his sense of individual fate, his pride, his ambition.

We never talked. He liked his life and rank. But he was bored (and restless) sometimes. On *San Lio* one day he came up and walked with me. It was formal—I mean he was after something officially, as *re della classe*. He asked me about Miss Murphy—did I think she was becoming stupid. I said she was a fake and that she hated me. He said, with his most *furbo* look, then with dignity, "Oh no, she loves *you* . . . She pays attention only to you."

"I don't want her to—she's horrible."

Then, as if only jealousy of her had driven him away, he slapped me on the arm and ran a short way ahead, daring me to chase him to slap him back. He never smiled anymore, or rarely—only officially. So, the outbreak and continuance of the game was a little grim in tone, running in the very narrow *calle* to *Zanipolo*, banging and bumping each other, chasing each other . . . But I had slowed down physically. I had been transformed into a strangely heavy, wounded, silent child . . . I hadn't realized it quite or listened to what others had said about it. I hadn't seen it in the mirror. I noticed it only now with him. Certain physical failures—and a certain failure of the chase—made it inescapable. But Onni, chattering in Italian or in his dignified male silences, seemed to accept it, oh, almost as a justice or a thank-offering from me to him. We ran toward *San Francesco della Vigna* where there is a courtyard and not much foot traffic, and often boys are there kicking a soccer ball among the walls and columns and trees and leaves.

No one was there. The wind blew circlingly in the enclosed space. Some conceit in him welcomed the present moment as a victory. A victor over me, with a victory at my expense, he tasted justice and meaning—did you know that feeling in another child when you were small? I told him I thought it was bad that we were not friends. I thought it was terrible to have whole days and weeks without being in the presence of someone whose presence wakes the otherwise sleeping world. Life is not interesting or good any other way, really.

Perhaps I had felt superior to him for some reason or other, because of the superiority of English warplanes to Italian ones —who knows—perhaps I felt superior still and did not really understand the movements of response, of anti-response in his face, the movement of feelings.

We ran in and out among the columns, and I was mostly out of breath, which was shameful really.

"Tomorrow . . ." I said when we parted. "Let's do something . . ."

He blinked and stiffened in an Italian way, rejecting this line of emotion . . . "*Ciao*," he said in a polite but assured and abrupt tone, soldierly and definitely.

"You're being stupid," I said to him.

He smiled and was still more soldierly and said "*Ciao*" again and ran off, sternly triumphant and leaving me stung and burning and childishly hollow, burningly bleak.

Then I set off, walking, walking with difficulty . . . Grief and hurt weigh you down, they weight your legs. I hated being hurt, and I hurt inside and outside myself. I walked in a gray late-afternoon light in Venice in empty and crowded *calli*, in a haze of sightlessness, my face stinging from bits of dead matter blown in the wind. The sudden spurtings of heat as if one were going to cry did not produce tears.

My mother used a tarot deck to tell her fortune day by day, a Light of the East Tarot Deck from the workshop of Li Ho, the Chinese sage—so the little booklet that came with the cards said: I have most of the deck still and the torn booklet. She bought it in Venice.

I was forbidden to play with it, but I laid out my fortune and turned up the two worst cards: the Nine of Swords: *Evil woes . . . Illness. Suffering. Malice. Cruelty. Pain. Despair . . . Pitilessness . . . Suffering, want, loss, misery. Burden, oppression, labor. Subtlety and craft. Lying and dishonesty, et cetera.*

And the Ten of Swords: *Ruin. Death. Failure. Disaster. (Almost a worse symbol than the Nine of Swords.)* [It said this in the booklet.] *Undisciplined warring force, complete disruption and failure. Ruin of all plans and projects. Disdain, insolence and impertinence, yet mirth and jolly therewith. Loving to overthrow the happiness of others, a repeater of things, given to much unprofitable speech, and of many words, yet clever, acute and eloquent, et cetera.*

My mother caught me doing it but was not angry. My mother said it was not Onni and Miss Murphy that was referred to in the cards, but matters that it was too soon for me to know about, and she gave me a sad, mind-on-other-things hug. "But you go ahead and think it's Onni," she said in her half-sweet, amused, clever-mother manner, a manner I usually liked.

I thought perhaps she meant the war in the large worlds of Europe and Asia and not my suffering or family upheavals here in Venice where all sorts of armament was on display, torpedo boats in the *Giudecca*, a destroyer moored not far from the *Danieli*, flyovers by warplanes in formation daily. It seemed the whole world was wandering far from hope, was drifting into a noisy and sickeningly thrilling and horrible striptease revealing a bony, a skeletal reality of *evil woes*.

Carlo said, "You'll learn . . . It's always like this with you . . . You only learn the hard way . . . You shouldn't have trusted that jerk . . .." I thought I was dying inside, my feelings hurt so, my sense of things was so shrivelled up. The loneliness I felt, the boredom when Carlo was nice or half-nice to me scared me— I mean its meaninglessness for me. I felt a cold, dry, clattering bleakness—of being unsheltered and young but not as young as before and not able to return to anything that had existed before the experience of "the nightmare teacher and the faithless friend." I had the conviction that I was a horrible person now— smelly. I knew this happened to a lot of children, to everyone, this thing that had happened to me.

"Do I smell bad?" I asked my mother in a whisper.

"You're all right . . . You don't smell, poor thing . . . Is your heart broken, darling Nino?"

That grief of loneliness and isolation when the fantastic and the truly pleasurable thing of deep enjoyment, of deep enjoyment daily, and personal meaning, is gone, is heartbreak apparently. Venice has no room for this sort of loneliness, no tradition for it really, no agreed-on postures of it—my father said of it at this time, "It's a good-time city gone sour." But he meant sour with politics. "It doesn't seem like Venice anymore," he said.

But the onset of private knowledge in me about the self's vulnerability, that knowledge with some finality in it, was like dying or illness—part of the self is dying; one is as if ill. It leads to an onset of private genius, to vows, to a reorganization of the self. One's feelings are seen against a backdrop—of nightmare instruction and faithlessness, to be repetitious. One is living in the real world (with its wretchedness) and your own hurt does not astound others but is treated as an ordinary thing. A knowledge of this becomes an openness to what is there . . . and to ideas, an alertness to hurt, a watchfulness. A bourgeois self is created.

Carlo said to me with cool jealousy, self-righteous and distant, said with his hands in his pockets, with a rushed impatience toward my unhappiness, "It's not the worst thing . . . your losing that friend . . ." He cleared his throat: "Worse things will happen . . . Worse things happen to everyone . . ." He started to get angry: "You're an asshole, Nino . . . You'll see . . ."

"You're disgusting," I said to him. "You're a big piece of disgusting shit. You're a monster."

Having to live out that period in Venice with such dreary feelings about Onni, about the attachment's being so worthless, I found that this stuff which seemed an indictment of affection, which seemed like a gray and endless emptiness inside the day, inside each hour, was part of my breathing, was part of the very substance of my life.

My feelings at the end of this episode of affection, my suspiciousness toward affection would be part of my life from then on.

The horror of the reality of knowing Miss Murphy and losing Onni's companionship and my new sense of emotions and my being thrust into a dark view of things was the worst thing that had happened to me up until then. The family disasters that were gathering—my parents would be divorced within two years; my father would become ill; my sister Ruthie would have a nervous breakdown—did not affect me so greatly when they occurred as this did; I would be toughened by then, and older. This episode had happened first, and I was stronger in many ways after it, and those events would not hurt me or cause such an awful, bilious heat of stormy and despairing and painful feelings and as much regret or burden me with as oppressive a sense of ignorance and wrongness-in-things as they would have if this episode had not occurred.

Still, all this was over my head, was too much for me to understand. My brother Carlo said to me, "You're too stubborn . . . You asked for it . . ."

"For the world to come tumbling down?"

"Family comes first," he said. "Blood is thicker than water. You cheated on us," he said. "Ha-ha . . ."

Nothing he said and nothing in his tone or manner or glance or touch helped.

At first, it didn't seem worthwhile to live. One lived stumblingly. But as I said, hurt trains us. Of course, one can be rebellious toward hurt and run wildly through Venice and try to be amused by other things. But hurt affects you—everything affects you, but hurt changes you with the most finality, and I became a rather stiff and quiet child. Children change a great deal when circumstances act on them. I overheard my mother say to a friend of hers of me, "The way children turn into something else is frightening." I became stiff and rather clear-voiced and a bit self-conscious and shy—and untouchable.

Of course, after puberty you change again. You get another chance.

THE MOVIES
IN VENICE

LOVE CHIEFLY and the actual moments of the day are my topic, and hatred and whoring and the nature of the body and revengeful or placable memory and the wish for innocence. Also, ambition and the stages of being and the condition of the world. I sort of sing of arms and the man, the arms of an embrace, the arms that are weapons. Not epically. Not with skill.

After the Fascist era, we returned to Italy, to Venice in 1946.

The ship docked in Naples. From the train windows going north we saw the visible reality of vanished battles in a war-worn country, the stone walls of monuments pocked by bullet holes, bridges cracked by bombs, by artillery fire, ruined houses and smashed and charred walls and ashes and untilled farm fields and military wreckage everywhere.

Hiroshima had been bombed, and the image placed in the mind of the eerily glowing column of heat. And the living skeletons in the camps had been photographed. And the ovens. And Mussolini had been photographed, dead, hung upside down, not from the columns in the *Piazzetta*, but at a gasoline station, beside Clara Petacci. Six years of the dead. Military airfields and armored-vehicle parks were still in place, rank on rank of armored personnel carriers and tanks parked in the sun.

The frameworks of the mind, the context of thought included

the military presence. And the black market. And Italian rapacity and energy and hunger. I was thirteen, almost fourteen. It seemed absurd to live one's life inside actual history. A people inhabited the caves at the outskirts of Rome.

My mother and Carlo and I were returning to Venice, life in the United States having proved to be unworkable for us. Although it seemed largely only that Carlo and I had chosen our mother over our father. But in the States, we hadn't fit in very well and hadn't been able to manage the personal and social politics, or even the language, the *Hi, how are ya*'s, or the social manner that asserts a claim of happiness and the conviction of local decency while having a suspicious and practical sense of realities. We were not shrewd, the three of us. And we had felt foreign and tended to see the California Sierras as not-the-Dolomites and the hills outside Santa Clara through a haze of remembrance of the Euganean Hills.

I was returning to my old sense of things, to the place from which most of the settings and details of my dreams were derived.

Venice in the distance, across the water, neared as the train racketted on worn railroad ties on the causeway. The train, the causeway, everything needed repair. We expected nothing to work. It was early October, the middle of a school term, the middle of the day. Time has no geometry of middles. The moment of arrival is mist and damp warm air, a lingering and uneven warmth from the leftover summer, a dank coolness here and there, familiar buildings looking worn, and no sun. And in the sunlessness, the shiftingly dirty water in the smaller canals.

Venice lay in a fog, a mist. Among the shapes of the mist moved apparitions, the sounds of footsteps were brooding and spectral. Carlo, who liked wordplay that year, said, "We ventured to Venice vainly."

We stayed first in the *Ala*, behind the *Gritti*, then in the *Pensione Seguso* while my mother oversaw the readying of an apartment in the *Ca' Giuliani*, a large, fragile, getting-on-to-decrepit palazzo just past *San Giacomo dell' Orio*. It sat beside a canal, the *Rio Marin*, and had a large, overgrown, weedy garden. Through the water gate and weedy garden, on walks bordered by tall, overgrown, crowded oleanders lightly dancing in the gray air, our furniture was carried from a red and purple furniture-van-of-a-dory into the building. That was how my life felt—a procession of old furniture in an overgrown garden in unevenly blowy weather in Venice.

My parents' divorce had not been amiable. My father had been unreasonable and self-righteous in the manner of someone beyond hypocrisy, an artist, who knew the truth, a man of power. He had promptly married again, an interesting bitch, and now he was dying a drunkard's unreasonable death, beyond redemption or change, angry with his life. It was death in any case, his death, and I didn't understand it, or did and didn't want to be part of it.

The fighting over who loved who and how much and what that meant in terms of money and over who was loveable and who was not had receded from outward, daily reality but continued in the mind. We mostly didn't talk about it; Carlo and my mother agreed that it was too stupid to be personal in the vicinity of the war.

So, in the emotional and intellectual aftermath of a dissolved marriage, among the broken loyalties and revised opinions, in a mess of lost intimacies, I had an at first bleak freedom in Venice, my own post-war world.

I was not close to my mother, who had become plump and rather warmly semi-emotional in a style my father hated—she was always a bit warm-looking now, and she wore not-young floral dresses and heels too high for Venice, and she flirted with elderly men—she wanted a life between the sheets, and this was perhaps incestuously irritating . . . I have always felt *Hamlet* was a disguised description of adolescence when one first discovers that one's parents and their lives are real and love-besotted and impure.

But, anyway, my mother became *worded* and Italianate, evasive, and her presence was physical or bodily and was unfamiliar and sexual and oppressive, an aural and visual and oral reality but not that of my *mother*. This woman wore Venetian pearls, highly-colored encrusted glass, and she talked a lot, uninhabited words, saddening. She was trying to regain her Venetian manner. She took my arm when we walked side by side and she spoke of my running wild, my being adolescent—a hint. We liked each other, she and I. And Carlo and I were on good terms. But he was too real as well.

I wanted to call no one. I had no energy or will at first, no clear desire, no particular will to live actively. I was ill with adolescence, with an infidelity of attention. In the shakey continuation of my world day by day, I walked a good deal, idly, not exploring so much as reestablishing in my legs and shoulders directions and the feel of the stones underfoot. I cut classes and hardly ever went indoors. I loved being unsheltered as moodily as I had once loved being sheltered, as I had once loved those who sheltered me.

Venice had not been bombed or bombarded in the war. In Padua a Mantegna fresco, a glory, had been lost to an American bomb. And a Tiepolo ceiling in Venice had gone, only one. Art saves lives, preserves towns except from the Mongols. Along its canals Venice had a small-town, gritty look. One wears blinkers, and one blinks at everything. One is staring with one's whole flesh, with one's thin adolescent spine, with one's eyelids as much as with one's eyes. It was as if Venice drifted toward and beside me at a distance, drifted out of the past, and floated by even in an enclosed *calle*.

I thought that if Venice proved to be too sleazy with recanted Fascism, I would leave. I was not quite free-willed, not quite independent, but only in motion uncertainly toward independence. I could go to school in Switzerland. There was enough money. Or I could go back to America.

I went to a State school, but my Italian had become clumsy and literary and, as I said, I preferred to cut classes and walk or sit. I sat a lot, staring at the water, in this *uncertain* orphanhood. I took "responsibility" for my life irresponsibly. I had a daytime flirtation with a sixteen-year-old whore. She was from Asolo and worked the Piazza. We went to bed a couple of times in a dingy room she used overlooking the Piazza. At that time, in the Italy I knew, drugs were everywhere. Only a few men go into battle sober, it seems. I doubt that she was on drugs all the time, but she used them, and she was, perhaps, drug-colored emotionally. She had beige skin. She was very distant, very strong in that whore's manner of being immoveably distant inside herself, and angry-willed and somber with distaste.

She was demanding in regard to money. And not generous in bed. Or affectionate. When things got going with me, she would lie back and be scarily passive. Paola would, at a certain moment in the act, *submit* to male wildness, to what seemed in comparison to her stillness an hysteria of dominance. It was part of what men paid for, part of coming, as she saw the matter.

When the orgasm was well along, she would begin prematurely to reassume her distant obstinacy and the active direction of her life.

It scared me that I didn't love her, that I wasn't fascinated by her.

She was very good-looking. She had beige-tan skin, as I said, and small high young breasts, and a sweet-featured, blank face, and pretty hands. And a wonderful smell, a mix of sand and cocoa. She would kiss, but not a lot. Her kisses were cool but not cold. Her foreplay was shy and reluctant but had glimmers of feeling in it along with the businesslikeness, the hating it. She would say afterwards, "Come back to see me."

Or she would say nothing, just look at me.

I was frightened that I didn't pity her, that I didn't feel superior.

I felt a goading appetite to fuck and then in the moments of doing it, a dreamlike inability to want to really, anymore, so that to continue to orgasm was hard, like wading in the muck in the shallows in the Lagoon. The loneliness of the act, the only companionship and accompaniment being a low murmur from her, and some tremors in her legs and belly, and the motions of her hands, scared me, offended me. She might straighten her hair in mid-fuck. I could hear the tourists in the Piazza. And the *Marangona* when it rang. And my own unspoken words and hear my unacted roles, boy with a whore, lucky American exploiter. I *knew* that I could scare her some, order her around, and that she would resist and then comply and that feeling would start then as in a sulky child but much, much more strongly and weirdly. It would be eery, a column of heat. That started to happen once or twice.

The reluctance I felt had, it seemed to me, something to do with the war and my father.

Haunted by the whore I didn't like, I read almost nothing. The newspapers. A few magazines. I spoke to strangers, shyly. My Italian, my child's Italian, creaked and moaned, and, then, without transition, became something else all at once, my speech now. Venetian dialect returned, almost an emanation of the buildings, an echo, or voices overheard, the shouts of gondoliers around a bend in a canal, the scutter of voices, then my voice.

And they, the buildings, began again, stone by stone, to be my old and new surroundings after their long sojourn in distorted forms in memory. Memory leaped, and reclothed itself so that in the span of gray, foggy days, the *Salute* and the *Palazzo Labia*, the *Libreria*, and the campanile of *Santa Maria Formosa* in their softly shrouded present forms were known to me as if I had seen them all along without remission in sunlight, clearly lit.

Shrouded, post-war Venice in the silvery gloom emerged prow-like, looming with accumulated emotion and beauty, an-ocean-liner-in-a-dream, but real, really my home. Everyone seems older and wiser after a war, for a moment or two, even me, but it seems each person is wiser in ways different from everyone else—there is an anarchy in the wisdoms, and empty places. In a sense, no one had been clearly instructed by the war—that nightmare teacher . . .

In Venice, daughters were nursing very old fathers for whom there was no structure of succor at the moment; the local men, often somewhat catatonic ex-Partisans, stalked the Right Wing, the Fascist bureaucracy; and soldiers and sailors who had returned were a whipped majority—what is charity now? The papers said *the nation must get on its feet*, but the joke in dialect was that the nation had only one foot. Italy shaped like a boot, has a single foot and is a nation-amputee. The nation hopped like a war grasshopper.

People without much power moved in the shrouded paucity of light, moved in the silvery drifting of the air, in the fog stained by the smoke from the city's innumerable coal stoves. At noon a yellow stain with burnt rainbow veinings of brownish tints discolored the fog over the glinting and shifting *Canalazzo*. Cloudy figures as high as the clock tower blew and swayed in the Piazza. The haunted carnival of the aftermath of war wasn't a matter of peace and hope at last but of the reality of horror and life going on anyway, as if concussed and distracted by what had happened. Or empty. Some human abdication in modesty and disorder left the days to be mostly a parade of the reality of time which was a kind of realism and of modesty, as I said.

The awareness that no limit exists to what might happen to you leaves a daily, perpetual sense of suffocation. The coal stoves were later banished but now in the fog one heard people coughing in the silence, people invisible to you. The wartime reality that your own force is insufficient and that you might be useless in combat, such a feeling is like an advanced starvation. Or tuberculosis, a hectic impotence in the shadow of apocalypse—like an echo of Miss Murphy. The postures, the movements of people walking in the mist near me had the same impermanence and unsolidity as the fog. And when you saw someone, there seemed to be something watery and ready for costume in them, in the figures already costumed in the silence enforced by the fog, in the faces already madly veiled in post-war surprise, post-war faces, some calloused and inhumanly hard, like fists, and others delicate and shaky with post-Fascist humility, repentent and sickening, nauseated, truly.

I struggled with the politics, but it seemed to me the parties were madness too, and that the issue was *Everyone*, not as a notion, but in actuality, and not the ideal *Everyone*, not an idealized and generalized *folk*, but the blundering and smelly and unholy and unexalted mess of Actually *Everyone*.

Onni did not resemble his childhood self. I caught sight of him on the *Rio Terrà San Leonardo*. It seems wrong to say I *recognized* him. My body tensed. My eyes tensed. A dim part of my mind produced a sort of murmuring of, *Oh, is it? Is that*

Giangiacomo? Sort of post-war bureaucratese: *Do I have his identity right? Onni Galliani?* The physical stirring, like ants running
along ticklingly inside you, nerves and blood somehow dully
thrilled at the idea that it was him. *Onni?* I didn't use the word
friend.

I halted in the afternoon light. I squinted.

He had on a leather jacket; he had rather long hair which
kept blowing; he had, it seemed, somehow, come to have very
large, white hands. He was walking boldly erect in a sort of crisply
defiant manner, boldly looking around him, here, there, showily.
Out of the sides of his eyes he saw me, saw someone he thought
he might know. And he turned to look directly at me. And in
the alertness, although it was much changed, although it was
adolescent and had full wartime precocity and wasn't childish at
all, still, in the alertness I knew him at once then, and with
certainty, hot certainty—no: with doubt but with emotional certainty and a rush of feeling.

I did not wave or call out. I made a face and my eyebrows
waggled. These weren't childhood gestures, merely nervousness—no: they were childhood gestures; you know, if you trace
an action moment by moment, it becomes harder to lie about it,
even to yourself. It is in the gaps, the compression that the lie
forms.

The passersby, the autumnal scutter of Venetian footsteps,
the somewhat poignant shabbiness of everyone in sight—this was
in the most cluttered part of town where the cripples and the
derelicts congregate as do tourists without money and migrants
from the countryside and sexual adventurers . . . Traffic, foot
traffic of course, is heavier here than anywhere in Venice. It is
the part of town that is most a continuation of the mainland.

Then, in the moment, you move toward ordinariness: he saw
me. I saw him.

"Nino? Nino-nini?"

"Onni?"

He made, he kept making truncated motions as if to embrace
me. I twitched a bit too . . . similarly.

He said, "You are *here?*"

"No. I am a ghost. You been bombed? I'm back in Venice for a while."

"I escaped. No bombs." He spoke with less ease in English than before the war. He seemed dull and dumb, defensive and yet sharp, even sly. "We only had one or two—one over there: are you going to be Venetian again?"

"Half-Venetian . . . like Venetian blinds," I said with some fatuity.

"Ah, you will see: the place is still here."

I nodded. In the indentation above the curve of one nostril was a mole I hadn't remembered. Maybe it was recent.

I think I smiled. "Hey. Is it you?" The transfer to other bodies of earlier selves is strange. But, of course, we were not our earlier selves inwardly either, merely omissible libraries of memories.

He walked nearer to me. He put his hand on me, on my back, under my neck, and he said, "A beer? Coffee?" He was suddenly the host, perhaps with mockery. But there were other tones. Perhaps it was a mockery of having no feelings in our new sophistications.

"Yeah . . ." I moved away from his touch. "Why not? So here you are, you bastard . . ."

"I was never a *bastard* . . . perhaps a little Fascist bastard-*cretino* but I am the child of my father." School, he said, the school building was now an art academy. California seemed to him very exotic; he listened staringly. He stared quite hard at the words, at the California that partly existed in what I said, not that he believed me about it. We grinned some from time to time, trying it out, grinning I mean. He offered me a cigaret and I took it.

"Juvenile delinquents," I said. He was not familiarly the same at all but I knew I had known him.

"Tell me what that term means," he said.

I did. We smoked and talked with lapses into silence. We did not talk about our pasts as children, or about any other past. He said, "I work. I go to school and I work." He didn't say what he worked at and I didn't ask. I guess this was caution on both sides and grating, such caution toward each other at first. His life was not my business. Or mine his.

I was tense. He was good-looking in some way that was interesting to passersby who kept looking at him as they walked by. We sat at a table outside in the *rio terrà* in the chilly air, bundled into our light jackets, the wind blowing at our faces.

We jockeyed a bit with each other. He said, "You seem so depressed I find you quite likeable."

"I'm too depressed to comment," I said grinning tightly and putting out my cigaret.

"I find you bearable," he persisted.

A conversation. Well, two guys talking, more or less, in the political framework of Back Then in Italy, a framework of sheerly functioning after a war, it was in the shadow of failed Fascism, the Ideal and its Coerciveness, and democratic messiness and victory, the whole thing was in a more or less complete style, a European talking to an American.

I mean Doctrine in some aspect with its sword or with its cross or with some formula is not part of my life. If it appears now, it can split the café table in two. As can some ideal longing.

We checked out each other's age. We didn't get personal or go beyond *passwords*. It really was clear in Europe, in Venice too, that everything visible lay in the shadow of destruction. Trying to talk under those circumstances had a particular allure. Maybe the belief, among the Doctrines and the Giant Forces and the sidling-along-just-trying-to-live stuff (and the grim self-absolution in necessity, the moral deathliness of it, the vast *shame* that clung to the elders) was that we might get a little bit of life in before the next, realer apocalypse. *A box of lips* is how the two ideas of talk and of a shaky world appeared in my head. The possibility of liking each other was slightly apparent in this tone and that look. One is easily fooled by feeling. Liking at sight, caution, caution easing a bit . . . It's interesting to *me*, the thought that freedom begins in wakefulness toward one's own history. Such freedom is a different building block for politics, personal ones too, utopian or otherwise. Nothing is the end of a chapter. There is no grand end. The appeal, the allure is not the end of history but lies in a wide-awakeness toward history, excitement and fear both.

And the personal—well, you know Ideals (and *Ideas*) are colossal and you sneak off behind them . . . The personal is just there—it is what is alive among the stones.

He spoke lightly about the post-war occupation of Italy by the Allies, and what came was a sense of *relief*; he wasn't out to fight with me. Then came a *self-conscious* sense of height and scrawny Americanness: no one in Venice was shaped like me, a gaunt kid-scarecrow . . . a tense, shambling, semi-collapsed teenager. It was not a popular type. It was too freakish. I lie. It was a type in wartime movies, tall kids, zoot-suiters, the kid in the platoon who got killed.

Some popular singers were this type. This perhaps laughable, gaunt, scarecrowy creature, perhaps *cute* if you were susceptible, was acceptable to him, this American type exemplified in me. He didn't sniff or stare or condescend. We kind of had cross-cultural moments. Each other's *style* was O.K. We saw we could be a little personal.

Talking to someone I knew affected me, and I saw that I was in a state of advanced madness of grief over the war, over the crimes, over the post-war shit, and over my life, my father, life and death-to-come, my parents' lives, and it was like realizing I'd come out to walk with my pants unzipped. I zipped up, so to speak. My grief stopped being so sloppy. It is as difficult to relate what goes on in people's minds as it is to relate dreams. He— Onni—was bluffing in a way the whole time. He had no grounds for confidence, after all, except visible physical ones—he wasn't crippled physically. He was good-looking. He was pretty taut, quite nervous—smoking steadily. The personal is where you have some say over things, sometimes. He was nervous about it and showily uncaring, or cool, about it.

Just before seeing Onni, I'd crossed over the *Cannaregio*, a very wide, straight canal, with high-arched stone and brick footbridges over it, higher than most to permit the passage of larger boats and barges with loads piled high. It's part of the workaday Venice. And the pedestrians, the throng of Italians and foreign soldiers and Blacks and cripples in the clothes or the rags of that year passing, were not part of any romantic image.

"You a Communist?" Onni said, trying to place the sympathy or whatever I was showing.

I sort of held out my hands and jittered and made an idiot-face. I did the idiot routine. He said, "I am." He told me that at one point during the war he gave a warm coat to a kid he'd known all his life who was the son of people who worked on a farm his family had owned. "The *ragazzo* was very short, very broad, very strong, not very clean—you understand? We had been children together a week or two each summer. He had put me to bed when I was very little. He took the coat, and he has a physical feeling. He puts his hand on my shoulder. He unbuttons his shirt, and he says, '*Are you a Communist, Giangiacomo? Do you like me?*' "

I said, "I think all ideas are impostors."

He said—not as insincerely as you might expect—"That is very interesting." He said it with the grave seduction of being interested, do you know what I mean?

Not far from where we were sitting was a palazzo with a Tiepolo fresco of Antony and a bare-breasted, staring-eyed Cleopatra, a magnificent woman, whorish, a bit bored, elsewhere-in-her-mind, sitting at a banquet table, with the wind blowing flags all around. Her sexual presence is surpassingly vivid, her sexual presence and mental half-absence—it is an amazing picture. The *Palazzo Labia*. Palazzo lips.

This conglomeration of things called a person looked at the good-looking, sharply dressed but shabby other kid, entirely unlike his old self and on edge and maybe *broken* and unrepairable like me.

Onni was kind of glamorous in a dim, foreign way, distant and unaffected by the idea of *normalcy* that was so powerful an idea back then in America at that time.

Was *Normal* the promise of happiness? Was abnormal the promise of intelligence?

I said something like "Normal is as *Normal* does . . ."

"Are you normal?"

"I'm not a collectivist."

"Are you trash?" he said using the American word, saying it in English.

Trash is for anyone who wants it, who picks it up. It's a specific question with an unclear purpose; it's maybe a flirtatious thing to ask?

One can always defend oneself, in a way, by being stupid.

I said aloud, "Poor, white, and twenty-one." But I was fourteen, as he was. No, he was older: sixteen.

Onni made a face and lit another cigaret and looked at me with disdain. My sense of him was one of attraction to him again with some caution. As I said before, the true history of anything is hidden in what memory omits about it. I had no conscious sexual sense but only the sense that he was interested in me.

Onni asked me, "What are you thinking about lately? You were always such a thinker."

I said, "A lot of nothing."

Then Onni abruptly suggested we go to a movie. Nothing had been said that was final but now it would be rude to part. This whole thing can be expressed as *we made friends again* but that would be saying nothing. Friends? In what sense? You can do anything you want with such a statement. It has no truth really, no keel, no direction. It is without meaning if you are talking about real life.

He wanted to see a war movie that was playing and which had some minor male stars in it. There is something droll in minor fame. We made jokes, fairly cruel, about the foolish look that not tremendously famous actors had in their publicity photographs.

I said, "Oh yes, he's big, that's a big name, can't hold back from seeing that movie." I was imitating a boy I'd known in California who'd had that line of prep-school sarcastic chatter and who, with the help of that chatter, had gotten along with a lot of different sorts of people without having to be in agreement with them.

I have forgotten the name of the theater, of the cinema. It

was probably too symbolic, the *Cinema Italia* perhaps. On the *Salizzada 22 Marzo* near *San Marco*.

I telephoned my mother from *San Luca*. Onni and I had drunk four glasses of wine by then. Five. It was dusk and only a thin mist hovered. The sky was a dark, dimly lit blue, but light still coursed wellingly through it, so that most of *San Luca* was as if lit by streetlamps, but it was the light in the sky that lit the walls and buildings and faces but in this dimly glowing way.

Onni and I were the same height that year. In the odd light and thin mist, we walked into the *Calle Fuseri*. The store windows were lighted.

Then, I swear, it was as if the odd spirit of elementary school and what Miss Murphy had taught him entered into him suddenly.

He said, looking around, "Nothing is changed. It is nearly as flabby here in Venice as in America."

"Yes?" I said with false humor, with caution, maybe with an inner fear of being disgusted by him. "You spent a lot of time outside of Venice where things got bad?"

"Bad? What is bad? You offer it to God. I think it must be silly to be an American. I am so glad I don't have your mind. I do not know how you live with yourself," he said smiling fixedly.

It was like being punched. "The war was bad? Hunh?"

He said, "I'm a cold person. I pay no attention. I paid no attention . . . to the war."

It would be like trying to notice everything at once to know why someone is saying what they are saying. It is enough that they're saying it. My blood ran cold: I was knocked out. "Yeah," I said in a fancy and sympathetic American tone, a good guy. "We say in English, *stuff gets to you*; we say the war got *to* us. But it must have slammed into you."

Things get bleak very fast when someone hates you. He said, "You don't have your own opinions. You didn't make that up yourself. You steal the things you say. You're pushy, and your parents push you. You leave no room for anyone . . . I am sorry but I have to be rude to such egotism—even in you . . ."

He looked at me brightly, with a stupid smile, assured of this truth. His neck was stiff, his head forward . . . proud. He refused to stop: he went on: "*Were you keeping your head while all about you were losing theirs?*" Miss Murphy's pet Kipling. "Are you going to be an intellectual, Nino-nini? That's a good thing to be in wartime, I think. No one around here spent the war *in California.* I think you're not the sort to die in battle. You are not so mistaken as that, as to be like that . . . Ha . . ." And: "Ah . . ."

It felt bad. To be hated. The Miss Murphy nightmare. Of course, by this time, my parents, other kids had done it. It wasn't impersonal in Onni; it was suitable hatred, suitable in that it fit me in a way.

I said, "I have to borrow money from you for the movie tickets. My mother is a loon about money, about me having any in my pocket. She thinks it leads to vice."

"I will buy the tickets," he said in a kind of darkened, low-toned and blinking-eyelidded wartime voice still.

He was treating me like someone who was good to a terrible sappy degree. I think that because I heard in his voice a *hatred* joltingly like that of my brother Carlo for me sometimes, and Carlo thinks that I am too good for this world, a silly idealist. Carlo likes me too, although not in a sympathetic to-be-taken-for-granted way, just in his way. He's been a shit to me over the years. So he's violent and guilty. This was like that but different, of course.

My mother has said to me, *Don't ever be in the right, Nino, with anyone you care about who has a bad temper.*

I was a pacifist or at any rate in a state of shock at out-and-out masculine forcefulness and its consequences. I never confess this to anyone because they test it right off the bat, and when they see it is true, they usually see if they can take advantage of it—it becomes the only drama between me and them, like a parable or something churchly.

The color or tincture of anger in him was such that I disliked him which was O.K. because of the magnetic mass of stuff adding up to attraction and because he could tell from my manner that I was something like a pacifist, which probably made him feel worse. But who knows?

From *Fuseri* into the *Frezzeria Barcaroli*, walking fast, frenziedly in the dim late light and mist in long strides, maybe trag-ically, who the hell knows?

"The two ex-kings of the class," I said. Then: "You rat on anybody?" Silence. "Turn anybody in? Jews? Partisans? Your parents?"

"It is all bullshit," he said in as carefully an American way as he could. "Please . . . do . . . not . . . talk . . . about . . . the . . . war . . . You . . . were not THERE . . . ." Then in a strangely huge—not loud—way, "You were not HERE . . . ."

He had a strong accent all at once.

Touching me on the shoulder as if steadying or gentling a horse, and walking slowly again, he asked me at that moment about American girls, California girls, their legs, their hair. He did it with polite patience, addressing a fool. He kept touching me.

I asked him about Italian girls, *their* legs, their hair. About Italian cars, Alfa Romeo, Lancia. He murmured back concerning Ford, Packard.

In the dusk, the dusk in Venice, in such light and lightless-ness, he looked eaten, eroded, like a battered *god*, well, a minor *godlet*, a Hellenistic thing dug up, dirty, a deposed godlet. He'd been deposed from his handsome childhood. He was still hand-some but marred. Used.

"I am getting dumb. School is boring now," he said in up-to-date slangy English with very little accent.

"You sound like California."

"You're getting dumb? *Nicht wahr?*" In German.

My comparative safety and his unprotectedness during the war perhaps underlay his examination of our comparative, com-petitive rank.

"It's all over for me," I said. "The firing squad," I said. "Bang, bang." And I clutched my side and fell against the wall, between lit store windows in the *calle* and hung my head and generally looked as if I were about to slide to the ground.

Onni smiled a kind of a hideous feral-cat-little-pointed-teeth-and-licking-its-whiskers smile, shamed as if after eating carrion.

Still, the fineness of the bones and the fine glitter of life in him and bits of yellow glitter in his eyes in the windy light near the store windows made up for it some. The moment kind of careered along as if we were on bicycles going downhill. But we were on the flat *Frezzeria*.

We were not emblematic. We were not emblems. We were people, kids, without fixed terms for the revised equations each moment, moment after moment, of what was going on.

"One can live as an angry, scuttling mouth or pair of claws," I said, tossing my head, making my hair flap.

My boredom had been truly eased by his presence, by his condition of unhappiness and his rage and hatred, shame or guilt, whatever the fuck it was.

What good would it do to say this was or wasn't homosexual? I don't mean actively. I mean just spending time together. I didn't know then, and I didn't care. Along the *calle* inside the moments, I felt time's obstinate omnipotence. No one and nothing ever actually retraversed a moment. "Look, a moment ago is dragging me—back—back—back." I walked backward and said, "*Swalc fo riap ro . . .*" Reciting backwards; I am dyslexic enough that I can do that. He blinkingly waited, not watching closely. He lit a cigaret, "A last one before we go in . . ." To the theater.

At moments he was so German-like, I thought maybe he had spent time with Germans; I wasn't sure I could manage that new element of the unlived-as-yet, the unlived-with knowledge about someone.

I figured that his hatred was incurable. I'm a fatalist—a predictor of dark things. I foresee evil woes a lot. I took a cigaret. Venice was a common ground for us, a common setting. The motions of the gathering and spotty rain mist, a few drops of sprinkling rain out of the clear but darkening sky were part of the mystery of the reality of an actual moment. His body and his mind remember that he can hurt me, he can outdo me after the mystic seven years of exile as he did when we were children. He has surges of hatred. I look at him with an obtuse stare of not-*friendship*, a comic or clownish staring in the direction of innocent infatuation for the moment.

He needs to be able to hurt me. He needs to be sure he can. I don't like him enough yet that he can hurt me in the way friends can. He can only horrify me. The old feelings are stirring, it's true; but childish love revisited is not much of a force in a large body is it? Hey, can I punish him? I did not know how much shit I could take or if I was willing to start over.

"Har de har har," I said aloud. Then as if in a bad dream, gratingly, or as in a bad poem, I said, "I hate whatever is beautiful—my name is TIME . . ." I cackled *insanely* and rubbed my hands together . . . insanely. "Candy bar time," I said. "Whoops: just candy—" Italy had no candy bars then.

"I have two Hershey Bars," he said. He answered my gaze: "There's a little PX for GIs near the station." Again he answered my look: "I would rather be a swindler than be without candy."

The person hating can rarely get free of self-justification. Emotions rub paths in the brain and in the nerves. Your life grows around those most travelled paths. I know him, but beyond words, in everything he says and in the way that he says it. The thing about being evasive and a pacifist is that you don't hate the other person, and, ha-ha, the laugh's on him, the one who doesn't *hate* is the cute one.

On the screen the action-filled movie proceeds in its portrait of war, and the lousy loudspeakers of the theater crackle with the noises of straining war engines and strafing and the sound of the fire of automatic weapons and of artillery. Also, there was a lot of creepy creeping-along music.

See, it was about these (*American*) guys in a photogenic platoon which in the first big narrative chunk of the movie gets shot-up on a grindingly fateful patrol in the North African desert, in Tunisia. It was a *serious* movie, not in color and recently made.

In the platoon, two men somberly, speechlessly love each other in a buddy fashion, tough and sensitive. Both men are tough and sensitive. The parts were played by minor stars. And four other actors in the platoon were also minor stars on the way up or on the way down; so, anyone in the cast could have a death scene at any moment. None had to be kept alive for the sake of the story or the box office. The actions of the men on patrol weren't clear; but there was lots of artillery fire and sniping. It was a *very* loud movie.

Onni said into my ear, "Ah, this is a good movie, very tense, much suspense, yes? If you were a girl, I would hold your hand—to make you feel safe."

"Shhh," someone said.

"Get off my back," I said to Onni.

I assumed that Onni like a lot of people in Italy at that time needed food, protection.

"My hand is much bigger than yours," he said in the flickering dark while the movie proceeded in its artillery-fusillade-punctuated way.

At the age I was, the comparison of parts of the body with parts of someone else's body was legitimate and common—it was part of boyhood.

"You got a small *cazzo*? A small *whizzer*? You have small hands?"

"Like the Leaning Tower," I said. My brother Carlo had told me to say this if Italians got funny about this matter.

I did not understand this stuff. I am sexually, masculinely, slow-witted, a pacifist, but I was patient with it. It kind of amazed me that Onni's awareness of his own body, skinny and taut and nervous and big-handed, was a heat in him, a thin buzz of anger, competitive, nervy. The movie bombed its way along. He said in the eerily flickering light and noise with sudden anger as before, "You are a midget. You are a midget in every way. You are an ugly midget boy whore."

We were measuring the strength in our hands by squeezing each other in a grip. His hands were muscular, calloused in the off-again, on-again light, but the callouses were partly worn away.

He said, "I worked on a farm near Udine, shovelling shit, *Americano* . . . Feel my muscle . . . *Squiz* it." When I didn't, he grabbed my hand and twisted my wrist. "I am very strong . . . *Squiz* . . . *squiz* my muscle . . ."

It seemed solid, but I am not good at locating such facts or feeling them tactilely the first time I try: it's a sensual shyness.

"Fuck off," I said. I thought he was possibly insane.

For a while then, he spoke of the movie as it went along: "Nice rocks . . . studio rocks . . . good job on the camouflage netting . . . Don't the insects sound real? Good crickets . . ." Then: "Soon they get transferred to Ancona . . ." That meant he'd seen the movie already. At the first shot of German .88s firing, he said, with male disgust, "German pricks . . ." Then behind his hand to me, confidingly and with disgust: "Germans fucked the farm animals . . . I like the smell of peasant girls . . ." Perhaps he wants to share the real world, his world, with an afflicted dreamer. Me.

I was silent, confused and at a loss, blinkingly scoffing inwardly inside my silence, defensive maybe, maybe entangled. The lonely grief of being afraid of someone. And of being lonely. I think the body has its own soul separate from the real one, its piece of the soul, maybe a subsidiary soul, its memories. The plane of his chest, his buttocks on the seat, the thin sprinkling of hair around and on his face which was partly hidden in the dark but one knew or sensed things in the flickering shadow— I think his body was angry. Does that sound too strange? The homosexual thing is always there, but so is just the ordinary thing. A lot of *No*s are involved, as if flutteringly.

Forty minutes into the movie, one of its protagonists goes to Venice after the death of his buddy in battle near Rimini. American movie companies worked in Italy right after the war to use money owed them that could not be repatriated. The movie had ten minutes of grief set in Venice. And a whore, played by a scary, very busty French actress, and a *nice girl*, who is curative and who wears less makeup and has a smaller bust, comfort the guy who is still alive. The dead guy reappears in special lighting in shots of Venice. Creepy. The soldier goes to a Mass in the *Frari*. I had felt the city to be a Venice of Grief, of Shabby Grief rousing itself; and now I saw a screen image of it. How powerfully real and unashamed, uninquisitorial and *persistent* it was, this Venice. The real Venice shone in my head, the multitude of bridges over the canals like small artificial Chinese hills, and the

crookedness of every axis of arrangement, the wandering hori-
zontals and uneven verticals, and the water, the movement of
water, wandering and wavering and wind-combed, waves and
wavelets, accompanied the unsensual images on the screen. In
the reality, the expertness of the decoration is affecting. It is not
all in the same style. Venice never had a ruling family. The old
decorative details were bought and paid for by different people
who were just people, not kings, although rich; and this, too,
generates a kind of heat, a lifelike thing, like that of a seashell
with the creature in it or of a mass of plants and lichens and
roots in a tangle among rocks on a mountain.

Then, in a shot of the *Riva degli Schiavoni* in front of the
Danieli, Onni appeared. His hair was blowing in his eyes, and
he was wearing white shorts and a visored naval officer's cap;
he was walking a bushy white Samoyed. A boy whore, an ex-
collaborator and Fascist hanger-on in the movie, he said something in that scene which I didn't hear. The real Onni resolutely
faced the screen beside me, not unhappily.

He was importantly shown. A few seconds later, he was
shown again in a party of sinisterly rich Italians going into the
Hotel Monaco. The protagonist, wandering sadly and having
seen the ghost image of his friend in a glowing oval over the
Grand Canal, sees them and stares. I turned and looked at Onni
in the dark.

He said, "*Io sono una grande stella—vero?*"

"Wow," I said.

I now felt I knew some more of what is going on between
him and me.

He was breathing through his nose. He smelled of the wine
we'd had earlier. You can know things but be unable to focus
them as syntactical thought—they have another syntax of sense
and of intuition. Then on a second look, and by comparison with
the first look, you can know something almost clearly enough to
accept it mentally as a possible fact.

I shouldn't try to understand, but an urgent desire to know
is there.

Onni in the movie and then the reality of his face in the

theater next to me, the outward curves of his lips, the bulge of his neatly roundish, white, flickering, actual eye are such different things that what is strung vibratingly on that difference for me is to be my sense of his personal reality from now on, him as having succeeded in entering an earthly paradise and Valhalla as an image or an archetype. He's not merely lost in his life like other guys. He is part of the language of the world. He is moored to a kind of success already.

Then I turned back to the movie to see what he was part of; I was caught in the daydreaming and teased thought from a sliding distance of movie-watching, of watching patterned shadows and the maybe heartfelt, maybe not quite heartfelt moues, smiles, *ricti* of the quasi-famous but maybe anyway too famous faces of the actors; I tried to comprehend the motions of the plot.

The physical reality of my head abuzz and the reality of my eyes watching and the flickering light lighting the theater became an obscure story of friendship and suffering. The giant figures on the screen had an operatic intention to thrill, to scald with feeling; and I was thrilled. I was scalded. I was one of the elements of *the so-called story* in one ill-boundaried moment after another. The loud voices of the actors on screen mingled with the whispers of my sense of things. The slim film of moisture of a *now*, of one's eyeball's movements, the sight of a gleam on Onni's chin, the saliva in my mouth, the *feel* of my eyeball under its lid when I blinked: I can tell I'm young. And the reality of the moment was *intense*; and I broke into a severe sweat.

Onni leaned over sideways like a grownup and whispered, "You want to be an extra?"

"NO!" I said, surprised to have said it, having thought I would say, *Sure, any time.* But the *no* is what came out of me, is what I said.

I said to Onni, "My father writes movies in Hollywood. He says the audience in a movie theater is a lot of sitting ducks."

On the screen, the nice girl's special eyes, slowed, glycerined, and holding simple and simplified (but not boring) sentiment, slide, pounce, walk and jump over a letter. The soldier is fighting in France where there was money owed the movie company too, but we were in Venice again. Outside her window, on the Grand Canal, someone, I think it's Onni, passes in a motorboat, a moving do-jigger. The movement and smile and flutter of the heroine's eyes and face and lips are on the way to a happy ending or maybe an instructive *tragedy*—the movie is so serious.

Then some more shots of the busty bad woman whore, her often photographed body in one of those special movie outfits that show a woman's body's movements as flittering light on photographed cloth. The ways her body was offered to the audience, the way such shots can't go on too long, the way real meanings are forbidden by movies, that paralyzed me for a while.

She too had a letter.

In a sense, narcissism is your defense against story, against what stories tell you to dream. Reality remained nearby in Onni's actual breath. I idly punched his forearm. He punched me back but really.

Resisting the story, I whispered to Onni, "The flavor of the candy is on the screen." The love story was saccharine, I meant. The political-emotional parable, the war portrayal were sourer than the love story. "Now we see the odors in the theater . . ." I said.

Then the sprocketted film slowed to a crawl and the soundtrack gave off a whistling and hissing and sporadically booming squawks. People in the theater talked and squirmed. The theater smelled of damp, of mildew.

Then the projector was fixed, and the film continued. I am small in relation to the screen in the sensual solitudes of the dark, small in regard to the giant la-di-da on the screen. My judgement of the *thinness* of the love story, the half-expensive images of it, was partly based on the sexual reality in my blood. The tissues of images made of wandering light, and untouchable and without odor or taste, claiming to relate a tale of heroism and grief tired me. I felt one's dimensional, sensory life was cheapened. Watching a movie, one is so penetrated by its eery effectuality and one's formerly best thoughts were so trampled that it was worse than being in a classroom for me.

"Are you getting it? He loves her," Onni said.

"I know the plot from movie reviews," I said.

I have no genuine relation to the movie but only to Onni.

The perhaps adorable lies of *the movies*. The subject matter here, too, is love while you live in real moments, actual love, a brainlike flickering, sentimental, senseless. If you have spent time in the presence of art, as you constantly do in Venice, art and long-term *kitsch* (Onni will one day, when he is a triumphant actor, call Venice *Kitsch-bühl*), what you see through to is yourself as one of the elements of a possible romance parallel to what is shown you in the art.

A public whoredom of the self, an exhibitionism, makes you an architect of the visible.

"Do you suffer at the movies, Nino, when someone is killed?" Onni asked. "Are you sensitive?" He had been biting his nails, as I was. Now he ran his tongue and then a fingertip over the bitten edge of one, scowlingly, as the light flickered.

"No. I never suffer," I said. I had not known I would say any such thing. To say next as I did, "I want to be *nice*," is funny: I was trying to explain myself: it came out as: *I never suffer . . . I want to be nice . . .*

Onni said, "I always had *una grande ambizione* to be *nice* . . . but . . . but . . . but . . . it always turned into me just being me."

"Do you remember the old newsreels?" I said. I was being sympathetic and referring to reality. On-screen a train made a great racket. The hero was returning to Venice. The sensory distortions, the sensory omissions of the dryly sprocketted, crawling film and the light and the racketting soundtrack were part of what was making me emotional . . .

"Yes," he said.

"I don't like this movie: that's not what being a coward is like," I said to Onni. "The old newsreels were nice and bloody."

"*C'è una storia . . .*" he said.

"It's not real . . . We have *real* lives," I said.

"Stars have real lives *essendo stelle*," Onni said.

"Bullshit."

"Yes, it is difficult," he said in the profundity of private experience. In the dark his face looked tragic and fallen.

I think the movie, and movies as a world, proposed a pragmatic, total absolution in the way they cheapened life and feelings. Everything was semi-bearable then; nothing mattered except the pain of being anonymous. If you accepted that, you could survive a lot of things. He was as serious about movies as Amedeo was about the Church.

And he had already visited and glimpsed salvation and paradise.

I said that aloud: "You're *serious* about movies."

"I couldn't live *senza cinema*," he said in distant simplicity.

"We're as real as movies are," I said.

"We are still children compared to them," Onni said.

The idea of a movie destiny gripped him tightly . . .

I was moved by his emotion, singularly so.

The movie had a windup notion of event and action, and it fired off results for the actions of the characters that were not very likely. It was a kind of baby talk in regard to fate. In a way, it had a sense of results, of consequences which, as reality, was a sense of the reactions of a big audience, real life reduced to that, to that and to the money to be gained from that, as if the audience voted on destiny. And established what reality was.

And that dry pragmaticism combined with the ghostly high-level sex appeal of flickering and skimpy images that were truly famous added up to a world. I could see, I could feel how the absolution, how the permission to live worked. The philosophy of no-philosophy, of no meaning but of this money, I didn't like that. I was hurt by it. I felt heavy, and my blood was cold in me.

"It was silly . . . I don't want to be influenced by that . . ." I said. Then in falsetto: "Save me, save me." Then, would-be wittily: "You see the light on the screen as the light at the end of the tunnel. And I think it's the aura of an epileptic seizure."

He couldn't always follow my English. I talked fancily and had since childhood.

•

Just before the lights went up, he'd played kneesies, ironically, and he'd stomped on my feet and groped me, kid-like, like
someone discharging the voltage of the movie.

He sat still when the lights went up. I punched him and
looked at him admiringly: "*Starino* . . ."

He sighed and said in English, "Ah what zee fuck . . ."

We rose and we left the theater, eased but not in a state of
ingénues' happiness. Still, the silliness of the movie, the motors
that drove it, the whirligig engines of fantastic wish carried out
and filmed, elaborately willed, handsomely outfitted, broadly created, and the unsnobbish and welcoming thing toward the audience, toward us, the language of excitement in it and even in
the ads outside as we went outside, had set us free, me too, sort
of.

We were unmoored.

Unmoored boy-balloons.

Onni hit me in the side of my biceps. I said, "Goon . . .
Baboon . . ." Then: "We're not so bad . . ."

In the *salizzada*, we pummelled each other. I faked my
blows. I am, in a sense, zero in effect, that is to say, almost without
effect like someone in a movie. Or like the point of a movie. On
two feet. That spectral, spectral me, a pacifist, sensually shy,
word-mad.

We lit cigarets, sauntered, talked big about money. Then
about life's *meaning*. Did it have any? He showed me how to
throw myself down on the damp pavement—it was sprinkling
and misty—to avoid rifle fire and not sprain my wrists or bruise
my knees. This was near *San Moisè*. In the passage toward
the *Fenice*, he performed; he was an actor making love to a
wall, the wall being the camera and the director. Then I was the
stand-in for a minute, and he stared pleadingly at me within the
scene. I turned away, disgusted. Onni called me *priest*. Then:
"You are peculiar, *strano, strano, stranissimo* . . . Worse than Joel
McCrea . . ."

"You dislike Joel McCrea?"

"*Unspeakably* . . ." We seemed for the moment, he and I,
to share the same angles of vision in a limited but warm sense.

I was greatly untrained in friendship—I was used to having an older brother, however.

"I like movies," Onni said dangerously; he was ready to argue for the as-if-religious truth of all movies as manifest in this movie.

I said, "I like movies enough. But movies are really full of shit, don't you see?"

"*You* are full of shit. You say *Don't you see* too much." He kicks me in the style of *savate*. I chase him *calle* after *calle* until sick from the running I stop. I was bent over gasping and swallowing when in the distance, Onni called out, "*Shit-teee*," and the word affected me. I suddenly smelled real shit and was aware of the real texture of real excrement; it was a memory. Also, the idea of wartime *shit* affected me. And I gagged and was ill in actuality.

Onni paused in the distance, turned, came back.

I suppose I already "knew" a lot about him although what I "knew" about him was a mood toward him, was a mood because of him, unwordable, as I said earlier.

"Uhhhh (ghhhggg)," I said. "I stink."

He mopped my face with his handkerchief and cleaned my lips. I twisted somewhat under his touch. It is interesting how many kinds of vanity there are.

He slipped the cellophane off a pack of cigarets and with a matchbox shoved some of the vomit into the cellophane pouch. Then he threw it in a canal. I used a stick to spread the remainder out and around, and then with the soles of my shoes I ground what I'd spread into the stones.

He said, "I will tell you something but do not ask questions."

He paused and then he just said, "I was raped in 1943." I remembered he had said something during the movie about being on a farm near Udine at some point during the war, so I immediately *understood* it had happened near the farm or on the farm in the course of the war. I don't know why I assumed that.

From the way he breathed and smoked and talked, in a quick, staccato, one-thing-after-another physical way, I heard an opinion: that just as with the paler events of my own life and my reaction to them, that once he was assailed and damaged, as-soiled, he felt there could be no cure; history went on; no one cured you; but who you were was determined by what had occurred.

He knew what people did next. The help from others. Or the no help. People made use of what he had become and pushed him further along in having been damaged. Or not. Not the fantasy of the thing undone or glossed over but another history of *along these new lines. I can live* was the cure-of-sorts.

He said dryly, "*Dunque* . . . And then . . ." He said he had been whored by his mother and his aunt. "There was no food—or very little . . . things were difficult . . . I should have told them *nothing* . . ." His mother and aunt. He shouldn't have gone to them for help.

A German colonel. He said, not fondly but semi-proudly—I mean with some warmth and some vanity—"He had women too. We did things, educational things. We went to Athens. Very interesting. Very good Doric. I like the Ionic as well. I admire the antique. Lucky for me, he was young, he was not unsympathetic."

That wasn't the rapist . . . That was the one who had whored him.

He said the last thing—about the German being "not unsympathetic" to shock or test the American; he didn't say it warmly. Or explainingly.

I listened, but I refused to hear or to picture anything or to vibrate in sympathy just as I had refused really to see the movie, *really* to see it. I could not, or would not, make myself or urge myself to listen to this account of his life more closely or deeply than I had listened to and watched and interpreted and believed in the movie. He hadn't told me enough. And I didn't want him to jerk my emotions around.

I did not want to know how sexual that stuff had been or how much had been a game with chasing and teasing and a lot of horror.

Then he spoke in a different tone, grim and businesslike but with some vivacity, with his eyes unfocussed, then looking at me obliquely and then directly, right into my face. "I did what they tell girls. If it is going to happen, enjoy it. Lie back, enjoy it. I did not enjoy it. Still . . . *dunque* . . . Afterwards I was welcome wherever I went. During the war . . ."

He raised his eyebrows, lit a cigaret from the stub of the last one. There had been no social shame, he meant. There even had been high rank. He said in dry, grown-up tones—a recitativo—that toward the end of the war, his father became a target for the Partisans and went into hiding and was caught and beaten and two of his fingers were cut off. Onni puffing and blowing out smoke, ghostly roundish puffs, thick and whitish in the half-dark. There was a light attached to the wall of one of the buildings around the *Campiello*. He said, "Then I was not welcome in many places." Then survivor's silence, a kind of moving over the grounds of one's own psychic being, a survey of the self unowned—unowned by family or by society, torn loose and cast *free*, that was in his face and manner. The self owning its own history as a mysteriously involved piece of ill-fortune. It is not worth thinking about is what one decides—who would want to relive it? Who would want to enter that abyss, that whirlpool?

I would like to pretend I behaved well, but I was an asshole. I nodded my head, looked at my hands, said, "Oh *God* . . ." And: "God . . . *Dio* . . ." And generally felt ashamed, horrified by myself.

I even muttered at one point, "It never rains but it pours."

The effect of a narration of his sort, a narration of such events, events of that order of trespass, is oddly comic grief at one's own fear. Because of such fear, one is often only a senti- mental element in one's stories about oneself.

His study of how-to-live afterward did not include suicide. Or love-of-death. He had no *doctrine* of the absolute. Death-love is how you move toward being absolute, by dealing in real death with its absolute closure. He wasn't like that. Neither was I. We were Venetian.

His was certainly not a prepared speech—you could tell. And he hadn't done the virginal stopping and starting of a first time either. He hadn't seemed to be pushed at by associations and associated words or by a new idea of what he was saying as he said it, or to be discovering stuff as he went along. He did not discuss or explore any of it. He did not say why he told me.

In my head, pedophiles and partisans, paternal bureaucrats and police, Slavs and Venetians, Americans and Germans, tortures and shocked flesh, hurtled along. That realer other book of his life, of kinds of *love*, after all, under other circumstances, kinds of love foreign to me, of death and war according to doctrine, of adversity of soul in severe circumstances, ultimate circumstances, lunatic, that book judges me.

That book came into his voice, hovered in my ear, entered my head, and never entirely vanished.

He said, "I was beaten hard many times by my father, maybe a dozen times to the point that I am glad *mio padre è morto*. He hanged himself, a catastrophe of a man. But living in comfort to the end. Subject, however, at the last to mockery by anyone —do you understand?"

I *guessed* that Onni was saying that he Onni was in rebellion against the ghosts of the events if not against his father anymore. Also, he was mocking my mannerisms.

"I grovelled and gave in like a child—the little whore was still a child. I was afraid. I have a loathing for pain. I gave him my docile love. I was very sweet—it was actual love . . . of a sort . . ." This tore at him. He *hated* a lot of things. He said, "Say nothing. Never mention these things to me." He lit another cigaret.

He had given an order, told me his secret name maybe, maybe not entirely truthful, certainly incompletely.

But it felt true enough.

He said he was doing some modelling. He said his mother and aunt still whored him, but that he lived away from them when he could. He said it was "difficult" to get a movie role. He said his aunt had a place on the Lido, "very good for assignations . . ." I thought he meant for her, and then I saw that was not what he meant.

I became ill again but this time I got to the canal.

I forced some of it, made it go on longer, to show him I

cared. I wanted him to know that I was a deep person and that I cared and all that. It was and wasn't entirely true, but it was true enough.

Venice is launched and is rocking lightly among the night-time hours . . . Echoing Old Night . . . Venice is breasting the thinned tide in its Lagoon.

"Will I see you tomorrow?" I said cleaning my mouth with my hand.

"Will *I* see *you* tomorrow?" he asked in a kind of whorey, strong way, sour. Some dim echo or redolence of childhood lingered.

He probably had more of a taste of bile in his mouth than I did. Love is embarrassing and uncaptioned, what there is of it. I punched him in the shoulder with my right hand, a straight jab—I'd seen this in John Wayne and Spencer Tracy movies. I did it in a movie fashion, not sincerely, but ironically-toward-the-movies: toward life.

Onni hit me back in my left shoulder. We then hit each other in alternation and on alternate shoulders, right and left, in a deadpan movie way. All is forgiven. Or trivialized to the point where it's the same thing as forgiven. Nothing matters. Who gives a fuck. We're buddies. Maybe. Budding buttinskies, butting bandits. This is exhilarating and is false-and-true; you practice it, you believe it for a while, it's true in that way.

I hit him with pacifist blows. He actually hit me each time. Aching, I finally dodged, backpedalled, sparred him off, turned and ran. He ran after me.

I slipped off my watch as I ran and tossed it to him. We played catch with my Movado while we ran pretty much side by side from lighted *campo* to lighted *campo* and under the suspended lights in the narrow, misshapen *calli*.

SEX WITH ONNI:
COSÌ FAN TUTTE

❧

IN THE WALLED GARDEN of his aunt's villa on the Lido, in cool-and-warm spotty and sporadic sun, in a grove of seaside firs, pagan copse, with no prior announcement and no explanation, breathing through his open mouth, Onni—ah, a smart Italian's pantomime-inflected silences—puts pinecones inside his shirt and holds them from underneath, like breasts.

And then in travesty, breaking into highly proficient Neapolitan song, obscene and coarse, he rollingly walks and holds and jiggles and partly rotates with both hands the uneven breasts of the pinecones inside his shirt.

He does this routinely or neutrally, being *interesting*, but with no focussed purpose apparently except mischief and showing off.

A neutral first step, partly cautious, exploratory, in some sequence of events I know nothing about yet.

Purposefully very self-conscious in how he looks at me—it is part of the travesty—he breaks off the song and says, *"Eccola, Signorina* Betty Coed . . ." Two languages: "Betty Coed, *la Ninfa*—blond *non una gorgone—non una grande stella puttana —non Joan Crawford . . ."*

Not a gorgon, not a grand-whore-star, not Joan Crawford . . . More a suffering and passively fleshy blond Betty Coed in one of the wartime Hollywood musicals then just being released in Europe.

Broadly, but like a real girl, a broad version of that, he walks as a girl we know in Venice, one who goes to his school, a slim-hipped, long-haired semi-child, Sandrina Spagna . . .

I exclaimed, "La Spagna . . ."

"*Signorina* Secret Places," he said and walked as if his butt and haunches had those cylindrical pouches or thumb openings, moist, dark, not entirely mute places, set there.

I had said the thing about secret places earlier.

He glances at me, tilts his eyes upward. It is airless and hot inside the garden wall, among the odorous trees, above the floor of reddish pine needles.

A decadent and punishable form of childhood, a version of dressing in your mother's clothes when you were seven years old, you and a gang of other boys in your mother's bedroom . . . *Ruffians*, my mother had said quaintly. *Don't tear my good slips . . .*

Sexual desire? The matter is mysterious. Curiosity. Friendship. A matter of no space between us. It depends on how you have been trained, on how you are shaped inwardly.

I was not chaste as my "friend" Amedeo was, but I was *Cherubino*-like, youthfully passive, well-behaved: this was perhaps a tactic. I knew the actual weight, the feel of actual girls' actual breasts. Actual girls, their wills, their moods. And actual whores now, not many. The whore I didn't like and perhaps this one that I do like. I suppose I was chaste compared to Onni. Sexual comparison in the rush of things is modest and dumb, sort of as if I had to be the chaste one if he was sexually knowledgeable; anything else was too difficult intellectually.

In sex, the roles given you tend to be extreme, humanly absolute, until you are dethroned—it's very Darwinian-shadowy-passionate-hurtful.

Exciting and hurtful.

Exciting and pushing at you. The sexual painfulness of school—the sexual fatefulness of the classroom as an arena of sexual torment, the bodies, desk after desk, the bodies with such soft engines of lift and of interment in them, such bullying sugar, the acrid and heavy sugariness of those young bodies, such constant pornographies of power, of powers, in a classroom—see, it is painful because I am innocent but he and I are not so innocent here. If I am instructed, I will feel less pain—isn't that so?

"The *commedia continua*," Onni said. Abdominally canted, he utters in travesty a sexual gasp, pauses, utters another, as if in a crisis of our daily and hourly sexualities a girl's dirty, quaintly germinated sexual promptness had appeared . . . It is a form of brotherhood among some boys to permit some sexual forwardness in each other.

He knows; he is *experienced*—he is someone-who-has-carried-on-with-grownups. The knowledge of sex hinted at struck me as talented.

He said in Italian, in travesty, "I'm just a whore . . ." And I wondered, and felt superior but stupid.

Translated, into American English, into Americanola, it was maybe like a kid imitating a line of movie dialogue and saying imitatively, *I'm just a piece of trash, Honey* . . .

He was portraying someone who claimed to deal in low-down pleasure; this was scary and alluring, this Neapolitan, big-fleshed, Venetian travesty-woman who was also a pink-and-beige-fleshed, handsome, odd-spirited, angry, violated boy, perhaps beautiful. I don't know. A boy I knew, and maybe deep-hearted. How would I know? I was as fearful as the male ingénue in a horror movie, the young fool with a candle walking down a frightening hallway past closed doors in a castle on a stormy night in a strange landscape. The sounds of the cold Adriatic on the other side of the garden wall, down the street, are storm-like.

Onni was not as frightening to me as an actual woman of the sort he was travestying was.

The darkness of sexual terror shutters the light. A little horror and doubt, and the moral misuse of the self and of the other is like childhood love. Pleasure is the past rectified. Friendship and love, *after all*, form a profane friendship in Venice. One knows that even a convent has its secrets. And forgetfulness and oblivion have an undercurrent of things some part of the self remembers, things in the past. Future forgetfulness seems impossible but it will occur.

In actual continuous moments, the pain of feeling and pangs of touch-me-not modesty—humble and unhumble—self-preservation, the self unsacrificed, form a comedy of young carryings-on, an American art form, a folk art, modern and neurally noisy. Pioneer boy, long-legged ingénue male from the frontier faces the travesty woman. I *believe* I had plucked a stalk of Italian grass and was chewing on one end of it in the fashion of the American West. I had one hand in my pocket. I stood with one leg forward . . . California heroic.

There *were* two of us, you see. (This is how you recognize truth, I believe.) We recognize each other in borrowed forms, in clothes. We are clothed in these forms.

In the Lido light, terror, sexual terror, is comparatively sibling-like, a competitive matter, and the role-playing becomes extreme—that is because of feeling. *The terrified one* can do the double thing of being calm underneath, the *best* gun in the West, while *the Italian-Antique tough and violent one* can be as if falsely palpitant with sexual and other terrors reexamined in a return of the reality of innocence dirtied, an extremity of such a state.

The sexual terror of men—full-grown men, older boys—is terror of the male mode as well as being a terror of women, but there is, by comparison, less terror of each other. But because of feelings, there is a great terror anyway.

In the politics of terror, are you being enrolled as submissive? Is that the way your inner postures go? Do you connive with authority? Is that your compromise? Do you resist it dumbly, whistlingly? Thunderously? Do you attempt to impose it? Are you nervous and not clear about what is going on? Do you expose your neck? Your lips? Your buttocks? Do you wait dumbly, not daring to find out who you are sexually in this moment of your life? Are you led around by a chain? *Did he put a hook through your balls, Nino?*

At the age I was then, one is used to truth, although not to hearing it spoken, but one is not so afraid of it toward oneself, at least not if you are freed from your family. In the garden the fabric of sexual terror which is in part a billowing tent of belonging to school, to sports, is being blown free, is sewn into stage clothing, into costumes.

And half one's amusement, half one's excitement is that terror half-placated, sexual courage played at, tested, ludicrously, *do you see?* And the shadow-masked but spotlit figure of terror of the other boy who is smiling in a bright onstage-in-the-Venetian-*campo* fashion, by seeming to be mostly in the *rush* of ornamenting the moment and displaying himself and praising life, is someone available but not to be trusted, do you see?

I didn't know what any of this meant, what it had to do with human rank, that he is being half a boy and half a *woman*, this travesty whore, and offering excitement, I guess pornographically, but innocently as well. But not really. I tried to make out the point of division of gender, the meaning. But I couldn't. I was terrified and amused, terrifyingly amused.

I would speak dryly here if I thought a dry account would be understood to include the above. I would like to write dryly here that I *thought* Onni was being very *interesting* compared to school . . . But beyond the innocence were realer selves . . . We-were-just-kids was our defense if we were observed. (Not everyone would mind what we were doing.)

Terrifyingly warm, I thought next beyond the innocence that Onni was a shocking intimation of hell, the devil, a demon I was making use of. Hot hell. Hell where we are travellers, immigrants, Gypsy kids in hell, refugees. I don't know. He is foreign, ruthless-careless, full of self-display. And he is full of power. This stuff has power. Thrill-mad angry kid . . . Angry at me . . . Maybe not.

The lower shadows of this garden where we were contained a hidden memory of a garden. *Giangiacomo* zestfully, *deftly* in a sort of display of Italian-sexual-despair, playacting I mean, unbuttons his shirt and shows one of the pinecones, and he sighs and turns his head to one side. We have crossed into the flagrantly dishonorable space that lies between play and sexual trespass. In the privacy of the garden, doing these things, one sees why the Venetians never built a hill in their city. Onni's is a seduction in a seductive culture in a permitted privacy.

A sensation of hot emptiness courses through me, probably visible through the water-surface of the skin as a movement of current underwater or of a fish gliding in shallows. The interested fisherman watching is a tainted Venetian, *Giangiacomo*, the industriousness of whose pulse is guilt itself in him.

I was erect most of that year anyway. Sometimes on the vaporetto just the shaking of the motor caused it—*Italy is stimulating*, erectile and responsive tourists say. It is a worldwide game, the thing of causing erections. Cars, ads, some sports, some little girls, clothes . . . et cetera.

He has a neat, smallish triangular distortion at the crotch. The moment is not a dream come true, nor had it been prefigured in fantasies of mine in any way. Soft globes of light are suspended in the air among the branches of the firs. I laughed. A good guy would chase Onni around the copse, would unzip while he did that, and Onni ought to wear lipstick and utter burlesque shrieks; then the good guy should wrestle Onni to the ground; and it would be a mythological thing, a country rite. This other hesitant thing, middle-class, is culturally perverse and has an element of love, uninnocence, love as the uninnocent conveyance of permission as if innocently—I would in no way guess at the future. The element of love is interested in the scene.

How far do you want to go?

One has only a vague desire. And no terms or habits for answering such a question of oneself. I guessed I wanted to find out if I felt desire.

Was the urgency vague-but-strong?

I didn't know how to look at these things. The feelings weren't cut-and-dried.

Answer in a cosmopolitan and cultivated tone: Is your desire strong?

Yes . . . if you ask it like that. I want to be sophisticated . . . No, if you ask it in Americanola: I wasn't burning up or anything.

What was the desire aimed at?

I didn't know. I wanted to . . . to know . . . I didn't know yet what I wanted to know . . .

Did you desire actual touch?

Yeah, sure . . . Yes. But I didn't know what kind of touch . . .

How far were you willing to go?

I don't know even now.

We each had rules, he and I. Sometimes in sports, you have to go quite far in order not to feel humiliated. A good deal rests on the curious thing of how variously in you a horror of saying no exists. One time, joking, Onni said, in a mockery of the essays we had to write in school, *Saying no causes wars* . . . And: *Nos cause hatred* . . . Even, if you can forgive him, *Anti-Semitism rests on Jewish Nos* . . .

I don't want to change my life.

The violence of some people who do want profound change in their lives attracts and scares me.

I will die if something doesn't happen, but I will die if "too much" happens.

Onni, in his travesty voice, in Neapolitan dialect, chanted, "*Sporcaccione . . . Sporcaccione . . . Ragazzo un po' sporco . . .* Nino is *dirty*. Nino is a dirty boy."

He brushed his pinecone breasts against me. Behind the rough wood of the pinecones is the weight and heat of his adolescent body which seemed to me to be slablike, repellent, supple-and-hard-fleshed, supply hard, bonelessly fleshy, fleshily real. He rubs *jigglingly* the many-lipped wooden cones *gratingly* against me. I am aware of my actual chest.

"Lay off . . ."

"Nino is a dirty, dirty boy. You want to jerk off, Dirty Boy? Jerk off, *Sporcaccione*, for *La Puttana* MADRE . . . *La Deessa comande . . . Vai . . .* Go on . . . *Per favore . . .* Nino, I would like you to jerk off, Dirty Boy."

He eyed me obliquely, and letting the pinecones fall inside his shirt to his waist, to his belt, said, "Let's have a race," making gestures with his hands. He unbuttoned himself with an edge of showy Italian comedy, a Pantaloon. He pulled himself out, small, pink, clean, decent, erect. "On the mark, get set, go," he said in English and began promptly.

He paused in a handsome, uplifted, pinkish stance and looked at me in a handsome way, lifting the hair out of his eyes with one hand and letting it fall again. He said, "Let's have a race—for the love . . . of *amore* . . . Let's jerk off," he said in a delicate way. Then he snorted. *"Per favore, amico, per amicizia . . ."*

"Alla commedia?" I said. On to the comedy? I didn't know what I meant to say. In speaking I forgot my speech. He gazed at me in a polite manner, and then less polite, more Teutonic and effective, he gave me a Teutonic smile, an imitation Nordic smile. He had almost an infatuated energy which had a tone, *oddly*, of despair and of strong-willed persistence: a *small* greatness—can you say that? A pinkening sparrow quality in an eagle-like face? An Italian energy of amusement in a Teutonic onrush? I breathingly half-laughed, almost laughed, suffocatedly almost choking on the laugh, on something, on *it*.

What was at stake seemed to have a shadowy thickness of meaning. A complicitous something-or-other on both sides. It was contained or translated into a sexual tautness that wasn't *sexual* so much as it was merely real . . .

He gripped me at the crotch. I yelped but cut the yelp short. He said in a parodic tone like a scary Italian whore of back then: "You cherry, Nino? You got cherry balls?" He palms the I-tool dickerer in my pants through the fabric. The presence of hard male flesh, or hardened or whatever, mine, is less striking and no more potent than the presence of hard male will in Onni— to me I mean. His will affected me like an erection, like my erection, but my erection was just there, without affect. I haven't got the nerve for real life.

Onni says in my ear of a guy in school, *"Beniamino* will *fuck anything."* Which is true. I'd seen the long-armed Beniamino fuck a soccer ball and come. In my ear *Giangiacomo* asks or commands, "Jerk off." He fumbles with my American zipper. A real person is real only in his way. A general thing *never* occurs in real life, but only in the mind. I was in deficit in regard to breath. *Breathless . . . A breathlessness.* Being swindled-forced takes the air away. Excited breath is joke-y, joke-y suffocation, as at the breast. Or as in childhood's spaces: under the bed or in secret corners in the house, hot, sweaty. I am weirdly and loonily in a state of *memory* at the edge of a dive into the future. Well, why not? One kind of sexual state can be described as essentially uncaring but willing. We invade each other's lives without *good reason.* Another part is caring anyway in spite of (or because of) all the real stuff, the engineering of parts, the negotiation of age and gender.

I pushed him away from me. I moved away from him and reached inside my pants and felt the waiting and ready reality there, the newly familiar flesh there . . . Onni did not keep his distance but came closer. Onni is married to who he is whoever he is. I am merely courting myself. I shake my head no at Onni. Saying no sickens me. "No," I said. "Stay back." I moved my hand and seemed in my physical sense to become disjointed, to be made of separate sections, some more alive than others in an unmoving but palpitant rain, the blurring of the physical world, and in a sort of hobbled but considerable leaping of sensation.

Genitalia dimly seen, and another person's sexual rhythms —it's almost a kind of babble. Are you a good dancer? It—the dance, the responses, the whole thing—went in and out of focus for me. It was repulsive and businesslike, the sexuality. *Giangiacomo* was sexually light-of-foot and he could jerk off and watch. He was *clean*, pointedly alert, alive the whole time, not blurred.

The sensations carry me off. I drift off out of sight or am yanked off comically, softly, violently, by then perhaps with some implication of further violence, soulful, irrevocable. That's just an illusion probably . . . I don't know. But I can't see him clearly.

Onni came very quickly. It was quick and pretty and *clean*; I saw it dimly, far away. I noticed it. I was *far gone.* I could barely sense the neat, quick terms of *his* pleasure. He was less deflected by sensation than I would have thought. Onni was not heavily weighted with sexual burden. There seemed to be no long-lasting twist of his face or twist in his posture of a particular yearning or of a question achingly half-answered.

I am haunted and drawn to a sense of meaning that it seems to me can be found in sexual sensations, in sexual minutes. His sexuality seemed to me to be like a racing swimmer's expert shallow dive. His masturbation was sexual differently from mine. His was some genuflection of the nerves, some throb of horror, or of habit, the quickness of a child, of a small animal, the taut, somewhat fleshy body, fleshily muscular in places, short-legged, strong-thighed, but quick, quick and only so deep but not because of fear, more because of bravery: a miscalculation . . . A miscalculation that was a fate.

I am embarrassed by comparison, and I was embarrassed to have seen him in a sexual moment, the silvery inner light pinning him, something feathery, or winglike to the brief spasms he had, athletic, boyish, cleanly rhythmed. He was proficient, pretty, given over to escape, unkillable.

That was profoundly enviable to me and I felt hopelessly stupid and cloddish. I was embarrassed to be seen. I was that year poisoned with sexual fumes and jealousy and envy of nearly everyone's state of sexual being. My own seemed bland and lost, incalculable.

"Do it," he said. "Now you . . . Continue . . . Go on . . . *I want to see . . .*"

From the middle of a passage of an emphatic quality of my heartbeat, embarrassed . . . it was *embarrassing* . . . I stared at him, almost instructed. I felt the force of his interest, in me, in the sexual moment; and resumed the motions. I fell into a pinkened-and-dark-gray inwardness of embarrassed sensations. I was filled with minor emotions as if with *dirty* clothes, the sort meant for working in the garage or the yard, for *playing around in*, that have no social or show-off meaning.

"Is *this* homosexual?" I asked him.

"*No, mai . . .*"

"I'm stupid," I said. "This is stupid."

"Go on, *Tesoro.*" He never wanted to be overwhelmed but

who knows? Maybe it was the one thing *utterly* forbidden him by his soul and his history, and, so, was a *raw* desire.

He was giving me an O.K. role. He watched staringly . . . It seemed a powerful thing.

Watched in that way, I felt hidden in me a raw and defensive tenderness toward this pleasure. The fundamental tone was one of study and of male companionship and of cheating on God-and-nature and it was a kind of espionage. And, of course, we were judging each other.

He had to seduce me. I knew that. What is a name for sex when it does not count for much? *Fooling around?*

I couldn't get my hand rhythms . . . "I can't . . . I can't get going . . . You're watching . . ."

"Yes . . . Yes . . . Yes . . ." he said. But his yesses didn't matter to me physically. And his will could not educe sensation.

"I *can't* . . . You win . . . You win anyway: you came first."

"No . . . no . . . *You are crazy* . . ." he said in Italian. He took one of the pinecones from his shirt and put it in my free hand: "Do it for the *boobies* . . ." he said.

I tried, gave up. "Close your eyes, *Caro Cretino* . . . *Do it* . . ." he said. He fingers my ear. Then my neck. The phrases *Onni is something of a whore* and *The war taught him things* excited me sufficiently along with my hand movements that I began to see the possibility of pleasure without having my real rhythms. A sense of his life, hallucinatorily unpictured but *felt* as phallic tremendousness, God knows why, excited me. *Real* life *excited* me but violently romanticized. Violent sympathy, disgust and envy, I pitied him so and I was so horrified for him and so relieved that he didn't mock me (I am not directly male; I am inhibited) that the shabby, fragile membraneous sensation took shape inside a frame of a fear of interruption, of some stupidity that would interrupt or kill the pleasure of the moment, a tender violence, childish; a girl could sing the role perhaps. The act suggests the word *violated*; the violence toward the self is suggested in the name of the act: *whacking off*. One's sexual nature was inspired and illuminated by a sense of violation in someone else. It was violatingly *profane* but a little childish. Indirectly exciting. In a state of interior sensation, one is given over nervously to self-assertion now, encouragingly watched by him.

And advancing, or mounting, in the farfetched electricities of the inner feelings, I approach spasmodic certainty. One is not intruding on anyone except, of course, in the odd factual sense of being there in front of him and revealed.

This event explained childhood's vanishing, that metamorphosis.

A localized, heavy, flashingly silver weight in the *cazzo* was unsteady (*oh . . . oh . . . oh*), the self and reality congealed around the unsteadiness and the weight of a gonadal optics such that inner vision became hot reality; the inner light is the sensational reality; and this becomes in separate flickers a newly instructed adolescent worldliness, airless and interior. Unspeakable. *I know how to do this.* The proud, upstaring, outwardly darkened boy is about to come.

Onni said, "*Come on, Pearl-of-the-day.*" He said it in Italian. I was white-skinned. I bet Onni had heard a lot of epithets in his sexual career by then, him and his young glory of good looks. His desires weren't specific and personal; so his sexual vision was uncertain. His desires had to do with his predicaments and not so much with an *interest* in a certain body or in certain eyes or specific lips.

Onni fingered my chest teasingly, my shirt, me underneath it, not intimately, not in a really bad way, not sexually.

"Come on . . . let's see . . . come on, Nino . . ." He had been with women.

His attentions toughen the feeling which slaps me inwardly like water. It is like a gesture of a coach's hand somehow affecting you strongly.

"Talk . . . Go ahead . . . Talk . . ." Onni bids me alluringly.

This causes me to make an agonized face and to feel interrupted. I shake my head. In the distance, I hear him say, "You are all pink and white." I'm not. He was daydreaming. Or trying something out. Turning my head away, closing my eyes, I tried to keep track of poisoned and lifeless, weighty sensations and their increasing weight and of life and of the reality of light, compromised light. I blindly feel the pure light as an impure lightness piercing and spilling the heaviness. This is an inch before coming, a Venetian architecture, a water stair, an inner stairway, a door.

"Say no again," he said in Italian. He was pinching me.

"No!" I said, too busy and too strained really to feel what he was doing. I pushed his hand away violently, thinking he was stupid. What he was doing was irritating as hell to the nerves at that moment.

Now I was in that last part which is so interesting and so beyond intent, that urgency without any urgency of performance, only of not coming apart at the seams while you eject and splatter. The arrival at the white sunlit summit is a confusion of dissolute and final hemorrhage, and rhythmic and forceful-and-yet-passive-somehow stepping out or over or up into and down into the explanatory light and into the evisceratory and skewering and screwy heat, sweaty, sweatily urgent anyway, jerkingly cooling, and subsiding—again like waves slapping on marble steps. "Unh, unh, unh . . ."—exaggerating it all, a bit, because he was watching and that affected everything.

Even before it ends, the sense of defect starts in, then the conviction of having been mistaken about what was allowed here.

I said blinkingly, "I'm sorry," before the last spasm of the hot snow-white slide, of the emergence of the lemon-milk mess of globs and strings. Blinking still, the smell like lemon blossoms, I said, "I'm a real asshole . . . A jerk . . . I'm no good . . ."

He patted my head: "No: it's O.K. . . . *va bene* . . ." as I finished off, silently sighing, bendingly gasping.

He was almost formal, almost professional.

I could make him out squintingly gazing at me as if in the dark. But it wasn't dark. I was merely in a state of vague postcoital lightlessness.

*

We went a step further that day.

First, let me remark that Venice and Venetian culture and eroticism had the charm of continuous safety over centuries; there is room for personal extravagance.

Onni said, "Are you feeling bad, Nino?"

"Not bad . . . just . . . hell, I don't *know* . . ." Austere.

"Let's go inside," he said. "The villa."

We did. We placed ourselves in the great *sala*. The immense green room was largely cold. Onni produced grappa and cigarets in a silver box—Venetian luxury. He lit a fire in the white stove at the far end of the room and went into a hall and turned on a gas-and-flame heater that poured warm air through vents in the floor. We drank and talked. Then he said he knew something better. He undressed in the chill while the fires caught and buzzed and blew. Distant, semi-excluded sounds of the sea, the Adriatic, were in the large room. I never saw such pinkness as his. The chill came out roseate through the organic prism of his skin. I was impressed by the mass and volume of his thinly meaty body, the body of a meaty boy.

It sounds stupid but I never agreed to go on. It was just that he said I could, could physically have more orgasms, and I hadn't *known* that one could come more than once on the same occasion, although I had done it. But I had not formulated the biological possibility; and, so, it was not clear to me; and I wanted to see it, feel it. His putting the matter into words gave the fact to me generously just as he had given the earlier event.

The quality of instruction and my partly resistant scholarship had a further quality of Venetianness; the myth is always gold, riches, a cornucopia, a miracle at your disposal, an unpunished event, a successful profligacy.

The envy and jealousy and curiosity that are forms of desire in the flux and flourishing, minor or not, of sexual event undergo a sea change into an almost passionate regard.

That too was Venetian—or seemed so to me.

It seemed that to be courted, the tenderness-sophistication and sexual license widened and settled you and made you sort of massive and a bit final. I don't know. It made you less nervous. Ah, the sound of breath is different. The soul becomes public to some extent and is invited into the world of actions. It is dressed like a Doge, the soul, but at the other end of one's time on earth, as a boy: a boy Doge dressed in youth and with his powers circumscribed by his ceremonial attributes of inexperience. The boy's soul is in the robes of boyishly upright and tough youth, in an *erection* as in the horned Dogal hat, as in the stiff, rich robe. The erection in a sexual moment, permitted and *ceremonial*. One becomes semi-aggressive with the almost giggling, maybe shouting of the sexual pulse in you then.

But the innocence is visible, too.

Onni soaped his thighs, the inside, near the crotch and lay down a towel on the floor near the stove. He told me he'd learned about this sort of sex when he lived with a working-class family in *Cannaregio* the last year of the war, after he came back from Udine. He said the guys did this *for* each other. Not *to* each other. He made the distinction very clear; to understand was one of the prerequisites for doing it.

That there were prerequisites reassured the scholar. It meant that this was not kinky but was a traditional folk rite; and one ought to know about it, experience it, as part of one's brotherhood among men. The male thing was a bit confused, but we were both acting male. He was the leader, the initiator. But I was the Top Dog, if I might say that. I lay on his back; he lay on the towel on the rug in the *sala* in the pool of heat near the stove at the edge of a glass-walled conservatory; and I fucked his legs, really in his hand which he cupped there below his smallish balls, on the other side of his legs.

He dutifully loosened and tightened his thighs rhythmically—this was supposed to resemble what it was like with a girl.

He said, "But there is no pregnancy, and the girl can't make trouble for us."

Here is the carpet under his head which is turned to the side. Here are my hands on the carpet. Now here is the sensation of my moving buttocks. Now here is a kind of unawareness of him and a kind of blurred yellowy-orange-ish-quicksilver-splattered sense, very vague, very distorted, of the light inside the glass roof in the conservatory, a drifting light, and in the air of the partly chilly, sea-and-wind-noise-filled room, the enormous green room, the grand *sala* where we were.

Such amazingly important and dear-to-me interest in a batch of silvery-warm-and-then-hot-then-ebbing-and-quickening feelings. Mounted on him. The stove's heat and the strange villa in its moment of abandonment and Onni's company and Onni's body and the feelings like a school of fish in the Lagoon, or like birds, larks, in a field lit by the afternoon sun so that they were like flying mirrors in their quicksilvery dance aloft and darting disappearance in the sun-glare. And their ultimately grave return, so explanatory.

The moment's drama is a progression into sexuality of a realer sort than before. The feelings are larger. The progression is difficult with a guy, with this posture, but the ugliness is effectually *sexual*.

This time one empties with less pleasure leading to worse sadness, much worse, to sad but quietly dance-like gray clarity and a statue-like stoney and stilled dismay and disapproval, an immense Adriatic melancholy. Perhaps it is despair.

But emptiness surely. And clearheadedness. The return of for-a-while distant opinion after the close-up opinions of the act, the engagement, the encounter. Afterwards one is a returned sea captain, a critic, a priest, a child grown this old.

The ancient sense of having been tricked and lured. Age, sorrow, Onni.

In the gray after-moment I realized that he had held me while I came. He had held me within the style of the game, of what we were doing. He had put both his arms up *behind* him, one alongside me, holding me at the waist with his hand, and the other acrobatically up and around my ribs and onto nearly the middle of my back, startling me and holding onto me as I slid a bit from side to side, and at one point, partly slid off. He gripped and constrained my nuttiness. It was clear then—to put it in the present—that he knows me now in ways I cannot yet know myself.

Touch. Touch can be like words.

I can, in continuous time (that means in *real* reality), play as if a sport, in a specific game against him to see what-he-knows, and I can know from that some of what he knows. I can see him and me in that. You learn in real life from what happens next.

Then it was his turn. In his knowing me, I saw myself. I saw in a way for the first time myself as male, a male judged by someone well along in being male in a special way, someone close to me in age, two years older but close to me in time. I took this information without much antagonism or doubt; I was a pacifist at the time, perhaps lastingly—one did not yet know.

But the instant, the very instant he climbed onto my back, the pink-and-tan slablike, muscular *reality* of him, I got studious and friendly-sarcastic, obstreperous and hotly-coldly distanced and wild and evasive, coldly difficult.

As if in order to remain unknown even to myself, I stay controlled, really as if controlled and cold, cold-nerved, because I am afraid to make it clear that I think this stuff is uncontrolled and disgusting. It repels and frightens me. It is scary and sad.

To be too disgusted is to go mad, is to be unable to live—I've seen this in my parents and in my brothers. And in myself before now.

So I keep shifting my weight. I make an issue of having *his* weight on me. I laugh a little and say, "It tickles . . ." (The hair on his chest, on his pubes.) I say, "Wait a minute—it's my knee . . ." (pressing on the floor at a bad angle) "Ow . . . ow . . . O.K., I've got it . . ." Then it was my *ankle* . . . I straighten my foot and positioned my legs and spine and he slid to one side. I said, "You're slippery . . ."

He says bridlingly clenching and guidingly pressing his tight grip on my ribs, "Slippery, dickery, cock . . ." Surely he heard that pun from someone English. Then he slides his arms under me and around me, across my chest: how do you say it? His palms on the towel under me: I have to hollow my chest against the pressure of his knuckles. I make a show of adjusting myself. He says, "Nino, you are acting like a Jew . . ." A Jew? A foreigner? Someone tricky and foreign in Venice? Someone unnatural? Ah, someone difficult and resistant, and, I saw, I was not sticking to the bargain.

Now here is the surprised sense in a bunch of recurring slivers and *slabs* of memory of him before, when I was on top serving my pleasure good-spiritedly and with discipline of a kind.

I am hopelessly astounded that he *watched*, listened to my ascent to orgasm and to the orgasm, to its quality. All at once I am afraid of him in a new way. Now here is that feeling of new fear. And here is the muscle-and-skeleton shift of spirit in my flesh which he senses immediately, dryly of course.

I am lying *obediently* but with the promise of disobedience now on two towels, two because I am tall, with part of my face still on the carpet.

I even say in Italian, "I am on the bottom for you."

"Yes," he says, busy, quietly astounded-unastounded, his style. One *senses* his fear, his hurt, his madness of correction of that stuff from earlier in his life, his rage of unwalled but active invulnerability, so vulnerable . . . like Venice.

He comes almost right away. The shiftings of his weight hadn't seemed even rhythmic. He comes before he can be learned. Or harmed. Or abducted. Winged lion *cub* . . . speedy. Very taut.

I start to move to get up but he says, "Wait . . . I want to come again . . ." He said it in Italian, and it should maybe be translated as, "Let me . . . permit me . . . I want . . . ah, now . . . *again* . . ." A kind of theft, courteously, of not permission but of *startled* stillness or undefendedness, permission in that sense.

I say grudgingly (and with stupidity), "Didn't you come?" He is already moving.

I huff under his weight and shift my own weight and am shifted while he mutteringly says he can come as often as he wants.

He is moving on me, and I am chuffing, and he is not—he has great breath control. While moving he says if he couldn't come whenever he wanted, he would arrange it with drugs and other things so that he could. He means he is in charge of his sexuality. He comes and says, "Wait . . . Let me . . . again . . ."

"What a cheat: look at all you get—my back hurts . . . I hate this stuff," I say.

He told me a dirty story about him and a grown woman, the Contessa, he was seeing, he said, while this time he huffed but briefly, athletically, hard male breath. Without warning, and all at once—it happened abruptly—I was excited again; I was very young; excitement hardly mattered, it was so easily come by; and I had to shift my position and straighten myself underneath him.

But my flesh, my spine became different again; and he said at once, "What is it?"

I said, "My dong was folded wrong."

He said, "Wipe your hands on the towel and you can do it to me now."

"Again?"

"*Bien sûr,*" he said, cosmopolitan, French.

And he rolled off me, pinkly, onto the carpet and in a kind of push-up movement got onto the towels while I sort of crouched and then was upright on my knees and then I—we—did it again. We were young. I was, anyway. I lay on his back, his slippery back. I hated it. His smell, his powerful, muscular (lumpy) flesh, the too solid, slippery meat of his buttocks, and the muscular flesh alongside the bone-bumps of his spine, the tickling wiry hair on his thighs, his hands on the other side of his soaped and tensing and releasing not-very-hairy legs, the heat under his balls and the feel of the slick texture of the soap, the separate units of smell, of his hair and of the back of his neck and of his shoulders, then of the carpet and of the soap and the lemony smell of the come.

His thighs were hairless enough for some pleasurable sensation, for a sense of a girl's legs, but hairy enough in a wiry way (and I was inexperienced enough) that my *cazzo* soon became abraded. Sore. In the sexual Venetian sense, I was shamelessly ashamed. It seemed inadequate, elaborate but inadequate, and only bearable because of the potently narcissistic sense of myself as young and naked and doing this in a villa on the Lido closed for the season with a fire going, the story-like, movie-like setting. The truth is in the moments, do you see? And not even in the shorthand account afterwards.

The pulsing in the peter in the companionship of this intrusively cockeyed act, and the maybe criminal energy of the madness of sexual hallucination carried me as did Onni's body beneath me in its somewhat coldly male approximation, not a travesty but a businesslike, Venetian joke-y/serious version of response and half-imitation of a woman. He was to some extent serious in giving pleasure. In trying to.

I had to get very strong images going in order to have the sensations of light in sequences of pleasure at a speed, a rhythm that would bring me to orgasm again in circumstances not directly exciting for me. The progress into deeper, or higher, sexuality was harder than before and dryer and more formula-ridden. The abridgement of humiliations in the *complicity*, such as it was, the semi-cooperative engineering of the so-called pleasure, did not hide the imbalances in the reality of the *pleasures*. The too clear evidence of sexual individuality and of the need consequently for technique and for soul and spirit to attenuate the technique, the absolutely incredible degree and number of variations of feelings, of sensations, the *absolute* blindsidedness of the moments here, or put it like this, the need for a technical approach as well as for some ludicrous amount of passion to drive the motors of the hips and the motor of the heart and the motor of the mind, such different motors, such different gauziness and solidity in harness weighed on me in an onset of adulthood. The syncopation and the sense of place, and the sense of movement, the sense of light, the sense of spirit, the sense of the darkness of sexuality, the desire to ride, to grip with the knees, to hold his arms *squizzingly*, to hurt and rein, even, to *explode* him, to explore and *explode* him, the need, the requirement that one *love* and accept the world, this world, this private corner of the world and the stuff one did here—well, add it all up, and being sensible, sensibly reasonable, I felt in the absurd calculation of feelings that *Giangiacomo*, after all, was loveable in a way, in his way, to a degree. I was shy and inhibited toward myself and a little unnerved by my desires, animal desires. I put it all into caring for Onni. This was a perhaps counterfeit sense of meaning, but it felt like a meaning, one to be chary about, in the way I was chary about my nutty sexual impulses.

The story was very clear even if unsayable.

The further result is an active cynicism about one's actions here even while one is being racked by *sincerity*, by sincerely sexual feeling with some holding back and some inadequacy in the absurd elaboration of *doing it* this way. One can say that the *sincerity* is torn with reluctance and distance like a Venetian scene. The compression of the sexuality of generation and the greed to live results in an architecture and perspectives of stone, of attachment, interrupting the dimpling surfaces of the water, of the flux of feelings.

Actual love, a free-floating sense of him, warm and troubled, is hesitant, partly to conceal other reaches of love, of love for dangerous *Giangiacomo*, and is to be found and felt only— only!—in the detailed reaches of the moments.

Dangerous, is he? Well, look, I am a man, a boy of zero effect except perhaps for images and the literal comparisons he, *Giangiacomo*, might make with his physical and mental reality and mine. These have an effect—to use an un-Venetian image —like dandelions in a field. They shine brightly in a kind of natural gold that becomes ghostly as a quality of the self, as seeds of effect. Ghost-seeds blowing over the water. I have this other form of effect, not at all the direct kind that he has every minute. But he in his life, after what he has done here seductively, he in his rage, his knowledge, his depth of will, abysmal depths, amounts to a tremendous bravery that I can accept or admit to. I see it now; it shines through his skin; it is the shine of his skin, of his eyes, his culture, his moods.

Little Mr. Zero-Effect Pacifist *Pink Buttocks* . . . the way I felt about myself now, phallic, phallically instructed . . . in gratitude for the dirty pleasure, pretty mild pleasure, which I don't want to repeat, is superior to the pleasure but drawn to its progenitor. *So*, the German *so*, the Italian *adesso* or *dunque*, it is love as mild rage on the surface, a rage of brotherhood, and mockery and concern perhaps like my father's and brother's for me sometimes—that was the model I had. What one knows is all one has to supply the crystalline shape, the skeleton, the structure for what one feels newly.

To instruct someone is to change them, always cruelly, in part, always stupidly in part, the hands inside you wrenching you, the masked torturer, et cetera.

And then the different air and gravity of the new planet

changes everything further. Everything is malleable and warm and can change more, in this new setting; everything is set on small islands in the sea. You can turn against an event or accept it or half-accept it, go halvers with it.

I accepted it. I am known to *Giangiacomo* by how I change in the quasi-metallurgical heat of sex. In the continuous changing of the moments, he is likeable, that whore. He is known to me by how he changes under pressure, or in greed, *Giangiacomo*.

The real feeling for him includes a species of rejection of him, of what he is. One has the wish that he be different. This is a raging joke-y thing of disappointment with him for supplying an inferior and upsetting and worthless pleasure and for being so egomaniacal in his survival all along, and in his powers now of further survival and likeability this way. He did not seem to have a cracking point as I did, and I resented his seductiveness, not just as a power that affected me, but as something that affected others.

I want him to be a greater and better example and a finer source of information. This is a form of independence while "*loving*" someone, part of one's self-esteem, although one is dully and paradoxically ashamed of this sort of self-esteem.

"*Giangiacomo e Nino*," he says in Italian. "Giangiacomo and Nino . . ."

"You're a whore," I say.

Naked, he sits on one of the towels on the floor, leaning back against the lower part of a sofa and smoking. He decided to take it as a compliment to his sexual knowledge and he said, "I try," and looked at his cigaret ash.

His face flickered. He turned his head away and told me to have more to drink. I pulled the other towel over parallel to his and sat as he did on the floor, naked and smoking, drinking grappa. The large stove was blazing. "Naughty Venice . . . Yugh," I said. He reached over and fingered and pinched my bottom.

I grunted and tensed stiffly. I punched him—with zero effect, just about. He persisted in punching, in shoving, because I'd called him that name. He was being unsexually sexual, establishing a rank. I bounced on his hand saying, "I'll break your goddamn fingers."

He went on a moment longer so that you "knew" he was a lunatic and to be feared and not a weakling.

It scared me yet again. The world of fear and worry of a pacifist is kind of a martyrdom, a juicy martyrdom to the craziness of others. Fear to a pacifist is a constant temptation, a way of judging the world foully and unfairly. "You scare me," I said mockingly.

He started to wrestle then. He reached over with one hand, a large, war-labor-enlarged hand, and jerked at my skinny, strong neck; and the force and the tone of it were war. He started to rise and curve toward me, up and half over me, to start the further wrestling. The fear of men, of masculinity, those routes and tactics of theirs, and my disapproval of it set in. I whispered, "Cut it out," wearily, apathetically. That stuff is really not in my range. I can't keep on when that stuff gets going. I said it wearily and I reclined there wearily, my face turned away now.

And he stopped.

That was my first inkling of mutual feeling, of the effect of zero effect on someone intelligent and wounded, on Onni.

He lies there on the carpet, his head against the leg and the frame of a dark blue-green wicker couch. He is still naked, not classically, really. "Feel my breasts," he says, using his fists as pinecones. I am half-dressed to prevent further play like the ass-pinching. Because he stopped the horseplay earlier when I asked him to, I now reach over and twist at his fists, but making a face.

"More," he says, looking up from under his eyebrows. "More."

I refuse to hear him. He balls his socks and holds them so they are breasts; and he says again, "Feel my breasts." I touch the socks which he jiggles while I touch them. I try to pretend this is not lunatic. I squint and try to look sexually grown-up, generous.

Finally I say, "This isn't what I like . . . I don't like this."

I emanate or radiate something: I treat him as a woman. He notes this—furnace-souled Achilles, temperamental.

"Casanova," he says moodily. He is on a different plane of reference. He says it *menacingly-mincingly*, a parody. But he held his chest muscle in that large pinched way to make a girlish breast, actually a pretty one, a very pretty one: "Feel my breast."

I snort, harsh and infatuated but distant, halfway gone off from him for good.

"Come on. Come, Nino, play with me."

It is not honorable to say no.

"Be like the rest of us," he says.

Bringing his head close, he asked in an ironic semi-weary-boyishly-*evil*-nosey way, "You like *tits?*"

"Hoo—oh— "

"Boo-oooh-beeeeeze . . ." *Boobies.* "You ever put a paper clip on—on a *BO*obeeee . . . *Nino?*" Muscularly set, busied-with-thought, with the stuff going on in him, between us in the moment, faintly swaggering in the manner, the set that his face had, boring-in-for-the-next-step-of-his-thought, in the *persistence* that had kept him alive, he stared forcefully at me.

To live, that will, is unromantic, isn't it?

"No. I'm a good Christian," I said and crossed myself, maybe in a looney way. The romantic thing is otherwise from his sense of things. I know more about it or can invent it or a form of it better than he can. He knows only what he knows so far. My embarrassed stiffness and knowledge appeal to him.

This makes him angry.

His stare, angrily, masculinely tricky is comico-romantic, darkly romantic. Sexuality occurs continuously. It is not discontinuous like thought or desire. His attention to continuous time is athletic and rests on his sense of danger, and it is jagged with graceful restlessness. In continuous time, as I keep saying, reside all good explanations and all one's true knowledge of things, not one's bookish knowledge, but one's real knowledge, one's Venetian knowledge.

He finds this stuff instantly intelligible, the continuous motionfulness of it: moments and love, love such as it is, love in reality, moment by moment, as, in a way, we invent it as we go along.

My attention to continuous time was not developed during

the German occupation as his was but with my father and brothers and in sports and longing.

I am American. I have no Gothic past. I am hopelessly democratic, from a country of no saints, no cathedrals, with a past of savage hell and wilderness, and with a high-flown hysterical sense now of a national existence that is utopian-apocalyptic.

In the villa, I feel from inside parts of my face existing in the air of the room. The dream-and-nightmare power of sexuality is attached to a sense of pain and dominance, exciting and staining and ruinous. Irreversible history gibbers at me. Phallic enslavement, *Onni on his knees*, or in genuine attendance like a servant and in nursery days. No. A broken slave. I feel *tremendously* pale, stirred up, distantly, pacifistically violent and maddened inwardly and outwardly. My knees, my dong, my skin are sore and burn in unsyncopated rhythms. If I start to weep and then am mean about it and clever, I will be, maybe, truly *interesting*. But I am interesting another way boringly. I don't think there is logically to be expected a category to be called *Halfway sex and romance that matters a tremendous amount to you*, do you? But there is one.

When anyone fights, each blow is sadistic, of course. Sadistic in an American or English or Italian style. Maybe it's careful sadism. Social class enters into it, and so does the history and psychology of each combatant. This is muffled in courtship sometimes. The degree of softness is the degree of courtship although not always. Sometimes it is the degree of harshness that indicates a great extent of feeling.

Onni now makes sexual *noises* intelligently, intelligibly to me. Such noises jokingly and seriously uttered suggest that his will to rule is close to his sexual promptness. I am not sexually prompt. He was still holding his chest muscle making a small, girlish breast off and on, holding it differently, making different shapes of a breast.

"Nino, you *like* tits? *Sì o no?*"

His actual sexual reality puzzled and repelled and startled me and interested me: I *hated* it. Men don't make room for each other sexually. He was different about that; he made room for other men, for everyone. I could get a glimpse of him, a sense and then an idea. My sense of him came through my feelings, through my soul if you will allow me to say that. His Italian reality in the sexual matter of fiddling with my nerves so foreignly is part of a guy's learning, is part of knowing how to handle shock, how to bear pain. You have to know that stuff, man or woman. Onni's reality is complicated, jolting, ridden with ritual.

He was still holding his chest muscle making differently shaped small, girlish breasts. He persisted, "Nino, you *like* tits?"

"Clown," I said.

"You like tits, Nino? The big soft ones? The pillows? The big sloppy pillow kind? Yes or no? Answer me, don't be Anglo-Saxon . . ."

"I'm a Celt. I don't know yet. Why do you think this is funny?" (He was laughing.)

"Tell me, Nino—how do you feel about tits?"

"That's private, you asshole."

"What is more private than my asking you? We are friends. We're here alone in my Aunt Clarelia's *The Green Villa*. Why don't you answer me?"

"It seems stupid to be honest about tits when there aren't any around and my prick is hanging out." It wasn't. I was being pornographic and chaste at the same time.

"Tuck it in. Put it away, Nino. It is so big," he said dryly.

"Breasts make me feel funny," I said in a studious manner, thinking hard.

"How do you feel about balls?"

"They make me feel funny too. So do pricks and chests. And rumps. And—spines and necks . . . But breasts are different."

"How? What do you mean?"

"I don't know. They look like custards that get thrown in your face in a movie. They have eyes. They make me feel deaf and dumb. You talk too much. Why don't you just go to hell. And shut up." Then, smitten by sensations, I said, "Unless I laugh at them . . . " Breasts.

"Why? Why is that? Tell me—I *have* to know . . ." Very Italian, very melodramatic.

"What do you have to know?" I scoffed.

He scooted over the floor and pressed himself against my arm which was just hanging there. I was pretty goddamned drunk on the grappa by that time in my sensual exhaustion.

He did it not sincerely, not embarrassingly, but jokingly-enflamingly: "What do you like to do with them? How many have you seen? You seen *any*?"

"Tits? Boobs? Thousands. Fuck off."

"Enh-anh-hmmm? You!" he said. "All the boobs they show at parties . . . *DON'T YOU JUST LOVE MY BOOBS—MY BOOBY-TITS—DO YOU GET A HEADACHE my BOOBY-tits are just so b-b-beautiful? DO YOU JUST want to DIE TO GET MY BOOBY-TITS in your face?* Breasts, uhh." He made a sucking noise. "They are nice. *They* don't bite . . ."

"I'm . . . not . . . as heterosexual . . . as you are . . ." Then: "I wouldn't want to be. I want to belong to myself, not to my *drives*." Then: "Why would you want—to put a *paper clip* on a breast? Onni, who let you do that to her? Was she pretty?"

"No. But I am a breast person, Nino, a breast *beast* . . . " he said in accented English, partly being German, for the joke. "Are you a breast person, *Ninohhhhh*?"

"I told you, breasts make me feel dumb. My grandmother died of *breast* cancer . . . I liked her . . ."

"You are so complicated!" He spoke with revulsion, yet with a certain courtesy of physical recognition, of acceptance.

I said, "I think it's bad to treat breasts like they're boys' hind ends—kicking a guy in the rump, it doesn't interest me; I don't want to hurt people. I don't know; I don't really know . . . This stuff interests me."

He leaned close—in curiosity; and he used his nearness to torment and make nervous and to extort truth. Italians, men and women, sometimes do that. He put his hand on my shoulder. He said, "Just stroking a breast is stupid—that isn't sexy. You don't like spitting on someone? You don't like biting?"

"No . . ." I said staring at him coldly. Dislike, excitement, disdain.

He said in my ear: "Breasts are nicer than the women they

are on. I like bad girls with big big *boobs*—great biggggggg *boobies*
. . . I don't like sweethearts. You know the American phrase *catch
your tit in a wringer*, Nino? I like a woman who can do that. Me:
I'm not picky. I'm tough. I'm a James Cagney kind of guy." He
was proud of his Americanisms. He smoked American cigarets;
he blew smoke now. "You know, Nino, a real man isn't picky."

"Bullshit."

He said, "Are you choosey, *Nino?*" He looked at me, blew
smoke. Came near, put a cigaret in my mouth, lit it with a silver
and onyx lighter, and said, "Yes? You are *snotty?* I'm not
choosey." This was a boast and a threat. He said suddenly, in
my ear: "You're like a girl; I can pick on you; I get to laugh at
you. You're always wrong about things— " About the male world.
The only reality.

"I'm on the wrong track . . . but lay off."

He used a further Americanism: "You are so full of the shit
that it is coming out your ears."

I said, "You're jealous. You're a *piker*." I realized he wouldn't
know what that was: "Big shots are picky, Sonny Boy. Not like
you."

"I know what you are like," he said. "You are a Gary
Cooper."

"Says who?"

"Stop being so sure of yourself! It is *very* ugly!"

"I'm right. Read a book and see." I spoke desperately.

"You are absurd . . ." he said Frenchily—and kissed me on
both cheeks, turning my head with a strong grasp. Then: "I am
a lonely person." He produced an unamused little laugh: "I don't
like sex . . . I . . . prefer . . . music . . ."

"You're so full of bullshit you deserve to be lonely. You
think you know everything? Well, a lot of men *aren't* just dumb
garbage-eaters. We pick and choose. Of course, a short guy like
you is a different story . . ."

"Americans can't be gentlemen," he said, coarse-eyed, and
he flicked his cigaret ashes on my belly.

"Jerk. Italian jerk." I reached over and pressed in just under
his ear, a judo trick, at the nerve in a little pocket in the skull.

You can hurt someone that way. He didn't grab my wrist. He turned his head slowly, making no noise—maybe a neat little escape of breath. He was testing my nerves, my ability to be violent. Pressing, I said, "You're a liar. Julius Caesar didn't fuck everyone who came down the pike—just Cleopatra . . . And Mithridates. Things mean something. What's the point of nihilism?"

Now he grabbed my wrist and twisted lightly. I persisted and so did he. We are both in fairly excruciating pain. He said, "The point? We all destroy ourselves. It is a world of evil. Of evil *shit*," he said, trying to sound American, gasping a little. I let up a little. He said, "Fucking is like putting out a match in an ashtray: it means nothing. I am a little cruel . . . you are very cruel . . . It means nothing."

"That's a cliché," I said, burying an *Ow*. But I assumed that his point was that to be cruel (and final) made sex real. "Come live in the real world," I said to him, jabbing again into the little pocket, accusing him in the words often used on me, saying it to him before he could say it to me. I said, "Maybe a man isn't picky but I'm a boy. I'm young: I don't have to be a man yet." Then: "Ow." His grip won.

"Is that American?" Then: "The word *American* means young." And he smiled one of his unamused but generous and genteel smiles at me. A strong person, someone who smiles like that.

These were the actual grounds of a profane friendship.

CHANGING

ROOM

or What a Profane

Friendship Is Like

❧

THE ROOM AT SCHOOL where we change for soccer smells like a cage—a cage that has been used for a long time for small, nervous animals, animals that won't be still. Nervous sweat and the drying sweat of effort and the acrid fear of error, of ugliness and weakness, fear of lack of courage and will make a terrific odor, a stink . . . it is stifling.

The stink of judgement, is it? The light in the room is starkly white. The room is old and worn. It throbs with the pacing relentlessness of the heart in a state of humility.

Onni—his this-year's-trademark look that year after the war long ago was prettyish, semi-antique Roman, curly-haired. It was idly arrogant, slick and old for his age but still very young. That was the basic thing of his looks.

But if you let your mind think about him some more, you might remember moments after a shower when he would comb his hair out straight and be an American junior serviceman—unarrogant and friendly with an undercurrent of toughness, but young.

It would be a good and a bad imitation—he was the wrong age and shape, and it was only a version of such a thing.

But he could harden it and be a convincing version, not the real thing, but he could appear to be very Americanized, not by me—I wasn't that American, although I was the real thing.

Onni did it with a softish, vivacious deadpan and with Italian dash, an unleashed and damned air and swagger.

Or a fine-boned melancholy and well-bred, highbred gaiety: that is Italian dash, too.

So, if I think of him as he was on a number of occasions, what emerges is his being and trying different things and his having a range of things he did fairly well; and the impression I have is of someone Nietzschean without having read Nietzsche, someone Venetian whose self was his fate, Nietzschean in that sense.

And yet careful: that Italian pussyfooting or mad sanity, that not telling anyone, one's neighbors, one's opponents, anything with your blankly beautiful face in any of its expressions, but instead threatening us all with his rather notable blankness and his erotic mischief, erotic vandalism.

He also had a look at times of weary patience plus disciplined vivacity; this suggested his well-bred fair-minded sociability—something he could do when dressed if he was called upon, asked, to be like that.

Let's say I have to pick something to summarize a lot of how he looked day by day. I'd say blankly that all in all he had a look of somewhat punished, slightly concussed and foolish physical triumph, just now, for a while.

But none of that survived into his nakedness when he took off his clothes in the changing room. In his pink nakedness, he looked smaller although he was grown and somewhat powerful in figure. He looked smaller because of the pinkness and a certain roundness—the shapes of muscle and in the volumes of his body.

Some days he looked harder and more defined.

I said earlier the ways the self changes in surges and spurts or by slow accumulation and slow or fast subsidings, the quasi-metallurgical self-distillation in circumstances of pressured in-struction on a *now do it or die* basis, a life and death thing in guys in actual moments—in *the line* of actual moments—is more his identity and real name than his actual name or lineage.

So when he is naked he changes adeptly, movingly—the

woman in oneself or the girlish part of oneself watches him . . .

Getting undressed and fooling around . . . in the changing room—*Giangiacomo*—buttocks, pink peter—naked vulnerability: a strong beige-pink self; a patterned sprinkling of hair; high-arched feet . . .

See, he has a bold shyness; then, abruptly, he shifts: you can observe a precociously concentrated power and allure of his motions. His looks and will, his dexterities, the maybe fairly tremendous heat of will and then the physical vitality, a vivacity of that—which grew great and changed in spirit and faded and came and went in various styles from day to day, hour by hour —he displayed that.

And the rumors-and-aura of his precocious sexual life, him as someone who whoringly aimed—I now knew—to be an actor in the grown-up world, together with the other stuff produced a densely magnetic power: the raw *Giangiacomo*, the vulnerable, pink, raw kid . . .

But that's me seeing it, and that's probably a form of me or of my brother Carlo; and I am aware of it because it's what people see in people around me. I know it as the pattern of what people see . . . the movie thing . . . And then, through that, I see *his* power, the thing that is specifically *his* . . .

The *presence* of that power rewrites everything scarily, and it has a physical effect on me. So does pink, ripe-fleshed *vulnerability*. It affects me physically . . . my legs and muscles—my voice . . .

His personal quality of power holds my attention and creates antagonism and resistance whether or not the power is malign and focussed or neutral and vague or careful or whether it is kindly meant or is half-kindly meant. This creates a *no* which swirls around him from me, a side effect, a side effect of life. His life in him is a disturbance, a disturbing allure of somewhat brighter air as if a key light were shining on him in the ugly changing room light.

Or as if he lived in a partly painted world in which he was the most foregrounded figure . . . the moodiest. Perhaps he is placed at the most forward edge with his elbow seeming to jut from the plane of the picture into my own space from the canvas.

And the strength of his back, the inverted crease at the spine set into the muscle, similarly extends outward to an observer a physical familiarity and way in or bridge to the meaning and perspectives and dramas inside the picture.

Is this a sexual heat—humanly? Is this *homosexual?*

A society of guys has an allowable slyness as of lion or bear cubs, an animal alertness of lies and pride and O.K. playacting —him as a scandal, as if he were effeminate or an advertisement for danger and for *dangerous* pleasures . . . bearbaiting in the *campi* of Venice . . . guys snapping towels at each other . . . who will survive? Which animal will win? He's often in the middle of what happens, but he is often left out, left at the edge. Then he teasingly and maybe heroically, since he is a scandal and dispensable, moves in painful earnest into observability—I see it . . . I see this life-and-death stuff in the gaggingly real present moment . . . He often succeeds.

My attitude to pain, men's, guys', and his pain, Onni's, and my own social deformities and odd despairs—my freakish oddity here, for instance, as the *American,* un-Catholic, and the sexual-physical existence of everyone and the comparative pallors and visible-audible presences, among these his odors, say, or his un-flinchingness or his nightmarish forwardness are like a lantern light on a ship's stern trailing dabs and dibs of light on the restlessly gouged, distressed water of the wake—that I erratically watched rather than watching him . . . that I followed his figure in, from inside that light on the water, as if I had dived in—or had fallen overboard—the key to reality that he was for me for a while, male reality for me—I was in that water, waterlogged, wallowing and following helplessly, near drowning . . . See, in this universe, people, us, we have only each other to look to to widen the area of light in the darkness or to see ourselves and our lives and what we might and can not do. Others show us what we might be able to do. Able or not, I was tempted.

By Onni's reality . . . I chose Onni, half-chose him as a limited model or example—much of this was accident, was luck . . . I had no idea if this was commonly done or not.

•

He showed off in the locker room: he slunk around on the outside of the group—the scandalous kid, the shamed one, the one not quite masculinely acceptable—and then, abruptly, he would be central because of his boldness and his energy and his *shamelessness* which I would swear was simply shame plus indomitability.

Changing for soccer, pulling on the long socks, looking at him still naked, I saw that he ruled, in mischief, in mischievous will, over the part of the changing room near him and he did this nakedly, not because he was phallic, but because he was unembarrassedly not so phallic as a lot, maybe most of the guys—him doing a tango with the abrupt, big-boned, blinking-riddled, big-lipped goalie, who was hairy, and who was embarrassed and clumsy until after only two steps or so when he did an amazingly deeply-felt travesty of a tall, plain, greatly sexual woman . . . But a Northern Italian *contadina*, not the travesty woman Onni had played for me.

I did not dream of *Onni* or long for him—not so far as I know. But if his body could have been flayed and peeled, unwrapped, and a glass forehead replace the skullbone behind the skin above his eyes so that I could have seen his sexual attitudes and known his true memories revealed in a pseudo-logical drama, as in a dream or as in a movie, tiny, bright-colored figures moving on blood-tinged platforms, pseudo-stages, explanatory, gracefully soliloquizing or gesturing in ways that would have told me what his world was, and what the world was, he was so much more embroiled in it than I was, then I would have had my strongest desire.

I did long for him to think of me as someone like the hairy goalie. But the desire was shaming to me—I still don't know why—and unacceptable to me and, so, it remained unclear, unformed.

How much humiliation and pain and being swindled and befouled by the world could he take? Even if one chose him because he was not frail and pure and was strong, one wondered how much could he take and go on triumphing? Are you prepared to live among the memories of people broken and in disorder?

His strength: I had a general impression of the good fortune that attends on beauty, in someone who represents beauty in history now, at this time in the world, in watching him. I don't want to misrepresent these things but I think beauty and fear and pain are primary forces—fear of humiliation, of the pain of humiliation, fear of masochism . . . Perhaps Onni's *strength* came from humiliation. I hoped it did. I didn't believe it did. Knowing me would—I don't have a word for it—tangle or abrade him perhaps.

I often feel I am invisible . . . not real to people . . . zero in effect. A girl, a tourist I picked up in the Piazza told me, *You are unreal* . . . We talked and necked in a shadowy *calle . . . I like women,* she told me.

What kind of *man* makes these mistakes?

Anyway, staring at Onni, I knew something that obstinately remained as knowledge beyond words, as a physical sense. It recurred even in memory not as mist or vapor but as presence, mere presence, great presence . . . *Great Presence* . . .

Like the sight of Venice in a mist across an intervening distance of as-if-smouldering water, the mist rising from it.

The knowledge had a quality or sense of loneliness and singularity but then also of universality, as if he was everyone— a strange thing, lonely universality . . . Again, like Venice.

I was still an amateur at being somewhat grown, at having this newly elongated stretched-out body, physically incomplete . . .

In a game, the soccer game with Padua—or was it Mazzorbo—I played very badly; but then (forgive me for boasting if you can), abruptly, with a starring sharpness of attack, which was a mix of self-expenditure and recklessness and a psychological sense of the other team—as a whole and of individual members—and of how the game was going and of my own mad, as-if-hypnotized possibilities. I hypnotized myself and then cast myself into the motions and shouts and tactics of the next several moments . . . Onni's friend.

I had a completely insane, physically impossible, half-hopping dribble, mad egret but in mid-run, having to brake only a little to organize himself toward the goal and other players. I could not think and do this. So, I am blind with immediate and busy physical sight and very specialized inner sight joltedly moving along with that—field sight—and I am full of sensation, I am filled chockablock with sensations, grass underfoot, moist air in my lungs and on my legs above the long socks and on my eyelids and in my sweaty hair—clear, slightly *crystalline* light with, near the water, the low-lying commonly known haze of the Lagoon, unevenly transparent and whitish, giving way when it parts to great clarity and brilliance of outline even at a distance.

I took off at a run, getting a pass from a tall, flabby boy, Cristoforo Limone, a self-important mean guy and a fool, ungenerous but cowardly—so he would pass . . . Also, he took orders from a guy named Gino who was very ugly and very smart. I half-knew with regular consciousness that this might be a moment in which certain things were possible in the game, but it was my body's sense of things that sort of hammered once at the regular setup and then got some sort of mad, blind, quick *go ahead* from me—or a passivity, a *let it happen, go ahead* of that sort . . . and I say I began running, but this other self did it, running and weaving in the way the coach had said was *inspired* (pardon me) as opposed to what he said was my stupid worthlessness, actually, *nothingness*—Italian and Venetian are untranslatable into English. They are languages of immediate action and of immediate judgement, of quite fantastic degrees of aggression moderated by an extreme courtesy based on the terrible discourtesy of intending to be heard . . . Heard, listened to, and *comprehended*, anciently and now.

They, the language and the dialect, are languages of comprehension rather than of expression—this is another thing making him sad—well, you see, in this closed universe of accomplishment or of death, among all the fucking moments you spend awake, in the avenue and blustering and swiftly silent onflow of a given day, you can be comprehended if you don't express too much. *Nothingness—a piece of zero—I do not have to think of you . . .*

A field full of wettish light and full of kids, fuckers all of them, and me, American and Welsh but taken to be renegade semi-*English* (after often, in California, being accused of having been Italianized), running and weaving, tall, gawky, roseate, as nakedly flushed, bossy and inspired, ruthless in my way—(one should be aware of narrators who pass themselves off as undemonic or typical or as innocent)—as if I weren't a pacifist, and without conscious thought except for little exclamations inside me (but never, almost never said aloud) of *YOU FOOL!* and *I WILL SHOW YOU, YOU ASSHOLE*, dodging and shouldering my way violently, elusively, me fooling the opponents with a sublimely upright self-righteousness of extreme trickery—inspired for once—and exhilarated beyond all likelihood of such a sensation being acceptably intelligent—happy and angry and savage and checking to see where my teammates were, panting, excited, elevated, sublimely and pedestrianly *winning* and gaspingly breathing the air of that afternoon, that grass-odorous, light-struck, mist-bordered afternoon—sweatily immersed in the action, immortally happy, it seemed, well, hell, guys, I scored two goals.

I scored two goals before I was cut down. In this passage of excited play, I had gone into my hopping mode to get off a pass; and Gianni Orgoglio, an oversized piece of shit—actually, a kind of not bad, crude, cruel captain of the other team—came at me, the killer for his side, the patriotic butcher, the one with the iron conscience, too broadly rooted in his own temper (and ruthlessness) to be outwitted or nonplussed or moved, or to play fair in relation to my feints and my exhilarated face and rhythms. My madly pulsing neck on which my head was placed: my head saw him coming and was aware of the power and speed (so to speak) in my arms and legs and of his greater weight and of his focussed will and of his purpose. He tripped me: he cheated; he did it hard and fast: and I went down before I could think, killed without a thought, the wind knocked out of me. Frozen by airlessness and thrown, I couldn't move even when tossed into the air, I meant to flail my arms and legs in order to land safely . . .

There is the grass, here is the faintly white-silvery air . . . Oh God the tremendous ache—the blow, the shuddering onward echo of the impact and the flying vibrancy of the impact of the landing on the ground. I fell in silence; I lay in silence, shut off, locked into the suffocation. Shut off from the common air of the world.

It is yet another form of Venice, this death, this extraordinary island, this shrinking and expanding Venice of darkness and isolation and of self-judgement without air, the riches of the world receding . . . the world receding like a *Zattere* of distant lights, golden, with guitar and flute music audible across the water, and girls visible far away.

To die to the world as if in thought or as if in monastic contemplation, disentangled from political and cultural moments and *shudderingly* unguided, unguarded . . .

And Onni bent over me, the light behind him, the outline of his head, the tangle, of hair, the lightly protuberant features of his face in noticeable dimensionality and clarity. I was too wounded to care not to see him for once. The presence of fate was in attendance already, death masked in appearance, dressed in the afternoon light . . . the encroaching darkness—a secret entrance, an exit . . . Unconsciousness, a daze; your death is unshared. It is not like birth . . . And you are visited by this other figure.

It sounds awful but I looked and saw *his* death and accepted it—and my guilt, such as it was and would be. His eyes and mouth are set for the soccer game unreadably except in this other frame. His athletic unconcern reveals an almost feminine, personal attachment, an identification of his luck to my well-being just at this minute . . . I am his. His child.

The curve of his large, flattish chest in the dark jersey with the light-collared collar bent toward me and over me in a *specific* physical meaning, a particular meaning which perhaps had never or rarely been shown him . . . He had no brothers. Who had ever shielded him?

The idea of tenderness, of clement attention under it all

finally—I could have danced what I saw. What I experienced at that minute I could have sung if I had been unself-conscious enough to dance or sing—I mean when I was young—but when I was young I could not have spoken of it.

He had a dreadfully *foreign* beauty now intimately entwined with the stream of murmurs of my own blood and death so to speak. The fluctuations of reined and unreined and of reigning and of raining emotion, feelings, tics, fear, pain, and sexuality as breath returns are like the emotions and moods of one's walking or travelling by boat among the hoary pink buildings in their grace . . . their slightly miniature marvellousness. Everyone on the field, all of them, all those *guys* have seen me in this state of helplessness, this isolation. Once you are publicly wounded, you are fair game. A dislocated shoulder, a sprained wrist, a pulled ligament in the ankle: myself worthless and in pain, now shockingly white and then blue and green and pulsing with faint whistling tortured breaths . . .

Nothing in his dreams, in the way he told himself stories in his sleep, would be comprehensible to me even if I knew about it, even if I could by some means or magic enter his sleep. I mean that if I could see his thoughts, I would still have to have him explain them to me . . .

But the concern in his arm under my head—and the limit of that concern, the harsh sensation I always had of a central coldness inside the fleeting heat and somehow swiftness of his touch —and in his voice when he said, in Italian, "You did well, you did very well, Nino, you are all right, you will be all right . . . You're all right—aren't you?"—those are not so rare and not so limitless that one can afford to say he would die for me or I for him.

The world is a scandal and worthless. Wearing bandages on my wrist and with my arm in a sling, limping home, accompanied by Onni and some others—but they went off—and Onni and I limped along the various *fondamente* toward the *Riva degli Schiavoni* with Onni singing dirty Neapolitan songs to me and stroking my shoulder and laughing, some, at my clumsiness . . . perhaps to a terrible degree . . .

No one mocked me as we walked; no one shuddered and looked away. I was in his company and under his devious direction; instead of being a helpless and embarrassed young man, I was that day a beautiful cripple.

And no one at all pitied me.

*   *   *

And so we go on to breathy May, the wind and the light, the flutter. Onni, handsome, a bit meaty but a well-shaped human being, meets me before school and says, "Well, hello, darling . . ." and cupped my neck with his too large hand. He brought his face near mine: "Ciao."

I said in his grip, "*Ciao, Porco . . .*"

"You are a grim person," he said.

I imitated a farting noise with my breath.

"You are a disgusting American person, you American pig . . ." He made an openhanded feint at slapping my face. "Am I on Your Hit Parade, *darling*?" The *Hit Parade* was a popular American radio program back then that some advanced European kids kept track of, of the popularity of American songs. *Hit* Parade, he said, and he knuckle-slugged my arm.

He was sensitive; he did this sensitively. "You walk like a tortoise," he said. He has a narrow-eyed, calm look . . . He was not calm in his moodiness, not openly a kind of whore, but plotty, aristocratic—"everyone" in Venice spoke slightingly of him, but "everyone" was available to him—he engaged with a nervous momentum in Love-Talk-in-Venice a lot. That look of calm is a lie but it is effective, that upper-level Italian calm.

So, then, I hit the sad bastard-whore on the side of the head with one of the textbooks I carry . . . ah, the flesh and cardboard-and-paper thunk.

Still, it was a pacific blow, and I dodged at once, but he socked me on the chest hard enough as I backpedalled that I started to fall. But he caught me by the arm and held me upright.

"*Imbecile*," I said in Italian in an upperish way.

That day that bothered him. He promptly pushed and backed me against the wall in the *calle*; and his face against mine, his body pressed against mine, said, "*Idiota platonista . . . Brutto.*"

"I am not a Platonist." Then, moving toward the unintellectual, since the placement of one's attitude changes one's vision, I saw him as a painter would, I think, eye-to-eye, the bones of his face, the forefront of the nose, the pretty gouge just-above-the-center-of-the-lip, saw him with visual innocence—it is like entering the world. "Goddamn fruit," I say in English, in the awful intrusion, so frequent in youth, of someone near you breaking into your feelings. He was doing it by force; he was pressing me against the wall of the *calle*.

He kissed me on the cheek, just under my eye, not quite entirely mockingly, which made it more of a shock. As a matter of feeling it commented on the comparative lack of feeling in the way I was acting.

In the awful intimacy of this invasiveness, as a lot of the time, I hated being young.

"*Asshole . . .*" I say, seeing him frontally—I was not always aware that he was shorter than I was and broader-chested. And stronger.

"Pretty scholar," he says and combs my hair with his fingers and releases me.

I was grotesque-looking: stylish.

I am blankly askance when he asks, "Did you ruin your book?"

As if I were a young man of action or a true wild American, a motorcyclist, I say "You awful *dago* lousy Wop . . . You fucking Eye-tie piece of shit." I swear a great deal but I am not violent.

"You talk like a Neapolitan cunt."

I said in Italian, "You *are* one."

Onni said, "You sound like an awful English person . . . I'm epileptic." He wasn't. He imitated a petit mal seizure; his throat, newly widened muscularly, worked in a snakelike way, and he opened his mouth and rolled his eyes and threw his head back and grotesquely moved his arms and legs.

"That's disgusting," I said.

His mother and aunt continued to whore him; he wasn't doing it on his own yet. He and his lunatic mother: in a Venetian

sense, he was for his mad mother a son-daughter, violent, violated, absurd, heroic and cool.

"Let's go have a *coffee*."

We went into a bar in the next *calle*, and he leaned way over
the counter, getting partway onto it, his feet off the floor, and
half-kissed the bar-girl. The lips did not make full wet contact.

She was an angry, stern-mouthed ferocious type, actually
Neapolitan; she was amused by him. She swatted him off; it took
six or seven blows: Punchinello stuff, abominable-wonderful.

Onni got his hand, comically, on her big breast and he began
to roll his eyes, but he was manipulating the breast for real . . .
dirtily; she thought about it for a half-second, before backing
away and clobbering him with a wooden bar spoon, a big one;
she hit him right between the eyes so that he blinked squatly.

Off and on during this she looked at me in the considering
way I had become familiar with lately, to see if I was eligible for
romance, as a substitute for him, a more reasonable version of
a tough, male, fairly wellborn adventurer-whore, or as a way to
get to know him, someone who could restrain him if we made
a trio, that kind of thing. Someone instructed by him.

In the politics of affection, especially among the young,
nearby corruption is irresistible because of its quality of truth and
because of the dare—you do not know if you can survive contact
with it. But it is outdoor life, all of life that is not in the *sala* . . .
that is how corruption seems: to be all of life and unsafe but
realer than family life.

I left the bar and smoked in the *calle*. After a while, Onni
joined me, and we set off; I set the pace and the direction, not
toward school but toward the *Zattere* . . . I veered off in *Campo
Santa Margherita*. It was a pale pollen-yellow day with a frail
powdery light, really a hard light at its center but with some
powdery yellowish quality to it that blew in gusts through the
city.

He said to me as we came out on the upper end of the *Zattere*,
"You are perverted."

"No, you are." Then: "Jackass." Tall, gangly, affronted—
amused.

"What does it mean to have your brain?"

He means I am stupid, fatuous, off-key. He is also jealous. "It means nothing, you piece of shit. You know that." But I am desperate for peace, and I sigh.

"Don't be pathetic," he says. He dodges my witless attempt to slap him.

I say, half-loudly, in the wide light, "Faggot! Faggot!"

People turn and look at Onni, who, in his beauty, turns slowly, showing himself to them all. He smiles androgynously like someone in an old painting at everyone who is looking at him.

If you do not use *symbols* to represent lovers, if you do not symbolize love, if you not *lie*, then you have the sting and abrasive hum and burn of *horsing around*, the mad fragments of speech, living speech, the love speech in horsing around, the perpetually reborn jealousy of it minute after minute . . . These real things are like so many diverse cupids playing in the light . . . And making the idea of love-as-sentiment seem absurd.

Bear-cub affection or fox-like affection, then the deeper, gouged attention when hurt, the humiliation, then harsh sensual or sexual attention—a tone, a gesture, perhaps crass or gross, touching—then complicitous attention, then the clemency of attention . . . often without gender.

It takes nerve to keep going while only half-knowing what any of it means. The incompleteness of it all is the eternal element . . . murder or utter-devotion-and-being-a-robot would be completion.

Can friendship make you go mad? Can it kill you? The yellowy light. The degree of harm we are doing to our lives is unknown, sharing drugs, sharing information about *fucking*, sharing political attitudes—the half-forgiveable and yet unforgiveable betrayals with girls, mentioning it to each other as a species of inattention to one another.

At night sometimes we share girls, not usually in threesomes but semi-serially. I made a rule against it but I broke the rule.

We have shared physical adventures: racing in motorboats, various dares . . . We have shared the humiliations in horsing around . . . Flat on my back on the pavement in Venice, on the uncrowded morning *Zattere* where he wrestled me to the ground . . . "Say uncle," he says madly.

Ah, he cares.

On the *Zattere* with him: the mind is as abrupt as fate. I spat in his face. He wiped it on me, on my face . . . I roared and roared with laughter . . . Completion is a ripeness forbidden to men. But engaged in and kept secret, fig-leafed, another male thing.

One is burning slightly in Venice.

—What did you do?

—We did nothing much.

A dream: *The flames cracked the domes, and the pall of smoke drifted over the water which itself was red and black twistingly as the heated currents seethed and veered. In the multitude of boats, half-undressed and weeping and staring people with disordered hair and with firelit eyes cried out or were silent as here and there parts of the city collapsed into rubble in the flames. The noise of the fire silenced the seabirds. Then snow blanketted the fire. Birds sang in the snow, and I awoke.*

Wrestling. He has shouldered me onto the ground on the chilly pavement near the gate of a garden. Light flares on the nearby choppy water. I kick at him bicyclingly. He backs off, pauses, lunges and grabs my ankles and twists me so abruptly and savagely that my spine cracks. Then, advancing inside my legs, he grabs me at the hips and pulls at my pants; and in dreamer's astonishment although I am awake, I shout, "YOU SHIT. This is SHIT! Stop. I'll kill you . . ."

But he knows the swearing I do is display without ferocity, usually. And since he is stronger than I am we both know that I cannot stop him from exposing my genitalia if he wants to do it. We suspect that such an act in its quality of profanation might end the friendship because of the unboyish degree to which I try to control my own flesh.

Weakness is an animal worthlessness. I am not weak overall

but he is physically more adept than I am. If I am too weak to stop him, I am comparatively worthless, and I cannot bear that. He jerks at my pants. I punch his head, his chest, in mad resistance, a madman-lion affectation in a tough-boy moment. I am surrounded by boy-smells. In physical effort he smells like what I imagine a dead lion smells like. He stank scarily in exertion, a somewhat sandy, faintly oily stink, acrid. His nauseatingly big, plumpish, newly powerfully-muscled throat works with breath. His smelly purpose and the air on my bare navel, thin spriglets of hair revealed, the upper band of my underpants now being pulled down . . . if I were a woman I would be a Lesbian rather than submit to male strength. I push with the palm of my hand against his forehead. In actuality I can break his neck, damage the vertebrae. We do a lot of life-and-death stuff actually. Perhaps I have become in this moment genuinely violent.

He was not clearly frightened of me but he was somewhat careful—in courtship. He had left fright behind in general when his sense of being untouched by fate was torn apart during the war. In the Venetian air, he is not subdued, not entirely careful, even in courtship, and this gives him a certain potency I do not have in a fight. He gambles with a sort of deadened nerve on life-and-death matters all the time.

Still, I *know* that he will stop in time. But I don't know it. Venice and the world are uncertain. When we are taking physical risks or tailing tourists and discussing robbing them it is not clear what will happen. He assumes I will not kill him, but that is partly contempt, partly love for me, that I am not a killer. I don't know the real male world very clearly. I press harder, calculating hotly that I have such a good reputation in the city that I can probably get away with one murder, one killing I mean, in my life.

What is the merit of Onni's being so tough, so willful in a shamed way? I thought it was a merit, a matter of character as a practical matter. His leaden resistance to nervousness or restraint is familiar enough that the moment wrestling is intimate and shocking.

I don't know if I will be finally humiliated or finally excited.

"*Vaffanculo . . .*" he says. He has me in a headlock. He mutters in English, "Why don't you ever keep silent? You never close your mouth."

"Go to hell."

He laughs somberly and bites my ear.

"Shit! You fucker!" I can speak only with difficulty. I bite the underflesh of his straining forearm; my teeth slide on the skin, then go in a little way. I butt his neck with my jaw. He jerks his body and his hand jerks inside my underpants and tweaks my dong. *It* shrivels. He laughs sibilantly and releases the headlock. *It* then thickens uncontrollably in release, in a return to self-will. It thickens in a bad way with that joyless and weird pleasure it sometimes has.

He starts to twist my arm; perhaps he can feel that the game for me is over, but all at once he lets go and backs away and says loonily, "*Give up? You Anglo-Saxon bastard? Give up? Say uncle. Say you love me. Say you want to kiss me, darling . . .*"

"Go to hell."

"Oh, are the gloves off?" he says in English. "Uh, uh, uh?"

I lie there. To make me stir he flicks his finger near my eyeball. I don't care. I am an oddity, a phallic, zero-effect boy. He is exploring how to manage me, how to manage his feelings . . . This is part of a *deep* friendship, love between friends, whatever. But it does not suit me, I am disgusted, tired of him.

He says, "You want me to suck your cock now, darling?"

In a flow of bile and adrenaline I say, "*Cretino . . .*"

He jumps and climbs on top of the garden wall. I see his motions of wriggling exertion, muscular distention and thinning in floatingly ascending arabesques as if very far away. He looms up there. I lie on the pavement. My wrinkled shirt and pants, the air on my bare skin, on my shins . . . I have a friend. Big deal. Venice has in it, for me, along with everything else, the reality of love . . . *Oh, is that what this is?*

A soldier-policeman is approaching, and I get up and re-arrange myself. Onni jumps down on the other side of the wall and disappears.

A moment later he re-emerges from a *calle*, adolescent,

power-flecked—independent. Perhaps at this time, he whored on his own.

He talks *a bit* like me. I talk quite a bit like him. When we are together, more and more we talk, perhaps because we now talk in a related style, changed along a certain arc of resemblance, but perhaps not a deep resemblance, only a cheap one. People, when they meet, judge each other as fighters, as ferocity. They judge your sexual nature, your sexual possibilities as weaknesses. They wonder about your family's money, your social rank. They wonder how well you are protected. In my manner, I try to suggest I am someone who is not pacific; I hide my true nature which, perhaps, is no longer my true nature; I am derived from Onni, from my sense and observation of Onni, both in similarity and in resistance, in apposition.

In Onni's presence, I am insistently aware of him as breath and as what I see and as mass and solidity. I feel him as a matter of touch without touching him. I hear not just his voice but his breath and blood. He has a smell of nerves most of the time. His presence, the bones of his shoulders, his face from in front, the curve of the back of his head under the hair, all this is weirdly *familiar* to me in wakefulness. But it is as if it had been often dreamed. His presence confers, and he himself is, an animal enlargement of myself—this is true *most of the time*. He is increasingly secret about his life with me, but at moments he refers to things in free carelessness or purposeful indiscretion or trust when we talk.

His voice, unidealized, is, in its music, its dissonance, an utter singularity that my soul does not always shy away from. Listening, I do not always distill his actual speech, or him, into an abstract similarity of announcement to printed things and remarks in dreams and to the speeches of characters in movies. Sometimes for long minutes I hear *him*.

Sometimes I do genuinely see the hazed clarity of his eyes. At some point in the winter, although he lives often with his mother and his aunt, he begins to have his own room in the same building but separate from their apartment. It has a large couch and a modern lamp with a three-foot arm and a black bureau.

Perhaps he has begun his rise in the world. His lazy, somewhat *odd* beauty, thin-boned in part, heavy-boned in part, is often ordinary, is often not present. He is not a boy but he can resemble a boy, be a boy—it is a form of acting. His physical quality gives an effect of symmetry, a kind of meaning to his looks, but his face is not symmetrical, and the meaning of his face, its statement as signifier, is variable.

Combat-courtship. Pride . . . Love . . . *Love*, in its animal smell, its heightened pulse, its qualities of erection, its death-feeling, its patience with itself, its patience with the way its patience comes and goes, its acceptance of limits, its disavowal of limits, its piratical quality, its brutality—these various things live in Onni's face, in his presence for me. And like his face with its neatly crafted *Italian* chin, these vary in meaning from day to day, hour to hour, they vary even in ten-minute sections of time.

His small penis is an advantage for the swiftness and clarity of his responses. His quickened secrecy in the stretched awareness of a moment may also influence the way he is photogenic. He is easy in his relation to light because he has less distortion of the self when he is stretched by internal pressures of nerves than I do. He is not wracked by the stirring at the crotch. Or by an ill-considered sense of power when what is needed is a seductive and sympathetic quality of being, of being almost zero-effect in terms of power but effective as a broaching of the idea of sex-as-filth or sex-as-romance. Yes, one has been stolen, abducted. No: one's shadow was taken and is kept prisoner in a lightness of boyish corruption, in Onni's perpetual readiness, a function of his genital size.

We had not repeated or returned to the early sort of sexuality. A male hardness of breath in excitement or in temper or in arm wrestling suggested the other, but the suggestion did not apparently have to be reshaped as genital gesture or even as conscious recollection of having known each other sexually to that extent.

But my quasi-innocence is a sexual lure. It has a particular sort of sensual reality for someone not heavily real sexually except in will and as an object. His own ignorance maddened him and was a large part of the knowingness of his gestures, his pretenses, his bluff. His assurance of knowledge is both a bluff and a reality if you press him. My innocence is a lure for someone who steals, abstracts, sucks out the reality of my being innocent. He uses people *usefully*. My innocence is a dare for someone corrupt—this is a particularly Italian matter. Curiosity moves him. My fate, and this month's fate of the world, are not equally important; and he is politically sound and is grown-up—he has the rudiments of an entire program of ruthless carelessness and of intellectual ambition—I mean my fate does not entirely concern him but it amuses him. My fate does. It interests him. Values and depths, options, priorities, his was more a French Leftism than an Italian one; it was more Sartre than Gramsci. Ruthlessly careless in a French existentialist posture (an Italian version) and in a mood, he moves darkly around his room, his posture polite, even humble—waiting for applause, for the drama to form here in his room. If he were entirely ruthless, it would not be possible to know him. He offers his weaknesses and vices as signs of approachability and availability—it is very effective, him maintaining his Achilles heel as a tourist attraction, so to speak, as a necessity if he wants to promote tourism, a tourism toward him.

He is sensitive about being a whore. He still is one but more strongly, more adept, deeper-voiced all the time. He was good enough at it that, not the words, but the actually fleshly thought that he was good at it still enrages me down deep and all through myself with various sorts of uneasy envies and jealousies, a large number of them, and with a sense of my having missed out on a lot of things. It is quite a feat, quite a fate, to be an extremely good, top-notch whore who doesn't whore around all the time.

Odious suppleness of soul, of flesh, of sexual mood. Odorous sunlight, a kind of drying stink from the damp walls and from the *campo* outside. A moat of air is between us.

I am supine on the couch; I start to count: "One, tooo-ooo, three-uh, fo-errrr, fi-i-i(ve)—"

"Wh-it ehr-rrr yuu dew-eeeeng, Neeee-no-o-o?" He had an accent like that.

"I'm counting—if I count to seventeen, I get to see God."

"No shit? *È vero?*" he asked cautiously, maybe, maybe awed

or touched or left out. He comes over and slips over the back of the couch and lies in the crevice almost, beside me, shirtless.

"I read about it. It's mystic—like St. John of the Cross."

"In the name of Goh-idd," he said, "Nee-nowwww, aw-errr y(ew) goh-eeeeng toooo see Gawidddd(uh)—*adesso*—like St. John of the Cross—here—in the *Sestiere San Marco*—on my couch . . . Nino?"

"No . . . NO—WAIT: THERE *HE* IS . . ."

He stiffened. Then he turned pale. Then angrily he pushed me half off the couch. I caught myself with my hand on the floor.

"You masturbate too much," he said. "Admit you are filth, you *merda* filthy infidel . . . You—and Winston Churchill . . . so pure . . ." pushing at me.

"Christ," I said, trying to get back on to the couch.

He grunted. He said—triumphantly, gruntingly—"What are you thinking about now, Ni-no? Are you looking for God now?" Then he pulled me onto the couch. He leaned over slightly to smooth my hair; he said, "I am sorry . . ." He was coked up; he gave me some coke a few minutes later. Now, he said, "It is your face. Your face is a mind."

My "innocence" holds a sweetness dreamily but thickly like honey, or moist earth for someone who feels dry. He can only stain such innocence—it is better to have such an attraction than to have none: it is leverage of a kind. One can comb it, tousle it. Or if it is a shape, one can exercise it, have postures of it, of innocence. Do I enjoy this as a superiority? Very secretly. Unwisely even if secretly. My will is stronger, stabler than his. I am much more open, violable—like Venice. I am older than I was. The body is awake—some of this is his doing. It knows it will be wronged, intruded upon because of love in various forms, hate, indifference as well. Onni is often cheered and yelled at as an athlete in sporting matches and in small parts in plays and movies, that is part of the story; it is a matter of story, the thing of being noticeable, second after second in Venice where everyone is noticed, where everyone is a star, a hero, just by existing here—to be more noticeable than that is part of him.

As I said, I am older; my no longer trivial hands hold a

cigaret. My eyes are breakable like china, vulnerably alert and grotesque with cocaine. I am aware, drugged, that my mother has said to me that people now say to her, *But he is handsome . . .* She says that she says, *It happened all of a sudden . . .*

I am not handsome. I am noticeable. I am someone partly created by *Giangiacomo* (now) *Galli*.

I am as excluded from ordinary reality as if I *were* a child or a girl or an angel. The *facts* of someone else's condition always interested *Jacques.* Not only mine but particularly and especially mine. Onni needed to triumph over the circumstances of others' lives, whorishly in part. He says reminiscently, "Let's play let's-die games, Nino . . ." At Cortina he had done a handstand on the edge of a gorge. I had too but more briefly, and I had not walked on my hands as he had. He had put a finger on my ankle for safety, in case I fell.

In Cortina, he played Russian roulette. We were fairly drunk with a party of vivid Austrians all of whom seemed to keep clearing their throats. I stared into the barrel of the gun and then said, "No, I am a coward. I don't want to die yet. Soon perhaps . . . but not yet . . ."

Onni had burst into laughter. Then they all laughed, and I was *permitted* to back out without being ridiculed.

If I win out over him too finally, if I seem to him to be too greatly superior, I understand he will kill me—one way or another. It *is* love, a risk. No one referees a *secret* thing of this sort. Who will save me? I will not let him finally regard himself as having a polished mind. There may be ways to live which do not directly include crowding someone else's ego, but I have not experienced living of that sort.

In his room, he said to me, "You impress me too much. I do not like that. You are not the Virgin Mary. You are not the Lord Christ. You are not holy. You are not sacred ground. You are afraid to show your true face."

Coked up, I had in me an arrogance, a pacifist's vast lunacy of assertion: "The meaty face? Or the spiritual face? What about cancer? Or lunacy? No one knows how they feel the way you say that you do . . ."

"Would you die for a friend?"

"It depends on the friend . . . Asshole . . ."

He rose and walked again in his room with a kind of genital-and-buttock awareness: more and more he is an actor, overtly superior to me physically, and a bit horrified by me, my middle-classness, my fine-drawn innocence.

Fear and horror are romantic for him. The path to feeling for him includes those things and some disgust in the Italian manner. In the ordeal of male infatuation, I made no promises, none, not one, ever.

"I would die for a friend," he said. I said nothing, just watched him. He said, "Are you afraid of me, Nino?"

"I don't know. Yes. I don't like the last-ditch in people . . ."

"Ah?" He blinks patiently, to make me say more.

"I am looking for an honest friend . . . an honest man . . . A serious woman—something like that . . ."

"I am not afraid of anything at all," he said dreamily. His hand moves on his brown skin, on his belly. "I love people too well, not wisely. You should be a Communist, then you would love me more," he said, still dreamily. His voice in the simplicity and colors of its artfulness is an extraordinary thing that warmed and amused. You cannot feel much guilt with someone as impure as Jacques-Giacomo—he had already done two films in Paris as Jacques Galli—only fear.

A woman I will know later, Angela Hoon, will say, *Go ahead, ruin me—I know what men are like . . . I will take care of myself . . . I can . . . I'm very strong . . .*

As Onni stares at me, something veers and I cry out, "Do you ever think about ideals as ideal?"

"Christian ideals? Political ideals?"

"I expect people to be what I think them. I expect people to be as clear as characters in books. But instead they are who they are. If I address people I see, I shock them. I am not patient about this."

"Everyone should sleep with a certain number of strangers," he said. He says it moralistically.

"I was talking about serious ideals—do you have serious ideals, *Caro Cretino*?" I began to cough from the cocaine.

He said, "I have *no* ideals—merely hopes . . . And good

ideas . . ." He was amiably haughty in an Italian-male conversational style, challenging you to be passionate and lucid and comic. Or something. His voice is pitched warmly in ordinary undistilled actuality. He went on, eyeing me sidelong, "It's all *merda*—" Then: "Except for love—and friendship."

The late afternoon Venetian brightness from the window is a subtle armor of light on his forehead and nose. He said more assertively, yet dreamily: "You do not believe in love?"

"It is the original real world . . . What else is there?"

"Why do you not want to be simple, Nino? Why do you never answer directly?"

But no one gives away what he or she really feels. Or thinks. I have watched, and I have never seen it . . . No one departs from strategy.

I said, "It's not like that with me." I said it driftingly, as if losing track of him. I was unfascinated . . . Maybe I was pretending that my attention was unfastened.

He and I are leery of the ways we think the other is a nut. Suddenly he hotly embraces my head. It is as if we are dressed in spikes, but he sees to it, and I suppose I am mischievous too, that feelings leap on us anyway, catlike or doglike, or fall on us like a horse collapsing crushingly and shatteringly on us, impaled on our spikes but weighing us down, making us breathe heavily.

"Will you marry me?" he said in English with a good American accent like Henry Fonda's, movie-like.

"Onni . . ." Then: "Do you believe, you know, in the old ideals? Platonic? In—I don't know what—in the Ten Commandments?"

He stared. He said, "Nino, I don't know. You think thought is immortal—is that it? Is that why you are so proud? You think that *Love* depends on Christ? I do not love God—as you know . . . I am often angry, I steal a little bit. If you obey the commandments, you have to be a priest, a not very popular priest. They"—the commandments—"are the opposite of what people admire—I get along with people . . ."

"I don't know that I agree. Maybe I agree. But ask yourself this: Are ideas bullshit? Is Plato an asshole? Or are you? What do you think?"

He laughed, without humor, wary that I might have the world on my side. "You are not Parisian," he said using his knowledge of that world. "You are old-fashioned." He often laughed at people to their faces in a deadpan way. He was greatly gifted at having a good time but he had little or no aptitude for happiness. He laughed in that form now.

"Well, I am a whore," he said.

"A *whore*," I said and put my hands out toward him, not meaning to touch him. I never initiated touch. I started to laugh. Between gasps of laughter, I asked him earnestly, "Do you believe in love?"

He looked at me while I laughed . . . Because of the cocaine I could not stop laughing.

"Yes it's funny. But I wonder what's most funny."

"Life is and you are, and death is and so is your Adam's apple. But chiefly cocaine is very funny. You a whore, God . . . God pity the rest of us . . ."

He blinks at me and has a toughened quality, and yet his posture shows he is afraid of me—that fear is an extreme luxury for him like the softest, slickest, most delicate fur pelt. His frigidly-hot attentiveness spears me with interest. His attention was the best attention I had known until then. "You are mad," he said. "I only like mad people."

I said, "I'm not happy being a Platonist."

He takes picayune little athletic breaths with no movements of his eyes or eyelids—it's as if he spoke while he listened in the way he listened; and I hear some of his silence and am deaf to some of it, to some of the elements of a love letter in it, to some of the intentions of his Italian vivacities of attention.

To be aware of other, less conscious intentions in him is to be aware of the dominion of the future. For a moment the dark failure, the ironic failure of the worthlessness of love to be worthless for me cripples my heartbeat.

And love is felt simply as a range of possibilities of companionship and duties, a variation of having balls, or courage. Onni's courage was part of the act of creation of the moment.

"Kiss my ass," he says in English, in an *intellectual's* tone. "You care too much about *Plato* . . . I prefer Pluto . . ."

I say to him, "You are what the Tahitians call *a creep.*"

He grips my wrist: "I am listening to you, you know—speak softly and carry your big stick."

Betrothed to his reality in the present tense, one has a sense of his *love* for one, such as it is, as dangerous and as causing real moves in a slippery and sliding focus as when you are playing water polo and you try to rise up on the ball and have, instead, a falling sense and often do fall.

Sooner or later one falls anyway. One's eyes blur in the symmetrical, wet, all-ways-dimensional now, the mind's and the world's and one's emotions' great sea in which one is amphibian or is perhaps a drowner.

He went on: "Do I have movie eyes? You are the smart guy I like. I want to tell you that I've gotten to be as smart as you . . ."

"It's a school ranking!"

His gaze drags across my cheeks and eyes—it is a roughened sensation as if he brushed me shiftingly with a sprig of mimosa, say. Coked up, I feel that his glance is tickling. And my breath has a glaring quality—I feel the glare in my nose and mouth. The smell of the room, the hot stone-damp smell causes an odd anguish. He says, "Where are we in this talk—you're so fancy . . . Americans of your sort are always so fancy . . ."

"Cut it out," I say.

He says, "Scissors, scissors," and he taps my wrist as in the *game* of scissors, rock, paper.

I feel myself to be uncertain-eyed but haughty.

"I want to marry you for a while . . ." he says. Not physically . . . I understand him: I know he likes to shock and hurt . . .

"You don't know how to be a brother . . ." I say as if he had suggested brotherhood. "We don't look alike . . . I'm the cute one . . ."

"You are sweet, you are genteel, *molto gentile,*" Onni says.

What limits do you accept to emotion while still being able to call the limited feeling *love*? How much of the Dirty World do you refuse to accept, did you refuse to accept when you were young? I can't untangle the threads of this. I merely say that in *that year* and *at that time* the boy was not general but was caught in his own moments . . . That year, at that time, Onni's face, his speeches, the coloring of the light are a masked whisper and rush, a hiss and whisking fluff, a rustle, materialized, real, not sentimental, the feathering wings and merely mortal body: one is tousled, pushed . . . Is he saying, *I sort of love you, Nino?* I feel it as heat. The sensations are large, feathered, hot and real. The sensations are the meaning.

At this time, I had a dream about love. In the dream I was of noble Czechoslovakian birth. I think this had to do with my not being Italian or quite truly American, but something in the middle, hence middle-European.

In the dream I was rather hard-minded and virile, a man of the sort I would wish to be, a noble realist in the mold in which such virility is described in the most sophisticated books, the books no one reads anymore, Tolstoy's books. Sometimes such a man is hinted at in movies.

The young woman I loved in the dream—Claudia—was well-dressed and subdued and gently reared, as fine-drawn, and as intelligent and quick-nerved as the most sophisticatedly sentimental description of a heroine would be.

But in the dream she and I were real and we experienced real emotion. The dream insisted that it was real.

In it, I could hardly believe my good fortune, but I was most restrained, unspeaking, but full of feeling. I was softly dignified with feeling.

She was brave and concise, graceful in gesture, utterly loyal, utterly sincere, utterly coherent. Marvellous legs. A calm face. Great, great beauty. Our castle had a black-and-white tessellated floor and an enormous grandfather clock which was a secret door. My fiancée came out of that secret door. I was flooded with emotion at the sight of her. Apparently, she cared for me in an obstinate and quite unquestioning and similarly astoundingly complete—and fine-drawn—way. Our castle had an enormous park . . . It was Arcadia.

It seemed real and deep and interesting, more interesting

than life but it was life. I remember the pleasing torment in the fullness and delicacy and restraint of the feeling in me at the sight of her and at every inflection and murmur of her voice.

Nothing was obscure. Nothing was tainted—or impure. The very rhythms of breath and of heartbeat were love synchronized, unquestioning, and entire. I cannot laugh at it now without subsiding, at moments, into the conviction that I knew such a love in life, that the dream was not entirely a dream, that no illusion was involved—what could be so cruel as illusion about a deep love, one's great love, one's profound—and unprofane—love, the one that explains one's life?

My emotion had in it no private or public clemency. The clemency, as in all such tales, was that of fate in permitting such a love to occur. The dream, in its perspectives of the castle's park, in its careful reproduction of breath, even of odor, made a great show of logical reality, so much so that if she and I walked too rapidly in the formal terraces of the park, the dream promptly replayed the walk at a more credible pace.

And then too, the dream, and some quality of the woman —Claudia—insisted that I must not doubt that this was all entirely real or I would lose everything, lose this ideal love because of my cheap suspiciousness, because I was not noble, but was a sly and grotesque spider or some such thing.

And I will confess here, in mid-dream, that I have always felt since that the dream happened in life; I have a very strong sense at all times, as of an unexamined memory, of a lost and perfect love.

And some parts of the dream were actually emblematically true, the feeling of being loosened by love inwardly while being toughened outwardly in defense of the love, and of being willing to be real to defend the love, and not a mere dreamer. German almost, so ruthless and strong, a warrior, imbued with country and cause. I had the sense of having been changed by love, changed *violently*, transformed in the most complete and irrevocable spirit. I was capable of anything. I would protect what I had with what, from stories of castles and spies, and to some extent from observation, I considered middle-European ruthlessness, that sadism of will, including torturing when necessary or maiming, and, certainly, shooting or strangling coldly.

I believe these were common story terms at one time, in movies and newsreels and news stories especially during the war, when Onni and I were living in different cultures and were not in touch with one another, these terms of reality, dreamlike but pretending to be life itself, these terms utterly separate from Onni and even holding references to life-and-death enmity toward *the little Fascist*. This dreamed love had as its proof of its reality the implicit claim that the dreamed figures were susceptible to death, really. You know real death does not occur in dreams; we are not buried in real earth because of our deaths in dreams, and others do not stay dead merely because they die in our dreams.

But rather one can ascend to Heaven or enter Hell, soldier-like, heroic. One can do all sorts of things in dreams and then, on awaking, re-enter the whirring and ticking actual room where your real death can occur. You wake to a much realer reality of death.

Subject to real death in the dream, I was an expendable male, a noble man in possession of true love of the realest sort, and was further subjected to war and to that also true but much lesser love, patriotism. It also was pure in the dream. The inner heat of wartime patriotic anguish was quite convincing, but then so was the sentimentality in the portrayal of such fineness in my wife-fiancée in the dream.

It was all a very fine sentimentality, and I was suspicious of it from time to time: the oddities, as of Claudia's mouth fluttering on her face like a butterfly. And certain phenomenally movie-like changes in Claudia's appearance, a more movie-like beauty, dramatic, a bit obvious.

The dream then devolved into episodes of espionage: I was the spy pursued by police and secret agents. A rather brutalizing and very repetitive necessity of cruelty, of sadism and brisk murderousness, filled those episodes. I was bathed in noble resignation. This part of the dream was repeatedly unconvincing since the chemical responses and the bad dreams one has when one is in danger and the high, almost feverish heat of the body at such times were lacking.

But the dream insisted that the actual meaning of life lay in this ideal love and in my ideal warlikeness. None of the opposing Nazi policemen looked like or acted like Onni. The dream wasn't of that sort. It was not clear even symbolically whether one defended one's feelings for him, in some way, in the dream, or if he was, in truth, the Fascist enemy or if he was in the way of one's experiencing ideal happiness with a woman. I was—I am afraid to admit this—the only good-looking man in the dream, but I did not look like myself but like a number of Central European actors, a detail of face from each one.

And there was an exceedingly, much too extremely confused scene, quite agonizing, set in Vienna, mostly at night, and chiefly at the opera, an opera known as *Anne IV*—Vienna spelled backwards—an opera filled with people and with music, Strauss, so that in the dream, sweating slightly, one clutched at *straws*, and a figure, not clearly man or woman, but dressed in black, gave me a silver rose which held the message I then had to transmit to London. And this scene was one of the very greatest nervous anguish, the audience, the music, the danger, the obscurity of the nature of the person handing me the rose.

Then in the dream, I briefly woke in Bohemia, in the castle in Bohemia with Claudia, now named Anne, who was not well; but she had made or gotten for me a marvellous pistol, a Luger of special merit that fired all the time and very quickly. The scene in the dream was without sexual overtones, but the next scene, which was all shooting and jumping through windows and into canals, was entirely sexual, was erectile—one acted continuously and without regret—and without hesitation—like a man, which is to say one was deadly and cruel . . . I believe, mind you, that in this part of the dream the character who was me was dressed in jodhpurs and very good boots and had a flesh-colored mask over his eyes.

Love banished terror. And sentimentality. Except that much of the sadomasochism was sentimentality of an earnest sort, a sentimental evasion and simplification of reality.

At any rate, at the end I was cornered on the roof of the

cathedral in Mexico City which was also Prague. The dome, the statues on the cathedral roof, like the statues in the Arcadian park of the castle in Bohemia, had to do with physical attributes—with physical reality. At the end of the dream it seemed I had been outwitted by the rival or enemy police chief, the Gestapo aceling, except he was old and a bit bellied. We were all in raincoats. He was about to shoot me, and I was filled with emotion at having to die when I had a true love waiting for me, although one who was dying, it seemed, and then, as so often in that dream, it became clear that love is not welcome to a creature who feels a great degree of terror; and so, if one feels love very strongly, one is not a creature of terror, love banishes or lessens terror and is quite dangerous. It is like losing one's fear of fire.

And then I woke, fearless but suffused with emotion, huge emotion. I could not believe the suffocation of it, and in the sense of piled-up memory the feeling of real love, of deep, deep love, of real worth, of worth underlying a realer love. It afflicted me. It seemed to have been a real experience, as real and much more valuable than a real experience.

For a few moments, on Onni's couch, because that is where I had this dream, I seemed to have no resistance to emotion . . . It is as if I were transparent and permeable with emotion—or not *as if* but rather that that was the case at that age: emotion showed in me perhaps as clearly as mercury does in mercury thermometers. But the dream and the evening air of Venice from the open window were blowing through the flexible and open glass of the skin and through the torn web of my sense of things.

Onni dozed, reclining on the floor against the wall. I felt I had been searched and ransacked, robbed. Only a few broken parts of me had been left for me to wake with. This cripple, crippled by dreams and waking, this war-damaged figure, chose abruptly, even angrily to care about Onni in opposition to the dream.

But in the moment one felt a greater other love was somewhere, was in one's destiny.

And then there he was, awake in the empty air of twilight in his room, a patch of yellow light on his face. He said, "Ah," and lit a cigaret. He looked like hell, dark rings around his eyes, lifeless, colorless lips.

"So," I said, or some such thing. "There you are." Something like that.

"I have come from Iesolo," he said without a trace of shyness, referring to the reality of dreams.

He blew smoke out among the blurs of faded light in the room. He had an unblinking look and enough cool pallor that one guessed at sex in his dreams, and some nightmare, and an indifferent locale, *Iesolo*.

But I had a sense of having dreamed in tandem with him. He rose and groped me as he walked past; he did that sometimes. When he groped me, I grunted with surprise at the savagery of it. I twisted away. But a faint treble note escaped me—a sympathetic animal squeal, a vibration across the moments, a synchrony, a syncopation between the dream and this, between his mood and mine of companionship.

He was never unphysical. He returned, fastening himself, and he simulated snorting more cocaine; and then he imitated, while he prepared the coke, nervously as it were, but he did not show nerves, a gondolier we knew poling along in the rain. He half-imitated him; he didn't do the whole physical thing. Onni did the friendliness-plus-brotherhood-of-a-sort of the gondolier; he held himself as if he were big; he had a coarsely full look, a ready smile, potently dishonest; and large, staring eyes, a thickness of will and a kind of impatient dishonor. Onni said of the gondolier, leaving the imitation, "A barnyard animal, without romance . . ." as he cut the line.

He sang like the gondolier, bold and loud, *un grande rumore* . . . Something in Onni's face, a fluctuation of something like a cloud of feeling or like a sheaf of the cold rain that comes and goes briefly in Venice sometimes around us in the shifting light, was the look of an inward scream phallically.

In reality, a person is full of shadows and force and of forces-in-the-shadows, and a portrait must show the madness, the horse's head of madness pushing and jerking in the self. The phallic reality, hips and muscles, the shouldering of the thinly beefy reality of the self when young, and the pink, wet motions of the mouth, Onni humming, ruthless-eyed but visited by the tossing horse's head of madness from the dream. Or from reality. Onni is still humming when we go out. Sunset lies along the stone curtains of façades along the *Canalazzo*. The adolescent sense of the crotch and legs in my clothes, my sense of my youth, the agreeable dirty smiles as you joke, the torture behind the still visible, the faked symmetries of feeling, Palladian, it is a moist, potent joke. We walk in the memory of actual dreams, dreaming side by side, in the odors of the twilight in the physical world. Onni-as-gondolier shouted and whistled and talked loudly in a not-young voice, a gondolier talking about pussy, *fiche*. The automatic and fierce assumption of friendship, one had a boyish sense of a flapping-like unfolding of a waxlike and perhaps aerial and slightly overheated immediacy like a waxed canvas marquee, that kind of warmth. Reality had that flavor. We walked in a cloud of ideas. He introduced me to someone on the street, an older man, dim-faced, but glowing-eyed and well-dressed. The formula of introduction was *This is* Nino *O'Hara, he is a school friend of mine.* Perhaps this is an obscenity. It is not of much use to pretend that whoring and *respectability*-and-chastity do not share the world peculiarly. He was an only child and could not bear to be alone. Inventive as a whore, he had a number of selves, of roles and not a single phallic role except as a young boy who was inventive and, well, you know, *Onni-like . . . putto-puttana.* He was maybe stupidly gripped by suddenly strong emotion, the sinful reality of such emotion, and maybe by the inclement attention such emotion brings you; it is not always sane.

Or it was a fleering sort of sanity, half-mad, and the irreligious quality of it held him, our companionship, the emotion, the moment. It battered me. I wanted to be corrupt, but I did not in my life ever match his corruption. I went only so far ever into his world. I am in this moment a target, or a possibility, a flavor of corruption in my innocence which he cannot stop thinking about. He urges the moment on in various ways: I am the object of courtship, *fresh meat.* But I am so serious . . .

Then afterwards, after he introduces me to someone or after

he sings, he waits to see how I judge him. To see if I am interested. Or upset. Or shocked. As we walk we meet a group of people from his other life, and I see how easily shocked I am, why he keeps watching my reactions. These people watch to see how I react. I am real to him and them as a figure at the edge of his world . . . I am drafted into some of his other stories as a figure at the edge of his world . . . I am not real to myself.

It's not easy to accept your own unsuitability for life. But if I do not accept it, I will throw my life away in resistance. Someone, luckily—or unluckily for me—has at times said I was suitable for life, that it is not true that I am so unsuitable for it. A compromise is reached, not the golden mean, but some middling thing, part of the duplicity of a world in which things change so much always and every minute. Each person's story is restless as narrative. Onni, in his pride, often tries for the brutal quasi-reality of a display of unchanging feeling, of something that claims to be that. Such a display in him drives children and dogs and women mad with restlessness near him, that brutality of claim. Such a wall-like steadiness is an art—a masculine art: it is not a boy-madonna stillness and fixity. It is perhaps the case that I had somewhat more of *that* as an effect. Its underlying flicker of restlessness and the extremity of life in it made it very strange in me. He says, "You always look like, how do you say it in English, the cat that ate the canary."

He holds himself in a pose like a young man in a painting of Veronese's. Such young men in those paintings are always examples of *vulnerability*, and of some degree of troubled or foolish or intense hope, a dreamingness. The ambiguity of life and the hint of motion in a painting, the illusion of life in a stilled object, is also like that in a young man—perhaps in me. Onni had a *friend*, a syphilitic *marchesa*, amusing and drolly lovely and bright although also infinitely mischievous and perhaps bad, full of bribes and will, and despair at her illness, and then with a sort of mean joy and then with a sort of crazy joy in it: *I will go to Hell soon*, she said once. We met her that evening, and she said to me, "You have become interesting, *piccolino*."

I blushed, leaned back on my heels, and said, "Oh God . . ."

She laughed at me, then, with appalling mockery—she wasn't mocking though—and she plucked at Onni's sleeve, "See, he blushes . . . *Il Prete Rosso* . . ." "The red priest" was a nickname of Vivaldi's; she was referring to my blush, my innocence. She said, "You have some of the quality of a radish, *tanto carino* . . ." Then she laughed rackettingly, putting her head back, showing her teeth and her tongue.

Again I said, "Oh God," and again she laughed. She beamed at me *delightfully*, sure in her manner, hoping to elicit talk. In the dreamlike moment—twilight, the pretty *marchesa* in black —I rode out my changing feelings, censoring them in order not to seem baroque or *inconceivable* to Onni or to her.

"He is *normal*," Onni said. I think he did take me to be *normal*. My reality for him embodied that other world as comparison but absolutely: the absolute thing is what is romantic.

We walked on in the twilight. "I think you will find that life is no good," he said pedagogically, perhaps jealously, perhaps controlling a jealousy. When he was in despair, often I would talk to comfort him. I want to argue him into a sense of that other life of *normalcy*.

I said, "I don't care that much." I did an imitation mockingly: "*Something terrible is wrong . . . I am not perfectly happy: make me perfectly happy . . . You ruin everything; you are not perfect . . . Please be perfect . . .* That's all so stupid, Onni . . ."

He laughed aimlessly but loudly; he clapped me on the shoulder . . . It is a bit dizzying when someone finds you amusing . . . For the moment, I have that value for him, the merit of comedy in the explosion of awful beauty that the world is in the sunset light anyway.

Then, in the dreamlike burst of blinking after he is silent, in the mind's after-grasp, I realize that I have been acceptably funny: *I see, I see.* Do you know? Manifestly eccentric, oblique and criminal, inherently but not actively sexual, insulting as life itself is insulting, and time-riddled and lovely-hideous, a noisy brightness of feeling: a bit of love . . . that's what it was . . . I hid this noisy brightness . . . I haven't usually the style, the nerve to live openly as a lover. Or as someone loved . . . I am very

young no matter what age I am. Everything has a different meaning in the grown-up world. Everything is rethought there, some,
many of the constraints of self-protection undone. I cannot show
emotion readily in the mad void of the arrival always of the next
moment. *What will I do next? What will he get up to next?* It is
better to pretend nothing is happening. The next moment will
be the end of me, maybe, if I am not careful . . . This is true for
me moment after moment.

When I was young, some years I was carefully young, *in the
mad void of the arrival of new moments*, in the unstill beauty like
that of clouds and sun of certain moments of emotion. The emotions, the feelings were as ornate as girls' breasts and as disorienting. Unemptiness, a summer-twilight-moment thing . . .
the odds of one's struggles in the world have been stilled and
become visible and are unimportant . . . Emotion, you ride it a
little sweatily, unsteadily, with a kind of laughter of the nerves,
with your face deadpan in spite of flutters of terror and of interest.

I wish I had an eternity of attention and real safety from my
own stupidity. A for-a-while-attention leaps down alleys and
through *campi* toward points of meeting one's daily fate, today's
bit of destiny.

"*Che cosa fai?* What are you thinking about?"

You. Me. "Nothing . . ."

Happiness is strange. It's just a tone on which everything is
mounted for a while, an unmalicious courtesy of events with
malice hidden in it, which is to say time, time and variation.
Maybe not a malice but a flavor of melancholy.

Unhappiness is not a common subject in Venetian painting—have you noticed? I said, "I like statements and sentences
that have in them the word *you*." Corny, no? Happiness half-
understood is the dark seductiveness of this: to see from a short
distance away *in the sharp-edged Adriatic light* of sunset a face
that matters enough that the sight of it jerks the moment into
focus for you: I like that.

He nods, affected.

A two-personned moment, a three-personned light.

"Pronouns are interesting . . ." he says announcingly. "Pronouns are for nuns!"

I startle him, a hidden laugh inside me suddenly bursting out, inanely I think, drunkenly pleased, deeply, uninnocently-innocently pleased, a laugh like sick drunkenness almost.

He said, "Nino has to laugh . . . One has to laugh . . ." Explaining and licensing me, a guy.

"I see why a Doge had to be old," I said to Onni.

"Yes. It is harder to seduce a mean old man." Then: "The ugly ones rule the world . . ." Then: "The young are martyrs . . ."

Tintoretto, the sad one, rarely painted Venetian light. He painted the light of the mind as a moonlight or as a light of transcendent meaning. Feelings are immeasurable—and variable. One lies seductively about how fixed they are.

Onni said, "I don't always know what you're talking about. But go on. It's all right."

I put my hand on my head, my no longer trivial hand.

His physical presence and his life as parable affect me. Safety from him lay in believing in the unimportance of (some) treacheries between friends and in thinking these feelings weren't important but were merely dangerous and had the importance only of danger. It was this dismissal of the moment that so disabused my heart and so indicated the incompleteness of my character that I kissed him, the only time I did.

"Ah, a flower," he said.

In a Venice of intimacy, a delicate commerce.

The immanent emotion is here. My interest in him colors my inward sight. But whatever happens, you realize truly in a later light, a different light, even if only a few seconds later. He has a somewhat irreversible, modest, basic, basically recurring clemency of attention about this time lag. Your moods, your feelings go up a hill, down a hill. The thing about being interesting to him is that, well, there it is; it is part of the world. Am I powerful here? Love is fantastic but real. This is not a liar's story . . . Yes it is.

This wasn't anything I could accept. I didn't believe in it—in love—but felt it as a witticism, a sharp truth concerning some of the small magnetisms that hold the world together.

The world and love, moments, magnetisms, a half-sexual

tie . . . rage, contempt, destruction, and the end of things . . .
But my own maneuvers and desires in sexual matters don't interest me: I wish they did. I want to discover other information
so that I can live in some other way—I am puritan and patient
. . . I don't want to know what fun it is to win out and hurt others.
I am ill at ease, somewhat provincial, and not passive, just unmoving, more than credibly motionless in these matters, almost
pious. But I am what I am. I was not always displeased when I
was young to be the person I was, a foreigner in Venice among
the hordes of sightseers—no, that is a joke.

But, I repeat, I was not interested in my own habits and in
my secrets. So I prefer talk and language to things and deeds,
and often to embraces. I have a particular desire to hear what
people say. Some people are rigorously silent and laugh from
inside their silence at you for wanting to talk.

He turned his head to me and said, "I like you."

"Let's talk about something that interests us," I said in the
fading light.

He said, "Yes . . ." Then: "I will be generous . . ."

"My price is talk . . . I would have invented psychoanalysis
for the sake of getting to hear things if Freud hadn't done it."

"Freud said people were filth . . ." He moved his head in
the dark. I was walking with one hand pressed to each thigh . . .
He put his hand on top of my hand, then removed it.

I said, "I don't care. I'm interested in how people talk; I don't
care if it's filth or not."

"We talk *all* the time," Onni said.

"But we are walking somewhere, or running or rowing, or
chasing girls—that's not talk; that's more a—a recitativo . . . No.
What do I mean? An ostinato . . ."

"You want *la grande conversazione* . . . sinful . . . from the
soul . . ."

I hated it when he was more graceful and more knowing,
more cultivated than I was.

"No, no . . . Yes . . ." Then: "Talk, just talk, no purpose—
just to *talk* . . ."

"That is obscene . . . Well, is that the rule?" he said. For him to say something was *obscene* was for him to want it. "What do we do in order to do this?" he said.

"You can't plot it—we have no goal. You just speak . . . You speak at no height of purpose. Doesn't the idea of being in a *dialogue* excite you? Isn't it something you have an appetite for?"

He turned his head and stared at me obliquely: "Yes . . . If you want . . . Why not? Let's talk . . . What shall we lie about? And then what shall we lie about *next*? Do you expect me to trust you? You are more vile than a Milanese. I don't do what *anyone* tells me to do . . ."

"Sexually? As an actor in a part?"

"That is different . . ." The quality of dumb obedience inside someone quick-witted and handsome and not subservient: I saw it. "Don't be too childish . . ." he said.

"I told you I like to talk," I said cryptically.

He said, with a sigh: "You are difficult . . . But everyone knows friendship is more important than God—everyone but you . . . You must learn. Well, we are friends . . . Do you know or do you not know that friendship—this friendship, our friendship—is more important than God Himself . . . Or than the Devil." I felt a twinge of emotional awe. He said, "Looking at you, I feel sorry for myself . . ." He sighed.

He was mimicking a grown man.

Then I stirred fretfully and felt a kind of neural impatience that this was so hard . . . that *he* was so difficult. He struggled like a cat against whatever tried to hold him. I said, "That strikes me as an unsound proposition . . . friendship being more important than God: Who is the judge? Who is to be the judge of whether you are cheating on *that*? Who runs that contest?" I said as the idea took hold of and wracked me. "Who governs *this*? Who decides if you're cheating on that? You can use that as a rule to pick on the other person and to boss him. We can't judge that ourselves if we're the friends . . . Your idea is *pazzo. Pazzissimo.* You are *Pazzissimo.* If you don't do what I want I can always accuse you of putting God first . . ." Then as the thought struck me of emotions so serious: "Ha-ha . . ." I said. I laughed nervously but exaltedly.

"You can accuse me of nothing. I am a good friend. I know about friendship," he said darkly. Then with a sort of Italianate *music* he chanted: "O.K.? O.K.?" Then: "Can you kill?"

"Under the right circumstances. I suppose." Then: "You are not talking aimlessly. You are using what we say."

"Bah, bah, bah," he said. "You are not ever direct."

"Bah, bah, I am a black sheep who has lost its way."

"You will never be a *black* sheep," he said.

"You of course can kill and care about friendship more than God," I said to the nape of his neck which bore a disconcerting velocity of something like beauty—maybe it was just life and youth. "Christ, I love the world," I said.

"Yes. More than God," he said, ignoring what I said, and testing me.

We bought *pannini* and some beans and some cold cutlets and went back to his room. I was a little dizzy, but I thought I saw that he believed that we are in a contest every moment with complications of darkness and evil and injustice mixed with further complications of bad luck, and we needed allies . . . He had a blackly triumphant air of knowing this, of being male and intelligent, a Venetian boy-man of victory. I did not want to believe him. He believed, very clearly, that a man's worth lay in winning out, in being an *iron man*—I don't know the Italian phrase for that. In the solitary importance of a masculine nature, in his loneliness, he believed this. He folded his arms behind his head and stared upward, sitting on the floor beside his food, uncorrected and unamended by my disbelief. "More than God," he said.

I sat on the couch, my feet on the ground, and faced Onni, the food beside me on the cushions . . . "Freud says everything is sexual, that sexuality is present in everything, all the time . . . Are you interested in that?"

"When I go crazy, I will be interested in Freud, not until then."

"Do you have *ideas* about sexuality?"

"I have a sense of fire . . . of fires in me," he said. The room was hot; there was no wind; the clatter of footsteps in the *calli* rose to the window. His shoulders relaxed, and he put his arms down because he felt he was talking well. He went on, he went further: dreamily he said, "I have a sense of fish swimming and snapping their jaws inside me . . . And in your eyes . . ."

The skull as a bowl or inlet or rock hollow in the sea, in the Lagoon; and the fish of sexual interest. He leaned his upper body forward and showed me his eyes; he demonstrated or displayed, with a quick jaw-like opening of his eyelids and a sudden look in his eyes, the gaping of fish jaws that he meant.

"I am not as expressive as you," I said.

The orgasms I had seen him have—four, five, six of them —it was possible that they were too brief, too painfully halluci-natory with whispers in them of further longing and of a sense of pleasure beyond the pleasure he had and without finality for him to like them much. I had seen that in him or so I say, but I had seen it vaguely and now it was clearer although still not worded or actually clear. It, this sense of him, it too was like a fish, but a large one, powerful-bodied, swimming idly and un-caught but blurrily visible. Anyway, he preferred triumph-in-the-world which included the sexual "triumphs" of coming often with a lot of people, people he wanted. And he almost liked being cold and unhappy about this and superior and lost. Contradic-torily, it supplied fuel and heat; it fuelled and fired his energies. He knew about comparative, worldly reason among men scrab-bling for places. He'd survived so far and meant to do better. His oddly classy Mediterranean *grabbiness* was visible but only as if in an underwater light, as something self-willed, something pow-erful and in motion, swimming along and foreign to me, not my species.

He was, from early in his life, a figure in the gossipy sensual shadows in which the secret sexual history of the world is written.

And I was not and had not been until now. But now in a small way I was part of the sexual history of the world because of him.

Onni stirred, lazily restless with self-display, with seduction. This is *the danger zone*, the zone of amusement where we are on the verge of sexual anecdote.

He said, "Do you know what the buttocks are made of?"

Actually then I didn't know.

"Muscle," he said. "It is the muscle you run with. You jump with it." He stood up, and he jumped. The dark and light in the room fluttered on the jumping *Giangiacomo*, the dark and maroonish-peach light.

"You're getting hairier," I said.

"Another snort." Then he told me he had fucked his mother. He was truly strange. He already had his shirt off, and he took off his pants, and, naked, he lit a cigaret and leaned on the windowsill in the streetlight from below that lit the upper horizontal of the window frame and outlined parts of him . . . He said, "Coming is boring." I then knew more of what I'd thought earlier. He said, "Sex is boring. I fucked my mother . . . And it was dull . . ." He turned around: "Nino, you want to fuck my mother?"

It is a weird brotherhood to be *friends*. It is O.K. to feel stuff, to go too far. But I resist that. He feels the power he has. Some of that power is over my imagination because of the unsafe beauty he has and because of the fluid energy of his eroticism and his use of it, of that fluid reality in him. The reality of that *energy of eroticism* had nothing snobbish in it and not much self-protection. I mean that whorishness in him had these consequences. He said, "My rear end is too big . . . I am built like a peasant . . ."

He moves around the room, practical, not heavily nerved sexually, doom-laden although not fragile, a bad guy, not such a bad guy, Onni.

I think I knew that the great story for Onni was the conquest of the world—that story interested him. His willful-snotty beauty. He was happy enough perhaps, or perhaps not; but scandal and thrills beckoned to him. He was a thrill-hunting Italian boy. He enjoyed going quite near the rim of death.

"Does thinking give you a hard-on, Nino? Does what you're thinking give you a hard-on?"

"Sure." I thought unclearly that erections were a failure of beauty to bring peace. But I was also aware of the eery linkage of modesty to challenge . . . the unsweetly luminous urge of potency to accept a challenge. Beauty is rarely the occasion of surrender in others.

How much immediate personal power in those moments did Onni have? I think that as a whore, a manipulator he performed well, even brilliantly, given the sexual illiteracies and shyness and hastiness of judgement of his clients, his partners and accomplices, his friends. Me. To be the object of such performance is like lying in a trough of a wave in the ocean and being borne up and up and then swiftly down by the power of the performance. I know this from later in my life as well as from him. A lot of stuff related to this shows in your appearance, in your eyes and in how you look at someone. We almost don't need to gossip; our eyes have already seen what is there. Our eyes establish our type. We see each other's male tactics in the world. My male tactic in the world is that I laugh when I want to be excused from my visible humanity. So, I laugh because he'd noticed I had dirty thoughts and was vain and was buffetted by his feelings and had an erection.

When I laugh, he says dangerously, disgustingly, *"Vaffanculo . . ."* He says it amiably, in the deadpan seduction mode. But he is irked.

I refuse the reality he proposes. In the below-ground geography of complicatedly fragile refusal, in the shiver of having my life, I clean my mind and my eyes of sexual response to him, perhaps in fear . . . It is a case of me in fearlessness and of a swaggering and self-revealing response of coldness.

"I do not live in vain," he says to me.

It is clear that this is a physical universe. This physical universe has Venice and tonight in it. It is where my chest and lungs, throat and mouth contain the motions of my breath just now.

He looked at me with that *a priori you-lose* or *you-come-second* thing of an adept at certain sorts of human ties. He has a sexual urgency about selfhood that isn't sexy in any direct way of the flesh: a *Why am I not King of the World?* and *You can't be important: I am* . . . that is usually but not always amusing, a form of erotic energy of a wrestlingly intimate or semi-intimate kind. But it isn't fleshly or hot with enclosure. It is hot with friction, with abrasion, with a kind of excitement, not my kind of excitement.

He said, "I can't lose my balls or let anyone cut *my* cock off . . ." He deals in himself, in others, a slave trader.

"La di dah di di dah," I say in falsetto, sort of singing something from *Lucia di Lammermoor*, but I didn't really remember the melody just then. My heart is jumping in that curious way of adolescence when it is so elastic and big and strange in its functioning. The way that blood moved in me changed the night air and set in the dark bits of colors, pinkish and red, red fire-lines and sparks, and reddish blue and pale blue-gray-white: delusions of heat, a mental and drunken sweatiness.

Then he said, "Dance with me."

"No."

He turns the radio on and comes over to the bed and puts his hand on my chest: "You have no muscle on your chest. Does *this* give you a hard-on, Nino? Dance with me."

I didn't yet feel my erections as urgency but mostly as embarrassment first and as a queer half-readiness that was embarrassing and yet which was unembarrassed.

One wants to conceal this and evade it.

"How about you?" I said, and he was erect at once—that shattered me.

I hadn't yet realized how the conferral of sexual power on someone, his on me, could seduce me so weirdly. I *saw* some of his history though, when I saw it now; but it was mixed up with my unexplored sense of my childhood, one's power then, not revealed but childishly known—now I was old enough and sensible enough and lucky enough to see, to learn.

"Erections are very easy for me," he said. He said it as if that were the most good thing, the best thing in life, and that I was stupid since I was not like that and did not know the stuff he knew, did not know what he knew about the common cheapness of sexual response and how to use myself and make my way as he did. Whenever he knows more than I do about something, he gets to boss me in the presence of that thing as topic.

He asks me, "Do you love Christ?"

"No. I have tried but I cannot."

"Touch me," he said. He was tirelessly erect; it was more a matter or image of pink readiness than it was phallic.

I said, "I'll touch it with my belt . . ."—meaning I would bump him with my midsection. I said it like John Wayne, a big guy, sensible, sought after, indulged, special, self-protective . . . a young hero—of a sort . . .

He grinned in the way he had and which he would later train himself not to do. I mean this radiantly dead peering grin of his would disappear later in his life. It was part only of his adolescence.

His fearlessness toward scandal is profoundly affecting . . . Some men, some boys usurp the traits and rights of beautiful women: *Love me, die for me—die with me . . .* Dictators and generals are like that, and bosses, generally. They rewrite respectability into this other heroism.

I am moved, not to a point of surrender, but to a wish to enter some of the depth of the distances offered, like the distances that surround Venice, to sail into them, or the wish to cross the Piazza, the call of the revealed space, the gaudiness of that . . . The path from a bystander's innocence to the hidden interior of the thing has its draw. A wish-to-know.

I reached onto the table for a cigaret and a match, and I lit up. Then, smoking, with the cigaret in my lips, I stood up, gawky and all that in my clothes, and instead of doing it by gesture, I spoke out loud, "I'll dance," and I just stood there.

Slightly plump-bodied, intent, he moves closer and raises his arms, "You can lead."

I said, "The little flower of the night." Then: "This isn't so bad."

He said, "I'm not the Virgin Mary—or Christ—but I'm not so bad."

I mimicked him: "I'm not the Virgin Mary. I'm not Jesus Christ." I got the words wrong of his speech.

Reality went on in The Great Silence of the music, a foxtrot, a song on a record of Fred Astaire singing songs of the

1930s. The harshness of boyish flirtation is in the testing in it. I said coolly although my blood was warmed, "This is more fun than I thought it would be."

We moved as if among curtains, warm curtains, into and out of curtained-off moments. The back-and-forth joggling of the body, the mysteries and flusters (and sometimes rhythmed nervous-and-muscular hysteria) of the fronts of the bodies and of the faces facing each other, of the heads riding above the bodies, the dramas, the dramatic judgements of what to do next as movement, is very close pantomime, both comic and passionate, lyrical too, of a notion of romance adrift in space, of attachment in actual air. It is experimental, it is a travesty, we are boys, staring into physical space and into the other space of the reality of another male; the spaces in male eyes are from experiences of space as boys and men.

This world of sexuality possibility was his property, like a villa on the Brenta or the Lido or like his sense of rhythm . . . his bait. The music set the terms, dissolving not the dictates of the soul, but translating them into some peculiarity of rhythm and possibilities, trailing one, trampling on the voices of absent mothers and of idea-ridden fathers and making us the whirling and marching keepers of our own absurdly muscular young moments.

We console each other in these silences of the mind with every step we take in the dance that is not backing away or an attempt to change the terms of the travesty. The double solitude of a turn in the dance taken seriously enough to be a bit musical and not just a joke is an anecdote, a physical routine showing discipline of a musicked sort, a discipline in regard to feeling. Neither of us was alone in the world at that moment. We could abandon one another, ironically and even nastily, spiral off into isolated comedy or clomping, as a show of force—in a harsh world—resisting the hidden harshness of the discipline in the flirtation, smoothed and rhythmic now.

The accomplicehood is a need and an accomplishment. Imperfect, I was doubleness jiggling, gliding. One doesn't make great claims for it in a dance . . . It is present and harshly real and yet dreamlike and unworded. No one now could define us as male or female, as serious or unserious, and persuade us of something about ourselves. We hear the music, each other's breath, heartbeat—that is the limit of audibility. The thing was, there were two of us . . . A scissoring of the legs in cooperative unison and a turn and I exclaim, "Ha!" This was like stabilizing a marshy islet with stone jetties and wooden piles driven into muck. I could bear some of the pounding of the watery phenomena of being young and male and in his company.

Overheated and intent, I became happy all-in-all. Not necessarily rightly. The judgement of whether I was happy comes down to a memory of his face and a sense of mine and of my chest and legs and feet circling around the room. Blankly I considered my luck, considered it physically, with my breathing. The feelings of the dance are that we are dancing in the insufficiency of the world, the insufficiency of others.

It is an odd position to be in, that of being a correction of others and of the world for someone. The dance of amusements and of refuge was very complicated and somewhat funny—we laughed when we stumbled. I was too self-conscious being led, when we switched. I would describe such an accomplicehood as a drunken presence in a scene foolishly and defiantly about physical choice . . . To choose each other in the end would be to choose this to be the rule all the time, would be to choose this to be the most familiar language. The rhythm and the motions involve the spirit and the heart—among the curtains, the curtained darkness. Dancing and lying-and-close-calculations do not suit. The movement is always reckless, always on the edge of the unlived future, always physical, never to be pure calculation. It is like combat or sport, a hard-breathing truce. The taint of this honesty, and the limits of the honesty, the taint of performance in this specific moment is delicious.

The physical reality of the hot, massy volumes of his body has certain aspects of the terrible as if we were dancing in a glass tower while the world burned and collapsed.

Onni, dancing, close, touching me his whole torso's length, holding me, embarrassing me, said ironically, "Nino, you see through a lot of the crap all the time? You a *good* guy? Why didn't you try Russian roulette with us?"

"It's not important." My reasons.

"Tell me . . . Come: answer me."

"No . . ."

The music pulls emotion into place which balloons like a curtain or like a leap through the curtain. He was businesslike in the way he limited the travesty, the comedy, and protected the dance, and then limited the seriousness of the dance so that it was a little hard-breathing or professional half-joke—a courtship . . . I had crushes off and on on him as we danced, on his life, on his dexterity, on other lives, on what I thought was a realer version of this, with someone else that I might have some day. We didn't share everything. I was aware that friendship often did share everything. We did not do that, but at moments I was ready and even longed to. I had a crush on the idea of it. Real life, peculiarities of destiny mean that being realistic you still daydream. You daydream more abrasively is all.

"Nino, take your clothes off too."

"No."

Being realistic when young is a daydream mostly, isn't it?

I danced experimentally, testing far too many things at first, but his slightly moist seriousness, as he persisted, shamed and instructed me. I purified my experiment bit by bit. The unease I felt was like that in my dreams when in the dream I am in a strange landscape. The landscape is not entirely strange: I have memories of the touch of men—from earlier in childhood—it was like this. But I'm larger now, freer: I can feel the years of my own life and my current height almost as if for the first time. My father and my brother are present in my dancing. It is almost as if I had Carlo's legs.

"You are not my type, Onni." Irony is my form of seriousness, is as far as I will go—me as Carlo . . . And yet I move, gawky, easily affronted, domineering, somewhat sharp-minded, softened in imprecisely expressed comedy and partly docile in the structure of the dance.

He is more *taught*, more given to doing what he knows. He

is a much better dancer than I am, but, also, he is not as good, not as present in the dance-moment, more repetitive. And more and more, he lets me lead; and when he leads, he concentrates more and is not so slick and arbitrary but follows the mood of the music and of our movements. He cannot improvise but he learns fast, he imitates what I do, and does it better, or differently. When we go fast and are showy, the excitement is tremendous; when it goes well, the dancing, it is all scary and tense, and full of breath. You don't want to fuck up. Some of this is sensual: his muscular suppleness from his shoulders to the side of his waist, for instance, when we turn makes me grin goadedly. I feel the redolent, slightly moist weighty life in him, under my hands, and pressed against me as well. And my own movements now feel *long-legged* and roomy compared to his. His shameless un-ashamedness and my being interested in this dance did not suggest sex to me but only orgasm at some point rather than frustration. The lawless moment had in it privacy and escape mixed with, I suppose, some of what Freudians call *narcissism* and *immaturity* but as a slightly angry music of serious escape for a while from a lot of differently oppressive things, escape into rhythm and movement, into the doubleness of the moment. The consolatory grace of not being public or so serious as public dancing was—this wouldn't lead to fatherhood or become public history—contained certain realities of vanity. I hated the reality of the vanity of sensual release on one side and the vanity of sensual release hated the vanity of austerity in me . . . Fleshly power and fleshly will were split into factions of yes-and-no. We stepped and spun not quite in rhythm, partly in step with each other. Youth, lonely, ripe, insufficiently instructed as yet, is a bribed mirror. Your body is a bribed mirror for the other guy—you can feel it, bribed by the flattery of rhythm and his strength, this music of feeling. The other person's body is a bribed mirror, too, for you, motions and rhythms and flatteries in a corrupted glass. My rhythms, my sense of music, my body, my face are reflected. Guesswork and local plausibility, half-second by half-second, a fleshed-out sense of a desirable finality of identity for a moment . . . I laughed in a weird way, tickled and both resistant and accepting . . . The flirtatious clemency was implausible but existent.

"Weird, weird, weird," I said.

Conceit, humility, love of a kind—ah, heated youth—I am semi-thrilled. My mouth hurts with the effort not to smile foolishly. My eyes are hooded, secretive. I am determined not to say mocking things about us, about the moment. I move, with him, in the parachute-shroud of lamplight in the room. To dance with him close generates a heat so that as we dance I feel I am making my way through a light, blowy, but warming fabric. The faint light of the streetlamps that overhang the *calle* below is in the open window. I am disgusted by his buttocks, the shitting muscle, but the disgust is not simple: it is proprietary. His imperfection makes him possible. The densely agile weight of him as he moves, his gross availability and beauty, crass with dishonor and worldly bravery and stylish honor, sickens me but confers a scary amusement, vaguely classical and fleshly. The hair stands up on the back of my neck, and my body holds haywire rushes and flushes and subsidings of blood, rhythmically—it feels like wire brushes rubbing against the inside of my skin. I am conceited at this intimacy and thrilled—and sickened.

The thing is, happiness is very peculiar, the shadowy thing of having a good time, things not going badly, if it is soberly considered, the good time, I mean, the darkness in it, the strain. Or the insane rush if you are carried away. Each person in the world has a different motor of response as distinct from all others as his fingerprints are. He is so alertly present in mood and body, in his rhythms, that I am discomfited in the weight and glide and shiftings of his body, braced or carried above his moving legs and feet. Onni, I think, pretends now and then to occupy an idealized moment of placated will, to be inside a dream come true—that is very seductive: his breath flutters on my skin. All of this is familiar ground to Onni but not to me. The side of Onni's head—bone and hair and ear—presses against me, near my mouth. One of his flexible, weighty hands presses on my shoulder—I am leading, and his hand twitches and flinches: it responds automatically—as if gasping. The ritualized automatism of rhythm cumulatively, the postures of heads and backs frighten me, and make me gasp. His naked body, his bare feet are part of actuality, temporary and uncertain. Discipline and secular awe hold him but I keep slipping from the dance, from formal attention, and returning. He focusses so intently that the rest of the world seems to be sucked into the dance, so it is like a dream, being in a dream this way too, the will ruling the universe . . . It almost is the sweet focus of a dream.

With one hand he carelessly starts to unbutton my shirt.

"Don't," I say.

"Don't, don't, don't," he says. And continues.

"No."

"I want to hear your heart," he says.

He unbuttons my shirt halfway and as we turn he lowers his head and puts it on my chest . . . At first, it tickles. I stumble— this fucks up this part of the dance. I am embarrassed so strongly then that I become an automaton, embarrassed and flattered, perhaps angry, and I start dancing rigidly . . . "Your heart is very strong," he says.

"Shut up," I say. Then: "Dancing is hard work." Abruptly he takes the lead and spins me . . . I feel honored all at once . . . An honor carelessly engaged in means I glide more largely, in too long steps. He moves quickly and balances us. I use a pun I've used before that no one has ever laughed at: "Jesus Crisis." I say it a second time: "Jesus Crisis . . ."

His big-fingered hands press on me and he says, "No, no, no," meaning I should not talk . . .

Now he pretends to be dreamily thrilled, to be content, as we turn in medium-sized circles. But he is intense about being that way. In the history of love, with Onni, dancing, I am partly choked in the near-simultaneities of feeling and heartbeat: of casual feeling and of not-so-casual feeling, of disbelief and of laughter-torn amusement . . . But the laughter is like little out-cries.

He says, intimately relinquishing the lead, "When are you going to switch over to being a man? No: don't lead so strongly. Switch over from being a boy?" He pushes the shirt off my shoulders. I am very skinny. This shirtlessness is cooler. The shirt hangs from my belt in back. "You have talent as a dancer," he says esoterically.

I told him *dryly-affectionately*: "I'll switch over to being a man and not a boy depending on when I get a heavy beard. I'll do it when I look it . . . when it looks right. It has to look right. Sometimes I do it now." I am more harshly sure of myself, cooler this way, perhaps vainer—like an infant—a tall, long-legged, phallic infant.

He says, "All's fair in love and war, no? Yes? No, yes, no," counting the beat, offering a capsule sense of how many times one changes one's mind before a change becomes final, habitual. "Take off your shoes . . . You kick me too often . . ." I slipped off my shoes.

For a few minutes in the dance, with me leading, he danced so responsibly, so heavily-supplely that his feelings showed like a bare self.

He was acting them out in danced gesticulations in his torso and in his neck.

"You hate being short?" I ask, slightly grinning, being kind.

"Now, faster," he said.

"Shortie," I said. "When will you change?" To being a man.

"I did it already . . ."

"When did you change?"

"When I feel like it, I change . . . All's fair in love and war," he said. He has a disguised self. A role. It never was any good to ask him what he meant. He never knew in the first moments what he meant. My innocence gives my body a certain value compared to the *value* of his . . .

"You sure about love?" I ask. Then: "Do you know a lot about yourself?"

"I plan," he said.

I felt tender, oddly gendered, male without remission but gentle, or if not gentle, protective. And a bit giddy . . .

He said, "I am a man who knows a lot—I know you'll always be terrible . . ."

"Yes. Yeah? Possibly . . . Probably," I said.

He said with august satisfaction and yet he moved slightly more urgently, "You will be a finicky man. I will tell you something deep. It's deeper than the ocean . . . I want to be the greatest man alive, the greatest man who ever lived." His pectorals in the dark move against me, now hard, like the tops of dogs' heads, and now soft, softish, like parts of a dog's belly or jowls. He didn't have a hard, scary body. Or a sly, whispery one at that time. He was beautiful, and ego moved in him like a blind light—no: like the spine and bones inside the impermeable skin, inside the muscle.

He says, "I could kill you . . . I know how. Come on, what makes you think you know anything?"

"I didn't say I knew anything."

"You can't know: you're only a child. Like me."

"Hallelujah hullabaloo how dee doo dee doo dee doo."

"You are a stupid American."

"Onni: hey. Stop being a fart. Stop being a great man. O.K.?"

"No."

"You're an ignorant cocksucker . . . you jackass . . ." I say.

"Piece of shit," he said. We pulled and jerked in the dance, pressed against each other; we began to wrestle almost motionlessly, not without some grace, still dancing.

"Onni, Onni, Jesus, you fucker, you goddamn pig-prick—you cocksucking asshole . . . Jesus. You—just—are—nothing—you are a pain in the butt—you . . ."

"Shut up now," he says; he triumphs. "Dance." He is leading; he makes me move backwards in the dance. "You understand nothing." I am dancing but I am entirely resistant. He backed me up against the wall, pressed against me, then punched me over the heart when I did nothing but look at him, because the tautness I maintained was not one of acquiescence. "A wall next to a wall," he said, meaning I was a wall. He walked away grimacing at my unsurrender at the end of the pagan sweet deathliness of the dance.

It is an egoistic and promiscuous appetite he has—I mean as well as whatever he actually feels for me . . . I am not outside all categories for him . . . Except at moments when he is afraid of what I might do . . . Like now . . .

"And now?" he says, lighting a cigaret and looking at me with twisted amusement, from a twisted posture—handsome, naked boy.

"Pasta and the Piazza," I say.

His final desire, when I have seen it, is quick and quaintly worked out. He makes none of his clients jealous phallically . . . He turns to the window, which is filled with darkness, and then he shrugs and says, *"Un momentino."* He does not stay long in the john; I would swear that part of things was not so serious for him. He emerges heavy-lidded and dresses himself at first with heavy, or serious, drama; but then he forgets and dresses quickly, amused after all, or unwilling to be bothered and sad.

*   *

The Piazza at night with the church-cathedral lit and the wind blowing the lights strung on guy wires high above the pavement, and a half-moon above the light with blowing clouds around it with moonlit silver-gray or bright silver edges in the dark blue, dark gray-black sky . . . And Florian's and Quadri's lit and an orchestra playing in front of Florian's, and Onni's face dramatically lit and girls everywhere, travel-stained or clean but pale with travel and with curious loneliness—my adolescence was prettily but dramatically set.

He is in a mood and has unbuttoned his shirt lower than he usually does inside his jacket. He seems half slotted into the dark, half rescued from it. Or as if vertically floating in an oblique but vertically flowering sea of darkness, the surf of which was bits of light here, there, everywhere, up near the moon or floating on the pavement . . . The night is so many-surfaced that one could not fix a shape to it, and lamp-and-moon-lit in depthless and heightless constellations: the weird dimensionfulness of the night.

My ignorance as a young man, my ignorance that year was like that darkness; it was everywhere and many-surfaced and flecked with light. I was wearing white pants and white shoes and a dark shirt, and I was pretending I knew what I was doing, pretending with my cigaret, with my *strega*, with my eyes and shoulders and my clothes, Italianate clothes . . .

The darkness, adolescent nighttime in Venice, has in its shadows girls. The mind remembering remembers them as naked although it was the psychological and spiritual nakedness, the tourist simplicity in them because I was young and because Onni was Onni and affected them, and it was the nakedness of their limbs and faces—their slender legs in the dark, the thinness of their clothes. Or it is some simplicity in how I see them, the elaborate fruit—forgive me—of darkness, of summer nights, and of our moods. Such girls grow into reality in the branches of darkness, tall, proud American girls, acquisitive and inquisitive, assertive French girls, too cruel, too intricate not to love and fear, and German or Scandinavian girls, gleamingly pallid, with skin the color of bones in the darkness, and English and Italian girls, shiny and dark or glistening and a bit rosy, conceited, knowledgeable, with young voices, and almost always with a noticeably foreign smell, a touch salty, and with an odd music, delicately unlinked, broken by travel—unless as sometimes happened they talked and would let no one else talk—how tough and boastful they sometimes were.

And often we could punish them by preferring each other in the end or by retreating into accomplicehood in the middle of the connection, but often then turning or returning our interest to the girls, to the back-and-forth with them, the mysteries and flusters and sometimes hysterias of their dramas, their dramatic judgements, and their comic or passionate notions of romance which we suited separately or together or not at all, although they might, to some degree, *settle* for us or for one of us.

That night, although it does not matter, one of the girls was tall and wore a black topcoat open and long, to her ankles—this was not the style then—and a white shirt and black pants and sandals on her feet: an English girl dressed in the French style. The girl I chose was short and English and had red hair, long too, and anxious and springy with its own curls.

We talk in low voices. Both girls were bold but in different styles. The short redhead was frequently shy, soaked with it, trembling as if with wet and chilled from a swim in the *Bacino* or perhaps the nervous vibrancy was a matter of energy and audacity.

Onni said to her, "What a dirty mind you must have to keep ducking your head like that." She hid her face, her head often, often, every few minutes.

And she turned pink, a russet kind of pink in the electric light, and her eyelids batted—oh, so often, so often, how they fluttered.

Compared to Onni's, her body had no weight. It was, if you will forgive me, all spirit and shy meat. Buttocks and pale breasts and hidden entries were palpable but spectral too—virginal, or nearly. Or this was an element of style, of education, of the hands of education on her, her odors, her small gleams, of the eye, of the skin, of teeth between her lips. Her will to talk—to flirt— had a winglike quality, of tethered wings, or if that sounds dusty and ordinary, of a tethered girl.

The tall one, Onni's pick, was oddly contentious and contemptuous toward everyone and everything, toward Venetian coffee, toward *San Marco*, not in detail exactly but in some hidden, inner tone. She was clumsily stylish—she was new to being stylish; her style was French existential and angst-ridden; and she meant to amaze and amuse and did. I had no intention of being so sad or gloomy that these youthful events were discouraged . . . I wanted something to happen. I had the real authority. And that irritated and goaded that girl crazily. She had a long torso and longish breasts with cone-like tips, quite hypnotic, but she was so assassinatory, so carping that Onni, in his aggression, seemed not only suitable for her and invited but in the right.

We talked about the weather, the weather in which their trip was framed, day by day. And their hotel. In the *Piazzetta*, we stood, our arms around their waists, theirs around ours, and we looked at the moonlight on the water and the floodlit façade of *San Giorgio Maggiore*. The air was cool. "I have a room," Onni said. The girls made terms. Onni and the tall English girl disappeared into the *calli* and never got back to the room it turned out, but we thought they were doing it, and this was aphrodisiacal for the redhead, Dora, and for me.

Dora followed the dictates of her soul, of her spirit—some war between her and the tall one, and another between her and her absent mother—and still another one with her hiddenly domineering—and free—companion, me—preoccupied her. We walked down to the *Arsenal* and necked there, kissed and kissed, and fondled and fondled far too expertly for our age and pretensions. When it was quiet where we were, we went further than kissing—but we did it as if we weren't doing it. The semi-weight-lessness of her body and some whiff of victimization when her breasts were touched sobered me into this nonadmission, into this introductory sexual thing.

We found Onni and Anna, the tall girl, who had very dark hair—did I say that?—in the *Campo San Stefano*. The girls felt or pretended we were not much and not of much interest to them now . . . They saw fit to tease or make it clear that we were not important. It was me they minded, more than Onni . . . This maddened Onni and made him a cold enemy to them. Onni and I could be real and primary for each other, and find each other's silences or anecdotes or routines of showing off of interest, making sure neither of us was alone in the world at such moments, but Onni wanted the attention of the world. Perhaps the girls were interested in violence in courtship, in teasing and ruth-lessness, in tests of strength. Perhaps the tall girl was merely unpleasant.

Onni and I kept glancing at each other, knowing also that we could abandon one another, ironically and even nastily, if we did indeed come to desire either or both of these women very much. Such accomplicehood is a need I had. One doesn't have to make great claims for it. As I said, it was that no one now could define us, these women could not hurt us much with their opinions or with their oddities. Or with their moods. The judgement of whether we were *amused* comes down to a memory of his face glancing at me across the café table in the insufficiency of the moments here with Dora and Anna.

He and I chose the more familiar language we had with each

other . . . This involved the spirit. Onni sang them a Neapolitan song and then translated it falsely; they laughed at the jokes he made up; and I laughed at them and him and what he was doing. It sobered the nerves and left marks on the heart. The laughter is on the edge of the future, of our memory of the girls . . . Once again the taint of the specific moment, a bit terrible, is also delicious . . .

It is that what I feel is what matters the most . . . It is arbitrary. He can escape. He is not imprisoned. But moment-by-moment what I feel is what leads in the dance. Even Dora half-hates me.

I do not love Onni enough but I love him enough all the same that I love myself some in reflection of his feelings for a little while.

Why not sex now, to erase the girls' moods—and to show our strength and freedom? Now at the end of an evening? We are walking in the *Sestiere Santa Croce*. A residual and constant pain or hurt runs through the evening, doesn't it? We can reach a satisfactory degree of painlessness. But the pain will recur. We'll live a while, a bit longer, more or less in this state.

Onni says in an approximate way, as a matter of encouragement, "Let's keep it up . . . up . . . up . . . up . . ." Unsmiling, he turns his liking toward me. In *Campo San Polo*, among the lights and the cafés, he puts his hand on my shoulder as we walk. The enemy-thing that love is, the eerily reckless unhappiness of it—what good does it do? I am the skinnily laughing one in the dim light, on the whole the less unhappy one. He laughs too, carried along by my strangeness. I understood this even then to be beauty you ought not talk about or to act on too often because it was silly.

He wonders about me. The force of his wonder knocks against me. The sexual thing. Well, let me be blunt, let me be explicit. I don't want to be worshipped, teased, laughed at, or otherwise be the object of revenge or justice. I could bear to be touched only on maybe half a dozen occasions with him or be a player in other people's sexual dramas, a girl's, a woman's—it has to be my sexual drama too: do you know what I mean? I am not clever.

Here is an example: he unfastens my pants and he peels down my underpants in a darkened *calle*. I am bored but responsive . . . I am larger genitally than he is and he is playing a practical joke on me *largely* by being the aggressor toward my reluctance and he is using, of course, my susceptibility to flattery. This, too, is lovely; it has a beauty; but I say, "Stupid, this is stupid."

"All right," he says. "We will stop." But he doesn't stop. We are simply jacking off . . . In some dim way, this is my choice.

Jacking off, he comes quickly. Except for a flicker of sightlessness, he watches me as he comes. Now that is a special thing: that sense of him in the passage of pleasure and still alert to me. He has great value. But I don't like remembering all the ins and outs of feelings and the slight sourness of the trickery dominance—and the isolation . . . There were too many feelings—and not enough; and the simple image of *friends* or of *the-beloved-and-the-lover* break down into actual characters, us, which breaks my heart, and which shocks me and makes me laugh, bitterly, but with some exalted ego—enough that in embarrassment I think none of it matters.

And some of it is shamed embarrassment, but that does not go very deep. The physical thing was gibberish. He was not simple enough. He had no central *physical* wish, and I do not suffer enough from boredom to like how unbasic he is. And I did not want to be serviced, seduced, or whatever it was. I screamed inwardly brakingly, *No.*

But I behave. I don't rub it in. I'm not honest—or uncontrolled . . . I don't push him away. The embarrassment and the subsequent physical and then psychological struggle—or seething in me—teases and feeds him . . . I don't know about his secret wishes. Although I suppose I can guess.

In the moment, his hands move; one holds my prick while I come; his other hand smooths my hair above my ear. A corridor of possibility stretches on, lined with doors to mutual transgression, new for me, not new for him, jealousies, gifts, blackmails, leaning on each other's regard . . . I do not want it! The seashell and echoing cave and absurd-telephone-to-wisdom of realer sex, one hears the roaring of the spheres in conjunction with the treble of the light of the tinier particles of the self . . . The world rushing and spinning in every metamorphosis . . . I am the seashell . . . I have power and no power . . . I don't trust his generosity enough to be other than wearily, secretly bold . . .

I am not strong enough, ruthless enough to slap him . . . or to boast . . . I suspect I know how to make him feel love strongly, wretchedly, imprisoningly. But it is not a prior desire. Or a day-dream of mine . . . I am young and merely curious, two-legged, standing by the unwindowed wall of this particular *calle* and lightly vibrant in my body and invaded as if by a disease by a *curious* sexual heat . . . I hold back.

In the act I waver physically when I am near coming. My legs stiffen and tremble and stiffen more. I am staring-eyed, perversely awake to the night—I can see the granules of darkness, see my fear, see my reluctance in the dark. See my restraint toward love. My hearing is sharpened. I am not enclosed in the act; I am in the world; I hear the murmurs of the air.

And then I am startled to be slightly faint, startled by weak-ness; I subsided into the act and was partly overcome.

But then I overact my coming so that he can see . . . I indulge his desire to see and know. I can accept it; I can feed it. The near vacuum of musclelessness at that moment, mine, I let him see it. He is never as vulnerable as that even when he is asleep, never so vacuous, so mindless.

He is of merit in the world, of use to the world, he is not gifted in terms of happiness. My startled pulse, or soul, slaps and leaps and sinks. A white-hot urinous concussion of a kind occurs. I spoke as I came: *"This is male horseshit,"* I said resenting what-ever of truth interfered with the ordinariness of what we did and made it shabby and yet excused it by the flare of nobility or sublimity no matter how brief in the friendship.

My balance returned. The flicker of heartbeat, of breath—the bird flutters of those and of dry eyelids—returning to the now dry garden of the world includes for a while an extraordi-narily clear sense of him, clear because drawn clearly, but not necessarily true. But it is as if the physical thing of even stupid sex and the mental thing and the flares of sensation inside sex give you a grid of clues on which a kind of map is drawn, a condition of sympathy. He is in a similar state of sympathetic knowledge, but this does not mean he is sympathetic—he is scornful or satiated or tricky. We are not matched symmetrically in these moments of mutual sympathy. Even metaphorically, we do not dance all that well together. If I imagine him regarding me—well, I shrink from it—but the self-righteousness and the half-satisfaction, the wall-like-ness and shyness in me, of me, it would be truly irritating to him, maddening . . . not to everyone; I don't mean that; but to him and to some others.

Let me go back a moment. He feels me come, the whole physical thing, he is aware—he feels it scientifically, not amorously. He has no mechanism, no experience of certain feelings, or a too fleeting experience of them to reproduce them. He gambles with his partial knowledge; he speculates on what he knows, with what has been given him—he is superstitious in a sense. If I make either of us a hero or both of us heroic as lovers, I lie about the moment.

I am the stronger one here but I am a weaker person than he is. *Afterward*, he is half-released, amiable dangerously, briefly protective, perhaps mocking . . . He is essentially wild; some restlessness is always in him. By saying this I mean only that the other stories that didn't occur, of anal sodomy, say, or of cock-sucking, or experiments in suicide, or in an overt pact of violent exploration, tease him as they don't tease me; tease him as likely or even as necessities if reality is to be real.

Or tease us differently. We have an alliance of some, only some, synchronicity.

With women he is similar but stronger in inflection. I've seen him, seen his feelings with them—they are not always stronger. But they are clearer. I *interest* him but what is inside that interest, what informs it, inflects it, gives it shape and aims it, is hidden from me, perhaps from him.

It is odd to have an unwritten role in someone's life.

But after sex on this or that occasion in the few times we did something, he is perfervid with a kind of semi-comic and very dangerous malice as if he has lost a game, not won one. He has not gotten what he wanted. Or he got what he wanted but it was not what he wanted—some contact with a moral sense, with an innocence, with a different order of mind, a different sexuality, a different sense of things.

With my changeable feelings toward him . . . So, being not entirely venomous or dark and trying to steal my soul, say, steal my life, he wants a romanticized tawdriness, a settling for a standard physical drama with malice attached. It is flattering to be eligible for this, but my skin now sometimes crept with fear at the sight of him. Fear of him. Of his will. Of how I might be hurt, changed . . . altered. If he feels such fear, it seems only to challenge his fearlessness, and to urge him on to dangerous *ressentiment*, pride, wildness . . . Drunken carelessness. Some handsome self-display that arouses envy. Trouble with the *carabinieri* . . .

I prickle with fear and dislike for him and with half-knowing sense about post-coital reality . . . Language lies when it speaks of perfection, of being without sin or flaw . . . And when it refers to an emotion as if the emotion were a single thing and were free of time—of years and of moments—as if anything at all was free of the vibrations of its near independence inside that irresistible rush of moments. My sense of reality is no match for his, or is, but I am too inhibited toward him, too clement, to use it—or too attached, too much in love, or too honorable, or too cowardly, or too cold.

The onset of reality here, post-coitally—and he comes often in the course of a day—is like an attack by the *acqua alta*, by gray roiling waves when the water is deep enough in the *calli* and the boreal wind—is that the North Wind?—when the wind comes from the mountains to the north.

Parts of me crumble, are washed away. In his nervousness because of me, he starts telling how an American girl I like, a Jewish girl named Lynette from Wisconsin, is hateful: "Her boobies are too big, that coarse hair, and she thinks she is a goddess—she smells of Jewish grease . . ."

Lynette is both nervous and sure of herself, in that absolute-absolutist way of someone who believes she is good, she is perfect, rather than real. To be "real" is to complain—it is something like that with her. She was also warm, suspicious, and intelligent—and funny. I hesitate. Sexually with her, well, it was anal, and she screamed. I am too large and she was not gifted sexually—only emotionally. Still, my phallic response was so immediate—shadows fell away; I was defined as by a searchlight . . . The nude dominance I like . . . The invisibility of ignorance and of all that one denies stopped. I made the mistake of telling Onni something about this . . . Perhaps I was being seductive . . . I told him how resentful and dry my emotions for Lynette were, how dark the game seemed to be, how forbidden and, as it were, behind the woodpile in a village on the mainland. And I was afraid of the looming story of the cruel dominance in me, whereas I knew he would not be—that he would attack it. I half-knew it.

But he is attacking her . . . He acts as if he can't help himself. The venomous juice of it twists his mouth and makes it actually moist . . . He dribbles faintly or spits . . . His eyes glare . . . He does actually *hate* her because of me . . . I feel humiliated, as humiliated as if I flinched at a feinted blow or were incredibly stupid or was so perverse that I ate garbage in preference to ordinary food, and ate it slobberingly. I would like once again to claim I was innocent. But, surely, no one is innocent by this point in any story. It is true that I did not have sex often. I did not want to be sexually driven. I was afraid of human attachments. I knew this, knew about my virginal coldness and the gustiness of it—I had a certain gusto about it. And a certain moodiness. A secrecy. My own malice. My own grief. I am not someone it is particularly safe to know.

I also knew that the love of God itself was not safe, so why should human love be? I felt human love, always, as danger and oppression, as invasion, as the approach of story—and as the end of loneliness, love toward me, love between others, love that I felt for others.

I was as fascinated by what gave him pleasure and by what he got away with as if I were a thief and those things were made of meltable gold. We dress in that absurd gold. In denigrating him I perhaps struggle to get to some simpler tie.

I say to him, "You're a whore."

"What is a whore?"

"A whore makes you love him for a cold reason, over and over and over."

I have noticed at times that he is quick to use pathos—pathos is a staple of Italian theater. He says, "Ah, you are a beast . . . stop . . ."

The pathos was leavened by a threat: he would get even. He always did.

"Jesus," I said.

I know now that I never truly pitied him, not for an instant . . . not for his life. Or for his feelings . . . Or his lack of feelings . . .

"Booby and boobies," he said as we walked in the shadows of a partly lit *calle*. I am determined to feel and act as if nothing has happened. He has something *ratlike* and unfooled in him, dirty, dirty. Still I felt drunken in his company, flattered, successful, lucky . . .

This part of the sexual history, the mutual or unmutual masturbation, was not repeated often. But it became masturbation without any touching at all. The stuff became masturbation in each other's presence while talking about our bitterness over life or some girl, or even less, me being private, doing it in the john and talking to him in the other room where he has a towel in his hand.

Then came a month when I felt too old, and even that was too disgusting . . . Except sometimes . . .

He is more expert in a great many ways in giving pleasure and in responding to a fairly wide range of kinks and desires than I am. I have only a daydream interest in being pleasing. Or in being pleased by a lover. But we are not lovers, are we? He was not a lover of mine, was he?

We are almost as different as we can be. "Do opposites attract? Do you love me more than you love your mother, Onni?"

That was a common insult. It was a mockery we used back then.

"You cocksucker," he said in English.

"That's slander."

He butts my neck with the side of his head, and I black out but I hang on to his shoulders. In that shock the truth of his presence, as so often, overcame me. He leans close and says into my ear, "A girl's mouth is strange . . ." He means a boy's mouth is just a mouth. It is an insult. He said, "Is your mind strange?" Then his lips pressed partly toughly, partly sinuously on my mouth, conferring conflicting humiliations—mockery, dismissal—and rewards, love, envy, appetite . . . He said, wiping his mouth: "It's like kissing the dictionary. When a girl sticks a tongue in your mouth, Nino, does she feel your brain?"

He does not know how to love. He does not know how to love me. He has to learn. Perhaps he will. Perhaps he will not.

*

The Pygmalion thing: well, he dieted, he exercised, he thought about clothes; he studied how eating certain ways changed his face, changed the features of his face. He wanted to be photogenic—he worked in Milan as a model; and he had small parts in movies. He taught me things as well. He got me walk-ons in two movies in Milan. On the train in a first-class compartment, Onni practiced shapes of his mouth . . . He practiced being hollow-cheeked or full-cheeked, and then he exercised his face to puff up some muscles and to tighten others . . . He told me how to hold my head when I smiled . . . "I am responsible for you," he said. This was serious to him, but it was a game as well. He mocked it. I did not steal his traits without his permission. He often stared at me. It is a bit *strano* to have your nose and eyebrows at your conscious disposal; it is both aristocratic, as if you were posing for a coin, and whore-like (and narcissistic) of course. I felt I had a peek at why Hollywood stars were called Hollywood royalty. Onni wanted lighter-colored hair. But he was already too noticeable and too much of a scandal in Venice; and then he did it anyway, lightened his hair and then bleached it nearly white for a month. I was ashamed of him but I hid it that I was. I was aware of how he felt when he was with me. I worried about it some.

The Contessa Wille-Perini—it was an Austrian title, Onni

explained to me—a notoriously unpleasant-tongued woman, made Onni's mother cry once with remarks about Onni's hair; those remarks drove his mother from a party in the *Sestiere San Polo*.

Onni said softly, ruthlessly, "I feel very sorry for my mother." But he did not mean it. Her feelings did not hold him hostage. We did not, I think, use our feelings to constrain each other. Or not lightly. Only ultimately. We did a lot of sports, rowing and wrestling and gymnastics. I did not like wrestling. I didn't like being touched in that direct reality of force by anyone. We ran. We played tennis and cricket. I fenced. "That is your nature," Onni said. "A fencer."

Onni read half a dozen newspapers a day. Or looked at them. He was often moody about the news. His ambitions had to do with an audience and its sense of a hero, its sense of men—for instance, a right-wing nobleman being cruel but being a great leader; Onni read stories in the papers about such men and then partly was such a man.

He cared about contemporary politics, and he also was at times the man in the Italian street, or *calle*. Even then he was also Onni-the-Great. We argued for hours and hours over Franco's senescence and the balance of power in the Mediterranean, and the rise of Germany from the ashes. And about Leftism. I said it was logically impossible, psychologically fraudulent. He could not live without it, the promise of solution, the Happy Ending . . . We quarrelled over Gramsci and Aquinas, Sartre and Husserl, Leopardi, Lord Byron . . . Sometimes he snorted with disbelief that his arguments could not shape my mind . . . To be honest, all his arguments affected me some . . . And do so still.

One time he called me at three in the morning. "Come and help me," he said. A scene, a semi-orgy, or real one, on the mainland had gone bad. He was calling from the railroad station. Someone had beaten him; and the drugs he'd taken were fermenting in him; and he was in an agony of humiliation and physical shock and chemical disorder.

I pulled on jeans and a sweater and ran in the dark through

the *calli*. He had made his way to the *Scalzi*, to the highest point of the high-arched bridge, where he stood pushing at his hair. He was not helpless even then, merely tormented. Or not so merely. We stood on the high arch in the black wind among the few lights at that hour. I put my arm around his shoulders and, for a while, cradled his head, and told him that he was going to be a great man while he breathed sobbingly against me and kneaded my waist in a fairly professional way, expertly, grate- fully, with *agonizedly* expert fingers . . . glibly, you might say. His touch was often glib . . . He asked me if I would help him kill the bastard who had beaten him. I don't think I thought about what it meant that he meant this. I said, "Sure . . . sure."

I think Onni did revenge himself on the guy later. Onni boasted that he had. He accused me of being a lousy friend, which of course I was. But I did not ever ask him to help me get revenge on someone, and he never offered, or did it for me . . . I never understood his one-sidedness except as part of his sense of power.

We were on the *Scalzi*, in the wind and faint light. And in the darkness of the incessant flutters of terror, I felt his true heat . . . Homer speaks of *furnace-souled Achilles*—that is a free translation—death-dealing Achilles, power and temper. The furnace-soul doesn't shut itself down ever. The sexual thing is a byway. Or one was off to one side—was temporarily privileged. I realized on the *Scalzi* that I did not take responsibility for blazing-souled Achilles except at specific moments . . . This re- sponsibility for someone's life, for someone's feelings, that some- one pushes on you in the name of their feelings for you, dissolves some possibility of deep accomplicehood, some chance for a dirtied but vividly effectual male honor that I revered. And offers this other guilty but not complicitous actuality. I knew that the more I knew him the more the tie between us widened in me until it was as wide as the night . . . And the pain was diluted in that open, dark width of itself . . . The emotion, the sympathy, the fear were like granules of the dark air . . . It was O.K. . . . . Neither of us was ever overly charitable to the other—that was not the ground of feeling. And that absence of charity when it came to exist noticeably was a shadow in the goings-on, in the friendship—to the degree we were friends . . . I don't know that "friends" is the right term for what I mean . . .

He is sobbing with hard-breathing humiliation: "*Do you love me? Would you kill for me, Nino?*"

In a surge of feeling, I take the responsibility for his life for a few moments.

"Quiet. Don't let the bastards get you down. We'll talk about it later . . . How much damage did he do?"

Onni's face was torn or abraded. His arms were bruised. His ass, he told me, was black-and-blue from being kicked. He had a sprained finger . . . Maybe a cracked knuckle . . . He walked with a limp: the backs of his legs were bruised, he said.

I don't want to speak here of what I felt when he asked me over and over to help him get revenge—the use one might make of attachment to explore one's violence . . . He shuddered against me . . . The bleakness, the sense of cold reason in even a profane friendship in the dark . . . Onni huddled against me, as his requests went from shocking me to boring me . . . Onni can be bright-eyed and clear-eyed, but his eyes essentially look like those in an old statue, newly dug up and still dirty with clay and soil, unrepaired. Now nakedly so. Heroic kid . . .

We did, in a later year, partly burn the boat of a *bersagliere* who stole dope and money from Onni and hit him too. But I was older and cleverer, and that time I saw most of the event. It was curious how Onni lied about what happened then even though I had been there and had seen it—he forced his words on it. I don't know that he felt there was a difference in the circumstances of the two occasions, one where I was complicitous with his rage and one where I was not. I don't think he took time to notice or remember . . . furnace-souled Achilles . . . with all the ins and outs of his moods, of his rage, of his pride.

Thoughts and feelings, like glimmers of light in the streets of Venice—or like the lights along the railroad tracks to the mainland—or on the water or the *Canalazzo* and on the façades in the wind—precede the passage, the distance of the passage to the concern for someone's life, the soft perspective of feeling.

The thing of its being temporary does not mean it is tentative or unintense. I helped him home from the *Scalzi*, in the dark, in the empty streets, and he leaned against me. In his room, he kissed my neck and said, *"Ti amo, Nino . . . Ti amo . . ."* Then in English as he lay down and I covered him with a blanket: "I love you . . ."

I sat on the floor while he hallucinated and I held his hand while he spoke in rage about the evening, and I dozed when he finally slept. We woke almost simultaneously at dawn . . . "You have an Italian heart," he said in a far-off voice . . . "You are a friend . . ."

The glare of rage in him was visible even then.

"I'm not going to help you kill anyone," I said.

He was quiet. Then he said, *"Caro Nino . . ."* And closed his eyes and dozed again.

"Disgusting sunlight," he said when he woke again.

By then I was sleeping across the foot of the couch-turned-into-a-bed. The other moment was over.

He said, "You are on my foot."

"Sauve qui peut . . . Shut up," I said.

"I will revenge myself on that bastard . . ."

"Fuck revenge."

"God, I am *morto . . .* My lip is cut . . . Make the sunlight go away . . . I can manage in the darkness . . . I will get up . . . And you sleep . . . *Caro Nino . . ."*

I crawled up and sprawled on the bed.

He said suddenly, "You are heartless, aren't you?"

"Yes and no . . ."

"I am not your mother . . . We are not married . . . You mean. Ah, you are *strano . . . stranissimo . . . mio Nino . . . Va bene . . . Dormi . . . Dormi . . .* Kiss me . . . *E dormi . . ."*

And that was all for a while.

THE NEXT PHASE
WITH ONNI IN
THE WORLD

∾

HAVE YOU EVER thought of the seduction in the idea of omnipotence? In memory Onni exists for me without weight, without
presence, without volumes and masses and moods and without
his own will. One finds no buried statues or old cities in the mind.
The mind carries nothing tangible in itself. Everything is memory
and opinion. Is ghostly. What a strange place to look for the spirit
and flesh of an actual love.

In the mind, in the *Bacino* inside the curved bone of the
skull, behind the *Malamocco* or *Lido* of the eyes and nose, I dive
splashingly, sparkingly and electrically, among wakes and spume
on a thousand planes of ocean through Omnipotence, if I might
be permitted to name Time that. I swim toward and around pearly
or fanged or stinging memories.

The distance to a tangible thought of a touch—honest,
unomnipotent—is like flying across the space of a canal to the
high *fondamenta* on the other side in a dream, a bit of omnipotence to reach a bit of unomnipotent truth. But some human
arts deal intensely in continuous time—seamanship and architecture and music. They are arts in which one lives in relation
to air and moments. The arithmetical stillness and fullness and
finality of mood of Palladian buildings show in stone and air—
or an astrolabe or a sextant—are not ghostly. A story is devoted

to the idea of love more than to the experience of it. What if memory and craft should attempt a written description meant to be like a building a mind could move in? With almost audible voices and visible and shifting reflections of geometrical stones in the ungeometrical water of the canals? Venetian art and the domes of Venice, the city itself I knew as a boy, the boy I say was me, and Onni: Onni had an accurate sense of disjointed, social time and of clocks; it was visionary, this sense in the mauled child, in audacious Onni. But he hadn't much tie to regular time except in sports and errands. An art, a mind without a strong tie to continuous time, to oneself in it, can't deal in actual feelings or living characters or tell you convincing stories, only seductive ones, only symbols and dreams, wishes, constructs of the mind and parables, rouged and polychromed allegories, truly strenuous, a realism without reality. So Onni was an actor. I knew it inside me: the realist without the reality of Omnipotent Time has programs of action which are only shadows-in-motion.

Thoughts, memories, flash into visibility like seabirds outside one's window. Here are the surfaces of the world and here is the point of embarcation for a voyage into the mind, abandoning real *calli* and *fondamente* for the Asias and Venices and seas in the skull. It is an old man's adventure of a shadowy and romantic nature to traverse the Sea of Vain Tranquillity, the Sea of the Memory of Onni.

What a strange voyage. It cannot proceed step-by-step but only flashingly and unsteadily, back and forth among hours and years. Memory can't unroll a strip of actually continuous outward moments. Memory is merely only a light, an aimed light, sometimes awed and shameless, a discontinuous light generated by the mind and broadcast into an attic-universe of antique moments, their traces in one's head.

One's conscious memory is will-driven along a line of linked moments sporadically visible, and it is tossed up and down on the waves, from day to another day, and among years and moods and ideas. Sometimes the shore is illuminated and the movements on it are almost clear and then the shore shifts drastically. Memory's light gives us only glimpses, a fusillade of aimed glimpses, but memory cannot ever give us the real moment, dear, irresistible, unknowable real time in motion softly and without letup and omnipotently.

These were my secrets when I knew Onni and we were young. I had a different sense of time from him . . . I lived in the moments differently . . . *Only the real is real* . . . In that art of continuous moments that love is—as in an all-day ballet—the real lives of the performers are a distraction. Love is perhaps a special performance in real life, the ideas of its music and the played music and the movements in the setting, that marvellous stone, inexplicably marvellous and ourselves walking under a dome . . . a large, vaulted, shadowy-and-lit inner space, with a gossip of meanings-among-meanings in those spaces and with Venice outside, ah, the mind crashes and reels. Artists and men and women and children go mad. We go spying on real life . . . in the arts, among memories, too, and we go mad.

Among ghosts, having invested our real life in ghosts . . . I mean this is real life, too. So, the wind seems to stir in this other light, the flags on the motorboats and on some of the buildings unfold and crack and stretch. Faces and bodies seem part of a real moment, a moment across a canal, that one glimpses. The pictured moment lasts less than a second. One fills it out with what one knows. Sometimes one sees the real more truly in these fragments than in life, in these brushstrokes and syllables and sounds and strange domes than among the breaths of real life. The mind inside the light of memory has waiting for us actual whispers that douse us in knowledge, in tumbling memory and knowledge. Only someone experienced in the real can recognize in the tumble that the light bears in it sweeps and ebbs of feeling . . . A strongly insistent, insistently unchanging feeling is a lie. To know the Onni I cared about, the real one, to know a little about how I cared and how he cared, I must make the movement of time real, continuous, that delicate certainty, and everything else must admit to change, inadequacy, to the darkness that is the edge of the as yet unlived future.

In real time in a real Venice, in real light, I am waiting for Onni on the bridge of the *Scalzi*. Venice, although it is a theater and now a theater of rendezvous, is *real*, or was once, in the soft brushing, folding, and unfolding of a present moment; and there are the tawny hues of sunlit walls and dark-red tiled roofs as I stand on the high-arched *Scalzi* with the great running actuality of the *Canalazzo* below me, the unstable glitter of the water, the absurd, water-walking, bow-dancing traffic in yellow sunlight. One waits in a moment real from end to end of itself and with the reality of there being no end in sight for a while of moments in which Onni and I will continue to be young. If I turn in a circle I see identified, massive structures, a railroad station, two churches, one on each side of the Grand Canal, a railroad hotel, and the sky and the Lagoon, domesticated here, intimate but not miniature, and the present-moment which you know by this, that in it everything is improvised . . . The world alters blinkingly . . . And in the sun, from my perch on the bridge, I squintingly make out among the various-sized figures on the *fondamenta* one white-shirted, dark-sunglassed, hurrying figure. He is in the kingdom of real light down there, walking with a continuousness of movement that one skips over in memory—the movements of arms and elbows, of breath in the nose, of knuckles and fingers as one swings one's arms a little. He is among five hundred moving figures, their faces unknown to me. They might have been made of glass and been without features and for sale on a glass shelf in a wind-ruffled store. No. They stir and not in pre-dictable ways but flutteringly walk inside the tinted realities of their lives and not as robots.

At a two-minute distance from me that plodder caught in the real moments, hurrying toward me in the sunlight, is a version of the glamorous, discontinuous omnipresent *you* of my thoughts of him . . . The hurrying real *you* in the unobedient structures of reality is propelled repetitively by dumb, fleshy legs in trousers in real air in an *ah-ah* continuousness and incredible fluster of minor movements of fabric and hair and hand-gestures . . . Ah, it is the real world that rends me with impatience. I think I have not seen real time in such emotional detail since childhood. I blink and my mind errantly flutters and flies and I look away in a sunlit storm of impatience and ignorance, wishing for the disjunctures and omissions and meanings of art, of dreams, of will.

One's breath, the wind, the repetitions of eye-blinks, one is nowhere when one is waiting. Step by step, Onni, climbing the *Scalzi* toward me, taking long strides, almost running—neck and knees, elbows—heroically persists in making something happen in the Venetian light, the Venetian wind, persists in the enormous uphill of everything moment-by-moment (from birth until silence). He clears his hair out of his eyes in the Venetian wind as he nears me. That gesture lingers in the mind, not forthrightly, but in overlapping ripples of different sorts of reaction to it, different moments of seeing it. His eyes in the Venetian sunlight squint and address me which in turn overlaps with the gesture. He addresses me with a half-smile and by his rush, his hurry— it is jolting, these syllables of approach, the approach of his presence, the extreme reluctance of reality to be like the mind's sense of things. The knees and lungs and the knuckles of his hands, the bent fingers, and the actual heartbeat, and my reactions, like gondolas poled by ghosts or strange squared ripples of response. The squirm of flags in the soft wind is like the flutter in real moments of false feeling atop real feeling.

I will not whore you . . . I will not idealize you . . .

Hello . . . , he says; when he is feeling good, he speaks English in a light inflection as if he were standing on tiptoe.

Hello, I say. Standing close, he is, of course, life-sized, slightly winded—his chest is shaking with his breath—bandy-legged, handsome as hell, morally obtuse . . . He is who he is. We do not yet know how we feel about today.

Ciao, Bellissimo . . . He likes the jollity of greetings and seduction, and he does a lot of greetings in quick order and a lot of seduction often when he arrives when he feels like it.

If I allow it, my sense of him is of someone huge, as large as a building, and of another species from me.

Come stai? I say.

Brutto day, *non? Belle idée . . . Ha-ha*, he says. He kisses me on both cheeks, says, "Ha," and then, in familiar immediacy, "Come, Nino—I have found two girls . . ." But when I blink and start to smile, he says, "Ugly, spoiled girls, no, not ugly—long, slim—just your type . . . Charming, yes, but little voices, mean eyes, choosey . . . I don't want to go. Talk to me . . . I am more in the mood to talk . . . Let them wait . . . *Bella giornata*, eh . . . What are you thinking—you are such a noble guy . . . *tanto gentile* . . . a sublime person . . . But talk to me . . . Nino . . . Tell me what were you thinking while you waited for me just now?"

He set the chance to talk, you see, against my going against my rules and being rude to girls I had not met. And who might not exist.

And it is like a laboratory test to see which bait the *aragosta* will prefer, but we are not in a laboratory. The sunlight shiftingly flickers among the movements of eyelashes, and the world rolls slightly in its customary Adriatic-afternoon fashion. One hears his vocal inflections—his trained vocal inflections.

"I was not thinking . . . I was merely breathing . . ." This is a peace offering. I imitate him: "You are such a noble guy . . . *tanto gentile* . . . a sublime person . . . talk to me . . ."

How much boredom, how much "love," how much knowledge of the world and the need to rule, how much embarrassment causes what we say? If one could feel deeper into the moment and slow it, perhaps one would see all the past and all the future and all the linkages and simultaneities that run through the world and hold it together. It is a general law in social matters that one ought not to think too much. What I see in actual moments when I look at them in memory in my head is the acute possibility in them that one might say or do anything. Concern, affection, laziness and fear, one's fashions of behavior at the time, the things that are in one's head, the power the other's company has for you, one's beliefs taken as experiments or suddenly, experimentally, as a fixity, and the slightly drunken pleasure of seeing him, the felicity after a day or two, of a week or two of being away from each other—it is bewildering in actual moments . . . I am excited and goaded, and I resent being roused, and I have a terrible ethical lust for pleasure, an excitement of the moral sense in pursuit of pleasure—of what we are given as pleasure—and I enjoy the light and air and wind of affection, of love. I am that sort of person, slightly unfurled, like certain leaves or like a pennon. I am proud of myself that year, anxious to maintain rule over my life, to control my life.

I make a joke: "You talk . . . I'm going to *Santa Maria Formosa* . . . How is the theater?" and I push him against the railing. He was working with a theatrical company. Now he must interpret my fake roughness. I start walking toward the other side which is actually shorter to the *Rialto* and to *Santa Maria Formosa*. I move without looking to see if he will follow me. The moment is alive in its instability. The *politics* of getting along with someone is a sleazy matter; it would not be *politics* if it were spiritual and noble. We are together in our guilt as men. This is why so many myths of love have to do with imprisonment and solitude. *Kiss my ass* is how things begin. He has taken on an air of superiority to whatever I choose—to talk or to go to *Santa Maria Formosa*.

A history of amusements and combats fills the background to the moment among the whistle of our new devices now that we are older. A breath of a kind of automatism of male absolution, lightly anguished and partly languorous—and corrupt—tickles in the bristle and rush of alternative motions of feeling. In the leafy, lengthy tangle of possible actions, in almost leafless, sunlit Venice, he is a young actor who has spent time preparing roles, making choices of revelatory actions. I smile with no clear meaning or purpose—this is a way of being agreeable. We are together for the first time in two weeks. He shrugs questioningly, examining my smile. I raise my eyebrows and twist my lips *agreeably* . . . "Ah, *sì*," he says and links his arm with mine; he steers, he drags me . . . I permit this. He marches me along and he matches his stride to mine which, with me in his clutch, is a little drama, flesh to flesh, moment by moment. I feel a depth to it, feel the furnace heat of general, male rage in his body pressed against mine; I am warmed, and I become queerly, perversely cold—and daydreaming, resistant, but not entirely, a young man aware he is a young man—you know? Young men are braided histrionically, explodingly into the history of the world, actually . . .

"And what have you been up to? Who do you see?" he asks.

I am the purer, younger, less worldly one—the ass. He is stained by the world. This is a form of "love" . . . He presses my arm and says, "Talk to me, Ninoni . . . What is new?"

Involuntarily I measure the degree of hardness or of sloppiness in his flesh, the health and wirey heat or slackness and degeneration in his arm and in the side of his body pressed against me. I see only a portion of his face: the half-light in the *calle* varies with each step. I judge him—this is the boy's role. The belovèd's role. We are approaching a slanted, bodiless, colored pier of daylight; and in it, the gloomy passion and somewhat angry and faintly half-asleep vanity of his face—he has a new vanity, a different vanity—registers the approaching light with a premonitory hunching and then opening or clearing. Onni's face faces reality now with an extreme hardness of will and speed and virility, with worldly ambition, with conscious self-presentation . . . He is wittily and masculinely self-conscious in an Italian manner . . . It is powerfully affecting—he is manlike, or is a man almost, or is one. It is shocking, the painful vulgarity of the beauty of the self-conscious young actor, the absence of any citizenship any longer in the republic of youthful fools and of male egos in abeyance even if only slightly . . . But I am a citizen there still.

One "knows" these things, one has feelings about things; one's degree of belief varies, one's scoffing irreligiosity—toward friendship, toward Onni's will—one doesn't necessarily listen to it. One has a wit in these matters that has come with time and familiarity and from the unclean intimacy . . . Knowledge seems to be the result of everything and is said to be a curse . . . Onni does not always feel I am accursed in my knowledge of him but sometimes he eyes me and does feel that: perhaps we are at our closest then. He invents an intimacy, a sum total of intimacies and experiences with others: I am an improvement on others— this is an invention, a falsification. Our intimacy has in it real knowledge, real guilt, which we deny separately or in sudden vortex-like totality, sucking us into moments of utter void. His knowledge, his tactics in the politics and motions of companionship are different from mine—except when he imitates me slightly.

I am avoiding saying I accepted my knowledge of him in part, scoffingly, but welcomingly, with some flinching as well: I was consciously a ritualistically naïve companion. I was also stiff with a complicated, ironic thing of refusal now that I was a bit older and more worldly in my way.

This is felt at once; he catches it at once in his darting eyes, in the nervous flutters of his cheek and of his neck. But it is not known inwardly in language. One's mooded sense of things, one's will watches the sunlight strike and ride on his face as he strides from shadow into light, and presents his face to it . . . One is not Onni as one sees the will in him unfurl its wings, so to speak, in the half-shadow again in the narrow passage . . . The wings of this self-presentation spread from wall to wall with feral will. He will learn an actorly shyness later in life, in his thirties, when his face ages. I feel caught in a subtly homosexual story in which the homosexuality does not matter except as a mode of truce in the world and as a concomitant of his extreme and more and more public handsomeness. I was perhaps a coward and too sensitive as a young man. It was my first year as a young man.

I obey his command to talk. I want to talk to seal off the future in a rush of words. What I say to him is obscure but not to him if he chooses to remember what we said before. The obscurity might be said to have a familiarity of odor as in the darkness of familiar hallways, the hallways being my cast of mind. Walking distorts the breath. "I have begun to think of myself as 'one.' " That is, as a neutral observer.

He jerks my arms to interrupt and says intently, so that the question matters in the day's drama: "Were you thinking about me?" It is a bit of joke but not really.

"I was thinking of you, yes . . ."

"When in English do you say *thinking about you* and when do you say *thinking OF you*?"

"When you want to say it in two syllables or in one." This moment is unfamiliar. Everything is new between us—and familiar. Life is as if gigglingly harsh. Passersby surround us. Onni grips my arm and hurries me along: "We are not so concerned with syllables as you Anglo-Saxons. Were you thinking *deeply* about me, Ninoni?"

"Christ!"

"No . . . Me . . ." Then: "I was thinking *deeply* about you . . ."

He had different feelings from mine, a different mood, a different mind. " 'One' should be suspicious of thoughts and theories of symmetry, Onni . . . 'One' doubts that there is a great regularity in the universe . . . *Dunque* 'one' doubts that your thinking and my thinking will balance if one starts to look at us . . . Thus spake Zarathustra . . ."

"What else can feeling be? But thank you very much for being so Anglo-Saxon," he said and laughed.

"I am not Anglo-Saxon. I am Celtic . . ."

"A druid? *Casta Diva . . . quel demone . . .*"

It is like walking on visible dark spaces among the atoms of the pavement when he carries on . . . His sense of balance is not stilled but onrushing, a balance borne on the charge of moments. Sometimes I feel I come on the truth tucked away in the interleaving of actual seconds, only and always in the actual fires of breath, footsteps, movements of eyelids: *Ah, so this is affection . . .*

He rushes on: "No doubt you are clear to the angels, but God and I think that what you say is dark. Give me a kiss on the ear, and talk to me about fucking . . . Who are you fucking this week . . ."

Amedeo said to me once that *Il Signor Dio* in the reality of His power did not need to claim power as men do. So, we start with an error of will if it is God we think we are imitating when we try to be powerful. I say to Onni, "To think about you—or anything—I must be very still, very quiet. I have to hide and wait for thoughts to come . . . I can't think now . . . I fuck who I can . . ."

"You are always so quiet . . . I think you are always thinking . . . I will read your fortune in this unquiet world: you have spent time with Amedeo . . . You are talking theology . . . You are in that mood of yours when you expect to be struck dead—or struck dumb—" Ah, he has seen me with Amedeo. Or Amedeo spoke to him. Or it is by deduction. He looks at me: "I am handsomer than you . . ." *Still* is understood. *At this time still I am handsomer than you.*

"Not by much," I say looking at us in the nearby shopwindow in the narrow passage in the heaving, shuffling crowd of tourists in the damp air among the close walls. "But we are different types." In the damp *calle*, in his grip, I slouch, no longer Puritan, not a Jansenist refugee, a newish young man.

"I cannot bear these tourists," he says. "All these tourists." But I am a tourist in my youth—as he is in his young manhood. "Why don't they go to Verona? Listen, I have some hash, very good kif, from the girlfriend of a Moroccan actor . . . Not here . . . I have it at my apartment . . . Here I have only a little grass . . ."

This maybe means he wants really to talk. Or is shy.

"Hash is a good idea," I say, thinking of the tactful veiling and euphorias and the ease of the improvisations of brotherhood in intoxication, thinking too of the drama of being with him moment by moment.

2

THE UNRESTING ONWARDNESS of the day is as beautiful as the motions of water in the light in the room. The light is like dimpling water when water is like the waving hands, the green palms of water-children. The delicacy of the universal earthquake is a mysterious irreversibility shoving at the walls of the chest and at the thumping heart, and at the world outside and the sky in the window. If the heart is stilled for a moment by touch or drunkenness—or companionship—one can feel the great sailing and lifting of everything, domes and transepts and streets and emotions, fitting together at times and moving apart at times, in a mad, bright explosion of vision and comprehension, or merely as the world's being slowly, blowingly unstill. Time is naked. I imagine it as experienced by Onni as pain in his new manhood, his new career, the shit and uproar and uncertainty, the loss and then all the newness he has to face. So, with Campari and a little champagne and hashish, I feel the principle of motion of companionship.

Onni stands by the window of his room, shirtless . . . The room is warm and stuffy. He has asked me to give him my shirt, and I am struggling in the time warp to take mine off so I can give it to him. He puffs on his hash pipe and he says, "I think perhaps my beard is coming in too strongly . . . And you are turning religious, I think . . . Amedeo is clever enough to convert a Neapolitan to Jansenism . . . Are you now very religious?"

I will tell you the secret of holy texts. They omit the moments entirely. He takes hold of my arm, and he elbows my thin bare chest: "Tell me," he says. "Yes . . . Have you been a bad boy? . . . Or are you very good? . . . You have told me nothing so far . . ." He is lonely on the peninsula where time has landed him.

"I have not seen you . . ."

I remember from a year ago him moving alongside me as we walked—a memory, the movements of his shirt, his head sailing along, his arms swinging, and I remember the heat and weight of his body . . . My sense of his mood, in his room, the sensations of feeling fly or snuffle or breathe, my sensation of being taller than he is, different, and in a particular stage of life, and the sensation of having changed, grown older, become serious in certain ways visible in a way in his reaction to me; and the structures of his face and the revelation, moment by moment, of manner and new thoughts on it were too difficult for me; I felt walled in, suffocated, too childlike; and, so, in a grown-up way I watched only his neck, his bare neck, and the motions of his hair; I read the news sent from those minor areas, those bits of Asia as I puffed on the pipe. In truth, the single supple filaments of hair and the spread of his eyebrows and the comma-like shadows in his eye sockets and in the flanges of his nose, were a little like written squiggles, bits of an alphabet, bits of words, inanimate bits of design that yet were animate and known as meaning.

"Ha-ha . . . Ha-ha . . . Ha-ha," I laugh at the nonsense of a face, at the nonsense of affection so separate from the feelings of the object of it. The strength of effect he pursued in one sense made enemies of us if I was independent of his mood, of his power.

"Ha-ha . . . ha-hoo, ha-hee," he said parodying me. "Here . . . Have some more," he said refilling the pipe and handing it to me. "Enjoy yourself."

I had outgrown mere admiration for that strength of effect in him, I saw as I smoked. What I was most aware of was something bony, a distention of will in his presented face and manner, in the alternations in him of contempt for flirtation and then of a kind of weary appetite for affection—him being a rough soldier although young. I was aware of a weight in him, a weightiness that was new, and of him sinking or subsiding into flirtation, like a heavy dog subsiding into water and muck. Or like when he swam, the way he had of putting his head back in the water, wetting his hair, but also the water supported his head and his gaze at the sky and his water-weighted hair, that other sense of affection. He had a philosophy of reluctant feeling, almost a philosophy. He was very male in this phase . . . And somewhat ungodly and habitually a bit enraged . . . Piqued . . . Perhaps tormented . . . As if a hook or a barb had entered his chest which moved rapidly with his mood, with his moody breath—now that he was a professional performer, lonely and male, and rabid with an inner weight of desire for all sorts of wishes.

He stares into my face and holds his breath and then says slowly, "You are jealous of my deep, deep heart, Nino . . ."

"Ha-ha . . . Ha-ha . . . Sure . . . Yeah . . ."

"Do you wish to be so stupid as me? You can be, *caro*, dear . . . You must give up your snobbery—like me . . ." I think he meant give up being young and become an earnest professional of some kind.

"Yes. I will give it up—like you . . . You are nothing but snobbery . . . ha . . ." I meant he was snobbish about all sorts of new things.

But I did not really laugh.

"You are a wonderful person, Nino," he said earnestly, fierily, strangely stupidly, feelingly.

I gazed at him, then drew my face together so that it was no

longer a net facing the world and him. His face flashed into
feeling and then moved into mere moodedness and was merely
an actual face. He looked at me from the blank cartridge of his
face then. But still it had in it some sort of intense longing and
a good deal of pain past all bearing in that pain's momentary
fullness of disorder . . . None of this was in any context of what
had been between us until now.

Lucifer and Juno in their actual omnipotence are shadowy.
Theirs—and the power of the saints—is the mere omnipotence
of storms and of armies at Chioggia but still it is comparative
omnipotence, compared to us, to Onni and me. Love is often
pictured as illumination. It was always strange for me, Onni's
powers of physical projection, his ability to project an idea or a
feeling physically. The nihilism of the world seems less at any
display of this Italian or Venetian trait in him, which seems to
come from his daily acquaintance with the gesturing statues
along the rooflines and in the courtyards of this pretty city.

He is realer to me in words that suggest façades and purpose
than he is in words of emotion. He was indelicately cursing me
for the existence of time and for the flux of emotion in him and
for the reality of his being too old and too serious to be a youth
and too young to be a star or a real artist just yet.

3

IT WAS SO STRONG an effect in the flux of moments this time
that it seemed the point. A particular expression of a melody that
kept being modified as we went along. The effect was so truly
pitched that I felt bound to him among the metamorphoses,
among the realities of the condition of such change. But I doubted
him and thought all this was perhaps in relation to a part he was
playing professionally. He has begun to move ahead in his life;
he is caught in the speed and guess-haunted darkness of the
spirit of accident that haunts grown-up events and projects. Bits
of glitter move on the active façade of his face as if his skin
contained grains of mica. We are fairly large young men. We
are at the age of adventure. It is time we joined the air force or

traversed a portion of Antarctica or of Africa. I always try to be a man of reason, but one cannot be logically obedient to someone, but only to logic, not to an emotion in someone ever. So, things become jumpy and illogical when you are sympathetic to some-one's feeling. He was studying my eyes, my nose—I tend to forget that I have features; his gaze reminded me that I had a face, reminded me of its reality-in-the-flesh around my nose and eyes and mouth . . . I think he was always conscious of his. He was probing as if to see what was valuable to me now. And perhaps to see clues to what I loved and feared as those things showed in my face and in who I imitated in the expressions of my face.

I smiled; a smile can be like an elbow fending you off. I am law-abiding, whatever the law is. I obeyed the laws of youth—sometimes. I think I knew in my stoned state he found me *"beau-tiful"* or some such thing—interesting to look at with a certain range of feelings attached, that I looked unlike him, that I was a different sort, but not "cute," not merely an old friend . . . This wasn't entirely unfamiliar . . . I had a mother and friends and I knew girls who did, at least up to a point, a point unclear so far. But it was new for me and scarey in this form—really new for me with him.

I was rattled by his face and by what seemed an artificiality in the moment, the degree to which we knew one another even when we hadn't been here before. The nonsense-gibberish of the *new* stuff and its underlying sexuality as *nature* was edged with comprehensible and nearly coherent diction—of friendship . . . It was realer to me suddenly, the change in me, for instance, and clearer too, and it was clearer what life was like—I could see it in his face although I hadn't seen it in this form there before. Then the strength and pungency of his combative masculinity and the variations of light moving on his half-seen face in the shadowy room and his slightly skewed, partly disarmed *new* sorts of vanity—these were an aspect of will in the private self sepa-rating itself from the world around it into private meaning for a friend because of emotion—do you know? He changed all the laws with his stare, with his mood, and I saw how, in this new phase of physical existence—me at this age—I could do that, too.

Lucifer and Juno are more capricious and *realer* than Jesus and the Virgin, who yet are capricious, so we still must pray and make sacrifices in the Christian dispensation. Pagan or Christian, we are not always prepared for emotions, even so. He was amused by me and pleased to be with me and he was bored by himself. He looked as if he was listening for my inmost breathing and then in the next half-second as if he was not listening but merely studied me in a half-dismissive, unlistening, but intent way. I would have liked to be with the girls in *Santa Maria Formosa* and have this diluted (or intensified) by them.

He looked into my face oddly . . . as if I were the *center* of his life just then . . . momentarily . . . It hadn't been like that before. Suddenly he jostled me and I turned away with distaste, being in truth peripheral even if *momentarily* central. Onni grabbed my belt with one hand and bent and encircled one of my legs with his other arm and threw me against the wall and onto the floor.

Then he grabbed me and lifted me and dusted me off while I hit him, and then I laughed and hit, and I pushed him away. All at once the sequence blurred and meant something else . . . What I think was happening was that he loved me more than in the past but that was perhaps because we cared less and saw each other less, and he missed the earlier emotion, and the regret in him was passionate and avid and new to him and rare now and pungent. But that meant a shuffling of intimacies as he knew intimacies. I mean his history of emotion held a lot of emotions and feelings that weren't really part of us but then, oddly, were or a certain feeling was because he was feeling it; this stuff got dealt like a wild card.

He had come to value me, to put a value on the moments of knowing me, a partly imaginary value, but you see, also a real one, and at that time, that day, a surface value as a young whore, which I was not, but which is one way he saw people, perhaps the one way he ever saw anyone he cared about.

So, his heart was set on seeing me, on affecting me, and that becomes, in the flow of seconds, a thing of being set on owning what aroused the feelings, me, but not me, but a plantation of feelings—what else did he know? Culture affects affections. I think too that his self-hatred was in hot bloom. Self-hatred and hard pride gave him a fueled rage of feeling. He expected me not to admire him. Onni who could not love, loved passionately in his way—I really understood it for a few seconds of sympathy. Clement sympathy.

Momentarily as I said. I half loved, half despised him—that means I was moved but also repelled by how his anger with himself and his anger at the world ignited the processes of this passion in him. I think he was showing a tormented and uncontrollable desire to exert mastery over the motions there are in an attachment. It seemed not like love but to be a moodedness and caprice.

In the shadows in his room, his face with its sharply excavated-from-darkness quality of good looks seemed to have inner staircases and to be difficult to see; but its eyedness, the way he stared and hooded his eyes and looked away indicated that he was very much the captain-owner of himself, of his room, of his feelings. It showed in the way he got out more hashish and more matches. And even in the way he smoked hashish, counting off the seconds he wanted me to hold my breath or that he wanted to hold his.

I turned my back to him and stood and puffed, blotting him out, I held my breath, expelled it, and puffed again. I don't mean to be presumptuous or conceited but there is something familiar in being loved. Again. It happened before. A certain emotional familiarity becomes a physical lightedness—one knows how to smoke, how to smile. One is another self, a self-at-home, and reckless and careful both. As I puffed, the walls of the room became a little like silk and wavery as if with wind and tinted with glare, even semi-transparent with Venice visible with changes through the walls to me—toylike memories of the place. Onni came over and embraced me from behind, and I absently tensed my back. I went on smoking, enclosing myself in a band of thought agreeable and not moody after all but not physical or active. If I allow myself, I can be jealous of everything—of Onni's physical strength and of his having strong feelings as a new adult. Or of myself. I can revel in my new power but how much power do I have? One time, at home, I was at my window, and I saw across a canal and down a bit, through an open window into another palazzo, into the room on the other side of that window, Onni unbuttoned with a girl I couldn't quite see, perhaps the girl, Gabriella, who lived there. Or her brother who had thin arms. Or her mother. Or her uncle . . . you see? I expected a wicked heat of jealousy and I did feel a stab. But nothing that triggered a sharper love and the great suffering that I expected from having read about jealousy-and-emotion in books and seen it acted so stormily in operas. I suffered that earlier time—and many other times—but I confess that my suffering was selfish: I wanted to be the one in that other room, the one seen, not the one who saw and whose mind was suffocated in sensations of loneliness and of having the lesser life.

Jealousy is self-concern in the light of ordinary reality. What one does not know. What one does not have. This becomes mixed up with a sense of *the ideal thing* as a cure which one, of course, has not experienced. That is because nothing is ideal, but when one is young, one does not know that. One still partly believes the lies of adults and one believes boasts of perfection. What Onni felt was unreal and what he wanted was unreal, was ideal, but he wanted it in reality, nervously, sweatily. Ideal, intense, sweatily real desire of some kind.

Onni was not ideal, merely Onni-whom-I-loved—in some ways and not in others. Whatever seems desireable, we desire. I wanted a good many things. But on the whole, I preferred my sanity to this and did not want to give up sanity and the past for a destabilizing emotion such as Onni's when he hated his own identity, and that partly became *"love"* . . . isn't that so? He was inclined to deal in changes of identity more than I was. He absorbed bits of me, gestures, attitudes, easily. In a sense, he had to be me at times, sort of, what-he-was had to include me to his satisfaction, although he disliked it that I was *bourgeois*—un-utopian, unapocalyptic, unshrewd. It is rare in accounts of love to describe being loved as a difficult matter and varying greatly from lover to lover—and as a responsibility, moral and emotional . . . And as a persecution. It felt dangerous, it felt illicit. I did not want it, any more than I wanted it from my mother, say . . . I suppose this was the automatic part of it all. I did feel it as a form of power and amusement. And I did want to be or to include Onni, not exactly as he wanted to be me, but to ease jealousy; I wanted to be like him without having to have his life or pay the prices he paid to have his life.

He had to take possession of that in me—of *the belovèd kid* or some such thing. He put his arms around me again, cautiously. The shy boldness in his embracing me for-no-reason except to rumple and display "ownership" of a younger brother—I mean that was the style of it—was physically unsettling . . . perhaps passionate . . . He was like someone setting fire to the room. And yet also he was reaching for the leash of an animal. I had no feeling that sexual desire was involved, only that vanity was. I felt my own value and felt that his passion toward that "value" was to overturn it.

"Be peaceful," I mumbled. Then: "Ha-ha, ha-ha-ha." I started to laugh again. I felt like someone buried in a war or revolution with him, and I was in an underground fort, under a garden, and I could just barely see and feel through a periscope that looked through leaves and tendrils at the world . . . I wanted to be freer to think and feel.

Then he said, "Your shirt . . . Your shirt . . . I want your shirt . . ." And he went and picked it off the floor and put it on.

"Leave me alone," I mumbled, deeply moved by love-without-love—or something. It made me want to be naked but not with him. I wanted to use this sense of myself with someone who was not him, who was simpler . . .

I don't think he understood . . . except sexually . . . In a way, we were comic figures . . . We were inclined, perhaps unwisely, as *collagistes* to be thieves . . . of ideas and of everything else . . . mere children, really, beginners, magpies, boy-crows, rapists, junior artists.

"Put on my shirt, Nino," he said in a sad voice. "Be me for a while . . ."

4

SO WE EXCHANGED SHIRTS. "We are going to be each other," he said. "You must use my name with the girls and speak only Italian . . . And I will be you . . ."

"Sure," I said and puffed some more and was filled with wild love but not for him in his present state but for him overall and as an average important event in my life that gave rise to the wild, unknowable, unutterable love I felt.

Narcissism? A bit. In part. It really was more for the half-comprehension I felt.

Leaving his apartment he somehow looked like me, a more tightly knit, a more potent-eyed me, but much shorter. Outside in the queer as-if-rhyming noises of the *calle* among the people and again in the closed-in meanderings of the *Merceria* he goaded me to pinch girls' bottoms as we passed them: "Do it the way I do it . . ."

He did it always as a joke, a little cruel. Then all at once, I began. I did it my way—well, a burlesque of him. I was good-looking that year, for a while, burnished and young—it happens like that for boys. I was admired. On the *Merceria*, a girl wheeled and smiled at the sight of me, at the joke, the joke being me, my face, my eyes, the ridiculous deadpan staring at her . . . the me she saw was me being Onni in burlesque—and in his shirt—but with my mind in my eyes, and the sexual possibility in me for us, her and me, like a tear in my silence, in my hard-eyed stoned fatuity and falsity and fullness of desire.

I did not really like her but I was drawn to her for that reason, that I did not like her or feel a need to protect her. Onni put his hand on my burning face from behind with my asinine smile on it and said to the girl, "*Ecco, il poverino satiro.*"

Onni had his other hand on the back of my shoulder, on the shoulder blade, the wing-bone of my back. So it was a puppet dance, a ventriloquist show, a bit of Pygmalion, a brotherly act of corruption, his urging me on and my being inspired by his urging, my willingness to do this to placate him.

I am, however, a deeply dangerous person. I said with a

funny surge of breath to the unknown girl, "*Ti amo . . .*" Then: "I have followed you for three days . . ." It was me-as-burlesqued-Onni speaking, not a direct imitation, you understand, but a modification, a failure and yet a correction, a mockery and a show of real capacity.

And I was not really a puppet . . . I was astonishing to him . . .

She said, "*Dio*, I have been in Venice only a few hours . . ." She was a pretty girl with a comic cast to her expression and a sensual quality that some girls have to being about-to-be-ravished. She was upper-bourgeois but perhaps without money. She had long, romantic, auburn hair and large, high breasts and slender hips; but she was a rather short girl, but fresh-motioned. Her eyes had a sad, bruised, shadowed expression but comic. She had large, fleshy lips. She gave the effect more of pallor than of color. I had a sense of saddened greed in her and of cleverness but not of poetry or of intellect. I would not have approached her at another time. Her style struck me as one of willful performance and pride and conceited ambition. She hardly glanced at Onni, whose manner alone, without his looks, was worth a glance of admiration. So, she was a bit stupid sexually. I said cruelly of Onni, "He's the rich one," and she glanced at him brightly then.

The mixture of fear in the girl, a kind of narrowness, with an Italianate audacity was very striking and pleasing. The fear was self-righteous and had a churchgoing tinge. Her sense of us as demons and then her eagerness to address the demons, and some self-loving quality of feeling safe, made a poor impression on me. But that attracted me strongly.

The soul's anguished search for autonomy, for its own separate power, separate even from goodness or from ordinary pleasure, is unending. I was in a mood to be autonomous.

5

MY INNER WORLD of consciousness was a little like a mad Venetian house, warehouse rooms and staircases and frescoes that moved and flickered and damp, truly mad rooms and staircases. And this house was prepared and lit for vanity and friendship, festively, everyone in masks, and, so, wasn't a home or private consciousness—or not exactly. The lights flickering on the water and the music in the rooms were for guests, were for this outward moment in one's life, one's first moments of general citizenship.

It is this that—forgive me—made me seem attractive to some people at that time, and for a while, to Onni—do you see? My anxiety to live and breathe was doubly and trebly intoxicated because of the time thing—*it was time* and one was restless and ignorant, but not entirely ignorant, and one was impatient in the blowy and luminous veils of all the intoxications that were as if caught on my eyes and lips and in my eyelashes and in the muted Venetian basso continuo of my heartbeat, a veil, a veiling more than any matter of secrets. Or of bloody desires.

The quality of defenselessness the girl had was, if I might say so, a bit showy. Silla had a harmed quality which she somehow tried to turn into the quality of having a charmed life and of being lucky—this created a very melancholy effect. She was a professor's daughter, and I very much wanted to be ruthless— or at least sophisticated and hard-to-fool. I don't think her parents were honest people. She had a brute of a young brother, she told me later, she had a complete set of family stories, she said she had an angel of a much younger brother, athletic and mournful and musical and quite emotional but tough and not a drinker like her father and other brother. She hinted at a family within her family—these were her descriptions. She was intelligent and quick, tactical, not analytical, not really subject to emotion, only to pride.

Her inner world, the Bolognese *casa* inside her, had a chapel but was mostly dark and was filled now and again by flashing lights, otherworldly, sometimes movie-like, and sometimes she was lit up inside in a hard and clear way, smartly. The rooms had an orderly alignment and seemed to be set out according to doctrine. Yet she seemed incredibly secret. She had a quality of bordering on vulgarity of soul because of her sentimentality about the deceptions she practiced with everyone, her politeness, her anxiety to please, her quickness of wit, her schemes. No matter how she acted, she remained in her own view, a marriageable, pious girl. But she was comic and wild and adventurous. In the design, the surface appearance of the laughing defenselessness, the deception, the way it was set out and lit up in display was as if she was secular and festive-nerved, which she wasn't. She never was like that at all except as raw deception, perhaps wistful.

Of Onni, I would say his inner world was a collapsed palazzo, very grand, very ruined, with many of the rooms of state and some of the smaller rooms still whole, but with ruins around them, towering staircases among empty rubble, and pretty rooms visible in the feral darkness.

And with new rooms being built. The willfully unsettling and theatrical arrangement of the lights were his conscious intentions, the roles he played in the world—a version from later moments of a general citizenship like my fresh, new one.

When the girl said she had been in Venice only three hours, I said "I followed you in Bologna." I said it as if with command and with the full weight of what presence I had at that moment in my life. I had very little confidence and I had all the confidence in the world, and this was like a vibration of polite liveliness, of rambunctious half-mannerliness in me.

She smiled, at first in superiority, and then brightly, like a child, at the nonsense. "Never in Bologna," she said. "I would remember your shirt."

As she talked, she hunched her shoulders. But then she restored their posture, showing the size and height and firmness of her breasts, and she smiled knowingly—as if festive-nerved. Then she put her head back and laughed: she produced a procession of Italian sounds that began as spiritual amusement because I had such a dark soul, such a liar's soul, although I was a mere boy really, and then she as-if-ran from room to room of feelings toward sad, greedy, secular amusement because I was a man really. "Never in Bologna," she said again. Then: "I know how much that shirt cost. I would remember it."

I am as a general rule physically shy. Usually I find life too complicated to lie and pretend. But I was impelled to masquerade. "My name is Onni," I said and stood with my hips and body noticeable.

But what was so strange and ugly was that I knew I should not choose her. She was not *valuable* to me . . . a difficult girl who would not capture my imagination and who was a problem for my conscience.

Onni *always* was in favor of my further corruption. He was fatherly or brotherly that way, male—but motherly in a sense since that was what his mother had done to him, you see.

Silla liked a lyric tone not like any tone in use among the people I knew but out-of-date, corny: "Yes, I remember your shadow sweeping past me when you followed me in Bologna . . ." And she laughed again, pretty much as she had before. She didn't have a large repertoire.

And then I laughed and was quite excited by all of this, by her, not by her directly, but by the little drama of good and evil. My sense of things is not that of someone wellborn, but it might be compared to that if one is not being carefully snobbish about it. As I said, I did not want to protect Silla or regard her highly —I was in a state of lunatic vanity—but I wanted Onni or God or some law that favored girls from Bologna to protect her. And me. Or not. You see, I believed or knew or half-knew that if one was "passionate," nothing, nothing at all, not a word, not a handshake was possible with any rationality. I think it was on this occasion, on a number of occasions at this time, that I first contemplated making it a rule not to write a book until I was old enough to know how things turn out for people—including me —that I would not be merely guessing at things in literary ambition but would be picturing them in some sobriety of information. I had a very strong sense, or a clear one perhaps, of Silla, and of Onni's "games," and of my naïveté and very sudden power anyway, if I might call it that. I had a very large store of undirected passion, of available emotion, and I wanted this situation to continue, and I thought I was very clearheaded, but I was not clearheaded at all, do you see? Onni *was* the puppetmaster of a scene that was a parody, a travesty in this new way, which he could not very well control.

Such malice and travesty have as always a sensual aura in the cheapness of the bodily self and the carelessness about kindness, or at any rate, they have a bodily quality which is patently corrupt . . . This was clear to Silla, too, I am sure, the blatant corruption in our flirting, the three of us. I accepted it all as a sexual compromise. All at once, Onni stamped his foot in the *calle*, demanding that I look at him. But I merely grinned and did not withdraw my attention from Silla. Rather, I walked on, my arm around her, talking and half-laughing while Onni short-leggedly stalked along being silent and imitating me—me at other times, another me—but then near *San Zulian* stamped his foot again and said, "I am going . . ."

I turned and showed him my face, my attention. He was an interruption. I wanted him to go. I was fed up with his corruption and ego and anxious to benefit from them without his presence. I was anxious to punish him merely out of autonomy and restlessness . . . And because he was "passionate" in this latest incarnation of him and not cool as he was before. I was anxious to make love to Silla, most likely not in a kind way. I did not want to face anything clearly.

It amused me to mix my travesty of him with my being myself in my turning to him and saying airily, as Onni, and then with uplifted face as Nino, "Good-by . . . *Ciao* . . ." I don't know why I was so vile. Love is unclean, I guess. Much of the time, some love, most love, all human love.

6

THE HUMAN MIND is not particularly sensible. Really now, how can it deal with the aspects—all the aspects—of things? Independence and autonomy mean you resist anyone's, everyone's power, perhaps all the time. Resisting, you are hardly free of anything except in a way; you are free from that power's having more say than it does. Running away seems like freedom, but it is also a form of helplessness for a while in which personal power—powers of attraction and resistance, real ones, not ones played at aphrodisiacally—command you and your fate spartanly.

The mind works with partly shabby and perhaps shameful tatters of reason in its own advanced calculus and geometries and its own local, rural trigonometries with an illiterate brilliance—facing and analyzing and working out very little—which is hard to explain and which creates a deserved air of emotional disaster.

A smile, the tonality of a smile, something in the gaze of the eyes and in the posture of the shoulders while one remarks to the pretty girl, "I am not a romantic sort," helps show you have a youthful, bold, ignorant, anarchic autonomy generating more and more power at the age you are. And arousing more resistance. The power thing keeps shifting—especially with Italian women. People with *fascist souls* hate this. In adolescence, a perhaps counterfeit autonomy and independence and power of choice are part of one's reality, are part of the supple excitements of one's physical reality—unchildish children, freed souls. Escaped Casanovas, a young-man version, a young-woman version, now in the *calli* of Venice, Silla and a tall young man, newly not a boy, are moving in the glare of their recently assumed autonomy.

I did not summon Onni's ghost-presence in my mind. I was him or me as I chose—I wasn't embarrassed with Silla or not much. I felt, oh, comparatively, that the light of consciousness-in-the-world was turned on in me, and that I was genuinely in the world. I could attract and fuck, flirt and defend myself autonomously. Was I afraid? No. Yes and no. I was strong and up-to-the-minute—lonely: reality is so many-angled and so motionful that though I want to say that I was aware of the issue of boredom, it's only half-true that I was. I was more aware of what I would say now was a mistaken sense of Silla's autonomy, her wishes. I mistook her desire to live, to have a good time, for autonomy.

To distract me from my usual reality, my role, and to attach me to her, she swept Onni's sunglasses from my face and she ran off with them in that ancient form of flirtation, that rough innocence, shepherdess and shepherd boy. I chased *her* through the streets behind *San Zaccaria* toward *San Lorenzo*, chased her twisting figure and whirling skirt, the unimaginably changeable shapes of her body, her flying hair as she ran and dodged between narrow walls among the tourists and the others, the local passersby. Running, using my hands and arms and shoulders to fend off the walls, bouncing and caroming, re-angling myself for the next part of the laughing, breathless sprint, along the straight canal near the Carpaccio *Scuola San Giorgio* I caught her, and the heat of running, its motions, arms and legs, this had broken into my face, my hair flopped back and forth. This modern moment of paganism—these were not childhood games, this weight of another person's will—their autonomy. The sensation of running, as a small child chasing another child, disappeared from my memory, running children in narrow spaces, and Onni, a pretty child, that was gone.

I laugh, "Ha-ha," in that genitalled, possessive way of a boyman—I offer no apology for these things: I was being bad, badsouled . . . warm-blooded . . . Silla put her arm through mine and leaned against me as we strolled along the *Riva degli Schiavoni*. As we walked, a lot of people, many, many people greeted me. The blooming of a young man is a commonplace of small Venice . . . All Venice knows . . . I was beautiful for a year, for one luminous year. Older women pandered me for friends. Most men liked me in some peculiarly direct way. But the strangest thing was that nearly everyone commented on what I looked like . . . It was part of daily language, a topic—my looks, my looks as clearly my character (for this little while).

The words, the attention-expressed-in-words, is as if wind-blown; it is dramatic; it is sensual, sexually goading; you have this vague role in stories, in a lot of stories, some with enemies, rivals, spies in them. What is so painful and ruinous day by day is the sensation of power in this personal beauty which is so troubling and ambiguous. It is a darkness in a lot of ways; you are in danger from others; at moments you are filled with impatience to get what you want; at moments you are filled with laughter. At others with waiting. It is a spotlit and temporary—and hot-blooded—state with no privacy to it and no real rumination about it possible; it is all action and sensation; it is all surface and reaction. Silla wanted to kiss in public, in front of people. "Kiss me now," she said near the Bridge of Sighs; huddling quite closely, we kissed and she twisted her breast against me, quite stringently. And she groaned.

The value you have in a moment when you bloom is based on your having no real value except that of attraction and purpose—it does not much matter who you are to the question of money. Now you are chiefly this one thing, a human sacrifice really . . . it has its giddy and profound sweetness too . . . And meanness, the needlelike thing of power, of power over people's awareness of themselves: this is an obvious part of the odd mixture that includes sweetness. I made a slapping *gesture* to show her I wanted her to stop. Then she said she wanted to pray and we went to *San Zaccaria* and she prayed for *twenty minutes*. And I gazed at the Bellini—it all felt very traditional. Then we went to the nearby *campo* and sat outside and had *apéritifs*. Children played near us, calling to each other and to a dog in treble voices, and the dog, self-consciously I thought, forced its own bark to a treble pitch trying to speak to the children.

On the way back to the Piazza, we ran into Onni who drew us down a side *calle*, where he and I smoked hash, Silla being game for a puff, a single puff, but no more. Inhaling, Onni asked how Silla's breasts could manage in the *calli*—he meant they were so big. He spoke with malice and snobbery and yet *permissively*. So that Silla told him to be quiet but laughed her fixed laugh, not entirely displeased with him. We sat at Quadri's while the shadows lengthened. Silla did not smoke hashish but she drank. A lot. An American Onni and I knew who lived in Venice in the summer, Drew Allerton, came and sat with us; for a while his chic silenced Silla. My brother Carlo came by. And others. In the faintly graying, late, horizontal light, in the tent of shadow which the hour and the architecture had erected over us, everyone at our table was drunk or stoned at least a little. The waiter hovered; Onni offered him the remaining half of a hashish cigaret; after the waiter took it, Onni treated him with that cruel and aware and humanly inhumane Italian way of dealing in Italian class differences that somehow excited Italians. Silla, at first awed by how chic a group we were, after the Camparis took on a spoiled rich girl's restlessness—perhaps she was imitating something in a movie but her being like that added to the late-adolescent chic we had. Drew said to Carlo who was boasting about some expansion in production that this was a suicidal age of history but, "You will manage," he said to Onni pointedly, which startled me. I hadn't been paying attention to history, to men choosing their roles or at least their opinions among the events. Silla's and my feet were entwined under the table. Onni began making eyes at an older woman at the next table—it was a moment of erotic massacre really. Onni jumped up saying, "*Ciao . . . ciao . . . ciao . . .*" and went off under the arch of the *Orologio.* The rest of us changingly sat on and ate and drank, and then we went dancing and drinking at a little bar back toward *Santa Maria Formosa.* People came and went, and it was very complicated, warm and blurred, very pleasant . . . I am lying. It was strained. People we ran into treated Silla as décor, like a pet dog of mine. Silla had moved on from her heiress manner to a sort of a loyal-hearted, sluttish, Bolognese party girl. She kept on being "sexy," rubbing around and nearly satisfying my un-sentimental excitement . . . That excitement grew leaden and a bit groggy and part of an angry vanity and general lostness. I told Silla that I disliked passion; and she clucked over me, became demonstrative, quite arch, and to my surprise sympathetically tragic—beyond romantic passion, sort of. She was, I guess, a fool in public in my view, a masochistic exhibitionist. It was flattering and sexual, her public availability to me, but it was peculiar too—I had not asked for it from her. The proffered sadism was enticing, but I had very little room to have my own feelings except as a sort of tantrum among all the people around us, all the events. I didn't want to be a fool. I became a villain defen-sively—in order not to be a fool. But I had hidden and distant feelings and a mouth of cool and still more distant idealism. Silla kept trying to kiss or touch my mouth with her hands, and I often turned my head away. She paid little or no attention to this except to be teased—she was dogged in pursuit.

So, a gloomy pleasure. Perhaps it was Onni's world that I was in. But he had left this world for that of acting and the theater, for those adventures in metamorphosis. Drew and Silla had more longing for adventure and meaning here, in these matters, than Onni or I. My brother Carlo had a ritualized sense of fun—he believed in this world of fun. The meaning and the adventure for me largely came from the sudden truth-telling: "No, I do not love you . . . No, I am not infatuated . . ." Or from lying, which I refused to do; I felt insulted erotically by having to lie. The music as background was often good and carried feeling, and sometimes in the heat and laughter a bit of imagination took off and flew and showered a sense of amusement and meaning. Onni showed up; I was eating a *pannino*; he called me *Attila the Hungry*—this was somehow very far from Drew's mood. I bullied Onni, too. Not deeply drunk, cynical and a bit bitter, I was half-erect the whole time and logy, heavy-lidded. At one point I walked out moodily; I wanted to be alone for a while. But they all came hurrying after me—Drew and Silla, Carlo, and some kids from school. Not Onni. At some point they were calling, "Nino, Nino, Nino, Nino," antiphonally, echoingly, loudly, ritualistically in the *calli*, in the lush, long-dying, palely purple twilight glare of the last light in the city. I was leaning against a wall in the *Campo Gallo* and smoking a cigaret. An effeminate old man with a bouquet of roses took one rose from his bouquet and bent over and laid it at my feet before he walked on in the glaring dusk. When they found me, Drew picked up the rose and handed it to me. We went and got slices of pizza; a tourist took our picture as we ate. We went back to the *Campo Gallo*, to the movies, a French story with a suicide in it, and two embittered, knowing lovers who outlive the ones they love who don't love them. Silla pawed me throughout the movie; and Drew watched us in the flickering light.

We went dancing again. Onni appeared, and we spoke and smoked hashish and parted again. My evening made no sense —it was a piece of a story of how I learned to live. You have to move in a gang of some sort—or people push you around. Also, you're too alone. You maintain a self-defense-and-potency bloc—some of it is bluff, is strutting . . . Some of this is to protect your rights to the girls you're with . . . My tie with Silla.

We went to a club in Mestre in someone's boat. The noise and vibration and crowdedness on the boat made me gravid with sexuality . . . all that throbbing . . . and Silla and I got into heavy stuff in the shadows, guarded by Drew and others. Still, we did not cross some line—we were probably showing off our self-control to ourselves. Onni showed up in Mestre, and people paid attention to me more than to him—my vanity was sated and gravid . . . Italianate. In Mestre, Silla and I actually made out on the dance floor, I came while we danced, which satisfied some elements of her exhibitionism, but I was pale and unsatisfied. She came with me into the men's john where I cleaned myself. She was floridly defiant and sleepy both. Guys came in and there were remarks and shouts. Silla tried to say all this was "love," but I refused responsibility for her scandal as I had all along. My head was pounding and I was utterly arrogant by then in a thoroughly youthful way . . . Fatuous, or not, I was a sort of hero—don't ask me why. In the motorboat back, people paid most attention to me, the hero of the night. Silla sat half on my lap . . . half on Drew's. I said irritably, "I like nothing." About the night.

"I'm like that," Silla said.

Bored—and it was very late, three in the morning—Drew and Silla and I were walking on the wide wooden railing of the bridge at the *Accademia*, not on the foot part. We had become accustomed to one another, and were friendly, sort of grateful for not being lonely by then. I sensed him. I turned my head, and Onni, *solo*, as he had been the whole noisy evening, was on the *Campo San Stefano* side watching us. He drew near across the pavement. It changed the whole evening, it changed the meaning of everything that he had been keeping an eye on us, on me, all evening. And had come looking for me in the *streets* of Venice as in Mestre earlier. It is hard to tell what interests someone, what suffering in this regard will grip them. Silla, Drew, everything was caught in this other meaning as well. Greetings hovered in the night air but were unspoken because of this other story—even Silla did not speak. In a posture of serious rudeness, a grown-up posture, a bit grief-stricken and menacing as well as rude, in his half-professional beauty as a young actor, Onni drew near in the incomplete darkness and climbed up on the other railing across the width of the footbridge, across from us and below while we waited, still in the silence, teetering statues, windblown drunks, high in the air at the topmost point of the bridge and a little beyond . . . I was above dark water, above wafting and scooped bits of reflected light in the unstable surface below, and he was separate from us—wavering, modern, un-certain evangelists—demoted now and focussed on him.

Physically and psychically, it is an extraordinary sensation in actual moments, the sensation of being liked and struggled for or over, the cause of emotion in someone else. An actor, perhaps any artist—a painter, a composer, a singer or popular priest or demagogue—is hardened at this. But for an amateur, a newcomer, a weight of shame and an obscure humiliation are implicit. The inner heat, and the inner brushings and whirrings of compassionate sympathy, warm, immediate sympathy only beginning to be trained into cool and cold distances, politic re-sponse, self-interest, pity, these things alive in you are frightening along with the other, with being liked. You do not know if you are being summoned to a story or perhaps given an answer to childhood questions—or a reward, given a reward. Childlike in-ner sobbing or gasping in the actual moments mixes with cold *flickers* of perception. The sense of power is warm and cruel, especially sexually warm. The blood flows in tireless exercise of will, as in a parade, but not a childhood parade.

To be erectile in this reality is to be potent not entirely at your will. It is someone else's will and feelings which are active, it is the "atmosphere" which is causing this; you are reactive. It is all a bit entangled and indirect but not really unclear. It is mostly lit up and clear. You understand it is not yourself but a self you might become, a role in this *obscure* carnival—perhaps for months or years or for much of your life. And then you might lose it. You lose a lot moment by moment. You have a sense in your blood, in your muscles, of your losing it . . . This was all obscure-and-romantic, you understand, and it was unromantic and unsettling and very real. One has been shaped or trained for power, for something like this, but one is inexperienced; one is dangerous—one's strength is that of a young animal.

But you do not know what your strength is. It is incompletely tested. One is vulnerable to swindles and deceptions and to various kinds of strength and coldness and menace. But one is feared moment after moment—feared like a tusked animal or a shout or like three policemen walking shoulder to shoulder, in unison.

One's glances have fearful weight, and so do the postures of one's head, and whether one looks down or up or to the side matters painfully. A politics is set up. One is amplified by the machinery of regard. One's scorn has great weight—it has the power to make someone flinch and perhaps hate you forever.

It is a form of musculature or of fleetness that leaves no sentimental decency possible. Hatreds, *flickers* of rivalry, a swollen sensitivity to being violated, the hint of one's own violence. Some women immediately grovel toward it, and some hate it and avenge themselves on it. Imagine that in an actual moment one is desireable, and that this desireability echoes and is reflected in the vault and crawl of moments, partly a joke, a *scherzo*, but yet it is something that matters, sexually, violatingly, if no other way. It is tremblingly, fragilely real in actuality, a form of adventure, and not in actual moments a form of wealth and safety except as offering adventure.

In terms of adventure, one is a royal figure. But one is so ignorant. Really such a vast ignorance and unsuitability and the heat of the bodies and the flickering of eyes—you at the center —and a certain stiffness in you caused by this as you are circled by the faint strutting or kowtowing of others' attention . . . By others' faces like paper lanterns in the warm dark. Everything is grotesque with life, with liveliness. The atmosphere of carnival, of knockabout and massacre in such phrases as *I knocked them dead, I was a knockout* is unmistakable . . . You shake some people up . . . The inner isolation is so complete that pleasure is a little as if the brain rolled naked from the skull and sensingly and unprotectedly, in exaggerated and massive sensitivity, among everyone around you.

It is a dark state, perhaps cheap or cheapening, perhaps self-emptying. The mutual massive ignorance is as perceptibly enormous as the dark around the discreet lamps in the *calli* and *campi* on either side of the bridge, on each bank of the *Canalazzo*. The intelligence, the wistful rottenness and malleability and longing, the corruption is like a slender light in a *calle* from an overhead lamp, set in motion by the wind.

This moment when the lights circle and sway in the wind, the wild tang of reality, this in the dark heat of the scirocco—it is the third night of the scirocco—in the wet stench that rises from the canal—holds an odorous fatedness, a Dionysiac readiness, a transposition to vanity, to an effrontery, unbearably unwise—and palpably present in the air. It seemed to form a cradle for the monstrous birth of events which did not need to occur.

Onni running up the other railing, on tiptoe, arms outspread, in the effeminate and neat postures of an acrobat, a *saltimbanco*, called out, "*Bello, no?* Nino . . ."

Silla giggled, one of those abrupt intelligent Italian girl giggles, an admission of sophistication. Onni went forwards and backwards; he scampered back and forth; he bent down and, gripping the railing, rose onto his hands; he walked on his hands in the dark-and-light on the railing, his legs in the air, his shirt—my shirt, a knitted polo, a faded, now whitish salmon or pink—sliding over his head blinding him. He walked on the railing, waving his feet, then singing the Fascist anthem, "Giovinezza."

Jumping down, he came over to our railing and jumped up and came running along the railing so swiftly and readily that one could see him as an apprentice-this-other-thing, this expert figure. He swung himself around Silla, holding her and swinging her out—she made a slight noise; she was a good athlete, quite brave—and he swung her in again, restoring her balance as he ran. Drew jumped down onto the bridge out of his way and into the bright light on the walkway. Onni ran on toward me, shadow and light, a motion of muscular mass and deft legs, in my shirt, this spirit of masculine beauty. Perhaps in pain. I have never for a moment felt finely made or shaped or handsome. I can feel only an aura pulsing in someone else's regard—the bribed mirror—but I felt it for a moment, felt my "beauty," mind you, felt it as particular and real but not explained to me yet in my life—when Onni, when that marvellous, gesticulating face—with the shadows bulging and fleeing over its surfaces, over his eyes —with the weak light slipping and silently popping on his cheeks, his nose, felt it in the heat from his wide chest in my old shirt, near and oncoming, when he was less than a yard away and beginning to reach out his arms to shift me on the railing. I felt it and I stepped off into dark space backwards out over the water of the *Canalazzo*. Turning in space as I dropped, I lost track of physical sense, Onni's shirt rising and flapping on my warm skin in the sliding air, the sight of the dimly lit façades along this part of the Grand Canal curving toward the *Bacino* while I dropped: this lost coherence. Venice and the curiously sexual heat of life at that time for me and the curious inexplicability to my senses of my motion downward was obliteratingly freeing. I threw my arms forward, and kicked upward; I curled into a ball and tucked my face into my knees; I hit the water face-down, or nearly so; and made a great splash and entered the real darkness, the treasure house of cold, slimy, real darkness, behind the shakey glitter of the soft surface plies of the water.

This was not so illegal then as it later became. The long descent below the surface, the sly embrace of the water, the embrace of death by drowning, ah, the un-naïve glamor.

When I surfaced, no one called out to ask if I was all right. The air slipped and slid twiningly around me and blew in my hair as the others dived in, jumped in, from the railing, from not so high up or high up, in silence or with muted cries, even Onni.

It was all so twisted with particularity, that my body became a hideous, vertical, mad smile. I was the successor to the amatory princeling I'd been as a child with something like that child's blundering grace returned as well.

I drew my hands over my wet hair. Onni said, rising from the water, "Ah . . . ah . . . ah . . ." Then, in my ear: "She is stupid . . . you prefer me . . ." His face and its moody suffering in the dark and half-light, my feelings of embarrassment, of lostness, of compassion, and of cold pity and repulsion—and of pleasure—and of fear and disgust—the Dionysian and Apollonian seconds ticked, and pride and assertion partly armored me.

One cannot breathe neutrally. And one's mind cannot shut off once life begins. In the unstillness of things one becomes protective toward Onni. Silla had lost her belt or taken it off, and her dress rose around her in the water where she treaded water and sang part of a Mozart aria about Poseidon. Onni was more interesting as a person to me than Silla was but he was not as sexually interesting to me. We swam in together, all four of us. The moon was shining. The hot wind blew. Silla sang fragments of baroque arias about conquering or defeated rulers—Caesar, Chosroes, Mithridates, Alexander, Cleopatra—mostly off-key.

We went to Drew's family's apartment in the *Dorsoduro* on one of the straight canals. His sister, his rumored lover, Margo-Donna, was there, a girl with hot dark eyes and bangs and a shapeless smallish body and who took a lot of drugs and a lot of lovers, and who was a good painter, in a way, and quite a good singer, with a very true voice. She was said to be very intelligent. She joined in on one of Silla's arias and corrected the tune and the pronunciation as too modern. She found bathrobes for me and Silla and Onni, who flirted with her at once.

He was groping Margo-Donna and playing footsie with Drew and chain-smoking. We smoked a hookah, drawing hash smoke first through red wine and then through vodka.

I did not want to be a romantic figure honestly or vulnerably. At one moment it seemed too brave and true, true to the heart and soul, and to human history, by God. I seemed cowardly and dimly American of the wrong sort, then at the next moment, not cowardly but *fine* and smart—shrewd. Onni's world, this corner of it, seemed disgusting. Silla's hand on my thigh inside the robe moved across the nerve endings and the little hairs and the loosened and unwrinkled scrotum. Onni moved and was beautiful and sullenly in earnest over there across the room with the others or was not in earnest but was mocking and not beautiful but difficult.

I think it is very difficult to describe the hard edge of will in people, the wish in each person in a group to have his or her own way, and then the contradictory weave of discipline and sense of rank and of putting up with not getting his or her way, and the differences between people in this, some like Drew being unassertive, and Margo-Donna being so assertive, and Onni being different, being a performer and "a man" now.

I had, for much of my life, been shy and private, and now I was this object and subject of study by the others, this power surrounded by everyone in their doubts and tantrums of cleverness . . . and their docilities. It is a little bit as if a Red Indian had become the Prince of Venice . . . a real-life variant of Tarzan's going to London: does Nino want a cigar, does Nino want a banana, does Nino want a backrub . . . Silla's hand was on my knee, then she stirred and her hand was on my abdomen . . . At one point I gave a Tarzan yell, which, of course, no one understood . . . not even Onni.

Margo-Donna, whom Onni had just pushed away, asked me why I liked Onni-the-beast. It wasn't just rhetorical. She repeated it. My mother has said that I have a punitive nature.

I said naïvely and egocentrically and, I suppose, quite ruinously, "He was the first one who ever loved me. Or thought that I was handsome."

"You're not handsome," Margo-Donna said. "You're just young. You're just interestingly grotesque . . . Onni *is* handsome. You're just a little puppet."

"Not so little," Drew said.

Margo-Donna said, "Onni never told anyone he loved them . . . He doesn't give compliments . . ." And she kicked him. He moved his leg away from her on the floor and went on watching her and me.

"He did not say it, he *said* it," I said, meaning it had been clear.

She shook her head. She started to crawl over the carpet toward me, saying, "Show me."

"No," I said, fending her off with my bare feet. Her aggression had been physical all the time. I said to Onni, "You show her." Silla threw her pale arms around me and began to kiss me, not inexpertly.

Drew put *his* arm around Onni and said, "No one can make Margo-Donna understand anything . . ." The eye, the eyeball is set behind the flutter of lashes and of the lid—this is in a world of violence among minds that are violent—and sometimes the eye catches fire from that world . . . But it also grows confused and resistant with rage and angry sorrow and contempt. The hot wind, the scirocco, came through open casement windows. Onni said in English, "Why don't you fuck the cow and get it over with?"

Silla, who was quite a willful, strange girl, said, "Yes, why don't you fuck me, the cow," and she looked frail and long-suffering but ready, and not insulted . . .

Onni's face, however, was awful . . . sincere . . . full of suffering . . . But he was never sincere. So what did it mean? The scirocco boomed dully and had the whining pertinacity of Arab music. Drew said with voyeuristic good-heartedness, "We have lots of bedrooms . . . There's a little bedroom behind that door." Margo tried to pull open my robe: "Let's see what it's all about." I pulled away and went to the door of the little room. Silla remained behind. I said, "Silla."

"What?"

"Silla, Silla, Silla," Onni said.

I never expected events in the world to happen in my style. Actions were as foreign as languages with their own style. In the small side-room, with its two small windows in which the wind howled, I undressed Silla who twisted and offered advice but who at moments paused and was lovely and still, pink, quietly alive. Silla's sexual wishes seemed self-concerned in the way Onni was jealous . . . for himself separately from me. In each moment of gesture that they made, you were not supposed to suspect the existence of private will in them or see how momentary and capricious they were.

Silla's were not whore's kisses. In catching her breath between kisses, she fumbled with my hair or my genitalia: "I never did *this* before . . . Oh, they will hear me . . . I'm noisy in bed . . . Nino, I will go to Hell for this . . ." Fumbling clumsily at my body: "I am risking damnation for you . . ."

I gripped her hard in the hope that she would be quiet, I bit her lightly. Finally I slapped her in a fake way and said, "Be still . . . Don't tell me . . ." But I was already lost among her roles and in my desire for the lovely back-and-forth of signals in sex and for body's response to body.

When I slapped her in the fake way, she grabbed my hand and kissed it. "Pull my hair," she said. "No. Don't. That just destroys me . . ." It felt like a moment of slapstick, of drunken youth—an indulged young man—but I pulled her hair with both my hands and kissed her large, fleshy mouth, harshly, trying to be a good lover in the other language of event, so to speak. It seemed exciting but it was an effort. Breaking the spell, I lay my naked self atop her . . . I don't know if all of me on top of her was suffocating . . . Sometimes airlessness is pleasure. The pleasure of such massive domination is not in being dominating but in one's rights to it being automatic, physical . . . Merely I was so much bigger than she was . . . I kissed her eyelids gently, but with command, and said, "Don't damn yourself for me . . ." while reaching for a cigaret in a rather cool display of who-I-was on this occasion.

"Oh you fatal Protestant," she said in Italian, melodramatically. Her large white breasts were of imperfect curvature but of fine firmness, pinkish in splotches luridly when excited and with a dusting of freckles on her upper chest. Her abdomen was very pale.

"Not in the rear," she said when I entered her from the front and met an obstruction. Also, then at once, she began to recite Hail Mary's. I muttered, "Ah . . . Ah . . . Ah . . ." in a wistfully sweet and then in a rather unsweet voice as I shoved.

"Don't pull my little hairs down there," she said. I was doing no such thing. But in the moth-swarm flutter of her protests and prayers, I pushed at the obstruction, and she cried out, "Make love to me, Nino!" in a false enough voice that I suspected something.

Leaning back on my heels, still partway in her, I say, boy-ishly, piggishly, "I don't want all this drama, Silla . . ."

She said, "Ah, ah, ah . . . I am overcome with passion, Nino . . ." Her fire-tinged and blushing body indicated some heat and was partly cold—slablike . . . She was in a pinkish and shadowy state.

"One-two-three . . . go . . ." Margo-Donna said at the closed door. "You're taking forever."

No matter how I shoved, the obstruction held . . . I did not get violent . . .

Onni called out in a harsh, Neapolitan voice: "Have you fucked her yet, Nino?"

"Get the hell away!" I shouted. I was not fully aware. I was stalled above her, partly in her. I lay atop her, the two of us pale in the lamplight, the scirocco howling at the windows. I was sweating. She smelled of cinnamon and of fish.

She said, "Have I a bad smell for you, Nino?" I must have sniffed. The belligerent intensity and completeness and quivering intelligence of her drama rested not on me but on millennia of Church doctrine, Church notions of event and of fate. It also rested on movies and books and ads and propaganda. The idea of mercy and of God's harsh protection as well as of Divine Love did seem even to me to outrank my erotic reality. At what point does "desire" have the cultural right-of-way? Where is an au-tonomy to match one's own seeming autonomy?

I was disappointed. I understood my Protestantism with a certain approval—understood it in my way.

She said in a soft, tuneless, as-if-sweaty voice, "Please, Nino, again . . . try again . . . *ancora* . . . *ancora* . . . *per favore* . . ."

Dutifully, and within the contract, I entered her again, shoved harshly. The head of the prick, now not so hard as it might be, ached. I started to pound and shove with the partly softened prick, and Silla groaned, lying slightly canted but not helping. I bounced out down there. Silla cried out, "Let it happen now! I want it to be you . . ." I slipped out again and on the shove to re-enter I bounced partway into the other entry, and she screamed, "No! You are too big! Never in the rear!"

I was not clearheaded, but I saw then the problem of semi-rape (or rape) and I saw that this had happened before, and I felt the honor of having been selected, but I was humiliated by the details of the problem and felt childish; and I was angry at her.

But I could not speak; that was partly the hash and partly my role: I did not know how to speak in it, and I did not want to talk to the girl. Silla addressed my silence . . . She explained, I think in practiced terms, that she was unbreakably guarded by a partly broken, but mostly unbreakable, protruding maiden-head. "The doctor says he will have to remove it surgically . . . The priests say it is from God . . . Do you want to try again? Maybe it will be magic for us now . . ."

7

IN MY VIEW I was not grown-up enough, and at the same time not simple and rapist-like enough for this real-life event to work out well. I hadn't the nerve or the will for the role Silla had chosen me for. My sexuality is very different. I felt that Silla had been clever . . . I felt humiliated, outwitted, used . . . And inept . . .

To have been Onni with Silla would have been far more suitable than to be myself. I knew this sullenly, practically . . . But did nothing about it . . . I was perhaps angry.

In the flickering of reality second-by-second, all this seemed to me to be very funny. Half-laughing to myself, snorting—stallion-like, but like a very young, very thin stallion however.

Silla kissed me, but when she touched me, I said, "No!" I disliked her, it seemed. But she might like that, like being despised and pushed around, while she had her way this other way. She had her systems. Each moment seemed a bigger space than one's thoughts and opinions and feelings about things in it could occupy or describe; so, one exaggerated. And melodramatized. In these loose, ill-fitting spaces of a moment.

She said with motherly condescension, "Do you hurt?"

My role was as the one who had chosen the wrong casket

in the fairy tale, who was not blessed in the fairy tale in her head.

She cuddled. She said, "Should I go to a doctor, my lord and master, and have it cut . . . Or should I wait for you—and God?"

My lips and mouth were swollen from necking. I climbed out of bed and went to the door and said with swollen lips, "My pants." They were handed in through the door. I said thickly to Silla, "Please, don't go to the *dottore* on my account . . ."

"Don't be cruel to me, my lord . . . *domine!*" she exclaimed. She scrambled out of bed and sank to her knees while grasping mine.

I peeled her off. Talking and walking with difficulty, I was still authoritative: "I want some air . . . No one . . . I don't want anyone with me . . . Silla, stop—" Margo-Donna said, "What is so bad about putting it in the hands of God, Nino?"

"Ask your prick," I told her.

Silla somewhat breathlessly said, "But, really, it was *wonderful* . . ."

I was relieved she was not publicly sarcastic. I was dressed in my damp pants and in Onni's ruined silk shirt. The others were talking, sometimes to me, and I said, when I heard my name repeated, "Leave me alone . . . This is too real . . ."

Sore from balked lovemaking, in a slightly loopy high-stepping way, I made my way outside. Onni was already there, sitting in a moored boat. Behind me the others watched from a window in the apartment.

8

EXTENDED AND ACCURATE descriptions of reality as in paintings and in the continuous moments of a piece of music are art. I did not speak to Onni or exactly not speak. I mumbled. And I did not look closely at Onni but I did not exactly not look closely at him. In the bubble and rumble of actual hot minutes, I saw Onni's face as a fish, armored with scales of foreign and watery feelings; it was the face of a creature of dim, great, strange depths.

But the truth in the moments is things change; and I also

saw a familiar face, simpler, and one I associated with a vacation from duty and from the possibility of guilt . . . I saw the absolution and illegality in our friendship.

Then I saw the person Onni was; then I went out of focus.

Onni said, "Do you want to go to Mestre?"

I pretended to silence. I saw he was in a mood similar to before, strong, harsh, focussed on me . . . I felt that he was not laughing at me . . . I felt my "duty" toward him, toward friend-ship. I felt some shame.

He said, "Do you want to go to the Lido? Do you want to go looking for girls?"

"They would only be real." They would have their lives. They would not be fantasies. Or simple. Now, in the flickering of the moments I paused and looked at him, but not importantly: I collected him, as we started along the *fondamenta*, his mood, his passion, the set of his lips, his lostness in his apprenticeship to art.

The lights of the *fondamenta* swung in the hot, strong wind, shifting the dark hollows from side to side around the sections of shaking light on the flat walkway of the *fondamenta* itself. I said aloud, "No such thing as a real fuck exists . . ." I did not know how to say that fictional and hallucinatory ones do not ever happen. I halted and stood still and said, "Give me a cigaret."

The wind was riffling my hair. "This *brutto* wind," Onni said lighting my cigaret. He said again, "Do you want to go to Mestre? Do you want me to find you a girl?"

I said, "No such thing as the kind of fuck you carry on about exists."

He stared at me. The wind was like a wreath of living rats nibbling at my hair. I started walking again. Onni said, "Perhaps we should all kill ourselves over you . . ."

I climbed down into a moored workboat and began to un-dress. Even the most ordinary reality is logical. I began to slip into the water of the canal over the side of the boat away from Onni . . . Onni asked, "Didn't she appreciate your white nakedness?"

Then, a moment or two later, he appeared in the cold water

beside me. His head was lifted; he was puffing on a cigaret. He stroked my trembling back as I swam breaststroke, my thin shoulder. Then when I paused to tread water he passed me the cigaret; it had some grains of hash poked in among the shreds of tobacco; I puffed and slipped away from him and off into the dark water . . . I swam far out into the *Giudecca*.

I jerked off in the water. The story slips into the silences of the errant mind paying little attention to what is real . . . The light from the *fondamenta* wavered on the crisscross pleating of the wind-ruffled water. Returning I swam in the shaking light. Fantasies and ideas were in my head. Onni put his hand on my arm but I shook him off.

Reality proceeds in its endless progression in the absence of miracle and the continuing untruth of fantasy.

I dressed and was still wet and walked along the *fondamenta* in my wet clothes. I had trouble walking—my knees had stiffened, my arms were tired.

"*Brutto Nino*," Onni said beside me. Trash bobbed in the half-lit water. The sky had started to lighten with morning. One has to say something, do you know? I felt inane and amateur. I did not know what to say. I said, "So this is what it's like to be eighteen . . ."

"What is it you want, Nino?"

"I want things to be ordinary." When I said it, it seemed incredibly stupid, my remark. It did not much matter that night if I was stupid, if I said foolish things. I would not be forbidden to speak. Everything I said had a real weight of practical importance in the actual world—of course, this is how fools are created in life.

He began to cry silently . . . God knows what his version of the night would be if he wrote it.

He lit his hash pipe, took one long puff, passed the pipe to me. I was hugging myself. He inserted the stem in my mouth and held it, and he said, looking into my eyes, "Are you happy, *Tesoro*?"

It jolted me that Onni was idealizing me. And youth.

I laughed jaggedly and choked on the smoke. "Shut up," I

said to him. One constructs male patience, male kindness. One creates its track in the motions of the world. "Shut up, my friend," I said and more or less relaxed into being with him.

"You asshole," he said in English.

The wind clung and pushed and whined in the passage. Onni, naked-faced in the lightening dark, looked around with darting eyes. We padded along the empty *fondamenta* of the *Zattere*, the *Giudecca* pale across the water, and in the paling sky, more and more brightly luminous, the yellow dawn came up. A broad band of glossily yellow brightness was in the sky to the east. The dawn poured pink and gray and pale-yellow light —Venetian pink—into the *calli*, hazey and tinted.

We found an open bar in *Santa Margherita*, a workmen's bar, the men with seamed faces and cracked, stained hands, and large, harsh voices—Onni and I knew some of them; you get to know everyone in Venice—and I had loved and hated them (when they rebuked me); but now they were foreign to me because I was young and my life had the shape it had. Two of them, *Matteo* and *Bartolomeo* . . . "Fucking all night, useless Leftists . . . Fools . . ."

I wet a handkerchief and knotted the corners and put it over my head against the hot sun outside. Onni was at this time half-talented, but only half, and half a clumsy fool as an actor. The men in the bar thought him insanely clever and were silent and awed when he said some threatening or boastful thing to them.

We went to another bar and drank a morning beer, stinging beer, and ate sausage. Onni talked, he muttered about the horror of being alive, the horror in life. He demanded a Utopia. He berated me in various derisive clichés. He discussed injustice— no, he only mentioned it—and the magnetism of evil and, oh yes, the validity and virility of rage, of political terrorism, death and blood and violence. He serenaded me dialectically in this way, paying no attention to me or to the recent events except in raising or lowering his voice, inserting a laugh or a snort, depending on my eyes, to increase his rhetorical effectiveness.

I ignored him. I opened myself merely to being outwardly who I felt myself to be, to being a real self, almost relaxedly, with him. The darkness of the interior of his mouth in the very hot early sun housed crows and blackbirds, croaking objurgations . . .

I said, "Let's not pretend to talk . . . Let's pretend not to talk." Meaning that silence was talk anyway.

9

CARTONS WERE BEING UNLOADED from barrows, and the stalls were being set up in the *campo* in the clear morning light when we started to walk again. The wind had died, and the sun was very hot. Onni bought the sunglasses of one of the workmen and gave me his. We pass *San Giovanni Evangelista* and I say, "Here we go round the mulberry bush . . ." The gathering morning strengthens its hold on the city. I walk in a spilled, taut quality of emotion—in an architecture of light. The noises of the city had a special quality emerging in the absence of the scirocco. Owned and goaded by my life, I walked in a painted city through painted air in a created world. I walk in step with Onni's perhaps lifelong caprice (one did not know yet). The ordinary, real, and ludicrous world has a sweet stillness, Venice as a continuous canvas with only sad, trapped elements of motion in it . . . It seemed that I alone lasted; everything and everyone else was brief, was condensed into fixed, clear meaning, and I was as alone in my continuousness as I had felt I was in earliest childhood. Do you understand me? Do you remember? The daylit canvas blows and stirs, picture-tinted, a flag, loosely curling and unwinding. Onni put his hand on my shoulder, then on the back of my neck, then on my arm . . . I touch him—his back, the back of his waist.

Onni said, "But you are as deadly as Christ."

"Hardly," I said.

In the creeping heat, we stop for coffee. Onni now hints he has killed a man. I listen. Has he killed someone? I am affronted as if I were a woman or a priest. Or saddened. Or jealous. I am not interested in his crimes but only in his condition of nerves-and-loneliness. In a small *calle*, he pulled a pocketknife, opened the blade and held it toward my chest: he said, "I wrong no one if I kill you—not even you care that much, you are such a dog," he said, and he burst out laughing.

I almost understand him. I leaned on my straightened arm, against the wall of the *calle*. Any remark I make will be low comedy in the light of the flop I was in terms of my refusal to be what he wanted. He is reaching for emotions he thinks I have—or so I read his face.

"Why do you make me unhappy?"

"Why shouldn't you be unhappy?"

"You have ugly feet . . . I have very good feet . . . I have narrow feet, nicer feet than you."

"Why are you talking about feet?"

"It is a common thing for lovers to talk about their *feet* . . ."

"We are not lovers." I ignore the knife . . . I start to walk away, but he blocks me with himself—he moves the knife to one side and he kisses me on the side of my face. Near the corner of my lips.

I flinched. Privacy for a young man in this matter, as in so many, is incomplete.

"You are always wrong," he says. Now we are shoving each other, half falling over, bending to the side, blundering against the walls of the cul-de-sac: "You are a piece of shit . . . *you*. *Stronzo, stronzo, stronzo* . . ." He is careful with the knife; he inflicts a long shallow scratch on my left arm.

"You asshole," I say.

He says, "*Fica . . . SPORCA FICA . . .*" and reaches for my arm and licks the blood.

I back off. "*Tu sei uno stronzo*," he mutters. "You need more hashish . . ."

In the shadowy dead-end *calle*, puffing on the hash cigaret, he pulls his shirttails out of his trousers and raises his shirt and runs his hand over his small stomach and its muscular markings, its muscular indentations, in a flare of exhibitionism as he puffs. He is erect in posture and sexually: "*Mondo stronzo* . . ." he says.

"*Nicht wahr*," I say inside some stoned role, leaning against the wall of the *calle*, my back to the wall, my legs at wide-apart propping angles. I mop my forehead. I fill the *calle* with an as-if-German heat, a young man of an insolent kind, not a good person. It is a role for me lately, it seems. I lick the shallow cut over and over. I stare at him.

While I puff on the pipe, he eyes me malevolently and struts a little in the narrow *calle*, patting his stomach and eying me. "*Sporco stronzo*," he says to himself. "Terrible . . . terrible . . ."

"Terrible, terrible . . ." I say.

He jerks: he flinches: there is a flicker passing through him. His face gleams sweatily. In the damp shadow in the *calle*, he says, "People throw up after fucking . . . *you* know *that, Caro?*" he says. He brought his head forward and made gagging noises. He continues, his face sweaty: "So, it is all difficult. *Dunque* . . . I wish to jerk off . . ."

In the motion of things, because of the principle of motion in companionship, it is his turn. He is the star again. In the dry procession of the moments, in the presence of *the-German-in-the-calle*, he will now go through the Inferno, Purgatory, and briefly gleaming Paradise of sexual sensation. In the plunge of moments—their speed and direction are uncertain—to be unjudging is male courtesy. I turn and face the wall, kiss it.

"Nino," he says.

I turn back. At the heart of everything I do is my *pink* embarrassment at the pig-horror of actuality. I don't share with him a kinship of longing although I too long for a *terribly* useless happiness and brotherhood, for a stilled, unrestless, final happiness foolishly.

To his misery he offers the distraction in the procession-in-place of his hand. At the instant of orgasm, he flinches . . . "Ah, the bitter angel," he says. An affronted angel who does not stay . . . "I need more angels . . ." He means that he is going to come again. I had forgotten that he liked to come twice in quick succession. I was never fond of his sexual reality. I remember now as if I never forgot, oppressed.

The way one is present, the inner mood, the posture, the look on the face are a form of speech. In the tiny space of the narrow *calle* we stand close, but the inner distances in us are like the distances in the Piazza.

10

WATCHING ONNI, I see that kinky and naked memories, sexual *acuities*, puzzle him. But he masters everything, his own reality now in comparison to mine, which arouses such a rage of curiosity in him that it becomes a cold, *kinky* desire in regard to me, to the reluctance and pride and fastidiousness in me standing there which, in turn, comes from my seeing my identity in comparison to his as he proceeds . . . I refuse to be what he thinks. I do this correctively.

Onni starts feeling his arm, feeling mine; he worked out in a gym. Reality has gardened him—his vitality, his vivacity, his melancholy shamelessness, the obviousness of his signals, his whore's excellence of method, his woe as a shadow inside that wonderful vivacity of surface of his is beauty. In that beauty, he has his own thoughts, his own drama, incurably. Like many very handsome people, Onni was quick to praise, to ease the strain of the difference in physical fate between him and you. He said, "You have a good arm."

I said angrily-dryly, "Don't tell me what you think of me . . ."

He pauses in his dirty action; it is very different now, how we affect one another. He resumes; he finishes at once; he can be that quick. He smiles dimly, a mirror of another existence inside the act. He cleans himself and is done.

He says, "You are a nice egg, a little cracked . . ." He is lost for a minute in the old joke, in the English . . .

Onni's particular quality—grim, strong, bony liveliness with a purposefulness in his being striking—is *quasi-metallurgical* . . . He's a real heartbreaker. A hammer. See, he's a striking young man with an indomitable nature.

The moments and my cold heart threw outward splashes of sight in the shadowy *calle*. I see the half-stilled motions of skin, the silken, healthy quality of the firm, unthin muscles of his face and the thick ones of his neck. I have the privilege of the company of the rivalry king who is also *the sweet obscene cherub* and *the dangerous, glowing giovane, the Italian boy.*

He says sadly, "You are handsome, *caro* . . ."

"Everyone is handsome at our age. Whoever saw an ugly colt?"

I am embarrassed and arrogant toward him. He will get even. Knowing him is a different story from any I thought I would ever live. He has now a tremor of nervous, lively performance. His avidity is perhaps uncontrollable. He is tightly strung but calm about being tightly strung—that is Italian discipline and an artistry of feeling, of vanity. I can control his jealousy only by letting him control me, literally . . .

He laughingly says, "Shall I tell you now what you really look like? . . ." He is protective of his freedom from me in a cheap way now.

"You are nearly made of tin," I say.

He bangs himself on his stomach and listens as if for the sound of tin.

For a moment, I felt the curious quality of the world in its holding everyone's fate, in the crowdedness of fates. I have a compromised, oppressive allure, a hint of fate.

"*Andiamo,*" he says strutting down the *calle.*

11

ONNI IS LIKE an angled piece of metal that can cast a flash of light into my eyes. His motions, his youth can inspire feeling. Do I wish him dead? Much of the admiration anyone receives is tainted. Onni is politically ferocious, hotly disgusted, coldly distant, and, as always, clever. To attempt to diagram the motions of his state would be to attempt to show Onni trying to emerge from time, to hold a still place for himself in a universe of wing-beats. He does not live in a universe of mysterious and epic flight that is without rest.

We go to a bar and I wash my arm in beer. I cover the cut with a handkerchief I buy at a stall. I throw up in a canal. I sleep for an hour, sitting on the *fondamenta*, and leaning against Onni. I wake to the real sun, the handkerchiefs, one on my head, the one on my arm awry . . . I am sweating . . . Onni wipes my face . . . I am ugly Nino again . . . In comparison to him . . . I summon my will, and we walk, and I am hidden and clear both. In the *campo* sounded the deep, bass bell-like tones of courting male pigeons, a boom and echo among those stones. Coarse-breathed, we emerge into the broader light again of *San Polo.* Venice, in its common way of this, opens this space . . .

Onni says, "Don't go home . . . Stay with me . . . Walk, walk . . . Walk with me, *Caro* . . ."

The day is gray now. Pigeons fluffingly flap softly on the stones as we scatter them in our pace. We walk stiff-faced in cooler and cooler wind among tourists until near the *Salute* the light grows grayer still in the false twilight of before rain, and Venice holds its profile outlined in dull luminescence against the darkening sky. Onni enters the church, crosses himself, stands there, then stands in the doorway, watching the rain, then sets off down the steps, and in the spitting diagonals of rain, walks rapidly in the stone passages toward *Santa Margherita.* Fitful swathes of sunlight appear, and they shrink and widen in the wind, bird-bursts of light, frail, nervous in the rain. Then the light flutteringly unfolds like cloth into damp, fresh-breathed sunlight. We sit outside at a bar in *Santa Margherita* among tourists. In exhaustion after the nightlong intoxication I feel the dance of Onni's self. Onni watches me and taps out the rhythms of songs he sings under his breath. Insistent discourtesy-courtesy, human and skilled, that temper of masculine artfulness, that Mediterranean obscenity of his is in an ascendant phase, part of Onni's tainted courtship of the world; and I respond passively—acceptingly, arbitrarily—almost without feeling.

Pigeons coo and paddlingly flap overhead inside and outside the story of feelings. The light in showy Venetian display strengthens to a glossy yellow fire. But then, as Onni and I sat in extended silence, clouds pile up again; blue-gray shadows like glass or like a powder are in the air; my eyes move pigeonishly in the glowingly darkening light. The sky's peculiar quality of light and dark in this moment of upper wind and lower stillness evokes a sense of personality, and of affection. This *campo*, this asymmetrical corner of Venice, is abuzz in the warm dark of the approaching rain, the array of stones and windows and birds and bells and light and children calling and rain coming . . .

People greet Onni and me, and some come and sit hurriedly with us, and Onni carries on with them and occasionally glances at me to see if I am watching him be the king of flirtation; he wants to make sure I know he is the king and that I am jealous. Shadows slide, a prologue-fish. Reality, reality itself, has a sickening, nervous fascination for me, but I yearn for the peace of unobstructed will in the flashing forward and sideways and backwards of a book. Or some story other than this. No one tells a beloved child how very real life is. Each person that sits down with us, teased or unteased, has a sweaty look and funny breath in the humid air and in Onni's presence. And mine. This is an excited nothingness, memory and imagination being perverse— girls', boys' bodies rearing up—what is the actual structure of your desires? Onni and I take shelter from the rain in a palazzo on the *campo* that belongs to an older woman. She is a rich bourgeois. We stay half an hour while a loud wind marches drummingly outside. I slept on a couch, unhappily . . . I did not like those people or want to live my youthful rank as angel and soon-to-die giant *cock*roach and young hero with them.

One is sane pitiably and touchingly—is it all right? Onni's voice oppressed my nap. I let myself out of the palazzo into a rain-mist, the stones of the *campo* damp, and the light very gray, the air and the wind mild . . . In the gray mist, the crowd reappears; the deep rhythms of Italian speech rise everywhere in the mist around me . . . Onni finds me and sits—I am in a bar —and says, "Do you love me?"

"Shit . . . You're full of shit . . . You are a woman at heart," I say. I mean he is too much trouble . . . No one can dance with the dance of such a self . . .

"*Caro Tesoro*," he says, "the penalty for coldness such as yours is women . . ." He is staring at me in a wide-eyed Venetian manner. He meant the pleasures of women are lesser pleasures compared to violence and ambition and feelings between men. My father believed that, as did Hemingway differently. Onni said in actorly broken English, "Onni love-ez Nino. I know who like-iss Nino and who Nino like-iss. Ha-ha."

It is unbearable to be unloved; it is unbearable to be half loved; it is more unbearable to be strongly loved—there is no stillness at all then. And, often, it is not quite workable love . . . I mean Onni never loved anyone . . . Except me . . . in a way . . .

The light brightens, becomes unendurable, we flee to the *Zattere* in the hot, damp, steamy, drying air and have complicated ice cream concoctions on one of the large floating rafts there while vaporetti putt-putted to the landing stage and rocked the raft, and steam rose from the waves. The air had a pearly residue of spume in it. We ate on and on, we rocked on and on—pizza and *pannini*, coffee, beer. The *Canale della Giudecca*, churned by boat traffic, is gouged by sunlight and glistens throughout its length, a mad, wet jewel.

"The kind of love you mean, you get from a dog," I say to Onni.

"I want to take your heart to Hell with me," he said to me . . . It was a line from a movie. He said, "Arf, arf . . ." A dog's love.

"Pure Anatomy and Cleopatra," I said in a smart-alecky tone.

He said, "Would you give me a big kiss with your tongue if I asked you seriously?" Then: "Friendship is hard, *Caro*."

He walks now bent-chested, strung tight . . . "Nino, do you ever long for the taste of blood? I am a vampire," he whispers into my ear. All of his past led to the remark but he speaks as if there were no past for it at all. In truth, I could not bear any further response to him or to his feelings. In his dance was the sentimental wish to have me be strong, and then to have the pleasure of overturning that strength. His will had an appetite that felt like a running current of poisonously cold water stilling and shocking me . . .

When we were young, before the war, I saw him torture a

boy who liked it . . . The boy gave him, so to speak, plump, sideways glances from his protuberant, dark eyes. The boy stood, eyes open, then eyes closed, while Onni tortured his hands with lit matches, strange marks appearing on the small, five-fingered, beast-like hand. Onni used pliers and a wrench to squeeze the boy's fingers. Onni pressed a tack into the pudgy flesh below the fat boy's thumb. All this was in response to the boy—it wasn't imposed. There was a workmanlike give-and-take.

For me, the first moments of watching brought blank incomprehension. After a while, the mind was expert in what it saw, in which cries were false and which were real. My complicity was of a different order at each moment that I watched. But I *gave* nothing to the scene although my presence was essential to it. Now that I have entered the grown-up world of active power, my comparative innocence is a surface that is constantly changing, my distaste, my absentmindedness, my hope, and this affects him in ways that then become tones or whatever but that do not affect me.

"Let's go to the Lido," I said, hiding from him. On the vaporetto, the prow of my face in the blowy air, among the passengers, in the categories of men, I am one of the banal executioners in Onni's order of things. At the Lido, the brown sand gleamed dully in a bluish light under thick clouds, the brown, bather-littered beach . . . the umbrellas . . . the cabanas . . . The gray water stirred and roared dully at the shoals. In my head was the memory of angelic bits of silence.

Onni's strides lengthen; his breath rasps as he attempts to outwalk me . . . One time in Sicily he and I entered a temple-not-a-temple, a rectangle of stone columns at Segesta, among wooded hills. The columns had a power of evocation of a superhuman presence, strong fluttering, animate, adamant, a pre-Roman acceptance of all of it, of phallic reality, sadic and rapt. It seemed to breathe of life and death, slavery, horror, fate . . . I have no male acceptance—only a hypocrite's knowledge. Onni talked obscenely about the figures we passed: of one pale, thin woman, he said, "She would look better dead . . . I'd like to bite *her* lips . . . I'd like to stick some fire in her *culo* . . ." Then, indicating an unusually strongly built man, loose-limbed and vain at the water's edge, Onni said, "*Vedi il cretino* . . . We should cut off his dick and nail it to his mouth as a tongue so that he can be a little intellectual . . ." Of a tall, fine-legged youngish man walking past us with a girl who looked like him, Onni said, "We should drown him and discuss Tasso with that girl . . ."

He is trying to frighten me. I fell onto the sand, and stretched out my knotted, rigid legs which twitched. A wind sprang along the beach, like a lion in this unsheltering church. Then through an opening in the clouds, sunrays descended—a distant radio played—the musics and gold-gleam and fish-scale shine of mosaics of an actual church are rawly mimicked here. Onni stood motionlessly, that boy-man. For him Christ and the martyrs return in violent pantomime to re-enact martyrdoms, souls eating souls, attacking each other in infinities of cruelty. In Venice, many have screamed in pain.

Onni and I are running along the sand, barefoot, heads upturned. We are of different species, he and I. No. We're not. His species has an *I-can-bear-it* beauty-and-sweatiness, an accepted guilt and aggression. We slow to a walk, and the wind grows cool again, and the bathers shrink into themselves . . .

Did I expect him to be fictional, subordinate, neat? His posture and his eyelids as we walk have a hard humor of precision beyond beauty. All his rhythms vary, of his walk, of his swinging arms, of his breathing . . . So, also, the rhythms of the semi-Oriental dance of light on his face.

"Let us go to my aunt's." But I refuse.

"Let's go back to Venice."

The vaporetto is chugging and wallowing and yawing in slippery waves, in the high wind of the rainstorm-without-rain. The vibrant obstinacy of the machine, its metal chatter and its smell, and the swing of the hull in the surges of water cause an erection. I long to be old and clothed in idea. Not desire. He leans against me: "Do you find the vaporetto *sessuale, caro* . . ."

I moved away from him. I stand in the bow. The scene, the little world of small islands and high masses of cloud and distant sunlight near Mestre and the blue-gray heaving water and the bluish mass of Venice makes me lower my head with sadness. Onni on the shuddering vaporetto while I rock as the boat chugs and twists says in falsetto, "You are Fausto," and he gripped and applied pressure to my neck. He does a thing I did once when I came when we fooled around sexually: he tolls like a city bell.

A month or so ago, one time, returning at night from a girl's place, I heard muttered bell sounds from a shadowy *calle* and I shouted, "*Get on with it, Giangiacomo . . .*"

From the dark in the *calle*, his voice came in English as now in the blue-and-green-and-yellow-green light on the vaporetto, "*Go to Hell, Tesoro . . .*" The actual torments of Hell are real to him, the remnants of his Catholic faith . . .

Fausto was a pale-skinned boy who wore glasses, a wrestler, a thin, strong boy with two selves, one clothed, one unclothed, each with a different maleness. I was in a private club of boys that he wanted to enter; I was in by special dispensation; but Fausto underwent the initiation. We sat in a room in a villa outside Mestre. Fausto was blindfolded and naked. Ordered not to speak, white-skinned, as I said, he was tied, hands and ankles. A neat spiralling and packing of muscle and the dotting here and there of moles, nipples, scars. Two boys lay him on the floor, and he was tickled and pinched until he was dotted by pink and bluish discolored patches of skin and could no longer govern himself. The rest of us sat silently. Poor Fausto tried to be silent too but then he roared and gasped with laughter and heaved himself up and down and tried to roll over—his butt, mere muscle and skin, heaved itself into something else, something that almost spoke in its articulated movements.

He wet himself. He shat on himself—he was mostly silent by then, crying only a little, laughing and gasping, muttering, "*Dio . . . Dio . . .*" Brown shit was on the backs of his white legs.

The living figure had a resemblance to the type of Hellenistic statue that shows the torture or death of a young man. There is only one form of attention, servitude to the subject; one can be mocking or wavering or practice waiting-and-watching, but that affects the attention. One cannot see clearly. Fausto's different servitudes of attention and the mingled slaveries of the watchers made an odd moment . . . This continuing helplessness of his coerced, enforced, confused, and darkened my mind as did the smell of him sweating, his unhappy, forced, gulping laughter, the embarrassing odor of urine, and the stink of his feces—I think cruelty is a human universal. But the degree of cruelty inflicted is variable. A hunger for victory and feelings of disgust and fear enveloped me with Onni. The disgust and fear were ambiguous and shifting; watching Fausto, I felt his *poor feet* tickled became his *disgusting feet*. One was partly, blinkingly-staringly cut off from any sympathetic sense of the other one, was fixed to a rabid sense of infliction, to watching the struggle of the boy except when, briefly, the mind seemed to slide inside the struggling boy and to feel a little of what he felt but abstractly although neurally: one undergoes, in some part, everything one sees happen, dreaming while awake, tasting everything as part of one's nervous sense of the world.

I thought I saw Fausto's humiliated surprise that his life had come to this. The twisted genital-obelisk (with its curious anchoring in a Gothic tracery of pubic hair) when the boy managed to roll over and was allowed to lie on his back, the obelisk was now erect. It had a partly corkscrew bend in it—poor obelisk, ignored, laughed at, pinched. The bound boy's known, unprivate self . . . one enters his heaving, gasping silence with sickened, involuntary sympathy . . . One backs off, disdains it all truly . . . Either way, one becomes a newer, more commanding self.

I had trouble with this stuff. I was shamed and hesitant, not always, not when given a sort of officerhood, but in general. One is aware that one must fight with other men over this claim. With Onni now.

On the vaporetto: toward Mestre, the sky beyond the edge of the cloud mass is sharply yellow again. Nearer us, massed clouds ride above the Lagoon.

"You are as delicate as a nun," Onni says and releases me.

The vaporetto slews and chugs and splashingly shoves its way. We disembark. "Boobies, boobies," Onni mutters as a tall German girl passes us. *Do not think about her life.* The crowd on the *Riva* smells of rain and summer. Onni's mind is buried slickly, hotly in his momentary condition.

We board yet another vaporetto, a black one . . . The boat goes grinding loudly and hypnotically and almost glidingly across the shadowed, placid *Bacino* under the massed clouds. The sunlight near Mestre strides swiftly over the water toward us, changing the sullenly gleaming blue-green-black surface of the water to glare, and the well-ordered face of *San Giorgio Maggiore* in a gloomy half-light into a tall church with pilasters and cornices damply sunlit. Across the *Bacino* behind us the bright city is only half-bright, and has vaporous outlines. Half the sky above it is dark. But vaporous brightness rises from the receding domes of *San Marco.* The water in the *Bacino* is touched with stirring and streaming vapors. I feel tangled in bright steamy, lightly churning vapors . . .

Onni strokes my neck and says, "*Pazzo carino . . .*"

To know someone is to be locked in some kind of easy or hard struggle with them. The absolution in being Venetian—in a way—guides me. "Fuck you," I said. And around us on the water stirs the expanse of damp, vaporous light. Thin tendrils of mist are streaming and vanishing in our passage. I am choked with the blind utopian-apocalypticism of my hope of sentimental happiness.

Now we are in very bright, very hot sunlight. A flood of poisonous heat is spread burningly over the fields of water of the *Giudecca.* The close-textured air was like muslin drawn taut in the wind and then loosening as the boat progressed in its course past the austere *Redentore* atop its tourist-dotted steps . . . on the bubbling fluster and liquid cries of the water toward the *Zattere.* The wind sluggishly whirred. The Venetian outdoors seemed to be an open window with a realer outdoors further on behind the hot blowing weave of yellowy light. The nearby stroking and tickling bunching of coarse heat, the brushingly palpable, light-tortured, curtain-like air hurt the skin, the eyes. To the south, visible in the bright, almost twinkling, almost evilly hot sky, was the dark cloud mass, domed and gray-blue-black, of the rain over the Adriatic. My head in its bell of rigid bone was clanging in hot, whited, bystanderhood, a moral posture, an emotional fastidiousness . . . a snobbery, a snobbish autonomy.

One day we went to the Zattere . . . On the *Zattere* we walked
in the direction of *San Sebastiano* in the other geography of
intoxicated, tested friendship, in the extreme flibbertigibbet in-
stabilities of sexual reality and in the dark grayness and light of
two separated, personal wills. Just as the *Giudecca* is wider than
the *Canalazzo* the drug-tinged moment is more outspread and
embraces a larger arc of space in its seemingly greater size and
duration than a moment shaped by sobriety. Time and the light
drag like a white fabric placed over my head and trailing on the
fondamenta. Onni walked with careful eyes behind sunglasses.
I walk bridally in that white drapery, in a kind of horror, alongside
the great flat leap of water of the *Giudecca* in a low-lying corona
of a blaze of restless reflection. I am distracted over and over by
an eye-widening, surprised, unkind feeling for each girl we pass,
a further unkind feeling toward her reality . . . the reality of
knowing her . . . But so too the men and boys and older people.
A bitterness of persecution by society, by reality sets in, a longing
to know and yet to have escaped—to explore, apart from everyone, a sentimental knowledge. Onni could still speak flexibly; his
lips moved in a sensible way; and he made a jealous joke about
love-idolatry for soccer stars and sports figures: *Soccer du Prin-
temps,* he said. One exercises the cruel right of ignoring the joke
as if it was stupid . . . And Onni does flinch in the moments of
my nonreaction.

"Drug-drag, drugged-dragging . . . wedding . . . Pale Paolo's
whosits . . . Jim Dante, dandy," I said, regretting the sadic silence.
We were dressed in drugs, I meant, and then, drugged and dragging the enlarged sense of the moments given by the drug, we,
or I, was being married to practicality, a virgin sacrifice.

He sighed.

We turned inland and passed the simpler houses here, but
at *San Sebastiano* in the sunstruck open space around the church,
uneasy, I said, "No. Let's go back . . ."

His face was as stilled as my own in the disorienting clarity
of this light. I could feel the echoes, but dimmed, and in a way,
mindless, of sexual reality as a martyrdom in him, in me—a
lightly sweating saintliness, a passive Christian rage in the hot,
blowy air.

The airlessness of the heat near *San Sebastiano* continued on the open *Zattere*. So much of flesh-pink and sallow Venice was visible that one expected coolness. But in its watery setting, Venice, the churches visible, *Redemption* and *St. George*, the city's humor of piety and erotic and forceful *wit* spread out in the heat was a matter of grief to the boy-man, less and less a boy, that I was.

I apologize now for my prudery then, which was essentially a half-man's sensual longing for what was, in the end, utopian-puritan. Apocalyptic. I desired austerity and common sense but some luxury and some sexual depth of real happenings and much, much, much less human nature . . . It is not clear to me in what way we are ennobled by love except in terms of patience with one another. I desired rationality proudly, commandingly, not as a supplicant, not whiningly. The young are dangerous. But what is the meaning of the massacre of the virgins if not the opposite of that? Is the point the universality of masculine *sin-fulness*? St. Ursula and St. Sebastian die prettily in Venice for the amusement of others. Sensations of dominance and of shad-owy wishes control me. Solutions to last night, to Silla's myth-y sense of love, occur to me . . . Docility in Onni . . . Him humiliated . . . "Don't walk with me . . . I'm tired of you . . . Go away . . ." In childhood how you obey or refuse to obey is central to your life. *Masculinity* in childhood lies in how you hold your brother's hand, how you submit to being bathed—in *wet* drama, wet water—by your nurse or your mother with her soft powdery neck and soft, weighty breasts. Onni trails behind me, fourteen, fifteen feet.

The ghostlike splashings of light upward from the pavement in this heat and the altered tenor of my breath in this tiresome and tiring display of love-as-torture weigh on me—I am tired of his games—while along the water, the nifty jumble of pretty buildings march beside the water-dance. Little that is visible is dull; nothing in the scene is awesome . . . This half-abandoned circus of a city, this dead city, my Venice in its lovely fields of wetly clanging, sunlit water, such a ferocity of decoration and appetite for happiness, for a lastingness of emotion, such a long echo of complicities, such a businesslike regard and appetite for love . . . and Onni drawing near and saying, "Let me use your matches . . ."

"Give me a cigaret," I say, autonomous, commanding.

Venice offers such a pretty suffocation of resentment, such a sweetness over its violence, that I, spiritually, gag on it . . . stupid, ancient, movie-oid Venice . . .

Onni's look of fate has deepened. He lights my cigaret. The strength of will in him fades, subsides, is submissive, but it returns, a texture, a weave of linkages . . . One would not want him to be defenseless . . . He will never be innocent and redeemed . . . That is, in fact, a fascist image, the controlled and beaten child or man or girl, pure, purified. I am so self-conscious a person that I tend to know when my ignorance and my absences of spirit begin. I am anxious to be apart from Onni, from the question of Onni, from questions about myself and love . . . I collapse onto the steps of the *Gesuati*, and Onni falls into a slouching seat beside me and says, "Fucking sunlight."

He says it in Bogart's voice. He leans against me, slides, lies in my lap as in a Deposition. "*Mamma mia, sono morto,*" he says. An odd Christ, he looks up into my face . . . I see the tilted and partly sunlit and partly shadowed inclines of his face as I drift toward absence, and he tries to hold my attention. He says accusingly, "You like to talk. I had a working-class boy—did I tell you this?—and I was being very nice to him, very, very nice, like a saint to him, and he said, *Do you like me? Are you a Communist?* . . . Tell me, as one Christian to another, how you feel about fucking now, *Caro Nino.*"

His voice is far away for me. "Uhn," I say. I say—like my mother—"*Do we need to think of that?*"

The weight of him on my lap has two parts, the skeletal articulation and then the scattered masses of flesh . . . The great flat leaping glare in front of me has a *white* color nearby and then a shifting pallor and then the blue of distance. The scirocco idly stirs in my Venice. Onni says, "You despise me . . . I am tired of it, *caro.*"

Onni sees in ways that I cannot. I do not and will not ever

have a sense of myself in that worldwide third-person way that he has of himself, of his rights, of his citizenship as a Christian, sexual soul. Sunlight lay across his tough torso; shadows tinted his nose; my reflection hovered in his dark glasses. He has a certain diffidence toward me but I am aware more of his willful confidence toward me and God and fate—he is a future movie star, for God's sake. The water danced and glittered, enormous, wet, and shining. He took my hand and placed it on the clothed, curved bed over his heart . . . The sunstruck and vibrating and light-leaking radiance of skin and the touch of fabric and the weighty and articulated volumes of muscle and flesh pass into my touch. "It is a crucifixion," he says. I touch him, martyred, both of us, tiredly friendly. But it is not truly different from any other touch, from him touching himself, since it is at his will that I touch his chest. The agency is reversed. One feels from a different position—one feels a threat of intimacy, of mythic entanglement, of prayer.

He says, "Do you love me? Do you know what love is, *caro amico?*" The accusation becomes a dreamy question, real and deeply meant . . . Onni gazes up at me, then at the sky: "Do you know what love is, *caro amico?*"

"Not when I'm sitting still," I say. The roughly sliding, broken and gleaming water shone more and more . . . "But sure," I said, "if I'm in motion . . . Give me a cigaret." I reached into the pocket of his faded salmon-colored T-shirt, my shirt; here is his body, flat, slouched, breathing, and warm inside the shirt . . . Here are cruelly abused saints . . . forgiveness . . . a hot, phallic sense of friendship and immediacy—a sense of the actual phallic reality. We light our cigarets. He rises into a squatting crouch and handsomely sits on the stone step. I keep watching *the roughly sliding, broken and gleaming water.* And breathing the hot, fume-and-salt-stained air and the tobacco smoke . . . Onni watches me. "Let me ask you something, Ninoni . . . Here, lie on me . . ." He pulled my head, pulled me, so that my head fell but I shifted my weight and I slide partly across his lap in a posture like his before with me, but still a little like a Deposition. His arm lies across my upper chest. I think he is more comfortable with me as Christ—who must die for him—than I was with him in the role . . . He asks, "Do you believe in 'happy' *love*, Nino-tchki, my pale and silent hero-Garbo, my old friend?"

I say, "I don't love you sentimentally. But look at it like this—you are what you are, and I love you . . . Ergo, I love in a better way than you do." That was not what I'd meant to say. Each sentence leaped at a different angle, freshly, from its birth in my throat—I don't know why.

"Of course," he said. Then: "Yes? You insult me? I don't mean that you love *sentimentally*, Ninon-chi. Can you smile?"

"I don't think you are ideal."

He gazed at me from behind his sunglasses. "Do you love me spiritually?"

"Sure," I said. "Why not? Well . . . to be honest, yes and no . . ." Sitting up, I felt a terrifying, slightly nauseated sincerity that yet was a form of clement hypocrisy. I liked him and disliked his body. Or . . . who knows?

He said, "What does it feel like to love spiritually?" He asked it with a male delicacy of interest . . . in the exotic. Then more strong-fiberedly and in English: "What does it feel like, old pal? . . ."

"It is a strong feeling . . . Feelings have no label on them —they heave and pulse—"

"Like the stomach?" Onni asked. "You feel spiritual love as if it were in the stomach, *caro*?"

In some ways, this was my first cross-examination in regard to love since childhood. "In the stomach and in the veins. Really, love is like the stomach of a horse grafted onto you. The stomach of a brute, big horse . . . And it is like a landed fish with large fins . . ."

We look into each other's eyes. I see that he reads my jokes, my speeches as indicating I do not have strong feelings about him like his for me. My voice, my body, really, they say too much. I try not to be embarrassed . . . I suspect my feelings are as strong as his but they are different. Now he seems to glitter with various kinds of listening and suffering.

I say, "But one just puts a name on it, puts a blue ribbon on it, gives it credit, or tries to, but it is just this brute hot stomach . . ."

He says sarcastically—sarcastically-dotingly-painedly—"People talk such bullshit . . . It is good to hear you . . . You have such a deep heart . . ."

He shifts his legs and slouches there, an assured exhibitionist.

I say with some feeling, "You try to get away with having this stomach, like a child . . . like a child dressed up and saying, *I love you*—but asking, really—you know how a child hits you when the emotion heaves in him? Or he runs off? Or does something else? I think feelings arise by accident because of all the things going on. They are brewed. Or formed. An offshoot of living. Feelings are odd with your grotesque stomach of horselike love—the question is can you be a graceful or only a horrific satyr then? How civilized do you remain—that is the lover's question . . . Some people are ignorant about *love* . . . Some never learn . . ."

"That is the lover's question?" he asked. "I tell you what I think: love is the murder of someone's life." He takes off his sunglasses, and his stoned, deep-colored gaze brushes me, and I feel my darkness. "Yes," he continued, listening deeply to himself: "Love murders the rest of your life . . . all of your life that is not the love . . ."

He has never loved . . . I am what he knows of love . . . He generalizes from me . . . He is filling in holes in his repertoire . . . And he suffers . . . The often loved Onni is working out suspicion, dislike, meanness, rage in the brute stomach; rage and obsession to be obsessed with someone in the rising and falling hot surges of intoxication, the pull and push of it, is tidal, more than tidal; I felt considerable fear . . . I felt the truth of *my* feelings . . . different feelings . . . I felt a resigned giggle and a wild inner giggle of exultation as in swimming out in mid-sea in large waves over great depths.

I think he is a lover who cannot love, and I am someone who can love but will not love him past a certain point.

I said, "What I feel is so secret that it has no name . . . I merely apply names to it . . . And I guess . . ."

"Now? Always? You are not upset by this inside you?"

"I don't know what is inside me—time changes things— often soon . . ."

"What does that mean?"

"I don't know yet . . . Why do you want to talk now? Hashish is not truth serum. Nobody can concentrate on love every minute no matter what they say."

"I can. I do," Onni said harshly-dreamily. He bent his head: "Even when I shit . . . And now with every breath . . ." He stretched and flexed, shrugged and spread his arms as if to demonstrate a self distilled into passion, into love.

But erotic restlessness and a heat of distraction were what showed. But perhaps I am wrong . . . He said wearily, "Have you seen *me* be unconcentrated?"

"Yes," I said. Then rubbing my forehead, I islanded myself from him.

"I say no," he said angrily, dramatically, "Why don't you just say you hate love?"

"You hate love," I say. "Be honest."

He says, "Why do you talk in the crazy way you talk?" He stared at me, then out, over the water—a serious, stoned stare. "I respect love. Of you and me. I am not the enemy of passion . . ."

"What passion? That's just a word you put on a lot of feelings in you . . . You asked me what I thought. I think what I said is true. I think your ideas of love are silly . . . I think people lie *a lot* when they talk about love . . . I think some people are good at love and some are not . . . some know about love and many are ignorant . . . I think when you talk the way you do, you are not talking from experience . . . You are being inventive . . ."

"Ah. I talk bullshit, people talk bullshit—but not you . . . Are you Papa Truth, *caro Nino*? You are the master bullshitter . . . I know this." He put his hand on his chest, near his heart, and he took on a look of profound inward thought; and then he looked back at me and asked cleverly, with a clever air, "So *your* mind wanders when you love? You cannot honestly concentrate on love?"

I felt the extent to which I was opaque to him, the extent to which he felt I fooled and misled him. It was strangely threatening, the sensation.

He said, "Ha. I am interested I think only in true love, in absolute passion," he said. Then he opened his mouth to breathe sunrays. He drew hot Venetian light into his throat; he said, "It is true that your mind wanders and you don't love—I have seen it, I know what I am saying. Your face gets very quiet; you become a figure on the other side of a canal . . . over there . . ."

The quality of echo, of him talking like me and playing with what I'd said and imitating my voice, trying to get at what he figured I thought was both intimate and chilling, loving and a display of hatred. He was sporting with my thoughts, stealing the doves and the dogs, if I might be allowed to say it like this, and the gross horse-stomach he imagined I had . . .

*   *

How heterosexual am I? I don't know. The rehearsal here with Onni of what I became can be shown from another angle. Let me mention here a woman I loved six years later, Angela Hoon.

Angela's politics and her willfulness, her wanderings and her career, semi-literary and erotic, were a tiny bit like Onni's —lives are similar in the same era. Let me present her physically, erotically—long, strong, well-rounded legs and thighs and hips, and a small waist and high, absurdly pale, tight breasts, and a shield-like, highly made-up face with strongly marked handsome lips.

Her mind and spirit allowed her a sexual acceptance of me perhaps as part of a reluctant politics of the real. Was the feeling real? She and I came to Venice. My mother was dead by then. I couldn't stay with Carlo—he is too possessive. Angela and I are in an expensive hotel. In the hotel room sexually she wants the posture of me on top of her. That is one sign of who I am. Another is that her inner walls are clasping and shifting . . . my obstinate and entirely clumsy movements . . . in that sleek enclosure. The extreme not-loneliness of entry when she accepted my physical reality—my phallic reality—has given way to a truce-riddled loneliness in fucking. The style of her doing this, her body's warmth meant both that coming was half-visible and that the bleakness of not desiring someone enough was not there but passion was not there either.

So, unadvisable further acts, let us say . . . sexual furtherness is in the room like a sleeping lion, a thousand-kilo weight of flesh on the floor, uneasily drowsing in a slant of light, a degree of sinful experiment in strong feelings filling the measure of what we had.

Ah, emotion is rehearsing its uncertain existence in the children. The unchaste, red-lipped Angela and I permit each other only a little but still it is very much, a lot, a great deal in the half-light of suspicious feeling . . . I was practiced in this, more experienced than she was . . . That was perhaps the ground of my privileges with her.

She said, "You are so sensible—and so good at this . . ." She was being *nice*, you know? But I *was* good at the atmospherics.

The reality of her skin and doubts about what each other might do were not so inhibiting as to be crippling. The trespass inevitable in fucking is moderated by a carefulness in preserving the alliance. One's impulses, toyed with and denied and partly released and sighed at—avoiding the extreme and the dramatic—are a hardened and sexually inflected breath and a flyingly intense sexual glare of sensation, a momentary cure-all.

It was something of a disappointment and a strain; also it boomed and shuddered and hotly shuffled along, being both honorific and horrific—acceptable as a degree of pleasure, even love; it was good enough to be called that. A good-enough sexual glare shines on lost landscapes and illuminates and explains, or seems to, much that was mysterious to me at one time or another in the past; and it reveals a new and strange as yet, not alive, infant and untextured future . . .

I am very sensitive to the blessing but not entirely tender to it or to her or to myself.

Is it a worthy affair? Is she worth it? Am I? One tries to take the measure of the event.

One has, one starts with diffused light in oneself thinking, a light as in a dream or as like real light in a thin sea-mist; this is in one's head, a form of thoughtlight. This sea-light-in-a-mist as in Venice in January is a light of sexual opinion, let us call it that.

Then in this diffused light the memory of an inward sexual glaringness occurs like a discharge of a flare in a heavy mist over open water.

While one fucks, or while I fuck, as later, one estimates how-good-it-was, the gabble of lights and shadow, of half-lights and ebbings into insufficient sensation. One can only with difficulty recall the factual sequence of clouded and even eclipsed suns and their slanting and vertical and horizontal rays, dimmed and gentle, that suddenly appeared to produce bursts of unevenly sexual glare, ascendant, toward coming. The deadnesses or sub-sidings that interrupt the ascent appear in oneself as dramatic landscapes of deadness—as in paintings of saints in lonely con-templation . . . Bits of moments of hopelessness and of taking breath and bits of moments of the piercing electric glare of emis-sion are thrown into the scale. Our mutual patience with the sexual discourtesies of orgasm. Simple release is weighed—as in the comfort that one is on terms with spring's nuisances of aphrodisia just now.

You walk in the cool damp *calli* and then you emerge into the sun among the sun-warmed stones of a *campo*, and it seems that the *calli* suggest to you your own legs dark in shallow, dark water, and the *campo* suggests your sun-warmed chest above the waterline.

On the *Salizzada 22 Marzo* one walks among the teased re-flections of one's feelings in the intent-faced girls and idle-bodied boys we pass. Some people stare at us. The comically private jangle of one's body holds gusts of emotion, a bulging false-eternity of heat and a weight as of wind in a canvas sail, feelings that are complex, compound, and made of corruption . . . You say, *Let's go back to the hotel . . .*

How crippling a moment of love is . . . the limping, half-ludicrous stride one has with an erection . . . the romantic shambling . . . masked as at carnival . . . One knows only the tone of an event as a measure in the hotel room, the shutters drawn, strips of light entering and sounds from the canal, sounds of boats and harsh voices, waves slapping wood and stone, and bird shrieks; and voices and footsteps in the *calle*, the world's tongues. And here in the shadows is nakedness taut with self-presentation—ah, a loose, almost stumbling, dim-eyed travesty of art in a city of parody. One stirs long-leggedly in the electric welcome by nature and this woman of one's physical existence for a moment. Almost any duration of this feeling for a while is love, isn't it?

My responses, taught me through Onni, are calculatedly naïve. A restored sense of clemency, the sensation of luck is a key . . . One doesn't judge the grotesque mixture of the filth of history and love.

Behind the eyes? Inside the buttocks? The tolerance of nothingness-in-a-way . . . the surprised, sun-teased, half-fragrant stink of greatness in her . . .

One's life is thrown away for this for a while . . . this has had to be learned. One has practiced this . . .

Angela was a girl of literacy who would call out, "For the love of God!" in an English accent which was for some reason very exciting for me. She played at submission. Her style is that she would drink a lot, too much, and act it out in intoxication that she is dryly and bitterly thrilled by what life is offering her. She is ironic and quite far to the left, in an English manner, of course, but she is ironic with a tremor of honesty in the too expensive hotel room in Venice. With someone new one reaches for what one was deprived of in love in the past.

"Do you wish I had been virgin?" she asks.

"Do you wish I had been?"

"Yes. No."

The slap of abdomens against one another: the slap of water on stone steps. The breath in fucking in full pitiability—the sound of *a beast*—sometimes sounds like thickly feathered wings that flap and pump in a barnyard way or elevated in a transparent and sometimes glaring air.

Details: In the intoxication and strangeness, the rosey rhythms of sun-glare off the water stain the inside of the shutters and my hovering eyelids and become small dizzying bits of prismatically broken, colored light along my eyelashes.

Among Angela's sensual realities is that she accepts physically *the One Who Had Been Onni's Friend.*

"I am a cunt man," I said and reached for a cigaret and handed her one. We fucked, smoking. She laughed some and was intent and awake.

Angela's inner concentration on her fingerless, oiled, cupping grasp and soft receptiveness impresses the lightly grunting, steadily rocking young man—it seemed to me very English. The act is not seeable, not shareable except internally, really . . . generously—but not visibly . . . The sounds of the bed—guh-creakitty, guuhhhh-crahkkkkitteeeee—the soft rocking motion of the light—Venetian pink behind the eyelids as if in echo of her spread cunt . . . the warm, stenchy jiggle-joggle . . . forgive me, dear God . . . she shifts herself, and the motion moves along her limbs and in her momentarily animate hair . . . The moment moves from a self-consciously controlled whisper of breathing to a mad lingo of breath in the sexual glare that eats up everything.

We rest. Passages of eagerness alternate with settledness. The reality of the sexual act, of fucking, is variously burning and collapsing but is re-willed after each collapse—Venice restored.

Again, in another moment, while I move in her, she looks at me—merely that: the addition of outward sight means I have to brace to control the shuddering along my back, my spine.

Well, let it go.

Naked after fucking, in a post-coital sprawl, we fail to talk. Angela sighs and I blink and watch the room and hear the sounds and smell the odors of Venice as they become solid again after the ghost-transposition of the senses in the fuck. The feeling in the overdecorated Venetian room—pale purple and purple-gray and pinks and blue—is akin to that vacation sense of the seaside; it is like walking on the Lido and looking at the Adriatic, except that it is mingled with the moods and moodiness of being in bed.

"Are you thinking of the Queen?" I ask her.

"Sssh, you . . . I love my Queen . . . And her mother. She is very fine, you know . . . A coarse crass asshole of a Yank like you would never understand the refinements and courage of our Queen . . . And her mother . . . Ooh dear, now you've put me on my best behavior. Mustn't talk about the Queen when I'm like this, you dear man." She slowly and delicately and incompletely amends the *indecency* of her posture. "Now we can talk about the Queen, you dear."

When I fuck, I fuck in fear of the afterward.

Her face holds feeling, unnamed feeling. She is somewhat lyrical by nature, skeptical, male-centered only at times. What is on her face suggests to me someone rehearsing the meter of a poem, a rhythm taken from experience. I am careful and limited in regard to her composition of that poem in her . . .

A tolerance for nothingness, for the weakness in all the elements of emotion in any given reed-like shuddering of time, I learned, I stole from knowing Onni, and patience, patience with the other's crimes, patience with my own complicity.

Still, I am more a virgin at self-surrender than Angela or Onni ever was. And what I learned from Onni may have been only miserable filth.

Angela and I were lovers for five years. Angela had a kind of cannibal-beauty-dining-out-on-flesh thing, and yet semi-totalities of flesh upset her even while they entranced her sense of duty toward being a woman. She surrenders more to her own flesh than she does to a man. Than she did to me. This was soul-deep in her.

We split up.

12

NOW HE HAS TAKEN a little cocaine, and his sense of combat is on his face, a tough anti-erotic-but-still-erotic look. (It is from actual moments that opinions and symbols and theories are drawn.)

We draggingly have walked to the ice cream rafts. I have the knotted handkerchief on my head, and one tied around my arm.

We order and sit in silence under an umbrella. The ice cream arrives and he spoons the elaborate ice cream from its glass into his mouth. Under the umbrella of the table he puts the spoon to the side of his nose and addresses me agreeably but *furbo*, in a state of unfooled shrewdness: "The way you talk is *too strange*. The way you talk is too much like you. I am an old-fashioned person, and you pain me." He gets a strong-eyed, very Italian look in the awninged light.

Essentially, I like only the courtship mode between people. That peace, that poetry. I say—swallowing a mouthful of a concoction of ice cream and whipped cream and soda and coffee— "Yes? But I'm the untormented one . . . So you can go to hell, you Wop."

The cold stuff slithers down my throat, a bright sensation in the Venetian pink throat. I said, "Onni, I am not real . . . I am too shy." I am intent in my drunkenness, hiding my exhaustion in a way, intent on being acceptable to myself among the people on the ice cream raft, none of whom are real to me . . . they are phantoms . . .

Onni says, *haute* pornographically in the bright light, "When ancient poets spoke of *love* as Venus, they spoke of her two sides—she can be face-to-face and she can display the part which is for dogs and tigers . . . for men . . ."

Two girls some distance away on the *fondamenta* are kissing each other . . . The shining movements of their hair in the light, the gleam of faces and legs, the colors of cloth that interrupted the gleam swim in me in an occluding darkness.

Onni reaches over and rubs my neck: "You are always thinking, thinking . . . It is good that we are friends . . ." His touch is *expert* . . . His lips are darkish in the light under the hot canvas. A sexual sense of him starts up . . . It is an enormity of intrusion into his reality . . . Acquaintance becomes sexual spying and a species of arousal. The sense is of his body, of his butt, his mouth, his practiced attitudes, his hands—servicing me, his bare back, me looking down on the skin of his back and spine . . .

This shoved me, bumped me—as if a whale bumped me in the dark, underwater.

He addressed a fresh-lipped young man's susceptibility I had, the courtship-drunken sensibility, a quality that offered a landscape of escape. Men escape into some such quality in women sometimes. I imagine his sense of this was complicated by the space-filled gaze of the young man who was so stoned and who was not actually womanly—me I mean.

The *Zattere* in bright light, the ice cream raft with its tables and people, us under the awning.

He said, "Do you fuck only your own life-as-it-is-included-in-a-woman—in someone—and not her, not her as a person—when you fuck? I do not judge this; I merely mention it . . . yourself in the act with someone . . . Is it *myself-in-them* I fuck?" His identity shines with a gilded whorishness in the light. And with a ghastly, true innocence. He is radiantly pale and strained—stained—from the drugs, dark swatches under his glaring eyes in the tinted light under the umbrella. We have, as it were, moved onto a long promontory, a kind of loneliness with each other. My mind is scoured, tired, ringing with words and phrases . . . With the hatred he is offering—or threatening me with. "What we fuck, Nino, when the beast in us *fucks*, is only that, is it true? In all the bodies and—and souls—only the same thing, *caratteristico*, this only thing that is available to us?"

I am two speeches back with love and its front and back sides which I say aloud, "Love and its front and back sides . . ."

"Yes! The sides of the self," he said, pale and stern . . . He is in a murderous mode. I am stirred by his honesty and depth, and by idea, an idea of love in the face and mouth-fuck part, the erotic *ambitions* of the front of the self, and then the back, the eyeless, sensitive spine, the unmartial and flexible rump, a different sort of "love" . . . "The back is the side of the person that does not judge you," I said aloud.

He stretched his neck and gazed at me in strict ferocity, in pallor. In the moment I felt an infinity of desire—but not for him . . . I was contemplating desire because he had led me to do it . . . Some of the heat of desire flowed casually toward his reality, however.

"The asshole," he said, pursing his lips lightly. He is leaning far back and his head is buried in light as if in the burning tail of a meteor. "It is a simple thing . . . simpler than a vagina . . . I see you with my back turned," he said thoughtfully. He angled the back of his shoulder toward me and turned his head away. "Yes, I see you," he said from there. His words flowed the wrong way, toward the people at the next table.

I, my intoxication, invented what he said. I said inside me, repeating what I think he said, *We are made of eyes. Like peacock tails. Flesh-eyes.* The eye at-the-end-of-the-spine, in the small of the back, *I can see you.* The mouth, which is near the mind, is an eye: *I see you* . . . It presses against, slides over the fact of presence, the amorous, temporally logical reality of presence.

"I talk too dirty for everyone who speaks English here," Onni said. "I talk dirty very well . . . Ah, aiee, *fucking* . . . I say the eye inside the vagina sees EVERYTHING!"

"I don't love you that way!" I said. The words spilled out in the light-filled moment.

"You do but you are not honest," he said. "*Dunque*, it does not matter . . ."

Venice shabbily glittered in its beauty here and there in the airy, watery-floored perspective along the length of the *Giudecca*. Desire in me was like water splashing and overflowing a cupped hand, useable sloppily, but only wildly . . . My head and upper body are in shadow under the umbrella . . . I rose and went back to the doorway of the *Gesuati*, leaving him to pay . . . Onni approaches through the sunlight . . . Every shade of emotion changes even the smallest particles of your self, all the micro-elements, every iota, every degree of amiability or of toughness.

"Napoleon had a small prick, a very small prick, Dillinger, the criminal, a very large one . . . The attraction of a criminal is very great, is perhaps the greatest thing . . . that we learn from the Twentieth Century," he said sitting down beside me. Male eroticism is actually always a matter of trespass . . . Nature created us as trespassers . . . My mood is violated by his mood in such close proximity.

"I don't want to talk about pricks," I said leaning on the church door.

"I was talking about the attraction of gangsters. *Their* pricks," Onni said.

"Ah, Christ, for the love of *Christ*," I said, "change the subject."

"Yes? I know life is *sad*," Onni said. "Venice is a whore . . . It is that now, isn't it? Whores and Venice and American ads and me: sisters of the backside."

"Jesus, ONNI . . ."

I rose and walked—unsteadily—toward the *Dogana* . . .

Onni followed me . . . At my shoulder, he said, "I am like the Sea Wolf: you know that book? I am something of a *Superman*. Not your comic-book one. I am a great man . . ." I blink and turn and see his head above the queerly *public* lines of his body. He is making a hash cigaret as he walks. He moistens and tightens the paper. "We care for each other, Nino . . . *very* much." He put the finished, lumpy cigaret in his mouth and lit it with difficulty. He took a puff and said, "You care for me a lot. We care for each other very much. We are truly friends. We are real friends. I am only flesh and blood," he said. I hated him, he is so adept in the arts of humiliation. We sat, and he threw his arm over my knee again and passed me the cigaret. He is one of the teased and brutalized and trespassed-on beauties of the world—like Venice itself. It is better never to go near the actuality of someone. In the shadow of continuance and knowledge.

Onni at the *Dogana* said, "Will you be buried with me? After all, you have been buried with me while we were alive . . . Aiee-me, I have always been too romantic for my own good."

The surprised, sun-teased, half-stink of the heat and the intolerable suffocation become a form of quietism toward the attachment to his presence. I trust him in a way, his body, his legs, his toyed-with nipples, his lurid need to win all the time, to avoid humiliation-from-now-on; he had that cast of mind, a *duce* and a whore, a magician. And *beautiful* and typical. And a hero and sad. The tight pull, drop, and nipped drape of skin, and the massy flesh, muscle tissue, bony hips, all of it . . . I think of him as used, lied to, robbed, snubbed, fucked over, recurringly triumphant. He grows stronger and stronger. His body is action and lies. And readiness. He is civilized, vivacious, and vengeful. And proud. He is good at hatred and grovelling and violence . . . He is loving and deadly. He more and more has a ruthlessness that is perhaps unlimited and eery, criminally unlimited . . . One senses it, how without limits he is . . .

The small sounds of physical closeness as we sit there, stoned, the sighing quasi-laughs, fleshy and distanced, inward . . . And nervous breath . . . like a wooden boat woodenly grunting . . . and the sheer reality of his bare forearm . . .

Onni told me of a scene in which there were four in bed, three tumbling away, while a naked and overweening *contessa* set out the next line of cocaine and then joined in again. "I was the bottom man," he said.

"Don't be so real!" I said to him.

The events he'd lived through were not easily reducible to anecdote. He gives me the menu of that occasion. He is half in, half out of the memory with a feeling of disgust and then with undisgusted amusement, theorizing in those alternate ways, judging his life. He says, "I will never forget . . ." He speaks in a dismissive tone with some disgusted and arrogant flavor of glamor as well . . . "Never . . ." Then one of the participants: "He was not repulsive . . . At least, he had no stomach . . . He was in a hurry to be shown that, while he felt freakish and like a spider climbing over you, he was the same as someone handsome in bed. I was what they didn't like in someone's being young . . . It was a game . . . 'We hate you, you are young . . .' Marisa the lesbian was sweet that night, the Contessa was more hateful than usual—she has skin like paper; she smells like ash and paper. The round-robin of slapping was awful . . . The women made us lie side by side while they compared us part by part like something in Homer . . . It would amuse me if they all would die . . .''

I knew of him that year that when he was undressed, and sometimes when he was dressed, his body, the body of someone *beautiful*, had a quality that I would say was that of someone waiting for a deathblow.

Anyone who is close to Onni is likely to be sadistic. And perhaps will fail in time in the face of his conquering will.

In a story, one omits reality. One picks one thing or devises a symbol and a symbolic kiss . . . And I will do that in a little while. But this that I describe here is what the symbol represents, the bright changes and the shadowy alterations and the attraction of a strong will, a story-like will that partly directs the meaning of the moments.

On the *Zattere*, at the *Dogana* the tethered soul, wingèd lion of one's acts, thinly growling and rising and falling, moves in and out of bright consciousness, bearing the zero-effect fool and bully I was as a man and the *life and death* I was, into and out of darkness and thoughtlight, like a movie light . . . I admire the narrow passages of sanity, the stanzas and metrical ins and outs of ordinary attention, the slipped rhymes of it, the sketchiness, the workmanship and egocentric assurance of not-a-game of it more than I like intoxication. I am always unhappy when I am drunk or stoned. Onni will be a big movie star, whorish in that grand popular sense; and the grotesque thing of *familiarity* with his body, with the spirit of it, the independent and foreign spirit, will be a commonplace of the era. I know his physical shape in part, and I know part of his ambitiousness. From inside the cubbyhole, the curtained alcove of the stoned moment, Onni offers a dim, pale, physically distorted smile: "Do you laugh at people, Nino?" he asks. "You are too quiet," he says. "Ah, it doesn't matter."

Being with Onni taught me to keep my nerve. I pass out at moments spottily and return to some consciousness almost as to a doorway, to the scene around me, the *Giudecca* and the *Bacino*, the brilliant light rippling in and out of my darkening and lightening intoxication.

"Are you happy, Nino?" Onni asks. "You are so quiet, *Poverino*." It would be difficult to guess at how much or how little of his life came from knowing me. I don't like taking responsibility for someone's thoughts—I chose him for his faultiness, so that I could not be closely judged. His interest in me is like breath on my cheeks, on my eyelids. Happiness, happiness is a hell of obscure ricketty elements shamelessly ablaze and drifting, rushing, really, like a raft of decorative fire on the *Canalazzo* . . . It cannot protect you for long or shelter you or offer a place to rest. In breath, a speech about a refusal to speak passes in and out through my lips. In childhood, you looked at people you cared about and now that looking has become this sort of looking . . . "A cigaret, *caro*?" he asks. He inserts a cigaret between my lips which are parted, half-smiling.

Love conceived of as a *motion* would be represented how? The creaking of one's breath? The delicate pomposities of youthful, intoxicated breath? Watery Venice, sunlit and fragile, and a wind-floored seabird's glide fill my eyesight at this promontory tip at the end of my strength . . . at the rim of the black flitter of the unconsciousness. Fluttering waves and flags of black absence from consciousness, a sea of this laps at me. Distances become opaque, but the wind and the sun are whispering, and the distance lessens, and I see the moment again in the light.

I place my dead hands on Onni's shoulder while he lights my cigaret . . . My thin shirt has come partly open . . . My skin burns from intoxication . . . Young skin is a mode of purchase in its stupid *beauty* . . . It is a blind, flinching, ugly currency in the sexual universe . . . The thermal current which is youth and the drowning shiftings of courage become a blackness but only thinly and waveringly . . .

Onni can take much of someone into his flesh as a woman does. He is an actor; he can do this with his mind. Also, the fleshy structures of his body are habitable. This is not true of me . . .

I gag on his reality when he takes the cigaret from my mouth and kisses me on the lips and touches my lips inside the kiss with his tongue a little—this is in the damp shadow of the stone wall of the *Dogana* where I lean my head. I feel in his breath that he is indulging this in himself. I think how the virtuous, and I too, exclude him, how we think him an enemy. I slide into the flittering black and then return to the light. The upward swift motion of the seabird against the hot wind into the blasting light is like a fluttering sketch of a gondola. The bird briefly is alight, the stammering tines of metal atop the neck of the craft of its own flight.

"A cigaret, Nino? Can you hold a cigaret?"

I shrug and let the stone weight of my head fall to one side away from him, from his breath. In the painfully foolish moment, my place as part of human reality is as part of everyone's reality in the glare of light that drives me back toward shadow. The preening and puckering narcissism of the lightly half-somersaulting, half-cartwheeling water hurts me. The palely cherubic, worn-to-invisibility wind cavorts. What-I-don't-know waits for me to study it in darkness into which I drop without warning, and from which I return to the physical slop of his hand on my chest . . . The stink of greatness of the real light—and of Onni—is not an element of theory: I smell it in the salt, damp, hot odors foolishly. The senses offer a lunatic hospitality to this lousy greatness, and one is nauseated. I shudder and tousle his hair and push Onni away from me . . . without pity.

"No . . ." I say inaudibly.

"You should be a priest," he says to a face and expression, mine, that I can't see or imagine.

He leans back. "Ah, *che orribile il sole* . . . The sun of suicide . . . I tried to kill myself twice—once when I was eleven, and last month . . . I have done it before but not so seriously . . . I slashed my wrists . . . I bled but not enough . . . I do not do it because things are so bad . . ." Something wobbles in his voice. "I do it to show I do not give a good goddam *fuck*—as you say . . ." Then: "I cannot take much more," he confides dryly.

He turned his head so that it rests sideways on the stone facing mine . . . The stone wall of the *Dogana* supports our profiles . . .

I shake my head no: I say inaudibly, "You are lying; you can manage."

A group of air force men from Foggia walked near, talking loudly, and stood looking toward *San Giorgio* and then the *Redentore* . . . They turned and walked back up the *Zattere*. They hardly glanced at us . . . One of them looked back at us.

Onni put his face near to mine on the damp stone: Onni pats my cheek. He whispers, "I tell you I love you. I am a beggar and not a chooser . . ."

I lost the day around me in a slow fading of outward sensation, and I jerked inwardly and the array of sensations returned filmily. I have in my nostrils the human, sweaty odor of his will. He is lifting me to my feet.

I blink and turn my head stilly toward the open water . . . Past two gulls standing on the *fondamenta*, the water dances in the great arson and streaming flood of afternoon light; Onni is lifting me to my feet at the *Dogana*. We entered a dreary, primeval epic of walking, a trek, in the wide passages, filled-in canals, small, pedestrian boulevards of this part of Venice. I walked crookedly and floppily, held upright to his side by his arm around my waist. Now we are stumbling into a gondola; in the smell of water, in the salt odor, Onni passes me to the gondolier who has a cigaret hanging from his lips. The beefy figure in the sailor suit and hat—his face looks like a dog mask to me—and his salty smell and his touch horrify me, they are so real and so far from any knowledge I have of such a person's life . . .

The gondola is facing the wrong way on the Grand Canal. The gondolier lowers me to the cushions and adjusts my legs, and then he is gone, to the stern, and everything is O.K. although treacherously flittering. Onni puts a cigaret between my lips and helps me smoke as I lie on the cushions and as the gondola turns into the canal and turns again into the sun. The gloriously yellow and cloth-like and rippling sky that rose behind the dome of the *Salute* and its stone population of figures high in the air now rises still more brightly above the doubled row of palaces and the doubled and erratic reflections. Far inside me the sounds of the Canal are ventriloquial, are spoken on the stage of darkness in me by my pulse, my breath, which are dream-thick, and which my mind parts like curtains, and I blearily stare through, while the gondola, turned the right way, and rocking on the wavelets, is poled by the tall, red-faced gondolier into the light.

I have never seen such glitter—in the light on the waves and on the prow of the gondola and caught in the feathers of swooping seabirds and tonelessly exploding and adhering to the windows of the palazzi alongside us. Up the curved road of water and in the air lay the fancifully buzzing explosion of actual sun into the heat in which we advanced blindedly and rockingly. I ache with helplessness, with the return to being a child. As in childhood, I am beyond fright.

Now we are in dark green shadow.

*   *   *

Onni had a thick bush and a thin pointed prick. A skinny line of hair went up his abdomen to his navel. His dick, as if muttering gesturally at being displayed and looked at, did not remain soft long usually, but asserted itself in its poking posture when looked at or displayed. *Viva Baffo*, Onni said. At times he called his prick by that name. When erect, it was, to be specific, the size of five or six cigarets plus an inch or so more of a businesslike, eyed knob, circumcised. The whole when erect formed an upward bent lever as for a train door or some other heavy door but strained looking and of uneven circumference and outline—unsatisfactory perhaps. He had trimly scrotummed, somewhat aerodynamically, sleekly shaped balls, and a very handsome although as-if-stitched anus with very little hair around it.

(Angela's anus was clear, with little discoloration of the pale buttock skin in the cleft around it. And the very regular stitching of it made it seem pure. It was very unlike her cunt which was lightly but sharply haired and slightly loose-flapped and then pink and a bit reddish and utterly strange, perhaps fig-like, but for me more like reddish water and shadow and a mouth of some sort . . . wicked . . . wickedly beautiful . . .)

Someone's sexual parts are not emblems, but they are often taken as such. In Onni as in Angela differently, the whisper of

phallic silkiness was a quality of attraction, story-like and cour-
teous, but sexual courtesy is a strange matter. I believe that what
drew their attention to me—for a while—was my zero-effect
brutality, if I might say that, and my sensual rhythm which was
amateur but thick and was complex with matters of my temperament, such as it was. I have no gift of sexual timing, of sexual
timeliness, but my public sexual quality at that time was *beautiful*,
was valid in the opinion of a number of people then . . . It was
valid that way for a while.

13

THE SEXUAL GIBBERISH of Onni's body, of the soul-in-nature in
him, in his room, murmured to me in the dark thrust of near-
unconsciousness, his closeness. To describe the inner senses is
to enter on poetry: I could hear the flashing of the flesh prism
in him. And in me. I lay drunken, mostly passed out, on a bed
in his shuttered room in daylight. The sense of rough sexual
territories and of hatred considered as truth where there are
separate lives—the freakish reality of individual existence—roll
this way and that as sensations.

Rolled physically this way and that, slowly, clumsily, one
feels the strained flutter of being undressed: feels the simplification . . . The skin breathes.

Then I lay there, my head floating and mostly dark, lay there
alone, and I felt dumped there, abandoned, dismissed as I rose
and fell and floated into and out of the dark and the present
tense in my intoxication, floated like a murdered body drifting
on the waters of a canal.

I had no choice but to be a body in the warm darkness. Onni
was moving about the room. The sounds he made were not concerned with me. I could not keep my eyelids up or turn my head
or make my head see; I had to close my eyes in order to breathe.
To try to see, to try to stay conscious was nauseating . . . It seemed
to strip the lining of the brain.

The whitish, heavyish, too straight, uncostumed prick in the
shadows, rude thing . . . too white . . . the jealousies and curiosities

concerning it are not universal but are widespread. My inner wish to endure life, to endure the complications of sexuality, to know what it is to love and be loved is in retreat in a body briefly with head upraised, a naked gondola of a boy on the bed.

I think Onni went down on me . . . He did something sexual or not-so-sexual with the prick. I didn't care. It seemed friendly and modest. And he was there. Someone was there. I wasn't interested enough to fight to stay awake to feel or to identify what he was doing. I was launched into an unradiant darkness, a *visible* reversal of light. The dreams were alternately as small as small paintings and as large seemingly as the sky over the Lagoon.

The reality from which we derived our ideas, our opinions, and the real moments in which we love one another to what extent we do love, are much more detailed, more nuanced than I have been able to show, are even further on the other side of telling a story in any usual way. Reality tells and reveals its stories differently from the way we do.

Anyway, this is the best I can do now at representing reality, and now I want to go back to telling a story.

THE MONSTER

IF ONE IS NOT JOKING, not joking and not lying, what is possible in terms of describing physical love? Is his slablike body moving atop mine in the humid darkness behind lowered shutters? Like a willful nudging snout . . . Is it moving slyly and carefully? Quickly and with rapacity? Do we have here the snout of will marking and perhaps breaking the mind?

Who has ever lived who has been unmolested? A bruise. A bite. An entry. Perhaps only into the mind. Have you ever told the blunt truth to anyone?

Well, what is a happy ending? A form of sentiment for the audience—derived from Venetian music? A license to experience affection?

The affection in the dark of a passage of drugged disorder, its meaning lies in its tone, surely. Clumsy, the tone that of a midget babbling, maybe nostalgically or dreamily, in a doomed, only half-willed assault. Or a daydream thing acted on—if it's that, that is a separate thing.

But the veiled act, perhaps a dream, how mysterious it is. Is it desire like an annunciation, a vision hallucinatorily real, your fate, transcendent strength interested in breaking the spirit of distance in the other? Truth . . . A god?

What I remember dreamily, nightmarishly is that it was real, and it was dreamed.

The abandoned mind is caught for-the-moment in transitory-and-changeable paralysis. Abandoned galleries of will are straggling off into the dark; they come alight in passages of sensation and show themselves outfitted with images, hands and penises, eyes and embraces passing themselves off as emblems of truth.

One contains a dream's vocabulary in a dreamer's movie-like speech to himself. Wanting to wake, one tries to decide in which direction to go to reach the outer surface of this paralysis in the real world. But it is not a literal direction. This space is without compass dimension.

I feel I move *upward*. One ascends angelically, demonically. My dreams are windows of theater through which I come to know the world but only as myself inside myself and dreaming.

The ascent into waking becomes a descent into actual breath. Are my dreams true? Are my true feelings what I feel in my sleep? Have I had a wet dream, that sort of abandonment, the self sexually fooled, that peculiar sexuality?

Ever afterward one contains this moment of one's history. One contains one's long history of dreaming. What sort of reality is this? A rat in the mind bites me. A rat's forepaw, five-parted, moves on me. A mass of heat, like lava, but merely human lava, lies on my ribs heavily. The horror depends on the quality of the animal's movement, on the expression in the animal's eyes, the degree of foreignness and of rapacity.

Is what is there on the face of the creature sad will or docility of appetite set free or malice? Or a wild, half-amused rage? Or trickery?

In the dark, before I awoke, what I felt in the motions was *curiosity*, and contempt, and solitude. An ambition to make the world as much a matter of one's own vocabulary of memory and experiences as a dream is. Sometimes contempt is an attempt to extend one's contempt for one's own sufferings to the seeming well-being of others.

•

In the dream I felt the mounting of superiority in the weight on me, a mounting into an actual superiority acted out in a few minutes. Really, a very few minutes.

When I woke I remembered crashing onto the floor at some point, a great crash, roiling and thundering in my nerves . . . Perhaps more than one body fell. The echoes and thumping of the fall were in more than one body. I came to a kind of consciousness and saw a wall and heard human breath; and I fell back, in deep gray-blackness, descending toward a new kingdom of dreaming. I did not wake. Do you understand the weight of complicity in that, and the emptiness?

The character of the soul seen by the dreamer is in the emotional intensity of the dream. In the dream *I* fell past angels in a darkness, past shapes named the Whores of Silence, past tiers of animals that maul and paw you if they catch you.

Then I dreamed again. This is the dream that followed the assault which may have been a dream. An owl shrieked in the *Piazzetta* where an ambulatory figure in a whitish light grew invisible while in the transparent campanile a naked goddess as tall as the tower stood, her eyes peering out at the top. The Piazza smelled of *goddess*. Feathered Indians in canoes were paddling down the deserted Grand Canal past animals swimming amicably in flat and mirroring water, wonderful-eyed giraffes and lions and shiningly wet horses among the ochre and silver palazzi in the windows of which flickering candle flames, orange and blue and white, moved atop bright-colored glass sconces.

Now *the reality* (in the dream) is of a sleeping boy in the deserted Piazza. *San Marco* is a silvery Neapolitan tin portrait of itself. An owl mates with a sparrow on the pavement. In a mockery of pictures of angels in tiers in the sky, pigeons, bugs, fish in the *Bacino*, bats, rats, the now pale horses in front of the cathedral, the Evangelists and the Infant Jesus unfold themselves or lift their tails and wings or robes in a universal display of genitalia. In the dream, it is visibly animate creation in all-out sexual exhibitionism in the universal sexuality of the genital all. A bald, big-necked soldier grabs the sleeping boy who breaks loose and runs through crowded *calli*, the soldier pursuing him. I don't escape but I find a gun and shoot him in the neck. He has a round face of great naïveté which beams sweatily and jerks in the agony of being shot. My body begins to weep, to exude a film of sweat and to throb with sexuality, wounded, near death, too. I have survived a beating. My back and buttocks and stomach and face ache. The dead soldier's spouting blood rises and becomes fountain jets of rubies tossed and scattered and falling redly in the Piazza. And people scoot and scramble to grab the jewels. God, overhead, watches. Butterflies flutter among the rubies. The statue of St. Mark, above the gilt horses and the crowd, begins to roar and shout. Peacock consciousness spreads into an immense fan. A yellow horse goes in a flying gallop around the Piazza. On it balances an intent bareback rider in a tutu. In the center of the Piazza, a large, bearded, bare-chested man, orchestrally conducts a *Kong*ress of giant apes.

The sad animal world is in the midst of cataclysmic drama. I cry out, *This is a box of lips.* The sky splits like paper; and ranks of angels—without genitals—appear, circled by stars and buzzing spirits of light. They are singing; it makes a bumbling roar like the pulsing of music in a domed church, noisy, peaceful, expressive.

And then everyone living and dead is blown or lifted or weightlessly and driftingly ascends. The angels of the Apocalypse quaintly sift the ascending souls which are winged and finned and pale like wisps of cloud with children's faces or else which leer and flame. The no-longer-sky, the empyrean beyond, black and holy, is filled with luridly lighted activity around one radiant point.

I sing, sing aloud, and am a very junior chorister near Deity not very far from Lucifer. Lucifer, leaden in color, is unshaven, hideous, and tremendous in size. His gigantic wings, his vast leather wings, in their ugly grandeur, ignite billows of sickened, uncontrollable *disgust* around him.

The scene was glowing with a great light. Eve and the Virgin particularly shone. The Virgin's cape was a sheltering structure, partly dome-like. Goodness and protection and mercy flowed from her; and handsome trees in bits of landscape tucked into geometrically shaped corners of things around her flowered and glowed, goodness clearly known.

The Devil's *vasty*, truly immense dirty sails, his wings, stirred the hardworking sweetness of that large part of the scene and blew and stirred part of the great population of souls ascending to the gleaming nets and sorting angels, and at the same time cooled his own heat . . . But then God tore holes in the Devil's wings through which the crucified Christ, hands and feet fixed to a cross, motionlessly appeared. But then He became a Christ of an enormity of motion, both blown and still, with *immense* artilleries of eyes and with an echoingness of speech, arms spread in blessing, and with a voice of inhuman, winnowing, harrowing, mercilessly real power, embodied and actual and yet more than human in effect. Murmurs from the Virgin had a merciful, forgiving tone.

But I must say that the mercies of Christ and His Mother were hardly separable from acts of corruption and companionship, and seemed to show more of an identity with this or that sinner or a sense that this or that sinner had favored them, than anything celestial and incomprehensible.

But this corruption as humane and human kindness, resting on prayer and on gifts, and on a community of interest, this method of measuring worth-to-God was doubly strange and powerful next to the Devil's great inhuman shape which was so stocked with objects and things near him or strapped to him that he was clearly visible; he was clothed in whips and chains and masks and figures that were not directly human but were freakish souls shaped like spiders, like rabid wolves, like octopus arms with beaky open mouths among them, falcon-headed women and men, men made of stone with stone breasts or human-breasted but with stone hearts visible, visibly unbeating, and mad, shrieking women and men, harpies, crows, attempters, forgers. He, the complexity of him, was unspeakable, was unseeable, was a gray blur.

In the lurid glow surrounding him where he stood, the Devil said, *Give the Devil his due.*

And here and there, bodies and various forms of light, the human and the reaches of meaning beyond the human rose flyingly near him, near Lucifer swollen past all bearing into an unseeable dark magnificence, a shoddy, outflung, defeated and deadened, leaden immensity of magnetic reality of presence.

Meanwhile a gathering momentum of wrenching, even rending, outcries of terror and grief which were like wing-beats and breath tore the scene. It was as if I were weeping and that this had become an enormous, universal weeping. Lucifer as the stolen pre-shadow of Christ, as time-defined, pre-the-coming-of-the-full-reality of Christ, as a sense of lightlessly orderly labor, *here and there*, grabbed and caught the discarded.

But Christ had come, the companion truth and aftereffect of the Devil, the shadow of light cast by the Devil inside the twining of realities, ours and God's; or, rather, the shadow of one cast light; and the light of the other was pure. And in that light, motion and will existed in the dream. And though the shadows shifted after a while, the light did not change; death did not need to occur. The knotted being of light as glow and glare and blaze without a boundary or movement was untranslatable into ordinary meaning, so many lamps of nature and of celebration illuminating the harsh action of the dance of judgement, the harrowing of Hell and of the dead and of the living. The very idea of motionlessness vanished, but I suddenly realized I did not believe the scene although in the dream which I did not know was a dream the scene was actuality itself.

The hope of final and unarguable meaning, to be mitigated by mercy, was acted out by a fantastically muscular giant—a figure of strength stronger than even the Devil, although the figure was quite small in comparison to the Devil's grayly leaden immensity. The daring and obstinate human who fought the argument of the scene and who was unfazed by the greater strength of the angels and of the Devil and the mass of others or by the operations of fear in himself, this figure of strength was striking with an oar and picking and choosing in a marine setting, in a *saline* odor, with utter, subcelestial assurance and finality, the souls, the anima, the final forms of identity for bliss or pain, for death or life of people as they lived as if he were God or Christ and the Virgin or the Devil in the harrowing of after-death.

Not God or Christ or the Devil stopped him.

But he, among the infinite stirrings and strings and wavering motions of the falsely real substances in the dream, became the sifting fingers of God but obliquely, through historical meaning, something like that.

Then the Virgin, and Christ, and then the Devil, formed aerially a final unity, a final dignity, as light but as light stilled and unified, a great unison universe-wide.

Then the light began to swing back and forth like the lamps on the wires over the Piazza in the wind of the hard rains during *acqua alta*.

Each proposal of meaning was stilled for a moment as if it was to be the last one, but then came the next proposal of meaning. All at once suddenly I felt the enormous kiss of God, the timeless and actually logical majesty beyond judgement or knowledge, and unyielding and unfaulty. But it had reality in time and was subject to judgement and knowledge and was yielding and faulty but was lunatic with hurt faith, the hurt choiceless faith of a child: Christ known in this fashion.

The moment passed into disbelief and into waiting which yet was belief, belief of a kind. One touches a window and one's hand passes through reality and law and glass and enters the visible, actual scene and the arbitrary law, dreamed of, obeyed, that was there. A spectrum of connections was implied. Stones that were clocks-of-geological-time were interspersed in walls made also of ticking clocks with ordinary clock faces. They were used as stones alongside yet another form of stones through which not light flashed but shade and shadows of comparative stillnesses that were not quite still but which were flutters of pretty beauty, various unstill truths of motion that were pretty.

On these walls were particles of unstill light, bits of shifting costumes of light, and through these walls came light and wind; but one was sheltered anyway.

And near were rapidly whirling spheres of gulping darkness

out of which came a sweetly unbearable hungry darkness that made one dead-but-alive, image-like. I *enter* the folds of a flag and am in a dark country of glory actually there inside the representative and blowing *fabric*. The lap of a statue of Eve became the naked lap of a real and naked mother. I lay my head among the odors. My head rested in the mooded actual tenderness. It was far stranger than the mighty images had been.

In now burning Venice the flames were dry, the canals were without water. *Dry sterile thunder and no rain . . . There is silence in the mountains . . . the red sullen faces sneer . . . from the doors of cracked mud houses . . . If there were the sound of water only . . . and dry grass singing . . . Who is the third that walks always beside you . . . There is always another one walking beside me . . . I do not know whether a man or a woman . . . Who is that at my other side . . . What is that sound high in the air . . . Murmur of maternal lamentation . . . What are those hooded forms swarming . . . over endless (Polish) plains, stumbling in cracked earth . . . Falling towers . . . Jerusalem, Athens . . . Unreal . . . A woman drew her long black hair out tight . . . And fiddled whisper music on those strings . . . And upside down in air were towers tolling reminiscent bells . . . And voices singing out of cisterns and empty wells . . .*

The quote was not exact and was anachronistically supposed to be an ancient text. Nor did I know at that time the phrases of the uncorrected version of "The Waste Land," so I am wrong to use them here.

We are escaping the end of the world in an ill-lit, sloping metal structure, a pipeline, in which rushes (and roars) a strong current of unpausing water, swirling, a tube of ocean. We begin slowly, heavily, with maddening difficulty, to walk in the dark rapid water and its massive current. It felt actually cold and wet—as if the dreamer had been mopped with a wet washcloth and was drying in night air. We moved in the eery glints of the metal pipe where the water and air boomed with horrible unremitting steadiness and while the surface sounds of the water were a tinkling and treble whispering like sad harps and drifting guitar plinks interfering with the booming. I never doubted the reality of love even in modern circumstances. A Viking galley sweeps by from an unexploded Northern Venice, but I drown. In absurd death and resurrection I drown and return to life. So do my companions. A girl sings to herself in Judy Garland's voice. A boy floats and sleeps, a girl riding on his wet chest, another boy walks ahead, his hand on the ankle of the sleeper, drawing him along, gleaming wet. We were far from a happy ending. We were free of the sentimentality of happy endings. But as I said, I never doubted the reality of love-under-any-circumstances.

In the dream I said I did not want to escape anymore, at least not in this way, in this lonely, booming, dangerous pipe.

I was returned to Venice. Fire balloons moved in a spectral light above the Piazza. Abraham Lincoln ascended the *Scala Giganti* and then appeared beside the statue of St. Mark above the façade of the cathedral. Then here is a dangling prick, not erect but thickened and enlarged, a slippery, sticky, slightly smelly dark-haired heft, life-sized but the view of it changed, and it was as large as a tackling dummy, as large as a person. Do you forgive your dreams their dreamlike nature? I have trouble being on terms with my dreams. I can and do forgive reality but I am accusatory toward my dreams.

I began to resent being asleep . . . *Rope, rope, rope your boat gently crown the stream . . . life is but a dream . . . But what are we hanging around here for in a dream inside a dream?*

The answer was given in a visual image that required words since it was of a *mind* suspended in a *crystalline* beauty of the air in a spill or curl of further beauty, a marvellousness of geometry, of numbers, pretty waves, sea-light; accompanied by a pounding; but one had to know it was a mind.

I am ecstatic and blind, blinded. In shame and embarrassment I think I wake and then I see I am still in the same light as before. I recognize that I am close to coming. The *ecstatic* peculiarity of it is shaming. I as-if-wandered into the final excitement, into a riverine orgasm, gray, heavy, sodden, breaking, with vast white light contained in it, a curlingly luminous foam.

I leaped onto the porch of death—*do you know?* I made the last few pre-orgasmic movements consciously and woke in a surge of disgust and in a spasm of bliss, jerkingly in the body's ejaculatory thrust, in that burst of light and disjunctures of flood and sensation, in a room's darkness throbbingly messing up myself where I lay, naked, still drunk, still high on hashish, half-sick and disoriented, on the wooden floor.

I don't know. Drunk, buzzing with the high—but not paralyzed—bruised, I saw the gray-white light from the lamp in the *calle* in one opening of the slatted shutters. Its light lay on the windowsill but darkness was everywhere. Bits of light lay on the floor not far from me. The smell of dust was in my nose.

It was Onni's room. I sat up drunkenly and vertiginously. I began to check myself. No one was in the room with me. Consciousness is as if veering and sliding and planing *drunkenly*, intoxicated still. On the side of my haunch was a stain of olive oil. I remembered the smell of olive oil. I remembered the smell of breath. The smell of sperm.

There was a small *dry* crust on my abdomen that might have been sperm, and another near my waist. I touched my mouth, my backside, my armpits, the skin between my legs at the top of the fork. Nothing was abraded or smeary.

I was shamed and scared for myself. Who survives untouched? A botched inch of entry, mostly balked—was it worse than that? A hand on my unconscious chest, his hand sweating in his drug high, something like a handprint of crud was on one side of my chest; another smear was on my cheek, next to my nose.

What romance moved him? Me, a lump wrapped in drunkenness—what a *tangential* desire. Was it revenge, to own, to ruin . . . How can I grow up now? *Fuck you*, and *up yours*, and *you asshole, you're fucked* . . . He's fucked me over.

My soul, my pigeon-like soul, one among the pigeon flock, and love and jealousy—I was cannon fodder to his greatness. In the half-dark room, the door to the stairs to the *altana* is open.

A towel is on the stair railing, thong sandals on one of the steps. Overhead I heard a chaise shift, and footsteps.

I rise and pull on pants, a shirt, unbuttoned. Barefoot I blink and squint . . . Walls rise, slide, shift, subside . . . I move like someone dead returned or like a shipwrecked guy, one of Shakespeare's tormented, half-murdered men . . . Among the clowns and gentles . . . The meagerness of the ravishment, that ill-begotten definition of *love*, a Jansenist rage of vengeance send me as if beneath the water for a moment, a drowned boy in Venice, yet another one: a deadened, violent self.

The bells of Venice rang in the moist air as I blinkingly came to the door of the *altana*. I held myself upright there. The sky bends down in narrow points among the roofs and bell towers. There is a full moon and small moon-whitened clouds. The first clanging from distant and hidden bell towers is muted, partly blocked by intervening buildings along the winding *calli*. But then the bells from the visible towers start up, *San Stefano* and the *Frari* and *San Marco* and its *Marangona*, unleashing a loud, urgent, nearer clangor mingling with the muted other clanging, filling the tight fist of the city with arrhythmic clamor. Around us, in the dark city, above a few lit, pale façades, stone figures stood and blessed or stared in the high, dark air—angels, the Virgin, the Evangelists, a few Christs—a stone population among the jumbled roofs, some with bronze wings and bronze trumpets and bronze haloes in the dark air.

Onni said, "Here we are—between the angels and fish . . ."

"Fuckface . . . You prick . . . You shit . . ."

He sickens me—sickens me. In me, in my vitals, the ferocious glare of consciousness pressed radiantly, *urgently*, stingingly. Spikes of consciousness seemed to pass through my skin at moments and to heat it with a hot sobriety while I am as drunk *as a lord*, sweating a little.

In the cold unrepeatability of the universe, a bottle of grappa is on a metal table and a pack of Lucky Strikes is beside it, dim white in the darkness, and a gold lighter . . .

Onni, not stirring on his chaise, says, "Come . . . I have grappa . . ."

"You stupid shit," I said, lost in ordinariness. "You're not the Sea Wolf . . . Shakespeare's dead." His actions have been old-fashioned, stupid . . . How unsexual other people's sexual desires are.

"Ah," he says in a weary tone putting one arm up over his eyes, elbow bent. He says, "Nigh-nigh," this was in an English accent, "your lips—you have exceptional lips . . . *extraordinary* lips . . . Have some grappa . . ." Then masculine blackmail: "Only fools sober up from such true hashish . . ."

Onni said slowly, "Imagine a drunken *god*—the Greeks had drunken *gods* who understood . . ." Then: "You are not as fond of me as you should be."

Pigeons in the dark, on the roofs and *altanas* and below in the *Campiello* coo, squabble, court one another . . . Venice seemed to plunge in a burst of wind, to be a flight-torn, trembling city . . . God . . . Imagine God drunken . . .

In me was a restless motion of a chronically enflamed falling and drifting sideways of bits of consciousness, an idiosyncratic litter of light and dark in motion. The clinging, warm-cool air in its little tides offered sensitive embraces. The clamberings of the wind under the moon brushed and tickled me like cherubs. Around me was moonlight.

Onni said, "Nothing happened. We were drunk. I am not a person of that kind."

"I can kill you."

"Che stupidaggine."

The night wind blew my shirt cape-like, exposing my back to the air. In some paintings and mosaics is one face among others that has eyes partly unfocussed with ignorance and youth, a face with a curiously compounded innocence and unfinal virility, but almost sleeping, daydreaming intently. Sometimes the eyes are alert. Such a face suggests the lostness, the sweetness of youth, not as rage and not as melancholy, but as freshly victimized and as still young—such faces are common in paintings, Hamlets waiting.

I can't find in myself the grammarian's fixed *I* or a daydream's starring figure; I am a committee of selves, a congress of young men.

The end-of-love is mercy—we will spare each other now. This is partly true, but it is largely an illusion.

"I might actually kill you, Onni."

In our moments, we breathed, not in unison. The practice of sight seemed noisy. My eyes' movements thunked and squeaked and whispered and whistled. "Will you miss me?" I asked suddenly.

"Don't be stupid," he said after a pause. "Are you still high, Nino? Very high?"

" '*Are you still very high, Nino?*' *Onni asked,*" I said.

He said, "I am sitting here. I have just found out something. 'To be or not to be . . .' I understand it . . . I understand the draw of death. I admire Shakespeare more than I can say . . . Shakespeare is the greatest of all writers, do you agree, Nino-nini?"

Onni is often without memory and so, in a sense, often without moral judgement. Instead, in a given moment he is in rehearsal for what he will be next, in the next moment, the whore Sea Wolf, a coarsened sensibility self-absorbed with watchfulness. His eyes, his breath in the dark. I suppose it is a common male gamble he makes, the stuff that he does. I suppose he is mad with velocity but in slow motion as if in an old movie, a silent one. A crazy sledder has banged into me and pulled me to the ground. *Will you love him?* Onni doesn't know much about love.

This stuff of trespass is familiar ground to him—I am *privileged* to be so instructed in this other reality.

"Ha-ha," I said aloud.

He says, "Shakespeare is so interesting—I could play those roles. I could do Hamlet."

What did he know about hesitation and love? The lovers I saw in the garden long ago I see now vertiginously as if down a shaft of dark wind. And the books with love stories in them that I'd admired, I saw again. I said, "I am like an angel in Giotto, a head in flight—Onni, I don't love you very much anymore."

He nods and says, "I see. I see," wearily patient.

"What do you see?"

"You are a madman. And stoned. You have the American paranoia. You are a nice boy—no one can do you any good."

I had realized only that it was dangerous and took a lot of nerve to love someone, but I had not realized how *hard* it was. Love silenced is indescribable in its finality.

I said, "You're an asshole."

"I understand," he said.

"You are a friend," I said, so carefully unironic it was ironic painfully.

"You are a poet," he said with satisfaction and in flattery. "But perhaps you are really a scientist in the end."

"Onni . . ."

He laughed handsomely and said, "You must understand: I have much in common with the soul of Hemingway."

The mind hovers like a smelly owl over the idea of dislike for him and amazement exhaustedly—and anger hovers among actual bats flapping in the Venetian dark.

His eyes, the shape and weight of the lids, near his *breathing* mind, were complicatedly familiar—this wasn't complete or pure. The darting and unstable phenomenon of near identity was palpable. The moment didn't have clear duration but flashed and had an aftereffect and bits of it re-occurred in memory in a different key, him and his realities of breath. I was confusedly drunk and stoned briefly his way as well as mine. My version of him in his drunkenness felt that drunkenness to be like an inner sunburn crisping me, so that I was inwardly sensitive and strange in this sunburn, strange and *handsome* in being drunk and careless—this was the sensation of it. His mind was as if tanned and experienced in drunkenness, *condottiero, bersagliere, gondoliere* . . . I am not laughing at him. I love him in a troubled—and limited—way, with a dismissive clemency still.

The limited love is dry and harsh. My mind poled along among narrow angers that opened into a wider loneliness, an empty sea. He'd been an easily harmed child, eager, half-foolish, playing at power. Now he had a man's ability to shift the world, the world of others, and was not clearly someone who had been a child. He was squinting. He usually squinted when he was drunk; and he usually breathed through his nose while his lips became enlarged. My physical sense of him is conditioned by long acquaintance. One harshly changes one's sense of him: he is ugly and without allure. One harshly, maybe with regret, feels this.

"You fuckhead," I say.

Forgiveness is strangely akin to permission, a different sort of dangerous amusement—I mean in real life.

"Are you a ruthless drunk, Onni? Do you have an Apollonian side? To balance that shit?"

"Do you do an interview with me?"

"We are talking."

"Talk-talk."

The shape of his imagination and the patterns of his constant revision of his life, I couldn't truly bear it that he was the way he was.

He reached over and placed his hand on the back of mine. I moved my hand away in an act of pornography—physical rejection is pornographic—but he put his hand on mine again. The pads of the fingertips like the tiny snouts of very small animals, shrews. The density of whored flesh, the dirtied strength. I felt contempt and let my hand stay.

Through the silent skin, the pulse, imprisoned in the veins, breathes its way, inside the walls of the rage-desensitized self. I might as well be a woman, in the shadow of Christ, I despise violent anger so.

The Napoleonic whore-of-destiny, so massive in ambition, cares about me . . . I can feel him caring about me. I am appalled. Thrilled a bit. He straightens himself with a sigh where he lies on the metal chaise, and he says, "You are not pretty anymore. You are becoming a man."

I don't truly wish love to be infinite.

He says, "I trust the *moon*. Now tell me the truth, really the truth, tell me, Nino, *Bello*, are you a Satan? Let us be clear; let us be honest: I know you are a Satanic American in the end."

I said, "The movies and the love of fine clothes have stolen my soul . . . ha-ha. You are right to blame me for what you are. Ha-aagh. The great whiff of the Devil . . . Huff-pufffffff . . . the scaley wings extend from America to the *Sestiere San Marco* and close around us . . . here in the dark."

"Yes," he said. Onni leaned over and kissed my hand.

The degree to which love is a willingness to accept pain is maybe sickeningly clear, maybe slimily enticing . . . Can you bear it? In some men and women it has a peculiar sentry-like quality or odor, the willingness to bear the slanted pain of love . . . *Enticing . . . dangerous . . . sickening* . . . An interest and curiosity about being pained is whorishly party-like, Venetian. But in him is the *sickening* and much more passionate totality of readiness and appetite for the soldierly—or saintly—thing of complete self-rending.

He is a much wilder soul than I am, a young man of greater accomplishment, of more power, a potent creature such that in photographs of him he seems priapic and importantly so: the self that sunlight reveals on film is more symbolically than literally true. It is almost like a boy being maternal, me being phallically assertive but in abeyance in this way.

That carefully, nicely outspoken flesh of his, him as a *folk* figure of seduction—an intelligent young Italian with a large amount of culture in him, drunk and dangerous, drunkenly-and-self-righteously-demonic-heroic, the thing about doing something rotten is that you're stuck with defending it inside yourself. Repentance, redemption, and change are rare and difficult and require a different intelligence. He wants to feel it is my demonism. Onni said, "Sit up, *Bello*! Let us talk about the satanism of SATANIC America! I believe in Hell, literally, the FLAMES, THE FLAMES—the flames are *your* atomic bomb."

It made my blood run cold, this other evidence, or whatever it was, that the thing had happened and was contemptible. "Go to Hell, *caro amico*," I mumbled. I put down my glass of grappa thinking I would never get drunk with Onni again. I would never sleep in the same room with him again.

He said, observing my gesture, "I did not really touch you when you were passed out. I cleaned you up a little bit. I treated

you like a human being. I teach you to be human, *carissimo*—
that is my role in life."

I was silent. One labors inside one's drunkenness to breathe,
to stay upright. He looked at me sharply and bluntly, drunkenly,
also laboringly.

He really did not believe in a world of judgement. He believed darkness ruled—he had a huge comprehension of this as
truth, a presumptuous comprehension that alternated with privacy and loneliness and supreme anger and varieties of courtesy
and doubt.

He said, "I *do* believe in Hell. I am frightened. I do not
believe in God but I believe in *Hell*. Do you understand? I feel
the flames of Hell on my feet." He shifted his feet gesturingly.
"I am fierce. I am damned. Do not laugh at me. I warn you."
This is post-courtship courtship.

"My aunt has very good grappa. It comes from her friend's
place near Bassano: her friend's mother makes it. My aunt is the
Devil incarnate. Here, have some more. America rules the world;
it bestrides the world—"

"For Christ's sake, Onni, I am *not* as guilty as you are," I
said. It is clear from my voice that I am free of him, that I am
maneuverable.

"America has more power than the Devil. It is as rich as the
Devil. Money, all money, only money. It is ruining my country.
The devil-country is ruining everyone—everywhere."

"I know, I know: there is no guilt but that . . ."

His long, solid arms lay loosely at his side. "No, but really,
Nino, truly, *Bello*, there is no peace, and it is your country's doing.
You are a little civilized but I want to talk to you, it is a serious
matter—Coca-Colanization. It is the death of culture . . . of MY
culture . . . It is the end of the world. I *hate* your country."

"Listen, Onni, don't ever tell me what to do . . . Don't ever
know better for me, you get me?"

He breathed rapidly, shallowly. "I am telling you the truth
about politics. You are a child . . ."

"And a woman . . ."

"Yes. It is true," he said.

It is hard to explain the reality of my body as misused, how it felt it had small, dark smouldering places, redly lit or orange with leftover heat, the flat bits of that in my nipples and on my belly, my waist . . . In the mind, in the flickers of nervous messages, I felt naked and real, used.

And ready to hate-him-for-a-while or for real, brutally. It is very different, the sensation of being misused, from any other sensation; it is a discouraged excitement that rushes along, the self overturned and scratched, semi-ruined, and struggling. Something like this is in Onni, too, of course. I felt the rushed syncopations of his nervous, stoned, physical-and-mental breaths, eye-blinks, his movements on the chaise, his pale muscular flesh. I think I felt the next step for him, the unknown next thing, was a truer rape, a truer humiliation of me. Or his rolling and falling into a faintly real rotundity of cherub-like or cupid-like finality of flirtation, almost a hanger-on, almost as if I were a producer or director or very rich man. Or a dominating woman . . . That is what he knows, those things are his limits.

The continuousness of the fine braiding of sexual heat with intellectual and spiritual appetite and the thin accompanying whistling of shame are distraction and curiosity, and perhaps a true sense of life-and-death. It has merit—this is what the life in him is like, it seems to me.

He said, "Can you defend the beast of a country your country is?"

He was like an elegant dog or foal scuffling in ashes, not restrained or leashed.

"My country is not bestial . . . it's an idea, a political idea —and it's a place, a location. It has become so powerful that now everything must be rethought, but no one is honest enough in this matter to be believed—so who will do this rethinking? Not you."

"You are right. No one is honest."

"Some people are honest about some things," I said veering from him.

"No, no. You are a child about these matters!" Then: "I am a realist! You have brought the Culture of Death! You are naïve.

It is a fight to the death! *You* can be civilized, you choose to be a lamb of God. But underneath I must save myself from you— you are one of *them*—it is a fight to the death . . ."

"Sure. Of course. I brought death . . . None was in Italy before I came."

"DON'T BE A CHILD!"

"I smuggled it in my eyebrows—in my balls—pure death. My existence is DEATH. BEWARE. Ford and Edison and Chaplin made Death and it has spread into your eternal life . . . Those aren't footsteps you hear in Venice, that's the clatter of skeletons, clatter, clatter . . . We are proud that we invented Death when you tried so long and could not do it . . ."

He leaned forward. He reached for a cigaret. "You . . . agh . . . *Merda* . . ." He clutched his head. "Don't be so crazy. You don't know what the truth is."

"Your clichés aren't truth."

"You are not innocent!"

"Italy stinks! You can't ruin what is ruined."

"You cannot deny that Americanization is death . . ."

"I do deny it."

"Then you are crazy."

"I'll tell you what the trouble is: you feel inferior. But what makes you feel inferior you little-pricked shit is that you're a little-pricked shit!"

"I am Italian . . ." he said. "I have feelings you cannot understand."

"You like white-jawed Adolf with his salute like a bowsprit? You like your mighty-jawed *Duce*? Ah, tell me about *our* gangster charm."

"You admire what you have done to the world?"

"Onni, no one and nothing can bring Utopia—Christ didn't, I'd like to remind you."

"Shut up. You are crazy."

"And you're a whore. Listen, I am not a Turk or a Mongol—or a Venetian. Why don't you build another generation of camps for Americans—for Americans without culture? The crimes are different, you fuck. One doesn't cancel out the other."

"You torture the Blacks!"

"I haven't done it tonight . . . Will anything ever be your fault? People should avoid cheap formulations of evil, Sonny Pie . . . You don't share the world with anyone. You and I are so implicated in one another that we are almost one flesh but you don't care. You don't notice. A person is his crimes, Onni. It is very democratic in my country, what the truth is. It's not a matter of the taste of princes and of governing ministers . . . The meaning of life is different for us. We vote on it. So, now, everything is a tragedy—a *democratic* tragedy—oh my God, what a tragedy. You're not utterly happy? My God, I *weep* for you. Your *kitsch* omnipotence makes me sick . . . Do you understand that tragedy is forbidden—*catharsis delenda est* . . . We're supposed to make things work, you cunt Italian. It is obvious. You are always so fucking obscure, you and your tantrums of deathliness. Be truthful, you asshole! Do you ever feel a bitter fright—at the comedy of the crap you do? I will die from *your* stupidity—do you understand? If we don't cut out the shit and settle into being sensible, we die in our spirits . . . You will ruin everything . . ."

"*Catharsis delenda est?* I don't speak Latin," he said. "But I think I admire only Latin women . . . I think you like to bullshit and dominate."

"I have no theories about myself. Only a theory about you. I am a child still . . ."

"You can talk the head off Christ: it amuses me to hear you. But will your fine ideas enrich anyone? Will I live well now and get rich with this new sense you give me, that democracy is so truthful in everyone? I will remember that and learn how to become a movie star? Do you approve, *Caro Nino*? Are you telling me a gospel? I wonder how smart you really are. I say you are as smart as the Devil. Tell me, is what you said here a speech made to me by my aunt's friend's mother's grappa?"

I burst out laughing, a little thickly.

"You laugh," he said. "But I am interested in *this* small truth."

"Yes? But how close do you ever get to telling the truth? Courage aside, just technically? And *who* would *you* tell it to? Would you do it on your deathbed when the games were over? Will you train yourself? The truthfulness will begin to be faked, a trick, too overtrained, like the rump of a broad jumper, do you know?"

"Ha," he said. "Yes—that is what it is in acting, the staleness of the truths; they get big-assed."

"It's not always a good sign, looking for the truth . . ." I said, thinking truthfully of what a shit he was; and without my knowing I would do it I reached over and slapped his face hard—but still it was more the gesture of a pacifist than it was a real blow.

"You are a piece of shit . . . You always lie when you talk about truth—" I was panting.

Onni's face twitched. He sort of oozed in small waves of resettling himself from the slap . . . Perhaps time tries to get at a torturer's truth—what do you think? Does truth get whipped and pinched from us? In shock, bloody shock? Or life as a voyage, a pilgrimage toward truth . . . that adds suspense, doesn't it?

He said, "Truth—*c'est difficile* . . . as Jean-Paul Sartre and Pilate say." Now he rubbed his face. I stared down at my hands.

He said, "It is interesting what you say about sin. I know two actresses at the *Teatro Rossini*. They are in a touring company—they are a bit Sapphic, maybe more, and they, ha-ha, are very good actresses—so you cannot be certain who they are. We go to bed, the three of us." Then he looked at me: "It is *the third kind* of love, not romantic, not family—in your term *kinky*, kinky and *nice*..." Companionable strangeness, he maybe meant. "I am never sexually cold," he boasted. He says, "But it is love. But who for who and which and what and why, that is a bit *oscuro*." He described the ganging up of two against one. "But I am the pivot. Perhaps the dupe is the pivot. But I find myself to be, you know, *the boss*. We have a cheap hotel room. I am naked but like someone in tall boots, with my six-shooter. It is a madness! You drown in cunt. In boobies. They love my hind end."

As he spoke he suggested more of the matter by suggestive twistings of his torso and with graphic alternations of his breath and a kind of glaring of the eyes like an actor. And he thumped his bottom on the cushion beneath him. He was trying to convey to me the love and squalor and heat, the heat of bodies, the heat of unvirtue, of acts separated from the two-personned act, and instead, erotic slyness and a witty namelessness, a less fearful sort of heat.

He added a gesturally explicit pose of crucified feet.

He said, "I am drowning in truth . . . And you are drowning in shit . . . It is not your world! It happens just as I tell you. *Vero, veramente*: I swear it. Did your father never have two women? I have to work hard in bed because they have their dreams, and they think I should make them come true. *Come* true. Ha-ha. I was very good, so they were very wicked . . ." He said, "One's sexual future is written in the stars. For the stars. But we are brothers. What happens to me you can share. But you are too strange . . ."

I could imagine it, the skin, all the heads, the knees, everyone getting in everyone's way, two and four of everything, but one cock, they throw their arms around it; they make love to it; they don't need Onni; they have *it*, nakedness, nakedness everywhere . . . But it wouldn't be completely visible unless you lined them up on the bed . . . *Turn over . . . You lie here . . . You lie this other way* . . . Wee pink, black-fringed cunts peeking out . . . and blotchy and pale and flushed hot skin—and who's making which noises . . . Cunt gobbling away, goblin-mouth-cunt, the suction, *sensational*—the glueyness, the entry-whisper everywhere, six places, and all the stings in all the salt burrows—the anxious, startled clutch of the competition, the hurt feelings . . . I bet it's all unceremonious and crude—nothing quite works— you laugh a lot—you can see what those old Hollywood backstage musicals were derived from . . . Cheesy costumes and flashing legs . . . naked, busy legs . . . cheap, busy music . . . And the scream of the peacock souls . . .

I said to him—he was drinking more grappa—"You should be glad you are not a castrato. Parents did that in this country once upon a time to children like you."

"*Basta*. You Americans think too much of the boring circus

. . . sex . . ." He was what he was. He was permanently angry in certain ways—that was all there was to it.

Listening to him, I— You know how the water churns if a number of motorboats pass close by each other on the *Canalazzo* among the echoing and tingling walls of the palazzi . . . It was like that. Or at the *Rialto*, the crowd presses on you, and you can only faintly hear the whispered bells of a friend's breath . . . It was like that for me with him.

I say, "Wow . . . Bow-wow . . . You are a gay dog . . ."

"Yes," he said. "We coupled like dogs. Like dogs. You are so silent really, always so silent even when you speak. Who are you? Who are you really? You are very smug in the end. You laugh at what we do to amuse our little selves. The world creaks under the wheels of America. I tell you that America stinks." He spoke in a milder way. He laughed his Italian laugh, not his actor's soulful laugh: "Ah, you naïve wonderboys, you *imperialists*, you break my heart . . . Nino, you have broken my heart."

The whole phenomenon of his great if slippery beauty is in this, that he has a semi-public body—one is addressed by his body. And his purposes, the scrawl of will in his actions, and him as a ruling exhibitionist figure, he is genuinely part of the glamor of the world. The gleam of fate, a huge hovering force in the dark, and the glamor and scandal of being alive show here.

"Your thoughts are making a noise, Nino—talk to me."

"We have been talking . . ."

"No, no, you are really silent . . ."

I do not want him to know me well, not as well as he had. Or as he did.

He moves to the attack: "No more silence—who do you think you are, *caro*, Gary Cooper?"

I am a certain sort of complexity out of which a voice emerges: I don't know. I said, slowly, in this post-courtship moment, "Remember when you first came to the English School?"

Sexual possibility and the electricity of attention—I had been the *re della classe*.

"I was a bright child—remember?"

He sat very still—a form of clemency: "Yes, I remember,"

he said. The brittleness of the clemency shows in the tone. And an enmity of a particular, looting kind.

I said, "I don't think the person you love—the beloved—is hidden. The self is the hidden thing. So, you see crookedly, as if you were general. I think we fool ourselves. One has no book to help interpret such terms as *I* or *my life* or *Momma and Poppa* or *love of country* or *happiness* or *a kiss* or *a little money* or *I love you*. The word *feel* in American English means *this is a hypothesis I hold*. The error comes when you pretend you're typical, just some ordinary presence, or I do. I don't like the obligation to be typical, Onni . . . I am me . . . This mystery of the self, the black hiddenness at the center of one's voice, and of one's problems in the world, is partly that you see no one from the same angle as you see yourself; and, so, it is the one thing you cannot compare; and, so, further, seeing yourself is the one thing you can be sickeningly idealistic about all your life until your fate compares you finally to everyone who ever lived. I think it is like dreams or any private signification, the ways people see themselves, and anything so singular is untranslatable. I don't think I am so expert in these matters. Perhaps each of us has a very secret motto, a self-formulation, something like *I who am loved and cheated and mauled, the youngest child, and reputedly smart, someone supposedly with a future, more or less American, someone with a prick and a profile, good or bad—not all that wellborn, but not of an anonymous background*—something like that. And those bits of opinion are secret like one's prick. They are bits of one's address, or one's old addresses. I can remember a whole abundance of others' opinions about me, which I've more or less interpreted, and which are ingrained in my body and my head. Someone says I am tall, says I am ugly, not ugly, smart or not smart. They are often corrupt about this but it is all the real information that I have. Someone I know or someone I meet and talk to reacts to me, not in any of the ways I would to me. They are inside their own lives. As if in another country . . . The future is all that's at stake really . . . It's always the only story now, the future . . . I don't know how to talk *sensibly*, Onni . . . I'm a freak—I know what I know. No one loves *me*. I always think with new people when I meet them, *You-won't-like-me-long-when-*

you-see-how-things-work-out-between-us: you ever feel like that about yourself? I do all right protecting myself from you, but I'm not conceited about it . . . I don't think I can manage much longer . . ."

Onni said, as if from a distance, outside of any pact, sort of somberly-childishly mocking: "You are so smart . . . Will you be king of the world, Nino? Will you wear wooden shoes with rubber soles like the ones nutty people wear?" Some clemency is there. "It's not good for you, *Tesoro*, such a burden: all that ambition. Who wants to spend his life like that?"

"You do . . . If anyone praises me, my brother says, *Let them pay for it and then you'll see if they mean it.* You are worse than my brother."

Onni said, "You are crazy, Nino."

"You know how we wrestle, you and I? The one who wins is the saner one because in the real world force is sanity . . . I'm a pacifist, though, and not a slave to the world . . . Crazy? Why not—it's part of the fun-house ride. My brother Carlo tells me every fifteen minutes that I'm nuts. He means it half the time . . . My brother tells me he does not want to have to rethink everything every hour . . . I want my own thoughts . . . My world is logical, not delusory . . . I'm strange, I know . . ."

"Your family should all let you alone: it is cruel," he said, denying me in his way as always, ungenerous in this matter.

"Onni! Help me!"

"I don't agree with what you say. Italians don't deal with things like you Americans. I have known you; I have known you well; and I think you are very—I don't know: you are an I-don't-know, that's all, *è sufficente* . . ." His bastardliness. His likeable, almost sweet bastardliness. He doesn't rise to the occasion in terms of love, and it's hard to admit that at every moment I expected him to change and understand. He doesn't restore the other clemency. Or the electricity of attention of before. He has no room for me as I am, and I cannot endure his wild freedom and his will.

But he had an air of fugitive affection. It is not really an Italian moment.

Onni said like an old man, an old Englishman though, "This is all sad nonsense." Then he became French, a French kid actor: "But your face *is* more a mind than a face. It's very nice . . ." Then he said, in Italian, *"Nonsense like this is like the Devil farting,* [*you*] *fool."*

"Onni, listen to me . . ." I no longer cared if I sounded like *a real person* or not: You know the little nervous clenchings of the muscle that make shadows in the stupid, thin, stretched skin of a skinny face? It looks feathery. I think I must have looked like that. "It galls my brother Carlo that I don't adore him . . . When I was little, he used to protect me, but also he would hit me until I was ready to blubber . . . He would say, *Now, do you get it, Nino? Do you get the point of the truth at last, Nino?* Now he knows better—he has stopped hitting me, and he is reasonable, but we fight . . . I will go mad if I have to live that sort of filthy life with everyone I know . . . I swear on my conscious mind, which is my one true friend, I try to fit in but I don't love him anymore. You don't *have* to like me, Onni. I do love Carlo —a lot—some of the time. He cares about me. But you see— don't you see—I'm not going to live my life near him . . ."

"Ha-ha," he *said* as if quick-wittedly. Abruptly he barked a bit of my laughter, an imitation of me: "Ha . . ."

"My brother says I hate everybody. He says to me, *You feel superior. Those of us with any pride ought to kill you. He* says I betray everyone. He says, *You're almost nothing but a Jew . . . You're worse than a Jew. You're like one; you do all those things.* I am embarrassed. My brother asks me, *Do you appreciate what people do for you?* I suppose I appreciate some of what people do. I get sarcastic. Nothing in me feels special *now.* Mostly it is how people react. I have one gift, for literal attention. Some people make allowances for me. Some don't. I don't get it, what this means . . . You don't want to listen . . . And that scares me . . ."

"You are very conceited. This *is* Jew stuff. We are all smart. Ah, this is a ridiculous life God gave us."

"You're the one who likes to wrestle to see which of us is the saner."

"I *am* more sane than you; is *that* conceited? You are too American for me. You are a *dangerous* boy, Nino."

"People often address one as if the other person was the same as them; they are thinking about themselves—seeing themselves in the other person. But I will never be Italian . . ." I didn't exist for him although he loved me. Breathing hard, I overturned the chaise he was on with him on it, and dragged him to the edge of the *altana*. He struggled and scrambled and escaped but I grabbed him again in my purposeful, mind-driven madness; I was full of adrenaline and had no thoughts, or only bits of thought, and was stronger than usual. He probably didn't fight full-strength; he was too stoned, too guilty; finally, I think he was curious; he had that other eroticism of getting to another dangerous place . . . I'd seen something like this in my Dad with Hemingway. My Dad was interested in tasting death or exploring dark things at the hands of people who interested him—often people he'd wronged . . . Hemingway guided him toward death a half-dozen times. And perhaps my mother had, too.

Onni in the dark, in my arms, as hard as an eel, or as an erect prick in a way, squirming and resistant, in my arms, against my maddened, sweating, truly engorged-with-strength body, Onni, his head out into space, his shoulders, said, gruntingly, "Nino, what are you doing?"

To be honest I had blacked out like a murderer. I am writing this coolly but, see, the body in my arms and beneath mine, pressing and struggling, and my own body are beyond struggle in the realm of fate. Organized and taut, they are near an orgasm of physical victory or defeat, death or real fear. Onni could have tumbled into a canal or his leg might have struck the wall or his head, met his death, I suppose, or been maimed. I shoved him further out into the air. I saw the relation between knowing Onni and being a killer.

It occurred to me that if I did throw him into the canal and if he survived he would love me in a certain way, be haunted by me always, by this moment. Something soft and seductive and *other* in me wanted to do that to him. But a harder part of me backed away from that, preferring another reality.

I released him, withdrew, I kicked him, *con mezza forza,* enough to arouse feeling—some love—and the kick was entirely real, but the forgiveness in it was as dazzling as a height in the darkness, the steep plunge, the backing off from love into mere patient forgiveness . . .

Stupidly, and feeling stupid, I righted the overturned chaise and sat on it. I wiped off my chest and arms with my hands as if to clean myself of him. My gestures said, *I cannot touch you without contempt now; you will only hate me more and more now.*

He aroused repulsion, disgust. He fell in the dark, grunting not shouting, into the dark water below—this was in my mind, in his. But he didn't fall. He did not seem startled by any of this. He sat up, swinging his legs over the edge of the *altana,* and he straightened his hair and peered down, seeing himself fall.

I said—stupidly—"*Pezzo di stronzo . . .* Shit . . . I don't know." I had become another person, nakedly.

He said, "You are not Italian . . ." It is true that the Italians have more forms of fidelity of attention than I do. I suppose he meant I was unable to avenge myself in an Italian way . . . I don't know.

Confession, with redemption possible: a love story. Well, I was refusing love. I often have, it seems . . . I am a very odd sort of romantic.

Of course, you go on feeling love but not in the same way. It's mixed up with rage and contempt, impatience, with refusal: you compress the feeling, dilute it to balance the compression (although it can explode in nostalgia or sudden moments of hurt loneliness in regard to someone or something else); you cover it with white paint or with mirrors so that it reflects the next thing, the next person; right and wrong, it is mostly over.

Being in the wrong in certain ways is a courtship ploy, and this can seem like that. But being firm while in the wrong and majestic and like a big-busted woman of a certain deportment wins out in the end: the *emotion* backs off even if the games go on.

The competition, the use of each other went on being real, as real as ever. Hatred, exile, love still in the new way. The as-if-brutal—and breakable, brittle—weary clemency, the *modified* clemency, ah, ah . . . *We are at arm's length.* He comes over, sits on the foot of the chaise, carefully soft and alert, aware of my rage . . . This is a form of respect and very winning. He leans toward me. I lean back.

"We are friends," he says, a little falsely, a little truly. He can't let me go easily but he has driven me away. I also know that if I tried to go on in his manner, when he turned and engaged with the situation and was truly present, I would not be able to manage it any more short of horror, I did so thoroughly, in some sense, "hate" him. I mean the history of our connection would go on being a live thing and ugly, and, in truth, to the death. Even embracing death and inanition and merely *backing off* I would have to undergo Onni's getting even now . . . I say I *knew* this then, that night. "We are friends," I said. "In our way." Then I muttered the next word: *"Profanely."*

"Profoundly? Is that what you said?"

"No, *caro amico.* I said *profanely.*"

OLD IN

VENICE

CR&

1

THIS MORNING I woke at dawn, and the place announced itself
immediately even in the near dark through the windows of my
room, water and façades, moored boats, boats at work upon the
glimmering surface of dark water. I wake nowadays once or twice
before I wake. I often dream I am waking and feel the half-dark
air and myself as real when it isn't yet the real world . . . I'm not
my age. I feel something like the silent clatter of my dreams, like
horses on a shore, on the Lido, or the inland rim of the Lagoon,
horses and armed men, often Oriental, usually silent. I have
discussed this with myself, who the silent Orientals are—perhaps
Huns. I am mean, *hungry* after a night's sleep. But men of the
East and not Lombards and the lumbering bombardment of the
feudal wars of one's career, of one's politics. Goths and Vandals.
Milanese. But Death. Or the dead. Or the barbarian young arriving in force during the night as Tartars and Mongols. And the
sound of my own harsh breath is the snorting and clanging of
war, of rage, left over from my night's dreams, from such invasion. Ruskin writes that Venice in the mid-nineteenth century
was, at low tide, in the middle of a lagoon of mud, of seaweed
and quaking, unstable muck. Desolation and uncrossability.
There were miles of creeks and rills and wandering channels of
deeper water which when the tide changed rose and overflowed

among the seaplants and stirred them and made the mud of the higher knolls gleam, and then it covered all of it with its own shivering, reflectant symmetry, with reflections of the sky. Beauty arrives. The beauty of the city in the sea.

In the dream I had just before waking, I was rescued from being hung on a gibbet in *Cannaregio* by masked figures, and then I fought in single combat like Sohrab and Rustum with my father or my brother Carlo on the edge of the Lagoon, swords clanging on metal, eyes mad with quarrelling, with nerves. The sky was deep red, maroon-vermillion, dark crimson, and purple, flames or sunset. And the dream, like most dreams, was shot through with emotion very clearly, with passion and fear, but this one was also full of contest and evidence of fatality, the fatality of close relationship.

Waking, I feel I have escaped from the rage and excitement, from the passionate focus and neatness of meaning of the dream. I half call out, half merely breathe the name "Nellie," the woman I live with now, in London, in New York, in California. I grab at the day, at the fact of still being alive, today's fact of one's continuing existence—I truly wake only in stages attended by thoughts and perceptions . . . City noises here resemble the sounds of breath, the sounds of someone in bed beside you, the sigh and shuh and creak of the mattress, the rustle of sheets, the clicking of eyelashes and the sough and slap of water, the flutter of wind, the clicking of footsteps in the *calle* . . . the sounds of familiar companionship mingling in peculiar neighborhood to each other.

Now that I am old—although people say kindly, hastily, *Oh you are not old*—I dress carefully always. I wear loose trousers, espadrilles in the old style, a thin sweater. I was careful to check in the mirror that I had no mad, thoughtful look. I was not creased with mood or fright. I added dark glasses, a floppy hat; I had a semi-Italian public look.

I went downstairs into the *campo* and walked inland—I don't know why. It had something to do with a too-much-eyedness in me, in my not being fully awake. Venice often seems to me to be inset with fluttering eyelids, the early wind, the half-light, the shuttered windows, the shuttered stores, and with what strikes me as the terrible wakefulness of the broad vistas of water, the murmuring wakefulness of the sea.

I walked in a direction opposite to the presentation of the naked idea of seamanship . . . The inanely entangled alleyways and high, humped bridges and stilled canals of sleeping-and-waking dawn-tinged inland island Venice represent clement shelter, a *tangled* clemency. One walks half-asleep in the empty *calli*. But ideas and sensations pick at one like the fact of the gaze, the *fluttering* eyelids of one's lover and her stare, waking one. Such unabstract sensations do literally seem like someone's living presence and gaze. So, in Venice, this least *Platonic* of cities, where for a millenium success had no conception of ab-solutes and was intelligent beyond any but physical description, one is ticklingly aroused by the ideas in the uncorrected sprawl and knot of streets and in the wandering façades of buildings matching the wandering paths of canals and of *calli*. Venice is human and eccentric, modified so little by touches of classical order that it seems to be free of any of the realities of modern absolutism.

Close by the *Fenice*, the *Ateneo*, so much handsomer before it was restored, so much lovelier before in its decayed, expensive Istrian stone, and curly cornices, is now stark white, and Scan-dinavian, and clearly outlined in cheaper stone and hastier work-manship than before . . . The Scandinavians largely saved it. It has their mark, that cleanliness. But the stone is machine-cut and too slick now, lesser stone than before. The building's beauty is milder now in its modern incarnation. Light touches the stone figures atop it with their bronze fittings, the bronze trumpet, a bronze halo. In Venice I am at home in my own life—this ruffles my nervous, aging heart, and its emotional reflections of the physical morning that I have lived to see. Onni lived near here; one saw those figures from his *altana*. But *time* is where one truly lives anyway; a city is where one's self is moored for a time: Venice-in-a-given-moment. In boyhood, after school and its steady thoughts—its Platonism, its Thomism—I ran off into the hours here in the *calli*, as if into the bushes and woods elsewhere. Into the rushing flood and tide of momentary reflections, into boyish comparisons, faster or slower, funnier and less funny, taller or shorter . . . Strongly familied or out-of-luck . . . More frightened or less, more tumescent or less . . . More unreliable or less, often beaten at things or not lately beaten at things. I remember, and it is as if one were softly buffetted or teasingly beaten now too; some of the blows of memory are not jocular. The two figures who loved me most passionately hated me the most violently—Carlo and Onni.

Onni had a defiant submission and a dark-eyed obstinacy toward the endless comparison of himself with everything. Perhaps a stilled hysteria. I know men who have become a little mad because they cannot escape the clutches of these comparisons. Fantasies about these comparisons abound, in movies, in sports and politics, in business, in cruelty, in love. For some women, the outcry is of the *perfect* . . . no more comparisons except in their favor, them being perfect.

The *Piscine di Frezzeria* is shadowed. Flowers bloom in a window box. Across a canal is a house that Mozart stayed in as a child—he was in Venice as part of his father's ambitions for him in European music. The high-arched bridge over the canal is being repaired and has plastic netting hiding one railing. Set into the placid water of the canal in an irregular perspective are workboats and reflections of façades. I am *in medias res*, in mid-sea, mid-drama, sailing in this double-comma-clawed city into one more day's new light. In this morning's piece of history, in this fragment of the history of the world, this narrow band of meandering water in the amphibious watery city is a pool of odors of moisture, night-damp and drying stones. The visual perfume of fragile sunlight touches the water and my mind which is sailing clumsily, disjointedly on its own voyages inside me. I am alone except for a few not very noisy seabirds and some silent, un-chirping sparrows . . . Ah, a street-sweeper ahead of me farther down the *calle* starts to whistle; and a garbageman with his rubber-tired cart is active. Around a curve and out of sight in this canal is the garbageman's moored barge, motor idling, waiting: I hear it now. I had not noticed the sound before, my own heart was so loud in me in the silence.

Comparisons have grown fewer. But how serious they are

now. I am as old as the street-sweeper but richer. I am older proportionately than Venice, closer to my death, but I am freer of violations. Some boys lived openly in the hours—I remember the maze and flux of moments, the shadowy immediacy as in this *calle*. The boys I knew would not have the lives of any other generation of men but would have the lives only of my generation. My awareness here is of the time and breath it takes to go from here to *San Luca* walking quickly or running, with small Onni. Or with Albia. The incantatory, jocular solemnity of Eliot's austere sentimentality: *Time. Time. Hurry up, it's time* bolsters my defenses against rage, an aging man's rage, the cheapness of life, the dim, faded, but still living greed of Venice . . . My God, I want to conquer nothing. I am staring at childhood. Schoolroom classes of so many minutes, the nervous moments of having to speak in class, my cowardice in fistfights, my flirting, my stealing fruit from a stall on a dare.

The light is in my eyes; I am squinting in strained, incredibly close, somewhat tearful attention beyond thought in the attention of memory. I am buried in the hasty other order of thought in giving and taking blows, *near tears*, tears of anger in the sunlight in the Piazza, in that other rage, in a fight, in the curious lost sense of having no other meaning but force, stamina, meanness, the brute astonishment of that, the *What does this mean?* when a blow unseated my balance or my mind—the pain, half-anesthetized—the pursed and jutting lips—the inwardly sucked and thinned lips—ah, Christ, the battered eyelids, the shattered nose and bruised chest, the erectile agony of fighting all-out in a rush of hot blood and fear and will . . .

Time plunges and glides splashing me, drowning me, the fool-pacifist . . . My moments are me, are my face, my arms. Like a boy I still live in the flutter and splash of overt time but I live now on the other side of my own history.

Venice! My body, my mind, and spirit veer in this morning's fever of remembering. I remember my phallic embarrassment, my covert readiness for the exigencies of rivalry, my startled—and partly *hysterical*—wish to escape invidious and insolent comparisons. In the melodramatic silence of the early hour, I walk crookedly and almost sightlessly and wake from that, sighing, and walk, alertly sauntering and staring . . . *We had no time for courtship in* our *Venice. We were almost Protestant we were so quick, so abrupt.*

Through the colonnade, past shopwindows I go and descend the three steps into, first, the shadow, then the sunlight in the empty Piazza. The glare struck me in the face, on the bones of the forehead and on the cheekbones. In a lagoon of glare, across the great, paved space in front of me rode *San Marco*. I found myself *squinting* as in a fistfight. How unrevised the bizarrely pretty façade of *San Marco* is, how comparatively uncorrected over eleven centuries. Never given a modern façade in any later period of the modern, untouched by any overall subsequent thought, an unrevised, *successful* idea, that long admired and accepted—it is disordering to someone alive in the moments.

And it is clothed in criminality. It wears the dress of stolen marbles and abducted sculptures. Clad in theft and pale in the early glare shortly after dawn, in the first sunshine of the day, there it is, standing in its sublime, inanimate confidence, in its lasting powers of seduction . . . It was unendurable. What lingers in Venice is the track or wake of success embedded in the out-spread architectural realities of the city. This is the surviving shell of an old criminal faith, a petrified and inlaid den of talented watchfulness.

Venice has no pagan roots. It is the primal city of Christian success.

I stood—victimized, martyred—in mood, you understand—captured by that millennium-old fragility, the disagreeably en-rapturing quality of its sugary, entirely un-Roman beauty.

The early morning light glittered along the upflung marble foam of the diadems above the entrances and among the Evan-gelists of the roofline. The dull copies of the marvellous Byzantine horses paced in shadow. I am tired of my religious fevers and of my terrors. I might even welcome death. In the end, I am not a clever man. I turned and ran—well, walked very rapidly in my older man's brittle stride—my stride is as brittle as my clemency—turned and walked very rapidly, feeling myself and Onni (since I always include him in any unfavorable category I am in) to be old in a less successful manner than the buildings here, to be just shimmery flimsiness, mere devices of life.

On the *Molo* four young policemen, heavily uniformed, and barbered, and capped, and hung with guns, showily fit, blank-faced, smoking off-duty guardians, young and young and young, the wind drawing the smoke from their mouths in extended whirls enlarged the terror in me but pierced it with further terrors, of the evils in the smugglers' Venice, the lunatics' Venice, the terrorists' Venice. This is realer than the old vanished Venice of my youth. The wind ruffled the crisp gray water and rippled the sleeves of the well-behaved young men with their submachine guns and pistols; and then just past them, in glare, leaning on the railing and staring out at the light in the *Bacino*, his back to me, was short-legged, bulky-backed Onni; not young, dressed in a baggy linen coat and a wide-brimmed Borsalino and amazing pants, paper-thin suede, some such dramatic thing . . . What can terror do in the face of suede trousers on a movie star? I caught my breath.

Onni had left his palazzo for a morning stroll before anyone was around to recognize him. His two bodyguards waited two meters from him. He was royal now—half a royal prisoner. We usually meet with precautions toward his public. And some toward mine. Mine exists. People turn to look at me, but they don't babble or carry on or clutch at me. And, of course, the numbers are different. Crowds tend to encompass him; they touch him, touch the familiar appearance present in unfamiliar flesh, flesh they want to be familiar with. It is the revenge of the senses denied in hours of moviegoing; the uprising of the body in pure reality in rebellion against dreams; it is always the Fourteenth of July in his near vicinity when he appears in public.

We were scheduled to meet at ten o'clock in his palazzo. Onni, the Grand Success, doing whatever passed for thought with him, was contemplating the pink-edged bowl of light between *San Giorgio* and the *Redentore*. He was standing near the telescopes, and smoking and staring down into the still dark, sliding water beside the *Molo* in alternation with gazing at the light. He has been forbidden to smoke by doctors and by insurance companies and by producers—he continues, of course.

He is so eaten, so devoured by a lifetime of pills and cocaine, alcohol and barbiturates and nicotine, that now he is grotesque physically, used, hawk-like—or like a starving rooster: a Gypsy's rooster about to be strangled—that dry, anguished, ready-to-fight, ready-uselessly-to-fight scrawniness—is set inside his bulk. But he is not scrawny; the crowing, ravaged will, though, and the damaged self are set in his eyes and his posture, thin, tense, starved, enraged, enflamed, confused.

One of the bodyguards said, "*Signore*," to Onni who turned and said, "Nino!"

Drawing near, I recognized his odor, his presence. The alertness he'd had as a young man had long ago become a less alert strength and weight of presence. But with the mad, starved rooster in it. Such intelligence and will, such a potently experienced man as force. The old star is a jolting mass of effectualities. But he is not pretty—he is raddled and sewn and self-conscious and a bit ashamed not to be a potent male beauty anymore. He has a broad, gruff style and a quality of caution, almost furtive. He is wearing a vest and a silky purple shirt and a white scarf around his throat.

I start to talk—I blither a bit—he is very odd now, Onni, and he seems odder even than usual this morning. I say, without preamble, "I am tired of my morning terrors, Onni." Then: "It was the cathedral that scared me this time."

He says nothing. Often nowadays as sometimes in the past he sulks if I talk like a writer. He seems to think I have a better life because I have been a writer rather than an actor like him, even one as rich as he is. He is still male, don't misunderstand, but he is also arch and petulant, given to heavy sighs, to heavy-lidded, almost 1920s stares from his famously heavily eyelashed passionate-and-weary eyes.

He does that now, sighs heavily, with a star's wit . . .

He too starts to blither; he outblithers me; he is wittier: "I think Aschenbach should have written for Hollywood and offered

Tadzio a job in a film and seen to it that his mother was run down by a motorboat . . . Of course, he must avoid a man named Guilty . . . no: Quilty . . . It is all the same book you people write."

Onni, obsessed with scripts, frets often over the unactability of classics; their sly pornographies elude the camera's grasp.

Then, in a gruff voice, this almost barrel-chested man says: "I was as beautiful as Tadzio, after all."

"Dark—though—you were dark, not ethereal. You were very healthy, very vigorous? Sad? Isn't that right? A gloomy little face? No. Not gloomy. Romantic." Actually I didn't remember his appearance as I spoke. I confessed: "I would have to sit down and concentrate to remember you in school."

"I did the part of a schoolboy wrong," he said, meaning he was miscast in life. He started to walk, and I fell in alongside him. He had a grotesque walk now, stiffened, with one side more angularly jerky in motion than the other—I think in the strain of filming he had had minor strokes.

A large white motorboat guns its motor, then glides parallel to us as we walk along the *Molo* . . . more of his retinue.

"Have you had your eyes tucked as I advised you?" he said looking at me and striding along.

"No. I bought very dark sunglasses instead."

He barked an unconvincing old man's laugh and walked still faster. "You droop," he said. "You look too serious. You look half-asleep."

Sometimes as one ages, the mind too becomes grotesque in its humors, in its ghostliness and fragility, and it is carefully minor and selfish, nostalgic and a trifle pitying, not particularly male anymore or truly sexual. The fondness that the old feel is tinted by a sense of tragic accident, not by surrender, merely by a sense of it. Onni is a famous face, photogenic, and so public, so distant now from childhood that it arouses my distaste, my disapproval. It was his fault that he had aged this way. He forestalls this with his remarks.

The surgeons could not do his hands which were old and

liver-spotted, wrinkled, unmuscular; and bony. The wrist emerging from the cuff of his shirt was old, too.

Onni looked at me now and said, "Well, the honeymoon is over." Then: "Here they come, the tourists." A flock of early risers were disembarking from a vaporetto at *San Marco Vallaressa*. The city will be full of the unseeing in an hour. I would not have thought that tourism had undone so many. Familiarity—with tourists, with Venice, with Onni, with Onni among tourists in Venice—is a troubled but unanxious and unwanted sympathy. One has a sentinel inside posted against a resurgence of childhood love of any kind . . . even toward oneself. But he was so clearly, perhaps not mad, but maddened and separate and moved by other considerations, and I so did not want to be alone in the Venetian morning with the tourists that the love came back anyway, permitted, a bit calculated, asexual.

The white motorboat glides parallel to us and disappears as we turn inland, two aging men, me in the bloom of morning terror, and him in his aged glamor and oddity.

Pursued or hounded, haunted by stares, by my morning's feelings, we walked in grim, eccentric tandem, perhaps inexplicably in step.

One time watching fireworks on the water here, I imagined the mosaics of saints and the Virgin and of Christ in *San Marco* become, in a sense, fireworks in Venice burning and cascading and falling into the *Bacino*. A far-off sizzle was audible in pauses of the booming overhead, the extinguishing of the light.

To the striding figure I say, with the bodyguards breathing behind us—I say like the host of an American quiz show, "Nowadays, all castles are called *Xanadu*. Name two movies with castles named *Xanadu* in them."

"*Citizen Kane* with Welles and *Marco Polo* with Gary Cooper and Lana Cooper, I mean Turner: she lost her eyebrows. She never had real eyebrows again. You are no longer somewhat cubic in the can, Nino—" Kublai Khan. Onni can make puns in four languages. He laughs, not without delight. The triviality is not consoling. I feel the shuddering myth of success haunts the cavernously beautiful eyes, the famous face; he must use common terms if he is to be listened to and understood. The vibrations of discontent and fear in me are like vibrations of water lipping and gnawing at stones. He talks like a woman . . .

"Do you know that you love me?" *Giangiacomo* asks me.

I do not answer. And then he doesn't talk for several steps: my not answering tacitly becomes an issue. We walk inland and then, near the *Gritti* after fifteen minutes of such silence and breathing, he says with grave gentility, "I have to go *casa mia* . . . You want the boat to take you someplace?" As if the only issue still was love.

"I don't want to get into a motorboat, Onni," I say.

"As you wish," he said crankily. Then: "I will see you at ten o'clock." He held out his hand, gracefully, grandly. Then he disappeared into the *Gritti* and re-emerged on the bar deck; and he boarded his boat from there. As I walked off I heard its motor begin to chug grandly and echoingly in the *Canalazzo*.

2

AT 10:39 I WAS in the Hall of the Mountain King, in his palazzo on the Grand Canal, in the *grande sala*. What light there was came in through high, leaded-glass doors and windows facing the *Canalazzo*, through purple-and-brown hangings attempting to shut it out. This thin, intrusive light moved dancingly in the mirrors and on the silks on the startlingly large couches.

He is handsomer in the gloom. He has had a line or two of cocaine. His aide, a youngish man, with a slightly loosened dark-skinned face, acute and alive with appetite and dressed in a black T-shirt and light-colored shorts and thong sandals, acted as butler. Onni was smiling more or less fixedly; he is still concerned with love. "Hello," he says in an intimate voice and laughs. I now feel the shuddering myth of success, of the boastful contentments of success in the cavernously beautiful-hideous room; the vibrations of Onni's discontent and fear are like mine: "Admit that you love me," he persists.

"What an accusation. You are being tiresome." Then: "You talk like a woman."

He lives in the monovocal world of his success. He says finally, "I no longer care what I am except in front of the camera. My efforts go into that. It is hard, Nino-ni-ni, hard."

He speaks as if he were lying, a form of irony, of not bullying.

He says, "My face is a little dead . . ." He is less photogenic now, that means . . . Onni's face no longer can compete in interest with those of young girls. Or young men.

"Work owns me. I am a dead soul, I think," he says. He has read my mind.

As when I was young, I feel something like a bird's body brushing against me; I blink; it is Onni's gaze, that bird's body's weight of a gaze on me, studying me, knowing me.

He is one of the most famous men in the world now, this man; and he could, in the recent past, cause two hundred million dollars to be invested in an absurdity, a film company and its studios which were, at the time, bankrupt; but he said he would work there and revive them; the company was bought on his say-so.

He failed. He was nearly killed by hit men hired by two of the Mafia investors. I was involved and had trouble, but it was not serious for me, although Onni tried to make it serious for me. Angela said to me once, *Some of us are dog-hearted, and some are cat-hearted. You have a cat heart, I think . . . You are terribly cat-hearted, Niles.*" I am hardly as adroit with power and coldness and revenge as Onni is . . . I am hardly as brave or as ruthless . . .

"I want to ask something of you," he says now. "Ah, you have the *no* look already."

"No-and-the-ark," I say.

Onni laughed in his usual Italian way, without joy and with as-if-coerced amusement. His movie laugh is the way I laughed once, a startled, somewhat helpless adolescent bark. He took it for his movie persona. When he is not around I use his Italian laugh. I try for that ring of power, for the Venetian rigor of his distrust of *everything*. Now he says, "You are comedy itself. I have a serious need of you."

It is dangerous to talk to him, he loves vengeance so. He has connections of great resource. He grants very little safety; and he never lets it be clear how much or how little he grants.

I said, "Ah, Onni, *the honeymoon is over . . .*" It doesn't matter what he asks of me; I will not do it. I can't.

But I felt an intense nostalgia; my heart skipped as when I caught sight of a drawing of him in a newspaper ad for a movie: *my friend.*

Over the years, year by year, I had learned with Onni that as in a horror movie, in breaths and actions, the patterns and the games of the earlier story would always re-emerge; the disguised, mad story repeated its judgements.

And this recurrence, this re-emergence of old knowledge, old feelings of dismay or disgust or distrust, is more terrifying to me than anything else in my life. An inner scream rises in me. I go out of control, not completely, but I cannot stay in the same room with him, I can't be near him, or sometimes near anyone, as long as the sensation of a fixed, recurring story is so strong and so sickening for me. It seems so stupid to be so echoing, so echo-like, so doomed. Triviality and the avoidance of story is better. Often, I cancel appointments with him, erase my ideas of him. Or I persist idly-ironically, while making jokes about being chewed up by the fan blades or about being macerated by the machete of the cokehead *cretino*-amok brute-Onni. Or out of respect for our lives I say to him hectoringly, *Character is destiny and so is lack of character.* But in his fame and as he ages he cannot bear this from me . . . He gets enraged. Sickened. Disgusted.

We often bored one another. We often had no time for one another, for the choking continuance of the story, for the echoes. His movie style became vivacity atop spiritual grief . . . Meanwhile the sunlight outside presses hard on the curtains that stir in the wind, and the light in the room swells and flicks, the thin light among the shadows. That room was *Bourgeois Dionysiac, MGM*

Bacchic. I don't think I ever looked at Onni without longing but it was not a longing for him; often it was a painful longing that he might be different . . . It insulted me that I had never been so close to another, better man as I had been to him.

I move to the window and shift one of the hangings and look out at the Grand Canal, at half a dozen boats and their glowingly pale wakes . . . How active the world is.

Onni, all those years before, sang for me in his newly professional voice. As a singer, he was both a technician and a spirit of song, a bit of a liar (about emotion) but truthful about seduction, adroit and physically inventive and subtle in regard to breath and sounds. It was clear how profound his ambition was, and his discipline, his reserves of extravagant self-use; it was clear that he was remarkable.

The rich man's room and Venice itself smells that day of water; it is as if an emanation of a water spirit, dank-fleshed, floats in the city, hovers near the balcony of the room. What a scrap of patched actuality his famous face is. One's physical sensitivity, one's ability to read presences lessens as one ages and is augmented by deductions drawn from experience, from sensory knowledge earlier in one's life.

He said, "Nino, the ghosts . . . the *Gottverdammt* ghosts." He swears chiefly in German.

"Ah, Onni . . . what can you do about ghosts?"

"You feel them too? Do they tangle themselves in your hair? Do they hang on to you?"

"I haven't much hair . . ."

"Do they tangle in your heart, *caro cretino*? Why don't you do something about your hair."

"Because of Aschenbach. And you. Do you have on lipstick?"

"A little. Nino, I am not—not an old coquette. Milliards of *lire* rest on my *viso* . . . You understand I am so famous I can do whatever I like provided it is bad enough—I can have you killed . . . But I cannot have my own face." Then: "I have done *The Sea Gull* in two languages . . . I have played Trepliov and Trigorin . . ."

"Do you want to do a Chekhov movie?"

"Not with closeups. *Caro Amico*, do you feel the ghosts in Venice?"

"Yes. My father. And Hemingway. He called me when he came here—he checked on me for my father."

"What a drunk that one was. Shrewd and dominating—and mad. He did not like me—I cried sometimes in the old days when I could not get what I wanted. Listen—" He offered me this: "I remember your father and other *rentiers* in white hats and white suits among the Blackshirts in the Piazza with the bureaucrats in dark-green suits and dark-green hats and dark-green glasses, all of them, like so many *Fascisti* . . ."

"And the Germans."

"And the Germans. I remember someone screaming, being arrested on the *Scalzi*. I feel an indignation, you understand. What was it all for if I cannot use it when I am old. What shall we do to be immortal?"

Suddenly he began to breathe loudly. After a moment it passed.

"I am writing a book, Onni."

"I want a little movie—shots of Torcello . . . Burano . . . I want ghosts in it . . . I want a few of our private spirits. I want none of your guidebook feeling about Venice." His breath turned harsh and he seemed to scream in a low voice. "I want my Venice . . . the ghosts . . . do you understand?"

I said—in a guidebook voice, high and as if pure, while the cocaine buzzed in him—"It is wrong for a ghost story, Venice."

"No." Then, suspiciously, grandly: "Is that something widely thought? Is that known?"

"There are no names, no biographies, just brisk, blowy air, and Doges and admirals the size of children."

"Yes? Were they that small? Of course they were. The armor."

"They were very small, smaller than the barbarians. And of lighter complexion than the Romans."

"A seaport of ghosts," he said stubbornly.

"Any place is that . . . vertically . . . Why do you want a *ghost* story? Venice is wrong for that . . ."

"Because of the way I photograph now—" Then he shouted something nonsensical, screamed it. Then: "Nino, you are driving me crazy. I must have a drink. *Pezzo di Scheisse* . . . Old friends are not worth the price of the funerals. Why are you not *un po' serioso?*"

I think he meant why was I not afraid of him. "Age is not cautious: the Doges were old for a reason. Your tough guys, the young ones—" His bodyguards . . .

"The fair-haired one is always cracking up, and the other one, the dark one, smells to high heaven of nerves."

"I like the smell of nerves—it is like on a movie set." The signs of age in him include the fleshiness of his back and the heaviness of the bone structure of his face. His stumpy legs and expensive shoes, too, make him seem old. "Movies are the hardest things in the world. Killing."

I have never worked with him except a little over the phone, only a little. "Killing," I say.

He said, rubbing his leg suddenly, "I have had to have orthoscopic work done on my knees—how are your knees?"

"*Men are men. Boys are boys,*" I said. "I shelter my knees."

He jumblingly, loudly, imperially switches to politics, then back to the movie business, then best-sellers versus *literature* or versus at least the plays of Chekhov. Onni, this universally famous man, welcome everywhere no matter how he acts since many people enjoy watching the famous decompose at least once, talks as he wants. He talks in gossippy and secret phrases and indignant quotes, bestowingly, conferring secret information, some from the presidents and chief ministers of countries, ministers of culture, famous actors and directors and the like, whom he knows and sees or has seen or sat next to at public occasions. Being famous makes up a large part of what he is.

His voice *confers* apparent order, coherence on the jumble, and indicates what is a lie and what is true. The force of his now technically impressive personality, if I might say that, is imagistically a riot for me, the human and the human actorily presented, then the actorly-and-almost-regal thing ironically grandiose, then the real power, then the mumbling of age, vocal miscalculation, then the correction, often cleverly unactorish and human, a performance element. Meanwhile he recruits me: "Do as I say. Do what I ask," he says. He says, "I am the emperor, *heil* me . . ."

He would have, he must have the last word, the realest word, the only word in an absolute silence of the others now that he was so famous and so alone in his fame.

Age. The bones feel exotically stiff and brittle; one's smile is no longer reliable. The old signs one hangs out are worn and creak in the wind. Fear makes me sleepy now.

Onni says, "*Cretino*—I dream of water, of earth—I wake choking, and I say, *It is a dream, un sogno*, but I choke. What is this silly business of being old? My childhood, my mother and my father, the war, people I worked with, people I fucked, my thoughts, my art, my skills—I have time yet. It is too soon to quit . . . You, I remember holding you when we were young, Nino. You shook. You always shook inside—*poverino*. You always had an earthquake going on—was it fear? It was nice, that, and the *cazzo*." The ruthlessness of the exaction of fear . . . "I saw a pig eat the face of a dead man, the blood, the flesh, the features—crunch, crunch. The fat black pig, you open the door of the pen, and it comes, Death, the pig, the black pig: it eats you. I am going to tell you about rape . . . It is not a long story . . . how long a story it is depends on who you are . . . On where it happens . . . Perhaps your mind is played with, there is a little pain—name-calling, contempt—then a little more, perhaps a broken finger, perhaps a crushed toe . . . Or perhaps a bruised head, ringing, ringing . . . Then a bribe, an order, a wheedle, a command—give up your will—and then the real force . . . the end of everything sensible. I was twelve years old, small for my age. Power is a great sin, corruption always. This thing that happened was a thought that occurred to an animal, a little thought for *una bestia*, a passing fancy in a war . . . first on his face, in his eyes . . . then in the act. Or it was something deep, a deep, deep feeling . . . I do not know . . . He slapped me in a friendly way, then harder for not being quick enough to— I don't remember. Like this." Onni reached out to slap me. I moved.

Onni stared at me stone-eyed. Then he slapped his leg. "Not too hard . . . Then hard . . . then harder. I killed him afterwards with his bayonet in his throat; we put him in the pigpen, the farmer's son and I—he had been mishandled too. I don't know. He was bigger than I was, and he helped me. Later he who helped me used me—it was reasonable at the time—I have never been bitter. I manage to find my way. One day, though, a party of *Fascisti* came to requisition food. *Udine*, the *culo* of the world. The farmer's son was slow—an asshole, stained with mud, like shit . . . I think perhaps he had come to think too highly of himself—because of me, his friend, his toy. Two of them hit him with the stocks of the rifles, knocked him down, they kicked him. I saw very little violence, you understand, but what I saw was concentrated and trained me—do you understand? They left and I opened his jaws and filled his mouth with pig shit."

It is not that I hadn't known; it was that I had known from a distance—except when I touched him. Or disliked him. *Giangiacomo*'s great face is without asceticism. It has power and discipline and a grovelling, violently immense sense of his own freakishness in it . . . He likes to use his great-faced power . . . And why not? His being a star is testimony to idea, idea acted on, acted out, testimony to success, a stoney power of self-defense and offense—it moves me, a creaky echo of the past. It moves me that he shows off, that he does it honestly, that he knows me so well, he and his fascist sense of power. He could not now play a young man, not even only with his voice, his face hidden. His voice contained much of the reality of his present face.

I can do a child's voice on paper. I think this has a quality of *pederasty* . . . of innocence . . . Do you agree that male love requires forgiveness? . . . Or that you have to be swindled or coerced by it? A man's love needs to be forgiven . . . My mother said to me when I was young: *You ask too many questions—you're an ask murderer* . . . Even I, a child, had a feral quality of emotion—the lurking ambush and the spring of it—my emotions tired her, tired my mother. Emotion had sprung at me in her presence first and had left me, the devouree, bewildered, amnesiac, absorbed.

Moved by him, I remembered him young. A memory, an emotion is never fully comprehended, never finally named in life, only in stories . . . This was a true memory of an incomplete and sprawling emotion flickering with reality . . . The memory I have of his young body is comic: it was scratchy, the slick, Italianate skin with the weave of cells and follicles was wiry somehow, not smooth. His oversized hands had large knuckles and nails but gentlemanly . . . His ribs and the muscle on the ribs, the post-war flesh, and his skull, his hair, his neck are mine in memory and are lost to him—he cannot remember himself from the outside. I remember the amorous *sexual* hilarities so close to a single burst of tears—and his too quick orgasms—well, you see, a child's love is childish; a boy's love is boyish. A man's love is unpleasant but can thrill you. A lifetime of love, like a lifetime, is long and rather sad usually and unclear in tone; anger and betrayals are arbitrary although sometimes they seem like curable accidents. Do you have a perhaps final sense of reward? Or a sense that it was a gyp? A whore's orgasms are financially viable. A man's love is terrifying and not to be endured. The violence of some of the scenes in his movies . . . Ah, well, I have not had a life of longing . . . I will not finish this thought.

Onni has shadowy possibilities as a sage, as a man-woman of exceptionally violent spirit, a successful Tiresias. Memory comes, goes, grows still, is unendurable, is opinion, is unphysical. Then physical, is cold and in flood ripplingly, an *acqua alta*, and it is not a stream, it is merely consciousness inflected by time in a number of ways: the pictures that memory presents are torn and angled and briefly present and changeable; they become untorn and logical; they seem to dissolve as I glimpse them. They seem to have arrived over light-years, so far are they from what we have become.

"You love me," he says. Then—in a peculiar voice, political or tactical and yet, in a way, stricken with memory: "And I love you."

The topic is politics and power . . . No: the topic is what he loves and possesses . . . No, the topic is love. How different it is now, that topic. Recurring outbursts of vanished love, love long ago felt freshly for a second or two again, the motion of hot feeling in the air in a small, sun-warmed room above a *campo* —this aging, surgically constructed, technically (and morally) complex, semi-unexistent and merely imagined man, this potency, this mechanism of famous performance . . . And the kid he was, vain, *brave*, awful and artful, hunted down, the juicy ho-ho horrors of love he'd known . . .

He said in the screwy present tense, "At one time I thought of doing a movie version of *Phèdre*. After all, I slept with my mother; I have the experience to draw on. Of course, Hippolytus did *not* sleep with *Phèdre*. But one can rewrite and use other names. What drew me was the *extent* of her punishment, the blackened sun in the Russian's poem. I did the *Oresteia* in Elis with Paxinou but I was never interested in Orestes and self-blinding. That sense of crime is not Italian. In Italian drama nowhere is there a portrait of remorse like that, that regret. We Italians are Roman and then we are Catholic—conscience of that sort is not the issue for us. Or is but— I cannot make myself clear. Certainly not our operas. Not like *Boris Godunov*. The universe and your own soul crushing you because of what you've done, *merda* like a brown dunghill, Venice collapsing on you? No. But my mother's madness, how you destroy yourself when you destroy someone else, guilt of a sort as large as *Zanipolo*— do you see the story? I would like a Graeco-Hemingwayesque tone. Ghosts. It is time you believed in what I believe. Don't tell me how *modern* the world is."

I said, "No. Absolutely not. But it is . . . You should look at Faulkner—Faulkner offers *doom*—the weight of the dead."

"Doom photographs well," he said.

"Yes. It is very camp."

"Ah, your irony," he said. You had to know about movie people's power and temperaments to realize he was drawing a line in his own monarchical way. He says, "Let us not fence with each other . . . We do not have time, you and I . . . I haven't time now or the will to understand you. Help me and I will reward you. I will make you rich, very very rich."

The sounds of the *Canalazzo* outside had their poetry. The sky through the windows where the curtain was open rested on the marble-and-glass façades across the Canal in their hints of semi-merriment and ludicrous wealth. In the small opening what was visible was tremendously clear, shockingly bright in the morning light, each element as clear as if named: *Sky... Water... Marble Palazzo, 15th-Century . . . Cloud . . . Chimney pot . . .* And so on.

The scale of everything visible, inside the *grande sala* and outside the window and across the Canal was limited; nothing gave a great effect of mass; or was grandiose in its geometry. The calculations, outside and in, were shipshape, and personal, and a bit silly. Fear and tension in me sometimes grow so large that they become a tremor as in the mountains when you are skiing, that enormous shudder in the air. Or as when a big wave pours overhead pounding and shaking when you are underwater. It feels as if the strain or excitement or fear—whichever it is, whatever combination it is—will kill me.

His dead eyes study me sharply. Power is the thing with him, that corruption. He is lying. He will harm me more than he will help me. I am less famous and in better shape than he is.

I doubt that anyone loves anyone enough. The fact of love as love actually exists—well, perhaps only grief brings you face to face with real love: as in a waking dream, alone. I discussed parts and roles with him. Lies are part of happiness, of ordinary survival and daily happiness, such as it is. Companionship? Masculine brotherhood? The shared love of women? The actuality of beauty? Jesus-what-have-we-here? It has been perverted in the ribaldry of age and money and will . . . in the partly involuntary pornographies of the world, our *friendship*.

Those pornographies have as much to do with power as with sex, with power causing sex. In his life, he has won so far. His unsettlingly sensible program of briberies, his years of the stink of makeup and arc lights and klieg lights, of love and contempt in public, the as-if-painted moments of affectionate presence have won everything, and everything comes only to this, that he is still full of appetite in the last chapter in Venice. Truth unsettles me. I love the nervousness of it, of truth, of its embodiment, but it is unsettling. The thrill of it is a shock as well.

I said to him, to this intelligent, power-rigged, power-jagged man who has dragged me into his story: "The mother is a clever woman enraged that life cannot be solved, that it is not a puzzle open to clever answers . . . Or to deep answers . . . I think the thing with the child must be part of that rage, that demand for perfection . . . It would be very daring to present the mother as a bore . . . I *think* boredom, to inflict it, is a form of malice— she bores the child, bores everyone . . . And is punished . . . She is a little bit Germanic that way . . . She goes mad at having been so wrong while having been so clever all along . . . She pities and abhors her child . . . Whoring the child to the German officer is something she cannot resist doing—she does it to be interesting . . . But it is something she cannot live with, it is the final proof that she is wrong, not great, not a great woman, only a miserable bitch, and dull . . . Her life goes out of control because she loses the love of her child . . . She does not know how to be forgiven . . . And the officer who fascinated her thinks her contemptible and is not interested in her . . . And she cannot get revenge . . . So she goes mad . . . ."

Onni said, "They go to Athens—for a visit—the 'fascinating' officer and the boy . . . A weekend, a week . . . I don't know . . . The German's uniform . . . it is hot, terrible weather . . . the aroma of that city is putrid, a stink, a nervous stink, urine-tinged like an ill man: and smelling of that is the uniform . . . No, they stay in Venice: it is the smell of Venice . . . and of evil . . . the play of the boy's *cazzo* and the German's—meat—the opera of the *cazzi* in the palazzo on the *Canalazzo* . . . The German *cazzo* . . . we will see it very clearly maybe as a guilty thing, a horror . . . The German's longing to be all one thing, good or evil . . . And the child's face, wrecked and surprised at being still alive among *these pleasures* . . . these nightmare odors . . . The German must be self-righteous, self-loving, tough, very stupid and very smart, but not smart enough . . . haunted and mad . . . Perversely beautiful—repellent . . . active . . . He attracts events . . . he will be tortured to death by Partisans, like St. Sebastian . . . I *believe* they will drive a bullet container into his skull slowly . . . after castrating him . . . after flaying his chest . . . the insane ecstasy of vanity in being tortured to death . . . Yes? Inventive Trevisans, yes? Do the women arrange for his death? Maenads? What do you think? Let us have him die in the woods outside of Asolo but hang in the Piazza, ha-ha: his dead, naked, mutilated body." He actually cleared his throat: "Ahem . . ." He leaned forward, "I want to see you masturbate . . . In my dreams I saw it last night. I want a photograph. . . . The aunt says to the child, *There, you are avenged.* The child says, *I didn't want to be avenged* . . . But he did. Listen, Nino, I do not understand these things. And now I must . . . I want to make the movie . . . a monument . . . a tomb . . ." He said, "I am king of the world."

In me was a silence after the morning's thoughts—no memories were in me. But I spoke: "The mother must commit suicide . . . And the German officer must be the hero in some way, like Humbert Humbert in *Lolita*, not the child . . . No one will identify with such a real child . . . The child is just décor, necessary décor, for the other story . . . You cannot tell a true story truthfully in a movie . . ."

"No, no. Do you have a sense of humor, Nino-nini? Do you have a sense of sense? Let me be wild this one time . . . Let us have a wild movie, a truthful one . . . Let us have a strange mad grandfather . . . who dances . . . with the child . . . too close . . . No? Too many old men, too many fat women have danced? Do you like old men of great power, Nino? Or only sissies with delicate minds? Are you finicky, my friend? Are you still my friend? Do you love me enough to be my friend in my old age? I must have a sympathetic part. It does not have to be big at the box office. It can be a shockingly terrible movie. But it must be remarkable. Not *kitsch. Kitsch* gives people cancer . . . Save me, my friend. Save me."

Some art, lesser art, is calmer than life. But memory, as art, finds nothing mild and no mild moments and nothing mild or tranquil in true recollection in the strain of events, of present actions. *I loved, you loved, he loved, we loved.* The nerves were torn, the heart pierced, the soul was rent and never re-sewn, never whole again. As in all real adventures.

Which is to say we grew up together . . . And we grew old side-by-side in a way . . . And he could always bribe me with the truth . . .

3 / LOVE

WHAT I KNOW, what I understand a little of, is that what the mirror holds, what Venice, old and delicate as glass, and Onni, toughened and rich, reflects back to me is half-proven truth, is a willed, partly fanciful, very old reality. A bridge, a canal, silence, a *campo*, a flow of tourists, noon light—I walk in noon light, in the whirring butter of such light and think of friendship and ambition, Venice and money. One has friends, resources—modes of protection; this is, in part, what adulthood is.

But the methods and modes of protection one has are perhaps not good enough protection against some people. It is always dangerous for me with Onni. People negotiate their favors, not always, but usually; and then, in real life, negotiate further; they own you; they deal in you behind your back—or over your head—like slave traders, like Venetians. Onni, older, was not morally different: he was harsher, colder, more able, more worn. I walked in the whirring light to the *Frari* and entered the enormous floating space and went to the sacristy and sat looking at the Bellini there. It is something I do in Venice—the Bellini, a Madonna with Child and four saints, is human but is super-human a bit, or touched with grace; the light in it moves from the human to the saintly to the nobly, gently, quietly, even silently holy. It has a golden architecture or geometry, a certain sternness of love, but the sternness is more like a spine. Love is very clearly love in it.

I felt a certain stale frenzy of stilled hysteria locked inside me that the picture softened or ignored. As I said earlier, when you age, the number of comparisons lessen but the comparisons are more final, perhaps more oppressive and tyrannical, older, younger, smarter, stupider . . . And the comparisons move in the moments, propelled by will and by plotting, by scheming. How strong still, how rich, how mad, how sane, how bitter and howling inwardly or how stilled and catlike, how frightened, how ferocious, how warm still, with how many fresh words left in the anticipatory silence now advancing in the increasing loneliness and *genius* that death is and which is given to us as death begins to take possession of us. How much then does one love the truth? Or love the intelligence of someone old? How truthful do you become? What would it mean to me if, in the end, at the last minute, so to speak, Onni proved to be generous-souled, great-souled, an artist of gigantic blessedness, as marvellous in his way as Giovanni Bellini was in his?

Or even less than that, an artist but a meanspirited one, one curled up inside, weird and minor but genuine. What would it mean to me to know that the boy I loved and who influenced me so was, in the end, deep, deep-souled, deep-hearted and, in a sophisticated way, kindly intentioned toward the world?

Or that he was a fake? A fake half-educated in truth? I have never been able to defend myself—from anyone—except by running away. I crossed the *Canalazzo* on a *traghetto*; my legs were shakey and I wavered when the craft shook and danced in the wake of a vaporetto, clearly not an Italian like the others on board. I went to my suite of rooms in the *Campo Marinention*. I am, as always, moved by the romance in what might possibly occur and constrained by a realistic sense of what is likely. My vulnerability, now a style, almost a duty, meant, I was aware, that I was evasive. And what originality in his work did I expect of *Onni*? Onni did not let himself have any ideas or feelings that were unlike those commonly recognized in the period among successful figures. He was in a way mentally made only of trademarked elements, ready to be sold . . . He meant to be recognized. What could one expect of him in the way of freshness and depth of thought now?

He had been a diligent Marxist. I could at best be silent in respect for the moral imperatives of the Marxist position. In actual event, so logic said, and so history showed, that particular doctrine could create only a culture of gangsterism and of *kitsch*, deaths inflicted in envy and contempt . . . Ah, Christ, the human carelessness that lies at the heart of any use of fixed doctrines . . . But what I am trying to get at is the unexercised mind and sensibility, the ways the self, as an artist, say, as possibly an artist, becomes crippled.

What is the real possibility for him now of art, him a straw man, burning and aloft and rustling with success. The light flickering off the canals illuminates the question. In Venice, I see Onni as an exemplar of will, will as in dreams, isolated in sleep and absolute in isolation. There is no end to what an actual man is guilty of. I was as afraid of exertions of will, although I made them, as if I could see in such exertions the exile and flight of the certain-to-be-ruined souls.

When we were older and we met, Onni and I, when we spoke, Onni would be thwarted by my character and by some surviving element of childhood which evoked strong feeling in him, admiration and then anger or rivalry, admiration buried in rage . . . I could proceed in the moments trying to be genuinely if calculatingly generous and not jealous but that was hardly more than an intelligent performance; and he needed a certain drama in all contacts, all meetings; and I, helplessly, or cleverly, damped such drama down in the hope of some other order of feeling and of reality; and he would be ironically flustered and partially re-seduced. I think these matters are interesting if you are not squeamish.

He had the tact and faith in the systems of power and vanity in the active world, and he had no shame; he believed in himself, in ass-kissing and in sycophancy—and complicity—in bald will and alliance-making and lying, in that patience with the eighth-rate work of others that allows one to rise. But one rises like burning straw. And what is learned has the wrong tonality for certain sorts of art. I did not have his powers of burning and self-destructive levitation . . . Or rather I was not self-destructive in any similar way. The quality of my work gave me a foothold and a living. And my mind, my perceptions were part of a historical continuum involving someone who was not manufactured, not trademarked. Much of life consists of lying about moral truths.

Onni envied me my life. I am not sure I ever knew, or know now, what the difference is between me and Onni, or between Onni and other men. I am not violent or realistic about dominance. I prefer a truce.

Or courtship. I have not suffered as much in my life as Onni has. One time, watching myself in a full-dress affair in Paris, it was borne in on me that I did not appreciate what was offered me. My behavior was at best tactful and a bit mad even as I avoided the center of feeling in the affair more and more. I fled with shame and embarrassment. I came to Venice, telephoned Onni, who has always kept an apartment here. I believe I wanted tacitly to apologize to him for the past, now that I saw a bit more clearly the sort of person I was. He was only by chance in Venice that weekend. He and a woman had been playing Pygmalion to each other. He had been working on his looks, shaping his face, his posture, his voice, his manner. His voice! The number of tones he could muster and display in speech! But I realized soon that only a few emotions were included in that voice. The varieties of tones were merely fluctuations of attitude in regard to triumph and humiliation, to your response or your unavailability and snobbery, or to his tactics of portraying some emotion or other. He had so many tones that it was hypnotic in effect, his limitation.

A good deal of his manner consisted of a new and, if I am honest, very handsome sad-eyed brooding that he lapsed into and rose out of with a smile that became famous and which, in a different form, had once been mine.

My jealousy was enormous and sad and perhaps pitiable. And it was of a compound nature. To be overshadowed and disapproving is dreary. And the advantages I saw for myself in being unlike him seemed dreary as well. My deflation was complete. Inside the actual moment one *shows* admiration; this is a perhaps fatuous magnanimity. One can't be a follower. One can settle on being arbitrarily, ritualistically, a bit inferior . . . as a form of tact. What this looked like to him I can only imagine. My jealousy alternated with simple admiration but he rarely left the situation alone. And I already had more of the world in my youthful favor than I had expected to have. So he was uneasy and aware. The moments felt like devastation itself.

Jealousy rests on an ideal notion of someone else's reality, a sense that the other's reality is ideal, and that reality itself is more ideal than one will ever be permitted to know and see. It rests on a belief in a reality we are less realistic about than the one we know. Everything I felt from the past and what I felt in the present I turned into a sense of mere life in him. It verged on condescension.

I veered from that back into my pathetic jealousy which then, because of his youthful brilliance and hardworking ease-in-the-world, became a sensual flare-up when he, seeing and noticing in his own terms, responded by touching me, by moving toward a sort of seduction, so that it seemed I could punish him, hurt him by being cold or overwhelmed with disgust.

Although I was overshadowed—and overwhelmed—it seemed like magnanimity to be *neutral*. Or it was a matter of saying no yet again. And once it began, it seemed obvious—an obvious way to be, or thing to do, not to reject him or regret his marvellousness or to hate him—at least actively—but to rejoice and be neutral and out-of-reach.

But it was a form of "no," and it was full of falsity . . . It was false to some of my feelings.

I should confess that he was at that time an actor, and a model and a sometime singer, with the persona of someone unusually frail, sensitive: an offshoot of the Montgomery Clift sort of acting-and-being (on-screen), as Brando and James Dean were to be. But he was more like me than he was like the old Onni. The footwork necessary for a career, the maneuverings among desires and enmities . . . and the pursuit of money, of financing . . . placating successful actresses and actors and male directors and financiers *when necessary*—and all the dramas of suspicion—justified suspicion since everyone involved was guilty from the start . . . And the attempts to find firm footing in public popularity as a comedian, or as a sexual object, or as a *serious* actor, the difficulties and excitements and strongly colored realities of his life had damaged him finally and for good and made him a hero, a heroic exponent of this sort of brilliance in life but in an embodiment, a style, this ur-him, that was reminiscent of me as an adolescent . . .

The awesome heroics of such persistence as he showed in the risks he took, in the gambles he made, and in his self-display and cleverness! He had such character and such capacity to learn in this other way that I did truly love him—and imitate him. And my earlier self. Following him to Naples, I saw him onstage in a burlesque revue. The technical elements of a performance, in the end, are subordinate to one purpose, a power over the collective responses of an audience. The peculiar mixture of pleading and then of command in such a thing was something already in him and already something he used in life, but he had learned to do it publicly. It was apparent onstage as soon as he sang, as in his earliest films, that he was extraordinary, unhidden and available to the audience and yet upper-middle-class, an unfrightened will at work. Talent is perhaps common. But talent and fear-put-aside are not. And then the acceptance of the life and of the lifelessness in being a subject of regard in someone bourgeois who yet is open to the audience is rare. From the beginning he accepted the damage done to the self. And then the submissive command of the audience's feelings, a kind of disciplined shamelessness. And the intelligence of selfless performance . . . It is a very rare combination. He lived onstage in an elevated and bitter and amused and beautiful way.

He was a new type in one sense, a traditional sort of male ingénue, with old-fashioned bits and pieces of Italian stagecraft, but he was mostly the new thing, the most extraordinary nakedness of feeling and patience with himself, and with a whoredom if you like, with his own deformities brightly used, if I might jealously say it like that; and he had a look of silent knowledge such that I felt obliterated in my own attempts to signify meanings in words by comparison to his human success at merely implying he could do it endlessly physically with his voice and his gestures and his well-practiced smiles onstage. He was faulty and young but marvellous . . .

Really, even in an undeveloped state, he was a tremendous, tremendous success, someone who would be a star, whose name would enter theatrical history, whose projected image would enter people's dreams.

How much of his success and how much of his ill-success

in life, how much of his obvious and towering excellence could I bear? . . . He was aware of this in me, of course.

From Naples, we returned to Venice in the company of two young women. In Venice, at one point, the four of us were included in a party of movie and government people. This party went in a flotilla of three motorboats down the *Canalazzo* to spend a day on the Lagoon . . . On the noisy boat, I was *aware* of his watchfulness toward me and the others. Some of the big shots knew my brother Carlo. And one or two had read my first book. Onni wore a white sweater, and I thought how calm he looked, but at one point when we were standing in the bow, and he was next to me, he placed his leg alongside mine, touching mine, as if to command affection or to be outrageous—he had become theatrical that way—and I saw that his neck was sweating under the ascot he wore. His eyelids, too, behind his dark glasses were damp, I think with nerves.

In our opposed forms of loneliness and self-recognition and recognition of the other, we touched each other often as we spoke; and on shore in the explorations of the past, we strolled with our arms linked . . . In those days he was transparently capricious, powerful already, often drunk, often on pills . . . It was clear to me he clung to the jealous-partly-magnanimous sense of him and of his enormous ability that I had, and of my patience with it. We sat side by side at lunch and dinner and on the boat, smiling at each other and occasionally talking art—Stanislavsky and the American Actors Studio, and how esthetics relates to politics. We smoked tobacco cigarets and some marijuana and took a little cocaine and drank cold *prosecco* and confessed various things about our lives and work. Often hiding a boastfulness. Sometimes exaggerating a despair. Twice he kissed me publicly, on the side and top of my head. Then in sunlight at the Franciscan monastery on the lips. My privacy, a neurotic thing, and his secrecy, a tactical matter, and my deflated state and his being a young man of an advanced degree of experience who recognized my state and knew its limits acted alternately like reverse magnetism and then like a lawful magnetism.

The physical excitement was enormous but not like the past;

it was not sexual, but was a restlessness of identity, a being goaded, criminally in a brotherhood of uninnocence at how much we had all-in-all affected one another. It was not clean, not workable. It was dangerous in its inner mechanisms . . . We were grown men, after all.

And the desire, such as it was, was of a peculiar order. He had become in his staged self someone like me but much more so, or more purely and visibly, more pictorially, perhaps too much more sympathetically to be endured by me. His nickname had become *l'Americano*. Frivolity and vanity: What I was had been absorbed into what he was like stolen marble. But also we lent credibility to each other in these few days. I admit I was narcissistic but it was in the fashion of an overtly philosophic young man. But I was not fond of myself. My alternations of state between being uplifted by matters at hand, and being quiet and suspicious of myself, my becoming a sort of human nothingness sitting there, potentially a speech or an embrace, potentially an actual person, but only if I am accepted as who-I-am, oppressed me. That lifted for a day or two.

The ways in which I was technically both his brother and his father governed the way he accepted me, which was as an audience, a special audience, and someone who was a friend; this frivolity left me room as a hanger-on; but he could not endure granting me life as a zero-effect person and a contradictory power over his feelings as well. This was not because of beliefs and psychology and ego only but also because of my deficiency in powers of action compared to his ability in such power. And because of some fastidiousness toward love he had begun to feel. I felt something and he had no comparable feelings. He felt very little except as an exercise of art or of artfulness, in an amplification and projection and elevation of emotion of that sort, part of his career.

I still don't know how to judge what happened, which is that nothing happened between us as adults, but everything was immanent as story and as clear judgement and as an implication of complicity. He arranged a movie job for me that day. I was tested in Rome. I saw the test and became ill observing the photo-

graphed "truth" of my person and my gestures, my personality . . . I fled . . . to Paris, and did not see him again for two
years . . . I fled without saying good-by to him, and he did not
call or write or ask for an explanation, which frightened me. I
heard in Paris from a mutual acquaintance that I could have the
movie job, but I refused it. For a number of austere reasons I
could not bear to have a public face . . . Years later, a woman I
knew said I had closed the mirrors in order to become a writer.

I don't know. Perhaps. When we met after that time, Onni
and I, I felt I knew too much, and so did he, about us, about
each other. We could not, in the end, even on the simplest level,
accept each other's world or manner, and abandon our separate
and distinct prides . . . He was *always* vexed with me . . .

That, too, however, reflected the story, the one I've told, of
trust, trust betrayed, of stern, involuntary reaction. In the years
that followed, he became famous. His work was remarkable
. . . Well, that's an exaggeration. It was sometimes remarkable.
Much of it was cold and calculated. The emotional implications
in classical speeches were beyond him except for those of longing
or boastfulness. His voice had already begun to hollow out and
to be mannered and movie-ish, an unforgettable, slightly hoarse
mutter. The one unchanging trait movie after movie was his
quality of patience with life. With that alternately weary and
vivacious tolerance, and his sadly canny attitude toward
everything—and my transformed smile—he conquered the world
as an actor. And his life became so complicated—a wife, two
mistresses, a boy adjutant he was close to, passionate friendships
with half the people he worked with and with a dozen journalists
in three countries—that it seemed to me his work had to be fitted
into a life and daily schedule of greatly creative calculation and
premature exhaustion. His work, the effects he got on-screen
were largely cut-and-dried except for moments, Venetian moments, richly revelatory, almost processional in their exciting
beauty.

After a while, I was not directly jealous anymore. But I was
determined not to work for such success in my field, the small
equivalent of his success that it offered, not to risk being devoured

in the ways he was and had been. I was anxious, not self-righteously, but in fragility and helplessness, to have a life in my work rather than expend my life in the attempt to have a major career.

But I did, in my way, compete with him—on a very grand level. I pursued a sense of art and with some success of a ghostly sort. Having inherited a little money and being, at times, subsidized by my brother Carlo (who outdid Onni in his use of cocaine), I managed to live and practice this pursuit-of-art; and in various small ways I was lucky . . . I prospered . . . Or so others have told me . . .

Onni, called *Gianni* by most people who knew him in this period, had a few breakdowns, and he had violent spells. Our friendship could be relied upon if it was not relied upon. Telephone calls could summon the other person—sometimes—or lead to sympathy . . . But you never knew. It was Onni who pointed out that my career, the one I did not have, was doing very well.

When we were both in our 30s, we met again in Venice. I was with a woman, Abigail Peuse, whom I loved for a while . . . But in her company I could not work. She wanted me to write a movie for Onni-*Gianni*. And he hungered for it too. And to boss me around and to get Abigail into bed. The 60s had come and gone, and the world was more in Onni's reflection than in mine, which was a reversal of the past. But he could not bear to have his and my story—and its repetitions—interrupted by Abigail whom I shamelessly used for just this purpose.

He became outrageous, a satyr. In a motorboat on our way to Torcello one evening in a great wash of yellow light, in the brilliant and watery and golden flow of light I slapped him—I didn't punch him . . . I was too much of a pacifist. I grabbed and shook Abigail and said something obscenely movie-like and feeble on the order of: "I want to enjoy the sunset without being sickened by your games . . ."

He was between marriages, and he was without his entourage. He and Abigail stopped teasing me. We got drunk at the *locanda* on Torcello and talked until midnight. We were silent in the motorboat coming back until at one point in the moonlight Onni sang. I made the boatman turn off the engine. Abigail held on to my shoulder, the moon shone, and Onni sang.

The blatant sentimental melodrama of it turned under the pressure of his hoarse, local, unmodified-by-nerves voice into beauty. A bit regretful, a bit showy, a bit false, that beauty. But it was beauty. It seemed to me that merit inhered in such moments, that such pleasure-and-falsity were final in a way. That here happiness and meaning, free will and taste, courage and honor were displayed and were to be found, in moments like set pieces, like arias set apart from narrative.

That night was a full moon and high water but the water was still and silvered, and Venice as we neared it was silver-white and black shadows—dramatically moonlit. The boat crept on the silver water . . . It seemed that night that our story had *some* of the peculiar honor of a song.

The gliding pliability of the moonlit water and the façades as they rose around us and our moonlit faces in the succession of seconds, in the linkage of moments, became the emblem of a story open to its own continuance. Onni wanted to come to Abigail's and my room but I did not want that. In that room everything seemed to rock in a continuation of the motions of the water; we turned on no lamps; moonlight was spread and scattered and reflected everywhere. My heartbeat was filled with the banishment of Onni, a successful villain who was merely human . . . Considering human imperfection, could you ever love someone in reality and not discover she—or he—was a villain? I had actually been raped by him in my soul . . . As I had by my father and brother . . . And Miss Murphy . . . And, in her way, Silla . . . Onni often used in his singing certain elements of my drunkenness, the giving up, or giving yourself over to the thing: he had the quality of near goodness of someone of zero effect. The shutters were raised. In the moonlight I observed Abigail walk naked in the queer half-lightedness of the trembling room. I was aware that Onni had successfully defrauded me. I was also aware that Abigail had said once or twice that she loved me and that she was very careful, on the whole, of my feelings, not always—Onni was an overwhelming presence—but much of the time. The power to arouse feelings, or a counterfeit of them, a lot of that in me had come to me through knowing Onni.

And the strangeness of the self did not prevent it that one might use one's vulnerability, might submit with a broad, bold smile to being defrauded, might offer this, up to a point, as grounds for love. And even the way I am naked, my style when I am naked, the vanity and the un-vanity, the anti-vanity, I learned that in relation to Onni. I said to Abigail, "I think that if Onni had been taller, he would have been simpler and not quite so intent on having the faulty mastery of everything that is all the sublunary world allows."

"Sublunary?"

"Under the moon, not inhabited by angels."

"You're lively when he's around."

"Your breasts cast shadows."

And so on. The phone rang not long after we finished. I answered and told Onni I could not talk just then. I met him alone for breakfast at the bar. He has never been with me revelatory or entirely truthful. He holds out as a bribe a series of revelations about his childhood rape if I will speak to him of my pleasures (or lack of them) with Abigail. But as I asked earlier, how near will *you* go, have you ever gone, in speaking the truth to anyone but especially someone clever? Or even to yourself? What he did at the end in Venice, speaking as he had, came from age . . . And cocaine . . . He wants the half-lies I might tell him. I don't know what he will tell me but back then I did not think it would be the truth. He was more truthful now. But it was not absolute truth. I do believe that to know someone well is to approach the possibility of murdering them . . . In revenge or carelessness, in passion or in justice . . . Or to save the world. Life is absurdly perilous. Swindling and betrayal and actions done in ignorance, these are included in the overt *charm* of his gaze. But the degree matters, the degree of shamelessness. In life one never comes on pure, stripped idea but only on the real quality of thought-and-feeling become actions and glances . . . and words. In this frame in reality, I love him fairly well, love

Onni, with emotional dexterity and with due allowance for the mysteries, but this is not reliably so . . . It depends on what he does. On how he looks—I mean on what his looks convey.

But at any rate after a certain age one no longer expects love to be a fairly sensible matter or thinks good sense is anything but the acknowledgement that love and the world are terrible and large-in-scale and almost synonymous with each other and not to be trusted. Love is most of what life is. One loves money or fame if not someone. One is always caught one way or the other by something.

I am glad on the whole that my life has occurred the ways it has. I accept my history pretty much. I am glad I have known him, and I trust him so little that I am even more glad of the separation, the islanding of myself apart from the massive story of my friend.

But I have not told my anecdote about that breakfast the day after the moonlit night. It is brief. We both wore hats and sat on the dock bar of the *Gritti* in the tremendousness of the morning every-which-way glinting light. His lovelessness is in response to passions he arouses. I have, as we eat, as he teases and maneuvers, the knowledge that I have already betrayed Abigail by making notes about the night before, notes to be used: *the moonlight, a silver transparency in the room . . . A's body, untransparent, volumetric, was electrically human—a matter of desire . . . Of shelter . . . Nothing infinite is conceived to have the form of a woman . . . Desire: the form of a woman in moonlight . . .*

It is very odd about lying. Or hiding things. That tends to be a continuing story even with the dead. I know that nowadays if I think of my brother Carlo, who is dead, or my parents, while I am thinking of them I hide some things from them still.

Among the undying elements of this profane friendship is Onni's trying to find out about my life, about my feelings. In our partly comic marriage, I lie. I pretend to a puritanism that is not quite the case. "Shut up, Onni," I say, "and let me drink my coffee . . ."

I have never told him anything, anything at all.

SO THEN THIRTY YEARS PASS, and we come to the point of all of it, to the conclusion, and a vivid and undying monument for his astonishing self and his life. He has always liked a cheap catharsis.

I said to him in my head, sitting alone, on the deck of the *Gritti* where I'd gone because of the past: *Whatever is good in what I write will arouse your dirty soul if you notice it, and you will force a response from yourself, or coldness. Essentially you will be angry with me and you will try to make me miserable. You will dig and dig at me, and you'll twist the script into something you can do which will not be much like what aroused you in the first place or what interests me in it and makes it important to me . . . Then you will try to get more from me than that . . . You'll want me to engage in sexual games . . . And you'll cheat on the money—and you'll pay for the finished script at the rate for a draft. The director you choose will react similarly with the same results —a steady and an unsteady censorship fighting with you and me. And an attempt to own and dismiss the ideas. Why should I bother with this stale love-and-hatred, and policing one another, this idiot combat? I am not as strong as a star is, Onni. You let me win when you court me. But you get even for that. I can't engage in these shenanigans—I can't do it even to pretend that I am young. It will not be good for us. It will shorten our lives and sadden us unless we fake everything. I mean real feelings will be devastating. Amusing in a way perhaps, but I don't want a period of great happiness and great torment now.*

And the movie, if we finish it, will be at very best, considering our energies now, a small but effective film, clearly a labor of love and unbearable for me to contemplate, perhaps for anyone to contemplate or merely view.

In the end I was curious and wrote a treatment, a sketch for a monument. I oversaw the script written by two young women. I was a script consultant. Then a man, a German living near Orvieto, was brought in. Then a Trevisan scriptwriter living in

Paris. I fiddled with that version . . . All this took ten months. I lived some of that time in London, some in New York. Then I went back to Venice, to the *Gritti*. The first scenes were shot in Venice . . . a movie in Venice: the slip-slop of water and the sloppy early work. Onni's performance was skillful in the first scenes; then, out of curiosity and professionalism, he began to try harder. You must understand that making a movie is very difficult. It is an infinite mass of daily contingencies that waste money and use up the souls of everyone; and the ghost-images are feeble . . . Nothing is clear; nothing is impersonal, or formulaic; it is intensity and mess and only ever falsely formulaic, which is to say a sense of order is fake and frightened on a movie set. The lights, the cameras, the minds and souls of everyone, the ambitions, the wills—and nerves—are an incoherence like war, a kind of war that has come to Venice and is out of scale and out of sync with the city.

I mean the portrayal of Venice fails.

And in the meetings and in the orders given, so much is talked about that one is embedded in business words and in jargons of performance . . . a false language of words and dollars, *parole* and *soldi*. The culture of moviemaking is a rush of emergency and improvisation, of *doing it* in actual moments in the shadow of an imagined success.

The nerves are out-of-hand. Everyone takes aspirin, wake-up pills, slow-down pills . . . Everyone smokes, drinks—but this is practical, this indulgence, not a luxury. It is not an indulgence in this mock combat against silence and invisibility. And against the boredom of the audience.

And no matter how many millions are involved or how simple a day's shooting plan is, the ruling element is ego, flickers of ego and hard bursts of it, so that the control, the constraint and aiming and encouraging and then disguising of vanity is much of what a director does, perhaps all that a director does.

And the humiliation is in the work, the failure, the cheating.

The script had become a story about an oldish man and a young woman he wants and her lover. Onni added to the script, to its emptiness, in his performance the old man's alertness and yet blindness to others, then his tyrannical behavior, then his suddenly waking up when too much is irrevocable. For a large fee, I had recommended in the first treatment I wrote that the audience not know at first which one of the younger people he murders. That was held to be impracticable. The idea was that Onni murders the woman and is left with the other, the man, who reminds him of the dead one, of his real loss.

Onni was complicatedly playing himself of seventeen or eighteen years ago—his forty-year-old self—in a scene shot on the great stone platform of *San Giorgio Maggiore*. In his 60s, he was supposed to be a fifty-five-year-old, but he was playing it as a forty-year-old in order to be a bit glamorous, I suppose, and to placate the lust for fantasy in the audience. Eighteen years do not matter in movies, in movie scripts. Beyond the ring of by-standers a vaporetto was discharging tourists, fragments of color and motion, peering heads and restless legs. Onni and the young actor were in the sun and shadow at the door, Onni inside and the young actor outside. And the façade of the church rising in architectural stillness. The light was very strong, was blinding, which was interesting.

Onni was not being the character to any great extent; he was doing his lines; but then in certain moments, with a time lag of a second or two, Onni suddenly saw something as he acted, and something happened to his face . . . He saw his life, the movie, Venice, himself as a young whore and would-be actor, saw some possibility in the part, some idea; his perceptions and his tech-niques fell together in a pile and were ignited by idea; and his face began to fill with sightedness—not just of the eyes—but of all the features, of the whole man synopsized in the famous and experienced face . . . He began, in *flickers*, to be someone mad and strained, so strained that something like the sensitivity of youth recurs; and every inch of the surface of the face is alive with a strange bitter swollen youth of jealousy and love and voyeurism . . . And power . . . toward the young man, an able actor and quite pretty.

You could see the bitter brittleness of life in Onni, the lure of this for him. It is not entirely a sightedness outwardly. And then you could see the lies gather, like flies, flies sitting on his skin, a true, almost buzzing, unstill opacity, and a fate—in the lies . . . He has had the wrong life. The beauty, the ugliness, the lure, the lurches of bravery, bravery of spirit, of dark beauty even in what he did, the truth even of that, of performance, the truth of performance *at the end*, and grief, he began to experiment with showing this . . . He was able to show this. He produced, his face registered such a tremendous tidal wave of grief that it seemed to me Venice was drowned. And I was. I was choked and drowned. He threw himself outward through his skin in a burst of glare that etched itself on film. He willed it as an actor. I loved him again as much as ever, not me, but the audience, the audience was me.

Then he made an attempt, halfhearted, to save himself from the intelligent heat and honesty of what he'd done and to find a simple, shrewd, swindling purpose for himself to constrain the grief and to catch hold of an inverted redemption, in wickedness according to his own will . . . this *cheating* was the meaning in the cruelty and rage of the character he was playing but of himself too, Onni, so it wasn't entirely cheap, but it was cheap in a way compared to the moment before. But then the deftness of the cheating strengthens and mixes with what went before and is subtly modified and becomes admittedly, projectedly convulsive, involuntary, a chance-ridden imprisonment the character undergoes. Then in a sizeable merit of perverse soul, commanding one's sympathy, a dark giantism of choice, Onni-as-the-character chooses hellishness . . . Then all there is, in the face, is the fact of continuance, of going on, choice in abeyance . . . Damnation assured.

I said aloud to no one, "That is very pretty."

I will say something else: Onni is a notably able actor. At times.

Onni and I in his boat went from *San Giorgio* to his palazzo. To rest.

Sunlight brightly fluttered on glinting water and on faded, famous buildings as we putt-putted into the *Canalazzo*. The

Salute, with its great dome of announcement and its airborne, motion-struck population of statues, gleamed in unreliable beauty, fabled unstonelikeness. In the middle of the Grand Canal, a flotilla of gondolas filled with Japanese surrounds a gondola with an Italian tenor in it singing mostly on key . . . A battered vaporetto laden with becamera'd tourists, red and beset, startled and numbed in their staring, avoids the Japanese.

In the *grande sala* of his palazzo, all the windows had been flung open. Onni was exhausted and stoned. All but the last scene so far shot was ordinary. He had a look of bravery not unlike the old man's look of bravery in the movie, of someone who would cheat on the issue of bravery and win out even at the end by being brave in another, hidden way, by fooling his audience, by some ruthlessness or other, by perpetual darkness of purpose and obstinate self-absolution.

He pressed his knee against mine in the afternoon light in the room; he grandly and professionally, and irresistibly, smiled at me. "Poor *Nino* . . . Poor sheep Nino . . . Nino like-izz the scene that has to be cut . . ." he said with tough complacency.

He meant that a good scene acted as critical dismissal of the other scenes that would look better if the good one was destroyed.

"Mediocrity is always unbearable—and ruthless," I said.

"Ha. You want to make artistic *integrity* the issue?" he said with contempt.

I stood up. "No. I do not make it an issue . . . It *is* an issue . . . Onni, I'm going. Fuck you . . ."

Wearily, he closed his eyes . . . He lived in a world of manipulations and power and blackmail. And of power. "No. Have some cocaine," he said.

"A little," I said.

He rang a small ting-a-ling glass bell, red glass, with a gold handle. And the wolfish, dark-skinned young man came in. I sniffed. They sniffed. I smiled at the young man.

"Don't look at evil Nino," Onni said to the young man. While they carried out the ritual of the cocaine further I went onto the loggia and into a scene of boats and sun-silvered, brightness-plated, blue-gray-green water, the *Canalazzo* in the last part of the afternoon. I was old, beset by age, and I saw tired, aging façades in glare, a concentrated shabbiness at the edge of a sun-gilded, filthy, immense ditch of water, but pretty enough . . . Then the moment changes, perhaps because of the cocaine, and I am in Venice inside the watery surround, in this trembling city of age and fragility. And to be old in this old city is to have around one a visual music of great, spectral suitability. My memories of earlier conditions and even shapes of the buildings as I have known them are present as a frame for what is here in front of me. Such memories are insanely real, as real as what is here, but they go sliding into specterhood quickly, into ghostliness, into being lost presence like everything that has existed in this city until now, like all that has been lost; but the city in its dress of this moment moves more slowly in its own giddy continuities.

The eccentricity of Venice is that the facts of tragedy and of amusement here do not co-exist, not in story-dissolving Venice. A perverse sweetness is part of Venetian style, the absence of accusation and of lament, not always but mostly—the absence of lament along with an absence of coldness. So that one is warmly without lament—it is a style of being alive. Onni's mistakes and Onni are more vulnerable to age than the city is. The elaborate secular grace and patience, the virtuosity of gratitude, in the great churches, the generosity in the amusement offered are a perverse sweetness in the criminal and unashamed and unafraid city. The nature of this kindness—this odd, boastful, shabby clemency of a city—becomes a form of obscure veiling, a dimming of the light on the architectural details of the old, fading, faded city. I am not angry . . . I have what amounts to a gentle longing mixed with melancholia and knowledge . . .

Onni called from inside the room. He called again. He came out on the loggia to me.

"Perhaps I will not cut the scene . . . I don't know what I will do . . . I am having trouble with my blood pressure, with my cho-les-ter-ol . . ."

I said, "It is surprising to me how Venice has changed in color over the years. In my lifetime. The paint wears out. The stone darkens with dirt. And loses color as well. All of Venice has faded and been rebuilt brick by brick in my lifetime. I can date my life and identify the years in which I had certain feelings by the colors of the walls in my memory . . ."

He spoke grandly, as if answering me: "Ah, a popular glory . . . is written on water . . . This movie is the culmination of my life. My talent," he said squinting, "I must protect it now . . ." he said toughly, but not unagreeably. "Stop staring at the city and come inside and talk to me," he commanded.

"Is it an issue of artistic integrity? Or is it a matter of wasting time?"

"*Stai zitto,*" he said. In the enormous shadowy room, he turned in a slow circle. Then he said, "You do not understand: what we have been given is being taken away. What we have taken is being taken from us. The very big ones always do as they like to us . . . I have never gotten my own way. I will not die without a monument; I am a Venetian . . . Do you ever think of the stupid stories *they* tell about you when you are dead? I understand the nothingness of all stories and you do not . . . So, *dunque,* I will spit in the eye of meaninglessness . . . Pig-death will have shit put in its mouth by Little Onni grown old. Now listen to me, *dunque,* you can trust me. I told you I know what to do with words on camera: the fewer the words and the more of the eyes the better. A little dumbness toward cheap thrills doesn't hurt . . . I will embroider the dumbness . . . I have the camera in my *nose*. I know how to act the man in this movie . . . But I do not have a movie . . . *Dunque* . . . The rage as the prick dies into the sunset in the west . . . Pig-death becomes ham . . . Ha-ha . . . I need some words . . . From you, Nino . . . Listen . . . *Senti* . . . Two monologues, I need them . . . one happy, one sad—the sad one says, All is lost, all, *tutto* . . . I want to do it *con tutto il cuore,* I will hold nothing back . . ." Then, "I promise you . . . The happy one I leave to you to work out . . . I have never been happy . . . Perhaps something a bit sad and easy about redemption . . . Or Paradise . . . Or kindness . . ."

Then he proceeded to outline, with force and cleverness, what he could do now in front of a camera with such monologues and some of what he could not do—be shot in profile, for instance, except for a special purpose: "It is comically sad, my profile. My nose is not so fine, and the surgeon-doctors can do nothing with it anymore. But I weep well—and I can be ironic, ironic-fierce—as if with mustachios, you know . . . And the ancient longing to have a young body and be naked . . . I am willing to show my old nipples on camera . . . without even music on the soundtrack . . ."

He was lying. He partly meant it. He wanted his own way. But I was agreeable . . . I was hungry for clemency . . . "I am hungry . . . I want dinner," I said.

We went in the white motor launch to eat in a fish place in Poveglia. He demonstrated his voice in the noise; he projected his voice niftily, audibly through the racketting of the motor and the wooden sounds of the hull bounding and bouncing, and cutting and slicing through the water, the slapping and twisting and as-if-living water. The boat bounded rockingly, suspended on the dancing lights of the sunset in the water, among scattered watery shadows, among shadows of clouds on the water above the mucky, untorn, violently polluted depths.

Onni asked: "Why are you not listening to me? What are you looking at? Talk to me about love. Or fucking . . . Fucking when you are old . . . I am in terror with this movie—which was not a good idea for me to do . . . I am always crazy now. What are you looking at? Help me. Help your poor old friend Onni . . ."

I began to talk—ah, what a slow, strange, helpful hemorrhage it was, after half a lifetime of not being helpful to him:

"It is Venice . . . lonely, old, trampled-on Venice . . . Queen whore of the world . . . The man is Venetian . . . Polite . . . Strange . . . What is here flowers here. Nowhere else. It cannot be transplanted . . . Such a trim, strange corner of the ocean, and this wounded man . . . Think, Onni, here was a city in which the lowest common denominator and brute human strength did not rule. Isn't that interesting? . . . But this man is the lowest common denominator and believes in and uses brute human strength to murder . . . Venice does not love him . . . *Gianni*, one is helpless in discussing love . . . Or acceptability . . . To be assured in such a discussion is to be corrupt—and frightening. Repulsive, old—do you see? The man is rooted here—but he is an intruder. Do you know old men who use a warmhearted repulsiveness for seduction? To threaten? But if there is no helplessness in the face, there is no love . . . merely the longing for love . . . Your face is not good for comedy anymore, do you understand? Except for dirty comedy . . . Low jokes . . . Perhaps your face will do only for melodramas and thrillers now if it is to be effectual on screen. But it won't work in the ways it has worked for you before, your face, not for love—a love story— high comedy or melodrama or not . . . So, we are doing a thriller, perhaps a joke, a bit tender, a bit silly but grim. It is not a tragic story, it has no poetry—it is only a movie . . . that is to say, an arm of commercial enterprise, as the wiley and pragmatic Venetians tried to make love itself . . . Do you know that? As an industry, it didn't take up too much room on these crowded islands for the income it produced. The women were the commerce of the city, glowing breasts. And the paled, sated men. It is not a joke, not a tragedy. No audience will let anyone show it what love—or greed—really is—in people—or what hate is . . ."

Onni said, "Don't talk that way. You are too pious really, *Caro*, for such bullshit. Go on about movie love . . . talk about movie love."

"But movie love is not real love, Onni," I said.

I looked at him. The shapes of the lips have changed, have narrowed and grown too curled, curled active slits. The barbered eyebrows are in new places on his face—that is from the face-lifts. The shapes and expression of the eyes, the eyes themselves, are those of an aging man burningly, somewhat *hysterically* alive, stubbornly alive, like the eyes of old men in Venetian painting.

He has an animal quality still. Or it has returned today. One feels in him on the boat and in the restaurant the animal presence of the star, not quite an animal of flesh, but partly bone, partly will, almost a matter of cardboard: a mask, a projection of presence. One can see this in him from a distance even. He is an animal spirit of an extraordinary force of suggestion; the potency is of a further quality of a ruthlessness of an extraordinary animal self-absolution—the thing that movies always offered him. And that an ennobling lighting denies. He was partly true and partly false, partly fantasy, real all in all, and old: the skin of his face and the muscles under the skin of his face have tiny puckers; the skin is scored by lines partly smoothed by the makeup he wears after the day's shooting, that he has not bothered to remove.

This animal spirit, an icon-in-the-world, hasn't the clean, safe look that money and power give, that mysterious completion, that satisfaction. One feels instead fear in him and appetite— appetite of performance, an exhausted satiety opposing his will . . . But the opening and clapping of sails of will on tall masts of institutionalized power and pride seem real enough that one can in one's dreams see him sail back across the Lagoon to Venice as an image alone.

The body seemed no longer to speak or to quiver like an ear. This animal spirit saw windingly, complexly; and then some- times, the posture brightened as if the body looked across water into the distance that it could traverse now as an image, a legend.

Moviemaking does make him crazy, naked, and poor. He breathed encouragingly as I talked. Or he snorted. He tapped his fingers, the nails, insensitive and made of horn, like birds' bills. His tired, aging body, the drying skin, the oddly shaped aging muscles of the shoulders and arms and neck of an aging man, his mood formed a figure of a dark order, well-informed; him listening to my storytelling was as if that storytelling was a dark wind ruffling old leaves and a strange tree that was a mixture of horn and breath.

He has no real sensitivity left. His strength ebbs and then re-forms. He is coldly not young, coldly not comfortable with death—comfortable only with the deaths of others . . . Can you love him?

I told him what I thought ought to be done to the movie to bring it closer to a truth he could project and impart to the whole enterprise. He had unamused eyes with hard exhaustion and a silence of feeling in them.

Then in the boat going back in the pale dark, where we sat in the back of the boat in the parenthetical bubblings of the bow-waves, he said in the dim light, "You know, you pretend to be, oh, so upright and so pallid, but you forget I know you, what a sluttish male you have always been, luring and seducing anyone you could get to buy your lunacy. You were handsomer than I was—oh yes, not like an actor, but so fine-boned, so long and frail and still so solid, so honest and uprearing and anxious to pound with your hooves, so anxious to own everything in the meadow. Always you care less than anyone cares for you—you have done this since you were a child. Always so quick to be affronted. And now you are much better looking than I am and more content. You are conceited about your mind and what you know, and look how you play with me, look how you play at talking to *me*, your old Onni . . ."

"Onni, a love story in a movie, my dear, consider the difficulties; the audience knows too much and too little; and you will frighten them if you are sincere. And you . . . Consider . . . You are practically death itself. You represent the tragedy of exhaustion, as in one of those plays of Shakespeare's that end with a battle in which the king is killed. So, what will you do? Sing and dance? Again? You have no real waist. Then, remember people live longer nowadays—romance in the shadow of a short life is gone; the courage of women risking their lives is gone . . . feelings remain but they are as if new . . . To show love as inspired or as ill-fated would not amuse the audience. Loving in that fashion is no longer done on-screen, and in life it is done differently from the ways it was done in the past. A traditional love story needs death, it needs social wrongs and wars . . . Nowadays if someone *loves*, it is a phase or a privilege they give themselves. They search for themselves. What do you judge love by? By what you've known, yes? Well, the audience too. By the love *you* feel and by other loves you think you've seen . . . By things you've read and seen . . . By jealousy . . . And its sense of ideal love somewhere else but not for you . . . Will you put your jealousy on-screen, your claim to know what love is? Such comparisons are a swindle—do you know that yet? Most love most of the time is nervous, sidelong, politic, then impolitic and headlong—or perhaps not. Do you feel love as a pressure of the skin, as part of your reward for being who you are in the world? Do you feel it as a series of wrong notions that you must correct? Do you never feel it? What is your experience of love that you can bring to the screen? Bring it and be done. Do you understand me? I dare you to show mediocrity in a character and then love taking you as the character past your own mediocrity, not the character's, and then past the stifling mediocrity of the world—love and hate . . . We are all mediocre. Conceit is a form of mediocrity. As is power. And dryness. The other thing, the getting beyond it, is an attack on everyone, is, you know, a truancy . . . from politeness, from ordinariness . . ."

"Ah, now you are Clark Kent taking off your suit, showing yourself, pushing everyone around."

"Yes. Your success—wonderful, isn't it, success? Power and success are gorgeous things. But a bit mediocre if they do not become gorgeous. The Venetians of the Most Serene Republic were very clever about this mediocrity: they executed mediocre admirals, assuming treachery, since the admirals should have managed to be driven and inspired by love and fear and pride toward Venice to rise above themselves . . . Do you see? The art you desire is not a trick; it is this other thing . . . To put love for this other thing first. I admit the control of mediocrity was helped by the age and sexlessness of the rulers in Venice. And by the ease of love here. Will you play the pander, the old person, who, in classical love stories, is necessary to stir the plot and the young lovers to invest their lives and then turns on them? A man who comes to place emotion above politics? Can you talk in a grand way to the audience? You want to star, to dominate, yes? So, we have a story of the pander and *his* love, and how he loves and falls apart, which is to say he loves powerfully but not warmly . . . this is what a movie about love with you starring in it would be like. This would be not a monument you could bear. I don't think you can bear to tell the truth about anything now except as a curse for others. How strange the world is . . . But you and

I could have done better in it . . . Something I have wondered, by the way, is: Were you lying on your stomach when you were raped—was it in a barn or in the house?"

"I never think about it, Nino. It is enough that it occurred. I forget it. I have forgotten it. You have forgotten things, too—you know? Do you think I am untruthful?"

"I sometimes think of how often we were hit, or hurt, as children, as boys. And how often we changed things around in our accounts of what happened. I sometimes think of how truthful you seemed to me . . ."

"It was in the kitchen of the farmhouse. It was not a seduction. Afterwards, I prayed to be ugly so that I would be let alone. But I did not entirely mean it, and I changed again . . . But for a while I carried myself differently, like a cripple. And I made faces. I had a dull, wooden self . . ."

"Do you remember the act? Do you remember the actual *prick*? The insertion?"

"No! Why are you asking? You think I whored myself? I remember only the smells. And the shock of being handled and thrown onto the table. And the feeling . . . the unrecognizable feeling . . . Then a sensation of distance as if I were unconscious. It happened at a distance. I was almost unconscious . . . And I remember more but I will not tell you about it, I promise you."

Was the original *love* between us well-founded after all? "Onni, can you act this thing in an aging man? Onni, all in all, we have done quite well, you and I. We managed, didn't we? We have known some truth—but now that we are this age everything in the world is in a foreign language for us. We must translate ourselves very carefully or we should be silent. What are you willing to put on-screen?"

"Nino-ni, old men rule the world. Nothing is over."

"You never did agree with anything I said. I do not think it is likely you will agree now. Which is why it is a waste of time for us to talk."

The next day in the purple and rose and crimson half-light of a slow sunset, enormous over the trembling Lagoon, Onni

said, "Ah, Nino-nino, you always like to make me jealous . . .
Now you want me to be jealous of what you know about love
. . . So, I am jealous . . ." He was in a mood of weary, potent,
pungent, perhaps terrifying nostalgia, of a theatrical sort. He
had coked himself up again. He says, "I was always jealous of
you, Nino." Again we were in his motorboat. Noisily, slidingly,
slipping in wet, cloven, sidling water, the boat in the dark maroon
and purpling and golden light pushed toward the line of lights,
the outlined campanili, the domes of the city. "I am jealous
of the way you have aged just as I used to be jealous you had
escaped the war . . . Let us slip into Harry's for a moment, let
us enter and see how important we are."

When I refused, he said, "Well, come to the palazzo, come
and tell me more about love and make me miserable . . ."

"But you will steal what I say."

"Why not? You will never use it. You see: I am Italian, I am
a realist . . . I don't believe in Hell."

As we disembarked, I looked at him in the early summer
dark lamplight. Youthful beauty has become shrewd exhibitionism, and that sometimes, rarely now, becomes beauty again as
time passes in the moments, a persistent but altered beauty, a
beauty of a new kind. Our hatred for one another is of a peculiar
order now.

"We might attempt a monster movie," I said as we walked
upstairs, footsteps echoing in the enormous marble stairwell.
"Can you be a beautiful monster now, Onni? A successful man
who has grown quite ugly in his power, and who, in love and
grief, becomes quite decent in a courtship way, attractive again
half as a swindle but not simply in that sadistic-masochistic ambitious way, but in redemption?"

"And then I will be humiliated?"

"Perhaps. I don't know." Two enormous blond dogs with
large heads—they stank; their pale-bearded dog faces were at
once expressionless and cheerful—came bounding down the
steps toward us . . . We walked past, shouldering them aside with
our legs if I might say that. The fresco overhead in the stairwell
was newly restored, hideous in bright, wrong blues and whites.

I felt my breath constrict with the effort of living. "If it is done crudely"—the character's humiliation—"it might soothe the jealousy of the audience."

"Ah, why can't an audience be generous in spirit . . . like you and me? Tell me," he said almost pathetically, "how does an old man *love?*"

"Well, what is your experience?" I asked cruelly.

"*Furbo,*" he said.

I sank into a chair: "Think how selfish an old man's love is if it is erotic. We are hard work for anyone now. We are not so good in bed anymore, will you admit that? No? Well, you are lucky or ginseng works for you. Does our hero fool himself? Does he feel himself to be a king who can devour other lives in order to have a bit more life for himself? David and Bathsheba as a vampire tale? In our story is it to be acted out that each of us doesn't know better than to believe ourselves? If the old man in such a story is beyond that and is not a fool or a villain, he must be anxious for proof, for evidence, for signs his love is not stupid and deathly—he must look for guidance that he is not wrong in what he feels. If he doesn't care, then he must be mad and cruel—or very stupid . . . Which do you prefer? Do you have any interest in playing the role this way?" Then: "The small-statured Venetians were like children riding on the ocean—think of them—think of admirals the size of children in those little suits of armor. Imagine them as little old men—in this Venice, around us—with their pictures and statues, their pages and slaves and local whores. They stayed alive differently from us. Only a few of the rich ones, of the rich Venetians married—did you know that? They kept the fortunes concentrated. The rich men, out of jealousy, made their wives wear high shoes, buskins, so high-soled-and-heeled the women could not walk but only totter. They could not swiftly duck in anywhere. The grotesquery of the tall, tall tottering wives with their dyed yellow hair married to the short, brilliant, jealous men in this clear Venetian light . . . The grotesquery meant they were beloved—at least in this sense—in this pretty city . . . The short High Admirals were rich and ruthless . . . *Come live with me and be my love* but in this way. And I will have my amusements—I will have those who are willing to labor over my pleasure. Tonight is *acqua alta*, tide and wind, tourists barefoot in the cold water; other tourists passing on temporary wooden bridges; clouds sailing overhead, the lights over the Piazza swinging in the wind . . . Was Venice a city of elopements as Shakespeare suggested? There was a surfeit, an overabundance of marriageable young women. They were put into convents where they misbehaved. Love is not a dreamlike sense of things but it is something dreamed of. I had dreamed of loving someone and then I loved you of all people . . . I loved you all those years ago, such a queer mixture of politics and the erotic. A dreamlike sense of things is not love. You would like to dream away old age; put it in a dream; dress it in words and images. Love is not absolute. Love has nothing absolute in it. Love can't deal in limitlessness except as death or suicide, to inflict death, or to taste suicide. Something else in us, not love, is absolutist, something like an outcry of will. The murderousness of wanting to be loved, loved totally, loved completely all the time, is not a simple, sentimental desire inside a real hour. It is a ruin, the simple ruin of the otherwise possible world. I am sorry for your sake and for mine that audiences are not generous." I said, leaning forward, and speaking with more force once I was seated and did not have to walk too: "If we do a movie in which the love is convincing, one or both of the lovers must die. Or the love must stop short. Or be balked. We are all of us too jealous to observe real love and not go mad with meddling and destruction. Real love is passionate but not so passionate as the rage of others to interfere. Love is passionate in real hours, in real bodies. When two people love, limits rule since each will take care of the other rather than risk losing this source of meaning, unless they are lunatics or are lunatic with guilt and want to die. The sensation of plausibility in dreams keeps you asleep, and the sensation of power and of having what you want keeps you awake and alive: so, too, in love. It is quite a tightrope or a bareback act. And then to hold an audience with truth about this! The audience has to be hypnotized into acquiescence and bribed and kowtowed to. It has to be given a sensation of its power. Isn't it true that stars must die or be balked in popular movies? The interplay of sadomasochism in stardom between star and everyone, everyone, is very curious—do you think we should have that in our movie? The old man and the world and all the sadomasochisms back and forth? To see the hero beaten, the heroine in tears and dead? . . . Or raped? Every day in the world, the wakeful go to war with the dreamers: shall we show that? Love and art believe in the world as truth. And politics too sees the world as truth but bloodily and cautiously. How do you *show* truth in two dimensions wearing makeup and in closeup? Fantasy rarely works well—except for Shakespeare, of course . . . Can we show the real world in which good judgement is never absolute, but it is often exact and inflexible: so the tragedy occurs? Shall we do it coldly and not as a tragedy, only as a sad thing? The melodrama of the Absolute Thing in this world and its wickedness and its fall, since it always falls, is that something you would want to act, Onni? You will notice that such melodrama is missing from Venice. And from you. You are merely a monster, sans doctrine—you are only a comically tragic thing no matter how many people you mislead. Have you ever seen Venice from the air, a compact mass of buildings, carefully higgledy-piggledy with no area for the assembly or barracking of forces? Byzantium could never have used the Lagoon as a substitute for Ravenna. The city is closer to the sea than to the mainland; it has no relation to armies. It rises behind the thin sand curl of the Lido, separated from the sea as if by an eyelid. In a small plane, the Lagoon is a half hour's flight from end to end—this is an enormous space for a city state. In the fourteenth century, Venice was as large in its way as Brazil is now. The waters of the Lagoon are a mass of colors—green, pearly gray, dark gray, blue-gray, bits of sun-glare. Venetian purple is visible in shadows, in colored swathes and tinted patches. The marsh shallows are sometimes rust-red. The water reflects the blue and gray of distances. And here and there are the greens of trees on various islets, different greens fluttering. And red-tile roofs . . . Until the 1600s, before the domes were built, the city was in outline somewhat like a marsh itself, like a marsh with reeds and grasses rising from the water, the verticals of the nonwatery; and not floating; in Venice the verticals, as if of grasses, were buildings filled, crammed with lives; but rooted and grass-like; except for a few of the churches which rose high like tents or ships' hulls upside down in the air. Venetian love is problematic. Is it love if you do not love someone best? My mother had four children. Yours had only one. How did my mother love us? Each in turn?"

"This movie will kill me," he muttered.

"Deal in fakes. Be a fake . . ." *As always* was implicit.

He put on dark glasses. Did we always try to hurt one another? No. We have become skilled with age. "I always get what I want," he said, mean, crooked, emotionless, deadly, lovely old man. "I will do a movie about love, and I will make a liar and fool of you again, *amore* . . ."

EPILOGUE

HIS DAMNED NEED to run things and his sensible terror of failure as well as his mad conceit meant thát his will, not just his words, but his will, his wishes, had to be the language of reason on the project as well as anywhere near him—it is his language, his instincts, his appetite for success—and love—that shaped the movie; and the movie was consequently diminished.

To keep me around, he sent a marvellous girl to seduce me. He also initiated, through intermediaries, tax and legal troubles for me, so that I could not leave Venice. He went to a great deal of trouble to get his way.

Onni's aging ruthlessness, his violence of domination, with its craven, splintery little pockets of submission, its periods of pained subjectivity, were changingly familiar to me. What upset me was that he saw no necessity to learn anything new at his age. A terror of the new overwhelmed the sensible hatred of failure in him. He had to be the chief interpreter and boss in part because he could not afford to be an apprentice to a new idea. Most of the movie was formula but not bad. Little of value was in it, but he did not discard the good bits either. It is important here to know about the seemingly half-accidental, time-ridden way a work comes into existence, to know how each event alters possibilities and probabilities in the light of the will, and how it transforms the silence in which the not yet done parts exist. Each day's light—each hour's moods, each shot's ideas and record, even if only of failure—gives you a different footing overall even during itself. The idea behind a performance and the ideas that make it up are at war. It is like Onni to be indomitable and indomitably improvisatory, moodily lunatic and guileful, temperamental and geared up and drugged, making his way from moment to moment in the shooting. If this process is entirely predictable, then each step holds only a false novelty. He was often good in his work and at times his leadership was able but perhaps on the whole not able enough. His was a performance largely without value, sentimental crap, not vicious and somber enough, not sufficiently truthful or intent on quality to be worth one's caring about.

Or it was my jealousy, my need for independence that felt the great scene he'd done at *San Giorgio* was unmatched day after day.

The young woman whom I liked? He trafficked in her and he troubled her mind. *He* slept with her when I did not. He inducted her into his own crapulous expertise of obscenity, and he watched me suffer over it. At one point he called me to his dressing room, and when I entered it, she was there; she was there, nude and drugged, lying on a couch, such a sad enormity of obscenity really, her breasts, her lovely, odorous nakedness, her weak stupidity, that wonderful-eyed child, no longer so wonderful-eyed, of course. One of the casualties of ambition. Onni's viciousness reflected his success and how far from success in some sense his work so far was.

But if I might be permitted to forget the crimes, the casualties, if I might be illogical that way, I can say that at one point in the shooting, Onni, in a black-hearted way, learned how to do the movie as a movie actor if not as a performing actor, but as a star, a cynosure. The old man blossomed unvirginally and had a newly burgeoning and ripening glamor that I watched with interest and some curiosity. He knew, he saw at moments what to do—and he did it, or half-did it. If you looked closely you saw that he was protecting himself. Then the drive or the idea of the moment that gave his acting its peculiar luster and quality of force died in him, killed by his energetic rage to win out over the idea . . . over the difficulties of the project. What genius of an ordinary sort his was . . . What a wretched fool he was . . . What a hatred and fear of art was in him and what longing to possess a place among its practitioners, what a longing to do it himself and what a reluctance to be as generous and as vulnerable as his capacities as an artist required of him.

But Onni was aware that his sense of what would work and be good in a movie and what would not wasn't guiding him. He had a great awareness of all sorts of damnation; and he had a number of interesting scenes, and one great one, and a number of ordinary ones, enough that one day he began to work in a dry, highly frightened, deeply skilled, and informed, and, I suppose, maddened manner, defectively at first, which is to say thinly, and then with more and more pungency, more and more urgency, more and more risk, and even with fullness, burning himself up, or burning himself out, black-rimmed eyes, hollow-faced, exhausted with thought, alertness, and hours of expressiveness.

One might say he worked without contempt for the medium or for the audience, or even for the cameras and the light . . . Everything was risky, the foolishness of the fullness he attempted, and then his commitment made him vulnerable to pain, and, of course, there were the physical risks, from the heat and the lights and amphetamines he took, and the psychophysical ones, the queer, jutting-boned submissiveness in his tiredness, the inevitable point in the arc of his mastery when he was willing to die and was genuinely afraid of the beasts in the dark of his mind and of all the contracts and bargains with darkness, let us say, that go into mastery. He would sit between takes, quite stoned with excitement and idea and unthinkingness—he was unthinking in order to hold on to his concentration—but he was feral still and ready to fight.

And he would smoke and eat or take a pill and sit and stare, and his fingers, on both hands, would be crossed, or he would cross himself comically and then again seriously, in a shadow of the first . . . Such a low submissive mastery—he might have been a peasant or a king with only the massive pride of dirty success and no other kind of pride at all.

Onni had two small heart episodes in this period, small aneurysms, but he hardly rested, and he did not give up. He shot one scene of himself when his legs were more or less paralyzed and he had to be strapped to a table in order to stand upright.

He bought his way, he practiced a flagellation of sorts in this scramble for at least professional redemption. He became ascetic in a sense, inversely saintly, duly fanatic. He sent the lovely girl to recuperate in Scandinavia. He went to bed early every night. He did not look at the rushes coldly but with a devastated power of attention, unshaken by the drugs and the strain and the emotions he was dealing in.

Then, shaken by those very things in other moments, he cried in my arms; this happened twice, once showily but sincerely, and once with a cold deadness beyond pretense that was also partly *sincere* rehearsal, if I might say that, but without making use of his tears in an extraneous way.

His work got better and then it worsened and then it improved, then it soared, and then it sank. But none of it was as good as the work he had done in the scene at *San Giorgio*.

I wept one morning outside the *Accademia* on my way to Onni's to join him for his morning ride to the day's shooting. I wept for no reason other than that life was frightening and wonderful and wonderfully cheap and that I was frightened and exhausted and amused. I believed in him—half-believed in him. I wanted him to succeed. I preferred him to fail, but I willed him to succeed. I did not apply my own judgement. I reflected his sense of accomplishment or of defeat. Or the crew's. Perhaps I deluded myself in that.

I cried because I would not live forever. I cried because Venice grows tiresome and old and ugly but remains beautiful in part, like Onni. I cried because I was beyond tears, really. I cried with nerves. I cried with anguish over Onni's ego and pride and his nerves and his limitations.

Then in one scene—I will be brief because this is embarrassing in sentiment—Onni did something I could not have foreseen or imagined or advised. He used the dry, carefully indeterminate movements of a French actor of our youth and long since dead named Ferdinand Jouvet, well, Jouvet anyway, and he used further, not his own androgyny, but his knowledge of it and of women to project a man that women told him about, or showed him, a man too manly—and cold—too soaked in will for there to be any possibility of response to him sensually in the young woman he was to kill—and had already killed since the scene had been shot early on. He had used the cold jealousy he'd felt for the lovely girl he had so damaged in life and with whom he had tempted me.

It was a movie sort of thing, this characterization unrehearsed and unwritten which somehow, magically, almost logically encompassed all the scenes he'd done so far and their various ranges of excellence and of ordinariness. It was an absurd idea, a stupid idea but so intelligently done that one could see Onni was a master of method, was a master technician concerning male force . . . This device of characterization had more meaning (in a certain sense) than could be supplied by any more systematically intelligent approach—except that of serious artistic intelligence which is very rare and much too wearisome to work with to be of use in movies. For movie purposes, this was superior anyway, and useful beyond mere utility, since it was photographable and was within the range of the chief cameraman to see and understand and capture.

It made the good scene useable in that now the gradation of intensities between scenes made story sense mysteriously. And it was not so different from some of the better other scenes: it was simply the best scene. Onni had moved toward this all along, although not with certainty, but gropingly. In one of the two scenes shot that day, he lit a cigaret and squinted in closeup and grinned sourly to himself and that illuminated a quarter of the movie. In the other, as that knowing character caught in his awareness of his own damnation, he spoke to the girl, and lost his knowledge, lost his purpose, and reassumed it as a rage of damnation and of hatred. His face had the double quality of blind *calli* running off everywhere, thoughts and moods and impulses you see, and then a blunted quality as if from fear, of having no possibility of thought—do you know how in a fog certain walls and corners in the city, in Venice, look impenetrable and dull and menacing? Impassable? Like that. It was some unspeakable fear of others directed at the girl. It was very good, amazing, really—it was movie-acting, the work of a disconnected moment, disconnected in scale and emphasis, not a theater actor's marvellous soliloquy, not any such thing as that. It was a star's work, full of information about personality, a familiar personality and using familiar imagery, but using it strangely and knowingly, a bit beyond intelligence, and far beyond worthlessness. The slanted truth of it was like a slanted light ray in a shadowy Venetian room.

Between him and me it is still love, of course, but in old men it is love-and-dry-knowledge. I recognize that he is using me as a model; it is an angry, corrupt, damned version of me . . . Perhaps it is me as I am now.

He worked more intently after that; making the movie was killing him. He had a dozen ailments every day, took a dozen pills. But he liked being amazing, and he was darkly pleased in a strong-willed way, and had a sort of angry and grubby gaiety. He was not grief-stricken about any of it. I was, of course. When enough scenes were good that he saw his monument as achieved, and not as good as it might have been, but good enough, say, for one of the lesser churches of Venice he began to show humor, not terribly impressive humor, but humor.

He said, between takes, "This movie is a labor of love . . . That is why it is such shit . . . More money and a decent script is what we need . . ."

"A decent script is what you have," I said. "Indecently high quality is what you want."

"I love your sarcasm. I love *you*, Nino," he said. "I love you without any feeling at all."

He loves me, ah, without feeling on the porch of death as before . . . It is funny, that, at least for me, but of course for me that is not a joke, what he said.

He reads my mind; after all, he is me in a sense just now:

"It is not a joke," he says after a scene in which he was hidden, slow in movement, jealous and indomitable—hence murderous: me, I suppose, but me and Onni mixed, surely. His actions and his stillnesses in the scene were grimly logical and yet he gave me credit in a certain gaiety of performance, a nifty undeniability of excellence of performance—really a niftiness, that gaiety was a matter of art.

Offscreen at night and in the morning and between takes, he was gray with exhaustion, brightening only on camera, and then sometimes ferociously, and often off key and strained, but sometimes on target. His old, partly trivial hands have a tremor but not on camera. His slit of a mouth, partly gay in the role even when murderous, looks mostly exhausted, is lifeless between takes and often on-screen . . . He has to gather himself. "I look like death—it is not a joke," he says sourly.

"It is not a joke," I agree.

His monument consists of extraordinary moments in a cheap script, not entirely cheap. It is perhaps like a too small monument with uninteresting details and set too high on the church wall. He says, "Write me a script, Nino! Give me a movie that is worth my effort."

"No," I say.

He says, "I have no heart but you are in it. This is a joke, Nino."

He then began to ready himself for the next shot. He now enters on the insanity of performance and passes offstage in this manner, a famous actor pursuing a form of willed suicide. I will say it at the end of this book, he was a marvellous actor who had a second-rate career and a very famous one.

*   *   *

One night during this time, after a dream of love, I woke and dressed and went out in the rain. *In Venice the rain was falling that day.* Rain in Venice wets the marbles of the cathedral and sets deep puddles in the pavement of the *calli.* And the canals sigh and ping. The noisy brightness of a rain with the sun half-emerged from Venetian clouds is like a noisy brightness of feeling, *la di da tra la la*, as in a comic opera of attachment and love with a happy ending, not as in a Grand Opera—that would be another story. A water rat, small and animate in the rain's mischievous light, runs along the edge of the *Pescheria*, a scuttering figure of animal wit. Workmen are setting up the market. Trophies from the massacre of fish are piled on shiny beds of ice on tables under the roof in the open-sided structure. The fish at the end of their story, silver-bodied, with open red mouths and staring and unreal eyes, stink of brine, of the salt sea, stink of boats and are very still, gleaming, and limp.

The early morning's wet odors of rain, the smell of wet Venice, and the fish odor and the dirt and leaf smells of vegetables, and the drifting smell of gasoline fumes from the heavy workboats carrying food to the wharfside . . . the rainy smell of the *Canalazzo* and of dirt-marked hands . . . salt-odor and fish-blood-stained hands . . . The eyes and necks of the other lives here . . . The colors of faces and of stones in the rain . . . Me with my head erect in the rain under a gray umbrella, my remaining hair damp, my dry eyelids refreshed . . . I am a passerby in a fish market, gaudy-scaled, stinking, among the brown-tailed, sharp-finned fish, and the pale *calamari* and slow-stalking green *aragosti* . . . In the rain, the carrots and tomatoes and apples and white celery and green cabbage are placed under paper, are loosely shielded from the light rain . . . I am not clever. I am merely alive. Carlo Emilia Gadda has instructed my mood . . . If he were here, he would perhaps understand me, my head suddenly lowered, ducking and staring at the stone paving underfoot to hide my tears, my rage, my embarrassment, my longing, my gratitude. I am riven with longing for that other world of feeling that no one has ever known, that other world of perfection, that world of pure and absolute love and of no appetite or heartbeat, of mouths that only sing. I am ill with longing—I who have not had a life of longing.

After a while, I lift my head, wipe my eyes, light a cigaret . . . I rarely smoke but have begun to, lately. The bitter smoke, the match dry my eyes. The restless surface of the *Canalazzo*, wind-chopped, low waves seesawing and puckering in the damp air, is a few yards away past the edge of the stone wharf and the stacks of cartons and the lounging figures in rubber ponchos and stocking caps. The shadowed, restless air . . . now it is sputtering and spattering and spitting . . . Moisture stingingly touches my face, my present face. The sounds of drops on the umbrella and my faintly noisy breath under the fabric, the soft fabric-walled echo, and Venice, the *Rialto*, hurrying figures in the rain, outside the dripping scallopped rim of my umbrella . . . the busy, polluted rain and an aging man in a state of comic desire to know finally *what real love is* became, *finally*, a very strong, very unreasonable, very comic conviction that I was an example of it, perhaps not a good example, but love is so stupid, is so common, is so common a measure of life that anyone can be an example of it, even me, even if I am not the best example in the world.

In the rain-tinged air in Venice at the *Rialto*, the wind blowing and twisting the drumming umbrella, the hunger to feel love unchangingly and to be a person of fixed quality, fixed loyalty, fixed emotion, with assured properties of trueheartedness and doting response choked me. The wish to have known people more concerned with stately love than Onni, people who would have created a lifelong love in me like a pyramid, truly a massive and immortal love, gripped me. The wish was imbecile, even logically impossible given the reality of time and the reality of feelings, sexual liaisons, and thought. It seemed to me that to be a great example in actual life of someone of unchanging feeling and fixity of will would be a ludicrous imposture. After all, in the rain, in the changing air and odors, with emotion prickling my face under the umbrella, I thought that, after all, *Onni* was one of the greatest exemplars of flirtation and love of the age. He was one of the great public builders of images of sophisticated-and-weary love in my lifetime. And I knew I did not believe in his images of love. I refused them for too many reasons for there to be a name for all those reasons . . . I refused them like a wife . . . as a wife might.

Such peering as this at something in the light of truth—and of the spirit—was Christian. The spirit and the ordinary, perhaps grace-filled, perhaps tormented body . . . this peering was Venetian.

At the *Riva del Carbon*, in that crowded, cheap place, among the early tourists and the souvenir shops and nearby, the lineup of gondolas splashing among pilings, and the *Rialto* rising in the rain-streaked air, I thought how Venetian commercial speculation arose from a mind wandering during self-examination. Venice rising from the waves commercially was trained by the catechism in thought-out gambles of the soul and merchandise. Self-examination and modern capitalism have the same root.

I walked then through *San Bartolomeo* and *San Luca* and into the not-very-crowded *Merceria* among umbrellas, and came across Onni as I had half expected I would. His two bodyguards were at a considerable distance away staring at hi-fi equipment in a very brightly lit window among posters of singers. Onni had on makeup, including a fake mustache and large glasses. He was in a yellow slicker with a hat. He was smoking a cigaret under the umbrella in the erratic rain. He looked like hell, dark rings around his eyes under the makeup in the dim, noisy light under his umbrella, while below the false mustache his thin lips were painted and gleaming; he was a strange-looking, oldish man.

"So," I said, in dim echo from before.

"You are a strange son of a bitch," he said in a hoarse voice. His famous voice is rubbed raw. He grabbed my arm; he put his arm through mine: "Come walk with the monster you refused to help."

"I helped you."

"It was not ideal help."

"What ideals are for is to make real life seem paltry," I said, meaning they help you enlist in death and avoid any real fidelity of a broken, possible sort to real feeling. "How can you love anyone, how could I have loved anyone, even my mother and father, if I did not distrust ideals?" He snorted. "I prefer being alive," I said.

He is leaning on me. I smell the oilcloth or whatever it is of his slicker, and his mustache and its glue, and the perfume he uses, and his oily makeup and his cigaret and his breath in the damp air.

"Bah," he says. "You are too clever by half . . ."

We walked in that narrow passage past the lit windows under the narrow strip of dripping sky overhead, tourists and Venetians bumping us.

"*Cazzo . . . pazzo*," he mutters in the rain. "*Pazzo amore . . .*" He is not being homosexual, or is, but it is in pursuit of an idea. He leans against me; he says, "Nino, did you know that you would live to have an old man's *cazzo*, a wrinkled prick?" And he grins.

A feeling of affection here with Onni is of a cold affection which, even so, hits me again and again.

"I don't know what you're talking about," I say although I do know. I begin to laugh. I am laughing beneath my umbrella next to his, and I am ringing with breathlessness, with cold emotion . . .

In the Piazza, in the peculiar light of half-rain, of rain ending and of blowy mist, in that damp light with distances opening across the *Piazzetta*, with the façade and campanile of *San Giorgio* pearl-colored in the fresh, limited, damp light, Onni says, "Will you write a monologue for me for my new movie now?"

The rain-washed, wetly freshened marble and the sweeps and curls of *San Marco*, the whole ridiculous, rising beauty of mosaics and statuary in the half-lit air are beside me. I say, "An old man's monologue on rain—would you like that? Rain which does not renew him: would you deliver that? A monologue of generosity, praising the world of others, the lives of others? The phallic freshness of the young, can you praise that and not the memory of yourself? I don't think you can, *amore, mio vecchio.*"

The boy I was, in this light, transparent, an enormous ghost in the enormous space of the gray-lit Piazza, splashes me in the present moment, the boy who had a nervously phallic significance for Onni who, in turn, had great amatory significance to the boy . . .

Pigeons whir, and reflected light brightens on the stones in the damply glowing air. The green-gold horses prance, and the wetted rose and worn pink and glassy yellows of the mosaics of the church and the flesh-pink *Loggetta* and the gray-white statues on the roof balusters of the *Libreria* against the parting clouds and the streaked whitened bluish gray of the *Bacino*, the dulled radiance of the water, its small movements, in the outspread, dim, fluttering fan of its distances, the spreading plain of travellers' water in the Lagoon beyond the *Giudecca*, the various bits of ruin and of modern ugliness only slightly interfere with the grace of the scene, the movement into perspective of the lovely city in the damp air, beneath now whitening clouds. The water at the moment holds more light than the air does. Brightness seems to rise from the water higher and higher, a semi-radiance without color. In the Piazza, the dully glowing films of water everywhere on wet stones gleam and shine, a muted, pale aura delicately and steadily brightening—the satisfaction for the eye and the mind at the sweetness in the success of men's work here and nature's decorative and significant docility, this, as so often in the past, amazes and calms.

"Can you reduce it all to praise, Onni?" Onni stares at me, a shiny old bastard in the gray radiance. I refuse to be tyrannized by love. I love and do not bother myself with its tyranny. Still, it is here, wings of light now and bits of mist trembling and fleeing, and the last few wisps of spattering and falling rain as the light spreads more and more widely on carved stone and brick. In the spreading gray radiance that is slowly whitening, Onni says as the wind blows, "I am a competent actor, *amico* . . . I can praise even you if the speech is well-enough written, *Cazzo* . . ."

Has it happened to you? Of course it has, love and no love and a gust of laughter in the Venetian moment, love which is not lifelong but is, and is pointless but which is love anyway, love in the damp air among pretty stones?

Ah, I can hardly get my breath. "I will do it for love," I said. "I will write something for you, Onni."

Poor Onni. I never wrote the monologue. I wrote this book for him instead.

So I have come to the end of my little book. A masked figure beckons me from the white light in the door of my room, so like a white page, and says, *It is over, Nino . . . It is over now . . .*

But I sit here at my desk and dawdle with my pen, and the

figure vanishes. I sit here and listen to my heart tick. Time here in Venice is an inconceiveably smooth, if watery, caress, full, of course, of light and glimmers of motion. It is almost as warming as light, time here, where history dresses itself by day and night in pretty monuments, in monumental façades and stone figures of considerable grace in a city of such monuments, a city set into the water like a stone ship in a dream and lit by night and day in order to see and feel its own grace in chill winds and fog and in summer heat and spring lightness. The enduring cleverness of the endearments locked in fine cornices and handsome windows and well-made steps, the unending power of amusement of thought-out beauty and ratio grants an often severe delight, even to fools, even to me.

For the moment I regret nothing. For the moment. For this moment. I miss the old colors of the stones here, the colors of when I was young here, and the old sounds of people in the *calli* and on the *fondamente*, the different footsteps and bustle, the old quality of local voices, and the busier and brighter-colored pigeons in the light of childhood, the sharper outcry of birds in the garden, the passage of boats along the *Giudecca* and the liners in their gigantic scale dwarfing the city, the awful smoke of the coal stoves, the numbers of children everywhere . . . I regret the disappearance of my life.

In the *Ca' Marinention* where I sit and draw doodles on the last page of the manuscript of the book I came to Venice to write, in this window-to-everywhere-and-to-beauty that Venice is— and that the mind is—I see the wall across the *campo* and the restless leaves of the small trees in the *campo*, and the softly restless, reflection-stained green water of the *rio*. Above a sequence of roofs sunlight rests on the upper part of the campanile of the *Frari*. It was the fortune of time given me in my youth that enabled me not to hate him . . . Isn't the love that the victor receives always laced with strange and ordinary bitterness? Onni's movie has been a considerable success . . . He said, *Sicuro, I am old enough and faded enough for you to like me a little at last, even if I am a great star; isn't that so, amico?*

Everyone has loved and been loved for a while. We lie about

this and pretend it was otherwise. We refuse to look at the truth. We want some other love than the one we had, some other history. But we have loved and been loved.

I do not praise or blame my luck. It seems as foolish to praise or blame what can't be undone as it was to set a story in Venice in the train of other stories set here or as it does to love an imperfect person in the first place in the light of so many passionate stories about "perfect" love and usually death that have been set here told us in the past. I try to accept the world . . . Sometimes this acceptance feels like love . . . For Onni, too.

I beg the pardon of anyone I have offended, and I ask patience for those parts of this book written in mischief or weakness of spirit. I say in all truthfulness of intention that I meant only really to entertain. If, perhaps, I had a few darker and more mischievous wishes along the way, they were merely aspects of a defense of actuality against the jealous destruction of truth by ideas used unkindly for the sake of power.

I intended to entertain and to serve God—not religion but God's extraordinary world, the whisper of His that this world and its light are and that we are. And to court Onni one more time, not the last time perhaps, since he and I are still alive, he especially in what seems an unreasonable liveliness of will. The feelings he arouses in me change but the love seems to recur. He is not always monstrous, not entirely. Even if he is, his work interests me, as I have said.

His movie was successful but not so successful as to separate us. He is afraid this book will be successful—I see it in him. I wish I were as innocent in how I love as I often am in my work. I am often largely content with the grotesquery of my fate, but that is, in part, a matter of style, and anyway, mine is not such a bad fate compared to some others, although when I said some such thing to Onni about himself and how things have turned out for him, he said, *But you don't understand, I have not been Napoleon.*

This little book is not meant to memorialize losses or to portray grandeur. I leave Marengo and Waterloo, Trafalgar and God knows what whiff of greatness to Onni to deal with in his next movie which will be set in Revolutionary France. Really, he is very difficult.

But this book is meant to be no more than an attempt to give one small aspect of love in its dimensionalities and color, its silliness, as a confession of its importance to me.

I did not dare attempt a serious representation of Venice but tried only to hint at only a small experience of love in this setting, in the marvellous water-shine and amoral sunlight of this place that is so dear to me. I did not dare to try to hint at the daily actuality of these islands, of these palaces and *campi* and the serious churches and the inhabitant paintings of the churches in their sometimes fearsome beauty. Instead, I drew on the city's centuries-old indulgence in the profane and its invention of secular grace.

I am shyer toward Venice than I am toward Onni . . . Perhaps I have loved and still love Venice with somewhat more steadiness than I have loved Onni . . . No. As I say that, I realize the story is not so different of me and Venice.

Very well, I am a fool, a cagey fool, in both instances. I hope Onni will read this book with feeling. I hope that Venice will adopt me if only in a small way now that I have admitted my feelings toward her. I hope you will close this book with an unmocking gentleness toward us who remain within it.

Niles O'Hara
Venice
1992